What reade

The Gl   Novels

"*Just finished The Glendale Series and loved it! I have never read a story that described the salvation experience so completely and beautifully! As a Christian and avid reader, I sometimes get nervous about starting a new book because I don't know if the content will line up with my faith and beliefs, but this was never an issue in these books. Thank you for writing books that Christians can enjoy! God Bless!!!*"
– Julie B.

"*I have read lots of Christian novels by top authors...but I find this series the best I have read. So well authored and covers situations that people are facing in today's world.*"
– Elaine P.

"*So glad I found the Glendale series. ...Your books have a bit of Kingsbury flavor and I haven't enjoyed a series like this since the Baxter Family books.*"
– Terri B.

"*I discovered Ann Goering about a month ago. I have read every one of the books I could find on Amazon. I am 70 years old and wish I could have read Christian books like these when I was a teen. So many lessons in her books that take so long to learn.*"
– Linda S.

"*Your books have been a blessing to me. So much examples and teaching, that we can get from your books for today's living. As for me, being God's minister will like to use your books in youth groups, women, family, etc... I pray that your books may be translated into other languages. I will like to have them in Spanish. Dios te bendiga Ann.*"
– Alida R.

"*This was a beautiful story of the transformation of one young girl, a love story, and two young hearts. This is a refreshing book that is enjoyable as it does not have all the bad language and other things that many romance novels have. Give this a try, you'll be glad you did!*"
– Mark Y.

"I am lover of Karen Kingsbury, Terri Blackstock. I gave this author a try and got all 3 books on my kindle and have zoomed through them. Love them all. Wish she had more to read!"

– Lisa B.

"Glendale is such an inspiring book for teenagers. Every young person should read it. It made my walk with God stronger."

– Hayley

"From Glendale to Promising Forever, this series is worth sinking some time and serious prayer into. I read all three in a day and went back to read it again, slowly to savor the words and message. Wonderful series, fresh author!"

– Angie

"While the stories themselves were well thought out and conveyed, the spiritual side of the book was an inspiration. I read a lot of Christian romance and this series showed the strongest faith I have seen so far. Definitely brought me closer to my own faith and led me to very uplifting answers when I didn't even know I had questions."

– Vicki R.

"I recommend this for all parents and teens. Parents will gain a new perspective while teens will see their own version of the story in it."

– Shelby C.

"I really felt like I knew the characters. It was as if I could see them and their facial expressions and their movements. The author did a fantastic job of showing the power of love, emotional, physical and spiritual. I am so happy there are more books in this series."

– Liz M.

"At first I thought this was a good read for teens and planned to purchase a copy for my niece. However, as I continued reading, I fell in love with the characters. I was able to relate and identify in some way or another with all of them. Jessi, the main character who at first just got on my nerves with her behavior & attitude, captured my heart. Ann Goering really understands and portrays the hurt and damage that divorce and lack of relationship bring. I was reminded of Jesus' compassion, grace, and ravishing love for us!"

– D. Lopes

THE GLENDALE NOVELS

The Glendale Series

Glendale

A New Day

Promising Forever

Mothers of Glendale

One Desire

Gray Area

Silver Lining

Ann GOERING

GLENDALE

A Glendale Novel

COVERED PORCH PUBLISHING

Glendale

Copyright © 2011 by Ann Goering. All rights reserved.

Cover design copyright © 2011 by Ann Goering. All rights reserved.

Edited by Eileen Fronterhouse

ISBN-10: 0989086607
ISBN-13: 978-0-9890866-0-8

Library of Congress Control Number: 2013934562

www.coveredporchpublishing.com

www.anngoering.com

Requests for information should be addressed to:
Covered Porch Publishing, Ann Goering, PO Box 1827, Hollister, MO 65673

17 16 15 14 13 CofO 7 6 5 4 3 2 1

*This book is dedicated to my Father, the
Giver of all good gifts and dreams;*

*My husband, who believes in me even when
I don't believe in myself;*

*And my grandma – thank you for being my
"sign from God."*

Prologue

"Jessi! Jessica Cordel!" Jessi froze where she was, stopping midstride. Her fitted black coat swung around her knees at her abrupt stop, her tall boots slipping a little on the sidewalk. People streamed around her in every direction, and she scanned the crowd for the one voice that had caused her to stop short. Suddenly, the pedestrians parted as a man pushed his way through the crowd, and she saw a face she loved – the face of a man she had spent five years trying to avoid.

The five years since she had seen Joe Colby seemed like a lifetime, yet as his eyes met hers, and he crossed the remaining distance between them, pulling her into a tight hug, it felt like only yesterday that she had left him at the airport, beating against the window with his fists as her plane taxied away from the terminal.

He suddenly released her and stepped back, hoping he hadn't overstepped unspoken boundaries. They both stood there for a second, unsure of what to say. He finally threw up his hands and broke into a grin. "You look great, Jess." She smiled and nodded, her eyes never leaving his face.

His laugh lines were a little deeper than they were the last time she saw him, and he had filled out. He looked more like a man and less like the boy she had known. Still, his green eyes were stunning in his tanned face, his chocolate brown hair fell just right, and his build was even more athletic. After living in a city, traveling the country and doing some work internationally, Joe Colby remained the most handsome man she had ever seen. "So do you, Joe."

For a moment, concern and sorrow clouded his face, and she held her breath, worried about the questions that would come. Just as quickly it passed, and his smile returned. "Jessi, come and get some coffee with me. I'd love to catch up."

After five years of being strong, she now felt weak with him in front of her. If only he knew of all the times she had thought of him, missed him, longed for him, and now, here he was. All she wanted to do was say yes and stay with him forever. Yet the situation was more complicated, and she knew the right thing to do was decline.

"I would love to, but I just returned from Kentucky and I haven't slept in twenty-six hours. I'm afraid I would be poor company and wouldn't make any sense," she said, reaching up to hold the strap of her laptop case, keeping it from sliding off her drooping shoulders.

By the set of his jaw, she could see he was not going to be deterred. His smile in place, he continued, "Well, I don't fly out until tomorrow morning. Go home, sleep and meet me tonight for dinner." She checked her watch – it was eight thirty a.m. She would have plenty of time to get some sleep before dinner. Still, she hesitated.

His pale green eyes were nearly begging. Without thinking, she quickly pulled out a pad of paper and wrote down her cell phone number, trying not to think about the repercussions that would follow.

Surely it had been long enough. Surely things had changed. Surely they could go to dinner as old friends, then go on as if nothing had happened. Surely.

She tore off the paper and gave it to him. "Call me around five and we can decide where to meet."

His face broke into an excited grin. "That sounds great!" They stood there for an awkward moment, with so much to say, but without the nerve to say any of it.

Finally, she stepped around him. "Well, I'll wait for your call then. Have a good day!"

He turned and watched her walking backward away from him, then gave a short wave. "Sleep well, Jessi."

She hurried to her apartment building and ran up the six flights of stairs, trying her hardest not to think of Joe or any of the memories he brought up.

Once she was inside, she kicked off her tall boots and dropped her jacket on the chair. She went to the kitchen to get two sleep aids and a glass of water. She washed the pills down and drank the rest of the water. Then she lie down on the couch, dragging a blanket off the back and letting it fall over her.

Her mind wanted to race over the events of the last hour and the last six years, but her exhausted body won. Within seconds, she was asleep.

One

Six years earlier…

"You have got to be kidding me." The young passenger's words dripped with disdain as she stared out the car window at the approaching town.

"No, actually, Jess, I'm not," Carla said, shooting an annoyed look at her daughter.

Carla's Lexus was packed to the top with suitcases and boxes. Hired movers had unpacked the rest of their belongings at their new house the day before. The tension between mother and daughter had made the trip from Washington, D.C. long and unpleasant, and now the reality of their situation was enough to make the angry feelings brewing inside them erupt.

"This town is worse than I remembered," Jessica pouted, staring out the window at a sign that read 'Welcome to Glendale.' Jessica reflected on how the small town, nestled deep in the woods, was the perfect definition of a hole-in-the-wall. For the past hour, the only break in the trees had been for a field of green plants that were taller than her. Even the cows, horses and occasional goats were forced to graze under the emerald canopy of the towering trees.

"That makes two of us," Carla muttered under her breath.

"So turn the car around!" Jessica cried, turning away from the window and toward her mother, seizing the opportunity. "Let's go home! We don't belong here!"

"Jess, we don't have a home to go home to," Carla said, her voice rising against her will.

"Don't say that! We can go home!"

"No, Jessica, we can't! There isn't room at home for you, me, your dad and his *girlfriend*!"

"It's all your fault." Jessica spat the words at her mom, her blue eyes snapping. "If you had been a better wife, Daddy wouldn't have a girlfriend, and he would still want us!"

The car skidded to a stop along the side of the road, and Carla turned to face her daughter full on, her face red. "You're right, Jess! I should have found the fountain of youth, pumped my breasts full of plastic, bleached my hair blonde, and then yes, he wouldn't have needed a girlfriend," Carla nearly screamed. "But somehow, every time I searched for that fountain, it wasn't to be found, hence I'm forty-two with brown hair, sagging boobs, and he decided to go to greener pastures! All we are now is baggage that he doesn't want."

"You, Mom! He doesn't want *you*," Jessica screamed.

Carla's eyes smarted with hot tears, and she lashed back at her only daughter like a wounded animal. "Oh, he wants you, does he? Is that why he didn't even try for shared custody? Is that why he said he didn't care where we moved as long as it was out of his house?" The words hit their mark, and Jessica slumped back in her seat.

After a few seconds, Carla took a deep breath, smoothed the front of her blouse with a shaking hand and pulled out onto the road.

"This town is disgusting," Jessica said, staring out the window again.

"It's not so bad when you get used to it," Carla gritted out of clenched teeth.

"Not so bad? *Not so bad?*" Jessica cried. "You're right – how could I ask for anything more? I'd gladly trade my malls, convention centers and friends in for *this* – some stupid po dunk town that has – what – fairgrounds and a corner diner? I'm surprised the streets aren't dirt. Or that they even mow their yards. Why not just let the goats do that?"

"Listen, I get that you don't like it here," Carla said, fighting to control her voice. "Well, I've got a news flash for you, Baby Girl – *neither do I!* That's why I skipped town as soon as I graduated. I know it's been hard on you, but do you think it's been easy for me? I was kicked out of my three million dollar mansion, had to leave my dream job, my country club and my friends to come back to the town I grew up in with my tail between my legs!"

"Oh, you're right. How selfish of me. Poor you," Jessica said, giving her mom a look of mock sympathy.

Carla continued as if she had not heard. "This definitely isn't at the top of my list either, but it's the only place we have to go right now."

"The only place *you* have to go, Mom!" Jessica retaliated. "I'm going home in a few days – wait and see! Daddy won't want me to be away for too long. I'll be home by Anna's birthday party."

"Okay, Jess. Think whatever you want, just don't come crying to me when you realize that your father has abandoned you for a lover who was born in the same decade as you," Carla said, getting in one last cutting remark before ending the argument. "For right now, let's just get a bite to eat, figure out where we're living and get some sleep."

"Oh, we're eating at the corner diner? How quaint," Jessica mocked, leaning back in her seat, realizing her mom was done fighting. Carla rolled her eyes and turned her car onto a tree-lined street.

"There's more here than a corner diner, but tonight we're eating at Mom and Dad's."

Jessica's grandparents were out on their front porch, smiling and waving, before the car was turned off. Jessi climbed out and slammed her door, only to stand beside it and stare at them, her arms folded. Carla gave her a quick pleading look over the top of the car. "Be nice, Jess. You don't have to like me, but these are your grandparents."

"Our baby girl has finally come home!" Bert Hill said, pumping his fist jubilantly in the air as he jogged down the stairs to hug Carla. Jessi rolled her eyes.

"Hey Daddy," Carla answered, giving him a hug and faking a smile. Bert released her to give Jessica a hug while Maybelle hugged Carla, then came around to hug Jessica as well.

"We're so glad you're going to live in Glendale, Honey," Maybelle told Jessi, squeezing her shoulder. "We've missed out on so much of your life, but at least we'll get to be a part of your high school years."

Jessica managed a tight smile that resembled a grimace. "I'm thrilled."

Jessica and Carla followed the older couple inside for a dinner of fried chicken, mashed potatoes and green beans, which was followed by blackberry cobbler and vanilla ice cream. Jessi couldn't deny that her grandmother was a phenomenal cook, yet satisfied her gloomy mood by identifying it mentally as 'hick food.'

"Dinner is great, Mom," Carla said, picking at her green beans.

"Dinner? You were raised to call this meal supper. Guess with as long as you've been in the city, we should have expected some things to change," Bert commented, his voice trailing off at the warning look from his wife.

Carla nodded, managing a tight smile. "I guess some things have."

"Carla, tell us about your new job," Grandma said, pouring Jessica more sweet tea. "When do you start?"

Jessica participated in the dinner conversation only when necessary, and as soon as they were done, announced that she was going to walk down to the 7-Eleven for a diet soda.

"That stuff will kill you," Bert said, winking at her with his merry blue eyes.

"Well, then I guess it's a good thing I have nothing to live for," Jessica answered with another grimace. With that, she left the house.

As soon as she was outside, she pulled out her cell phone and dialed a familiar number.

"Jessica. Oh my god. I totally just got the cutest new skirt. Think trendy meets hippie meets…your blue and green halter."

"Really?" Jessica's voice was suddenly wistful as she listened to her best friend. If only she had spent the day back in D.C. shopping with her friends, instead of driving to this horrible town.

"Yes. *And* the guy who checked me out was so totally hot! He totally asked me to go out with him tonight, so of course, like, I said yes and gave him my number. He wrote it on his arm. Like a tattoo." Anna sighed dreamily. "He was totally gorgeous, Jessi – like dark hair and huge muscles and totally had bad boy written all over him. I nearly died!"

"What are you going to do when you hang out tonight?" Jessica asked as she kicked a stray rock with the toe of her high heel.

"He's twenty-two, so he said he'd get some wine and then we'll go back to his place and…." Anna giggled, her unfinished sentence making her plans for the evening all too evident.

"You just met him, Anna."

"Oh my god, Jess, you are so naive," Anna said, making it sound like a disease. "I told you he was hot, right? He totally is! I can't wait to see him tonight!"

"Yeah…I bet," Jessica answered, the familiar sting of inferiority starting to build. "That's going to be awesome, and I can't wait to hear about it," she continued. "I mean, but you totally took your pill today, right, Anna?"

"Ugh. Thanks. I totally forgot again. I'll take it before I go tonight. Oh my god. Jess, you're not going to believe what I'm seeing out my bedroom window," Anna continued, her voice turning disdainful.

"What?" Jessica asked.

"That woman is on an inflatable in your pool totally naked!"

"What?" Jessica shrieked, drawing a curious look from a lady watering her flowers.

"What a tramp," Anna continued, disgust dripping from her words.

"I know. She's unbelievable," Jessi agreed, matching Anna's tone.

Who did her dad think he was to kick them out of their house and bring that woman in to swim in their pool, eat their food, sit on their couches and sleep in her mother's bed? He had done a lot of stupid things, but she thought this had to be at the top of his list.

And what was Jari thinking, tanning in the pool *naked*? Didn't she know that they had *neighbors*? The woman didn't have a shred of decency. As if husband and father-stealing wasn't enough, now she was tanning in the nude. Jessi shook her head in disgust.

"Oh, by the way, where are you, Honey? Like, when are you coming home?" Anna asked.

"Hopefully soon," Jessica answered, looking around at the houses she was passing – all split-level with two-car garages and trees in the front yard. There wasn't a single house on the street that had been built in the last decade, and all of them looked exactly the same, except the color of the siding. It was so quiet that

she could hear her heels clicking on the pavement, and there was-
n't a moving car in sight.

"Will you be home for my birthday party? I hope so – it's
going to be so totally fun! Oh, Jess, I have to go – Mr. Hottie is
calling! I love you, Babe, and I'll talk to you soon, okay? Bye!"

Just like that, Anna was gone, and Jessica put her phone
back in her purse. If only she were home, going on a date like
Anna, getting ready in her spacious bedroom with the walk-in
closet and attached bath. Instead, she stepped into the 7-Eleven
parking lot.

As she rounded the corner of the store, she saw a guy about
her age headed toward the door. He had brown hair, tanned skin,
a white t-shirt and jeans, and green eyes that were electric, even
from fifteen feet away.

"Not bad for this rat hole of a town," Jessica muttered under her breath. Just then he looked her way and flashed her a
friendly smile. He held the door for her, and she held his eyes as
she entered, giving him her most charming smile. Then she
headed to the back of the store to grab her diet soda, and he disappeared.

She glanced around for him as she walked back up to the
counter to pay, but didn't see him. As she turned to leave while
sliding her credit card back into her clutch, she was startled to see
him standing right behind her.

He flashed her his friendly smile again. "You're new
around here, huh?" he asked.

"How could you tell?" she countered, her tone sarcastic.

He grinned and pointed to her shoes. "Not many of the lo-
cals wear high heels to 7-Eleven."

He was even more handsome than she first thought, and as
she surveyed him again at this close distance, she realized with
surprise that he was probably one of the most attractive men she
had ever seen. Her sarcasm faded quickly as her mannerisms
turned seductive.

"I doubt I'm much at all like the girls around here – in fact,
I'm willing to bet I'm unlike any girl you've ever met," she told
him, her voice like liquid honey.

He tilted his head and considered her for a moment. "I believe you're right." He stuck out his hand, the friendly smile

back. "I'm Joe Colby."

She shook his hand, giving him a practiced smile. "I'm Jessica Cordel."

"You just passing through?"

She grimaced. "Just moved to town."

"No kidding? Where did you move to?" She pulled a slip of paper out of her clutch and gave him the address of the house she had yet to see.

"Really? That's right next door to my house! It's a great place. It's been sitting empty for a year or two. Mr. Mekelburg lived there before going to the nursing home, and his family didn't want to sell in hopes that he'd be able to move back home someday. When the LORD took him a few months back, they put it on the market." As if she cared about Mr. Mekelburg.

"Well then, since we'll be so close, I'm expecting to be seeing a lot more of you," she said, flashing him a flirty smile and letting him interpret the statement however he wished.

Again, he tilted his head and studied her. "I'm guessing you're right – seeing how we'll be neighbors and everything," he answered, his words measured and careful. She opened her soda and stepped around him.

"It was great to meet you, Joe Colby," she said, walking backward toward the door.

His smile returned to his face. "You too, Jessica Cordel."

She paused. "For you, it's Jessi." With that, she turned and left.

An hour later, Carla and Jessi were driving down a curvy gravel road lined with trees. The shadows were falling in the woods, and Jessica stared out the car window.

"Do you see the fireflies?" Carla asked, glancing at her. "You used to love them when you were younger and we'd come to visit. Remember how we spent hours chasing them? When we caught them, we put them into one of Grandma's jars. Do you remember? Maybe we can spend an evening doing that again sometime." Jessica quickly averted her eyes from the flashing bugs she had secretly been admiring.

"Maybe not. I'm not a little girl anymore," she said dryly. Carla didn't respond.

"Here we are, Baby Girl," Carla said thirty seconds later,

turning the car onto a long drive. At the end of the driveway sat what looked to be a cottage.

"Oh Mom, it's beautiful! Does it come complete with elves and fairies?" Jessi asked sarcastically.

Carla gave her a disdainful look. "You might end up liking it here more than you think."

"Doubtful," Jessi answered, taking in the details of the house.

A shake-shingle roof, flowerboxes filled with colorful flowers, shutters wide open to reveal glass windows, a front porch with a porch swing, and siding hidden by green climbing vines made it look disgustingly close to some woodland cottage from a fairytale.

Carla shut the car off, and Jessica got out, following her mom up onto the porch. "Where's my room?"

"At the end of the hall," Carla answered as she unlocked the front door. Carrying her purse and duffel bag, Jessi walked to the room at the end of the hall and shut and locked the door. As she did, she heard her mom mutter, "Welcome home."

Two

Jessica kicked at a clump of dirt with the toe of her tennis shoe as she waited for her mother. They were supposed to go into town to get groceries, but Jessi had been outside for five minutes already, and there was no sign of Carla.

Tired of waiting, she called for her mom, cupping her hand to her mouth to make sure she was heard. It was too hot to get in the car, but she was ready to go. "Mom!" she yelled again, hoping that this time it would encourage Carla to get out of the bathroom. When she still didn't come, Jessi dialed her father's number.

"Hello?"

"Daddy, it's me."

"Hello Jessica, how are you?"

"Not good. Mom is so freaking slow, and I want my own car," she told him.

"Sweetheart, I'm at the office right now. Can we discuss this when I'm at home this evening?"

"No!" she cried, taking her long hair in her hand and holding it up to allow air to reach the back of her neck. The air was hot enough, and the humidity made it sticky. "I want this fixed as soon as possible!"

"What do you want?" he asked, sighing as he conceded.

"I want a car."

"You have a car – a nice one."

"Yeah, back in D.C."

"Well, when you come for visits you can drive it."

"I need one here, Daddy," she whined.

"You want me to buy you a new car? Just like that?"

"Yes," she told him bluntly.

He let out a deep breath. "Do you think I'm made of money, Jessica?" His voice was testy, and she felt her irritation rise.

"You have plenty for Jari to use to blow her boobs up like balloons," she challenged.

"Jessica, stop it! Don't stoop to that level."

"Well, why not? If you have the money for her to have plastic surgery every two weeks, why don't you have enough money to buy your only daughter a car to drive to school?"

"School hasn't even started."

"It will soon."

"Well, maybe we can think about this when you actually turn sixteen," Bill said, taking a new approach.

"I have my permit. I want it right now, Dad," Jessi demanded, her tone final.

"Fine," he said, giving in. "Don't get yourself all upset. I'll have one delivered."

"When can I expect it?" she asked.

"Next week."

"Next *week*?"

"Well, Sweetheart, Jari and I are leaving to go to Ireland for the weekend, and I won't have the opportunity to deal with this until we get back."

She stood up straight. "Daddy, let me come to Ireland with you! I've always wanted to go!"

He let out a long, long sigh. "Jari and I need time to discover each other, Jessica, and I don't think it would be fair to her to bring someone else along – even if it were someone as sweet as you."

The phone call didn't last much longer, and as she slipped her phone back into her purse, she smoldered over her dad's words. So he thought she was sweet? She shook her head, her eyes narrowed. "I'm about as sweet, Dad, as you are faithful," she breathed.

She was pulling her hair back into a low ponytail off to the side, when an idea hit her. If he wasn't everything she expected him to be, why did she have to live up to his expectations?

A plan started to take form, and by the time Carla finally emerged out the front door and they left, Jessica had made up her mind.

~~~~~

After they returned from getting groceries, Jessi hurried into the bathroom, leaving her mom to carry in the bags of food. She stared at herself in the mirror and ran her hands through her long, thick, dark hair. She turned, determined. "Mom, can I use the car?" Jessica asked, walking into the kitchen.

Carla had just set the last bag of groceries down on the counter. "Thanks for your help," she muttered.

Jessi blinked slowly. "Mom. The car?"

"You're fifteen, Jess – you only have your learner's permit."

"I know how to drive, Mom, and this isn't D.C. – it's Glendale. You told me yourself that you drove when you were fourteen."

"Where are you going?" Carla asked, pausing to look pointedly at Jessi as she put a can of black beans away.

"Into town."

"What are you going to do?"

Jessica popped a chocolate-covered raisin from the dish on the counter into her mouth. "Stuff."

"Stuff?" Jessica nodded. "Why didn't you do your *stuff* while we were getting groceries fifteen minutes ago?"

"Because I didn't," Jessica answered, flipping her dark hair behind her shoulder.

Carla shook her head, clearly annoyed. "I don't have the mental energy to fight with you. The keys are hanging in the cupboard." Carla turned her attention back to putting the groceries away in their new kitchen. Jessica grabbed the car keys and started toward the door. "Be home by dinner. We'll eat, and then I want to hang those shelves for the orchid and bamboo arrangement. I need your help, okay?"

"Yeah, sure," Jessi said as she shut the front door. She jogged to the car, got in, started it up, and drove to town.

She parked in front of a small beauty salon, pulled the keys and went inside. The hairdresser was sitting in one of the spinning chairs, turning herself back and forth with her toe, talking to a lady who was sitting under a hair dryer. They both looked up when Jessi entered, and the hairdresser stood.

"Good afternoon! What can I do for you?"

"I need a haircut," Jessi said, her tone steady and even.

"When are you thinking?"

"Right now would be best."

"Laura has another thirty minutes under the hair dryer, so

come on over." Jessica warily measured the lady up, concluded that her haircut wasn't half bad, and decided to go for it. She followed the lady back to the spinning chair, where she strapped a cape around her neck. "What's your name, Sweetheart?"

"Jessi Cordel."

"You're Carla's daughter?" the lady asked, surprised. Jessica nodded. "Don't know why that should surprise me – you look just like her," the hairdresser continued, pulling Jessi's hair out from beneath the cape.

"Haven't heard that before," Jessi muttered sarcastically under her breath.

There was no doubt that Jessica looked like a younger version of her mother. Down to her dark hair, crystal blue eyes, the slight point to her chin and the shape of her fingernails, she looked exactly the same. If it weren't for the few wrinkles that had gathered at the corners of Carla's eyes, they could nearly pass for twins.

"I've heard about you two moving back here," the lady continued. "I'm Christina." Jessi nodded. "So, Jessi, what are we doing to your hair? Just trimming the ends?"

Jessica shook her head. "I want it cut off," she paused, "but still in a really cute style. Maybe like this one." She held up a magazine clipping.

Christina studied the picture and then turned to Jessi. "This cut would look great on you, but Honey, your hair is beautiful. If I had hair like yours, I wouldn't cut it off."

"Well, it's not your hair, is it?" Jessica snapped, her hands starting to shake.

Christina straightened and took her scissors out of a jar of solution. "Seems she's got the same mouth as her mother, too," the lady under the hair dryer said, flipping the page of a magazine. Jessi ignored her.

The truth was, she didn't want to cut her hair. She loved it long. It had been long since she was four years old. She had never had it short before, and she didn't want it short now. But she did want to hurt her dad like he had hurt her and her mom, and this was one way she could.

He loved her long hair – he thought it was how a young

lady was supposed to look. With long hair, she looked proper standing behind him on a stage, waving to his supporters. She nearly snorted. How perfect would Jari look standing there? He had traded his beautiful wife and daughter in for a young play-girl.

Christina snipped and cut, and Jessi bit her lip and blinked as she watched the long strands fall to the floor. Christina cut and measured and cut some more. Then she flipped it all under, and pulled little pieces this way and that until it looked just like the photograph. When she stepped back, Jessica stood and leaned close to the mirror. Her hair didn't even come close to touching her shoulders, and the floor around her was covered in silky brown strands. Tears nearly came, but she swallowed hard and stood straight. Christina had done a good job, and Jessica tipped her well.

After making a quick exit, she sat in the car and looked in the mirror for a long time. She hated it, and as quick as a flash, she began to blame her father. If he hadn't run off with Jari the Harlot, then she would have never had a reason to cut her hair. It was all his fault…like everything else was his fault. He had ruined her life.

The haircut itself wasn't bad. She liked it, in fact, if it had been on someone else. It was kind of bobbed in the back with long dark pieces hanging straight down to her jaw in the front. She tilted the rearview mirror for a better look. If she hadn't loved her long hair so much, it would have been cute. But the fact was, she had loved her long hair.

When she got home, she crept in the front door, not wanting to deal with her mom before she got a picture sent off to her dad. "Jessi, is that you?"

She stopped. "Yeah."

"Come here."

"I have to do something. I'll be out in a bit."

"Okay. Make it quick. Dinner is almost ready."

Jessi hurried back to her room and grabbed her digital camera. She went into the bathroom, held the screen toward the mirror, and snapped a picture of herself. Then, she plugged the camera into her computer and attached the picture to an e-mail. With a satisfied grin on her face, she typed,

Dad,

Just thought you might want a picture of me to take with you to Ireland! Hope you and Jari have a great time discovering each other.

Your Baby Girl,
Jessica

She sent it off with a dramatized click, then waited to make sure it sent. She signed out of her e-mail and shut her computer.

"Jessi! Dinner!" Carla called.

"Perfect timing," Jessi responded under her breath. She let out a sigh as she spun away from her computer. She wiped the palms of her hands on her jeans, fluffed her hair with her fingers, and walked into the kitchen.

Carla's reaction was more than Jessi had expected. Her mom's mouth fell open, and she dropped the bowl of salad onto the floor, the glass bowl shattering. She didn't seem to notice. "Jessica Nicole Cordel, what did you do?" Carla asked slowly, her voice cold and angry.

"I got a haircut, and *you* just broke a bowl."

"Your father is going to kill you!"

"Really? You don't think he'll like it?" Jessica asked, her tone dry.

"Jess! You did this to make him angry," Carla accused.

"And?"

"It will work."

"I hope so!"

"Jessi, you cut off your beautiful hair," Carla moaned, her tone softening as she crossed the distance between them and touched her daughter's cropped hair. "And for what? He'll yell, get mad, and then what? You'll be stuck with short hair for months!" Jessica shrugged, pretending her mother's reasoning didn't make as much sense as it really did. Carla shook her head, and knelt to start collecting the pieces of the bowl. "I hope you think it was worth it."

"It was," Jessica muttered.

"Did you already send him a picture?" Jessica nodded.

"Well then, I guess we can expect a phone call from him tonight," Carla said, almost throwing the glass pieces into her hand, her face stony. "That's just what I need! As if unpacking the house, cooking the meals, and wading through all the paperwork from transferring wasn't enough, now I get to deal with an irate ex-husband. Beautiful, Jess."

Feeling suddenly small and maybe even a little in the wrong, Jessica knelt to help her mother pick up the shattered bowl. "My hair really isn't so bad, do you think?" Carla straightened to take a second look at the new haircut and let out a long sigh.

"Its darling. I just liked your long hair."

Jessica nodded. "Me too," she said, the words coming out in almost a whimper.

"Oh, Honey," Carla responded, touching her cheek. Jessica turned away, not wanting to cry.

Carla swept up the little pieces of broken glass, lettuce and tomatoes while Jessi tossed a new salad. Then they sat down to eat together at the dining room table.

The dining room was just off the kitchen, and the patio spilled out from its French doors. They had the doors shut as the heat outside was oppressive, but Jessi imagined on a spring day, it would be nice to open them.

Carla stabbed a tomato and a leaf of lettuce, and reached across to feather Jessi's hair. "The hairdresser did a nice job. Who did you go to?"

"Christina. She knew you."

Carla nodded. "I went to school with her," she paused. "Jess, I always thought I was so much better than her. I was the prom queen, the captain of the cheerleading squad, the star volleyball player. She played the clarinet, had hair that looked like it had been brushed too much, didn't have a date for our senior prom, and I'm pretty sure, failed PE. I went to college, had a great time, brought home a boy with a promising future and wore a rock on my finger that she'd only seen in magazines. She stuck around, started cutting hair for people, married a boy from just up river and settled down."

Carla set her chin on her hand and stared at the wall behind Jessi. "When we used to come back for our yearly visit, I'd see her and I would pity her. I was living in D.C. in a gorgeous house with a pool and a maid. My husband worked for Congress, I had a job that paid enough to keep me in a new Lexus, my beautiful daughter went to the best school that D.C. had to offer, I was an active member of our country club and…I had it all. Christina still lived in Glendale and cut hair," Carla paused and watched Jessi as the teenager continued to eat.

"Now, Christina still lives in Glendale in a beautiful house in a nice part of town. She has a husband that loves her and would never think of cheating on her, two sons in college, a daughter in high school, and a dog that she walks with every morning."

Jessica didn't say anything. There was nothing to say. They ate in silence until the phone rang. "I'll get it," Jessica offered. Carla nodded and wiped her mouth with her napkin.

Jessica grabbed the phone off the kitchen counter. "Hello?"

"Jessica Nicole! What happened to your hair?" Bill Cordel's voice was close to a growl.

"Daddy. Hi. How are you? How was your day? You all packed for Ireland?" she joked.

"Cut the games, Jessica. What did you do?"

"I got a haircut."

"I can see that. What were you thinking? You know I like your hair long!"

The words formed cold and harsh on her tongue, and she never thought twice about saying them. "But you're not here, are you? Let me make something clear to you, *Bill* – I don't care anymore what you like or dislike."

"I am your *father,* and whether you live in my house or not, you are still my daughter!" he yelled, his voice shaking.

"That's what you think!"

"Do you have DNA tests to prove otherwise? Do you know of any other man who was in on your conception? I don't think so!" he bellowed. She rolled her eyes. How original. "You are still my daughter, and I still have control over you until you turn eighteen! You will ask for permission before getting any future haircuts or…or doing anything else!"

She toyed with a piece of her short hair. "Daddy, I have to poop. May I?"

"You," he paused, and then let out a dry snicker. "You are

not funny. Not one bit. You are a disrespectful, rude, fifteen-year-old girl and—"

"Oh no, do you think Santa won't come this year?" she asked in mock disappointment, interrupting.

"That's it. I will not speak to you when you act like this. I deserve to be spoken to with respect."

That lit Jessi's fuse. "Respect? You think you *deserve* respect? Why? Because you ruined our family for some tramp that worked in your office?"

"*Jessica Nicole!*" he paused and took a shaky breath. "You will cease to speak in that tone and with those despicable words. You will talk like the young lady that you are."

"Stop trying to intimidate me, Dad," she told him, but he kept talking.

"You will speak to me with respect and a respectful tone, because I am your *father*. Is that clear?"

"Loud and clear," she told him through gritted teeth, and pushed the off button. She called him a name she didn't dare call him to his face, and dropped the phone in its cradle.

She hated the way he tried to control everything – the way he tried to control her. With big words, a loud voice, and formally strewn together threats, he controlled their conversations – just as he had controlled her life for the last fifteen years. Well, she didn't live in his house anymore and she was tired of it.

When she took her seat, Carla looked up. "You got what you wanted."

"I always do," Jessica answered, a sharp edge to her voice.

"Yes, you do," Carla murmured softly.

Three

Carla came into Jessica's room without knocking. Jessi was lying on the bed in the middle of a phone conversation with Anna. Carla hurried to her closet, opened it, and rummaged around. "Hey! What are you doing?" Jessi cried, covering the phone.

"Looking for your duffel bag."

"Why?" Jessi demanded.

"Where is it?"

"Under the bed. Why do you need it? You have your own luggage."

"We're flying to Denver in the morning for a long weekend, Jess. Get packed."

"Why?" Jessi asked again, her tone changing to show her pleasant surprise.

"I have to go for business meetings tomorrow and Friday, and I thought it would be fun to make a trip out of it."

"What are we going to do there?" Jessi asked suspiciously.

"Oh, probably some shopping, a little sightseeing, maybe see the symphony or opera."

"What will I do when you're at your meetings?"

"You can go to the mall," Carla offered.

Jessica considered it and then nodded. "Okay."

Carla smiled while pushing her dark hair behind her ear. "Okay." She left Jessica's room, and Jessi packed.

The next morning their flight was delayed, and Jessi took a short nap in the airport waiting area. It certainly wasn't the first time she had slept in uncomfortable airport chairs. Carla woke her when their call to board came, and she walked sleepily onto the plane. When they had taken their seats, both Carla and Jessi pulled out sleep masks, put them on, and promptly fell asleep. Neither woke until the plane landed in Denver.

Carla had arranged for a rental car, and they picked it up at the airport. It was a red sports car, and Jessi ran her hand over the dash. "I like this."

Carla gave it an accepting nod. "It's nice."

"Better than your Lexus," Jessica countered.

Carla let out a short laugh. "Hardly!"

"Think Daddy will get me one?"

"Think he's forgotten about your hair?"

"Nope."

"Then I think that's your answer for the car." Jessica couldn't help but agree. Looking back, she wished she had waited for her car before getting her hair cut.

Carla took Jessi straight to the mall and dropped her off for almost four hours, promising to come back for her once her meetings concluded for the day. Jessica was perfectly happy. Her purse was loaded with credit cards that her dad paid, and the whole mall spread out before her.

She bought three pairs of shoes, sixteen tops, two pairs of shorts, six pairs of jeans and two new dresses. She almost laughed as she slid her credit card through each machine. He could take away her walk-in closet, but she could still make sure her new one was full.

After she finished shopping, she treated herself to a manicure and a pedicure. Next, she visited the food court and sucked down a root beer float while people watching.

She was finishing the last of her drink when a young man in his early twenties sat down in the chair beside her. "Mind if I join you?" She considered him, then smiled.

His hair was brown and wavy, his skin tanned, his shirt collar turned up, and he had bottle cap holes in his jeans. She was bored, didn't know when her mom would be back, was at a mall that she would most likely never return to, and he was cute. "Not at all."

"I'm Chase," he said, offering a charming smile.

"Jessi," she answered, smiling back.

"You look lonely," he told her.

She leaned forward. "I was."

"Where are your friends?"

"I'm going solo today."

"You from around here?" he asked.

"Washington, D.C. You?"

"Here – I'm going to school downtown."

"What year?"

"Junior."

"Hmm… Sophomore," she offered. It was a game, much like verbal ping pong – the kind she had seen in the movies.

"What brings you to the mile-high city?"

"I'm on a quest for some entertainment," she answered with a flirty smile.

"Looks like you've been here awhile," he said, gesturing to her bags.

She shrugged. "Nothing better to do on a Thursday afternoon than shop."

She watched his eyes run over her. "Especially in a short pink skirt and heels," he commented. She shrugged, pretending not to feel the butterflies in her stomach.

Anna and Kayly, her two best friends, would hardly think feeling butterflies was cool. They were much more advanced than she was and teased her about it mercilessly. She had toyed with boys more than a few times, just like she had seen in the movies, but Anna and Kayly didn't just play around – they were the real deal. It took more than a bold glance to give them butterflies. Jessi pushed her thoughts aside. "You have to look nice to go shopping," she answered.

He nodded. "And you do a stellar job at it." She rewarded him for his compliment with another flirty smile. "You seem bored," he observed.

She stretched her legs and rested first one high-heeled foot and then the other on his knee, sitting back in her chair to watch his reaction. "Very."

He gave her a questioning look, one eyebrow raised. "Do you want to get out of here?"

She smiled at him. "What do you have in mind?" she asked.

"We could catch a bite to eat and then see where the night might lead us," he offered.

She pointed to her empty glass. "Not hungry."

"I know a great club downtown."

"Not twenty-one," she told him, faking a pout.

"I know a great park," he paused, his voice taking on a romantic lilt. "I have a blanket in the back of my car, and we could watch the stars come out together. Have you ever seen the stars come out over the Rocky Mountains? It's a sight you don't want to miss."

She wrinkled up her nose and shook her head. "I'm allergic to grass pollen."

"We can go back to my dorm." He was getting desperate.

She titled her head and gave a teasing smile. "Mmmm…I don't think so."

"You've shot down every idea I've had," he pointed out, looking suddenly impatient. "What do you want to do?"

She shrugged and flipped her hair. "I guess if there's nothing to do, we'll just have to forget it." She stood and bent to pick up her packages.

"Are you kidding me?"

She looked over her shoulder and shook her head. "Nah."

"So, after leading me on, you're just going to walk away?" he asked, clearly irritated. She blew him a kiss and waved, doing just that. She heard him call her a name before turning on his heel and stalking off in the opposite direction.

Her phone rang as she neared the door where her mom had dropped her off. "Perfect timing," she said under her breath as she checked the caller ID. After confirming that her mom was waiting outside, she went out to get in the red sports car.

"Did you leave anything for anyone else?" Carla asked as Jessi placed her purchases in the backseat.

"Not a thing. I offered to buy the mall, too, but they said it wasn't for sale," Jessica answered, drawing a chuckle from her mom.

~~~~~

The next day Carla only had meetings in the morning, so Jessi slept in, went for a swim in the hotel pool and was fixing her hair when Carla returned. After Carla secured her briefcase in the hotel safe, they drove into the mountains to have lunch. They stopped at a quaint little restaurant surrounded by pine trees, and Jessica felt like very much a lady seated at the white linen-covered table with a napkin spread across her lap.

Carla and Jessica made small talk during lunch and then planned the rest of their day. After eating, they drove through the mountain town, taking in the rustic charm and marveling at the splendor of the majestic peaks towering all around it. After doing some sightseeing, they went back down the mountain into Denver where they stopped at several stores, always coming out with purchases. As the afternoon wore on, Jessica convinced Carla to drive across town to 'another store.'

When they arrived, Carla sat motionless, her hands still on the steering wheel, and simply stared at her daughter. "Jessi, no," she breathed.

Jessica sat straighter and looked out the window. "Mom, I want one."

"Jessi, you tricked me."

Jessica shrugged. "I knew you would never drive over here if you knew where we were going." Jessica had told Carla she wanted to check out a new store and had given turn-by-turn directions. Now they were parked outside a tattoo parlor.

"What do you mean you want one? You've never wanted a tattoo before!" Carla said, her voice rising. "Your father would have a cow if he knew we were even parked outside of this place!"

Jessica couldn't help a small smile. "Exactly!"

"Jess, I don't think I like this rebellious attitude," Carla said, worry flashing across her face.

"Mom, who's he to say what I can and cannot do? He abandoned us, and he abandoned his authority over me. It's up to you now." Carla couldn't agree more. Instead of arguing, she changed tactics.

"Remember when you got your hair cut and hated it? It's not worth getting something that will never go away, just to make your dad angry."

"Mom, I really do want one," Jessi answered.

Carla sighed. "Is it even safe?"

"I researched it on the internet, and this place is the safest in town."

"You've been planning this?"

"It's not everyday that we're in a city, and Glendale doesn't exactly have many tattoo parlors," Jessica answered dryly.

Carla put her head in her hands. "I don't know, Jess."

"Please, Mom? Please, please, please?" Jessica asked, looking up sweetly.

Carla took a long time answering. "Okay, fine, if you're sure you want one."

"I do," Jessica said, already out her door. She already knew what she wanted, and had drawn it on a napkin while she was at the mall the day before.

Carla signed her name on the permission slip without looking, hoping that she wasn't making a huge mistake. Jessica took a seat in one of the large chairs and smiled at the tattoo artist. He had tattoos covering his whole left arm. Diverting her eyes, she cringed inwardly.

She had never liked tattoos. Still, she knew her father would hate it. All she could think about was hurting him like he had hurt her – and she would do whatever it took. Maybe, if she hurt him enough that he understood the pain he had caused, maybe he would kick Jari out and beg for their forgiveness – ask them to come back, and they could all be a family again.

"Ready?" the tattooed-man asked in an Australian accent.

"Jess, are you sure, Hon?" Carla asked, her eyes doubtful.

Jessica looked up at the man with the needle. "Yes. I'm ready."

It hurt more than she expected, and she bit her lip against the pain. In less than an hour, she had a small black butterfly injected into the skin on her shoulder.

~~~~~

Jessica didn't tell her father about her tattoo as quickly as she had told him about her hair. She had decided she would not make the same mistake twice. This time she would wait for her car before telling him about her tattoo.

She was sitting on the couch, flipping through a magazine late on a Saturday afternoon when the doorbell rang. She got up to answer it and found a man in a blue button-up shirt standing at the door. "Jessica Cordel?" She nodded, and he held a clipboard out to her. "Please sign here." She peeked around him and then quickly signed her name. He handed her keys, and then climbed into the car that was parked behind a brand new yellow sports car.

Jessica felt her hopes deflate as she ran out to inspect it with her mother. "It's sporty!" Carla said as she ran her hand over the hood, obviously approving of Bill's choice. Jessi didn't answer.

It was a nice car – brand new and very cute. It was even a convertible…but it wasn't what she had been hoping for. She had been hoping for a rich, expensive car – anything to show her that her daddy still loved her. Jari was driving a Corvette. This was cute, but fairly common.

Jessica sat in the driver's seat and pushed the button to make the top go down. Then she searched the glove compartment, the center console, the floor mat in front of each seat. There was no note, no card from her father. It was a completely impersonal gift with only the insurance card and registration to show he had meant it for her.

Jessi blinked slowly and surveyed the car more closely. It was a two-seater and the stereo was impressive. It was an automatic, and the black seats were plush. It was the ideal car for a teenager, but Jessica wasn't happy.

Her dad hadn't bought her as nice of a car as he had bought Jari. It made her blood boil. She was his daughter, after all. Aside from the cost of the car, there wasn't any sign he had been thinking of her when he picked it out. In fact, Jessica wouldn't be surprised if he had asked his assistant to pick out the car and wrap up the details. She swallowed hard, put the top up, and got out. She had watched her father spend hours at car dealerships, deciding on just the right car for Jari. He had paid to have it filled with red roses and balloons, with little love notes tucked in every nook and cranny.

"You want to go for a drive?" Carla asked, getting out, her face hopeful.

"No." Jessica's voice was dull, and Carla put her arm around her shoulders.

"It's a nice car."

Jessica looked at the ground. "There wasn't even one flower or note."

"It was such a long trip the flowers would have wilted," Carla assured.

"What are you doing? Why are you defending him?" Jessi cried, stepping away.

"I'm not, Baby, I just don't want to see you so sad."

Jessi shrugged. "I'm fine." She turned away from her car and went back in to finish looking through the magazine.

That night she had her mother take a picture of her in her new room, her shoulder tilted toward the camera, her new tattoo obvious. Carla looked worried as Jessi sent it off in an e-mail, but Jessica didn't bat an eye. She would enjoy every minute of him yelling at her, of him telling her how disappointed in her he was. He hadn't even sent a card or a flower.

After Carla went to bed, Jessi tiptoed through the house and stood looking at her car.

Why couldn't it have been a car like Jari's? Why couldn't he have sent a note with it or a flower or a balloon? Why couldn't he have done *something* to demonstrate that he still remembered and cared about her – that she was special to him and that he loved her? If that was too much to ask for, then he could forget about having a relationship with his only daughter; after all he had done, after all he'd thrown away, *that* was too much to ask for.

Four

Jessica turned her snow globe upside down and carefully shook it before tipping it up again. The glittery snow fell over the cottage house and trees within the glass globe, and Jessi was in a daze watching it.

"Jessica?"

Jessi blinked and looked up, quickly setting the snow globe on her dresser. "What Grandma?"

Maybelle walked farther into Jessica's room and picked up the snow globe. "This is beautiful."

Jessi smiled a little, her eyes sad. "Dad got it for me when I was four." Grandma sat down beside her on the edge of her bed. "I remember sitting on the floor in my room and shaking it, then just watching it for the longest time," Jessica continued, her voice wistful. "I always thought that this was heaven – like nothing bad could happen in the cottage. When Mom and Dad used to fight at night and wake me up, I would shake this snow globe and wish we could all go live there. They would be happy, and everything would be like it was supposed to be."

Jessi felt her grandmother studying her and kept her eyes diverted, feeling vulnerable after sharing the painful memory. When Jessi finally glanced over at her, Maybelle's eyes were gentle. The older woman kindly turned her attention to the snow globe. "It reminds me of a fairytale I once read," Maybelle told her.

Jessica nodded and smiled. "I know there's a real cottage just like this one in some mystical forest. The forest is full of streams of sunlight and little elves and hidden woodland people who peep out from behind mossy rocks, and gurgling streams filled with beautiful rainbow fish. The deer eat flowers from the flower boxes on the windows, and birds sit and sing to the cottage people each morning to wake them up," Jessi said dreamily.

"Perhaps we read the same fairytale," Maybelle said, giving the globe a gentle shake. They both watched the glitter land.

"Do you think this house looks like the cottage, Grandma?"

Maybelle smiled. "I do see a resemblance. Something about this house is almost magical, Jess. Something good is going to happen here."

Jessi pushed herself to her feet, the moment over. Maybelle did the same and carefully set the globe down on the dresser.

"I finished decorating."

"I see," Maybelle answered, following Jessi's lead and looking around.

The headboard had been pushed against the wall, the right side almost touching the windowsill. It was made up with a charcoal gray down comforter, white sheets, white pillows and bright white, dusty charcoal, and jet black throw pillows. It looked soft enough to jump into.

The black dressers and end tables were stylish, and the lamps were stainless steel and modern. White sheer curtains hung at the windows, softening the room, and a plush black wing chair sat in one corner. Bottles of perfume sat on a silver tray on the large dresser, and pictures of friends from back home were stuck in every corner of the large mirror. A large painting with a deep red background and beautiful white orchids hung above the bed, and the Chinese symbols for love, peace, and happiness were hung in black frames in a cluster on the north wall.

"I like it, Jessi," Maybelle said. "But where are all the photographs you had up in your old room?"

The corners of Jessi's mouth turned down as she was reminded of the dozens of framed pictures that had lined her walls. They were pictures of her mom and dad and her, starting when she was a baby and going up through the past year. She looked away. "I haven't found them yet."

Jessi saw Maybelle glance at the cardboard box under the bed labeled 'Jessi's Pictures,' but nothing was said. Jessi wasn't ready to deal with the pictures from her old life yet, and she was grateful that her grandmother was kind enough not to force the issue.

"Your mother actually sent me to get you. We're going into town to have supper with Pops." Jessica nodded, and slipped on a pair of flip flops. She walked down the hall with Maybelle, quietly, and met Carla in the living room. Maybelle and Carla had finished hanging the walls with Carla's oil paintings, and it looked good. Jessica didn't bother to compliment their work.

She ran her fingers through her hair, and grabbing a magazine said, "I'll wait in the car."

"I'm almost ready, why don't you just stay in here and wait for us?" Carla asked, straightening a picture. Jessica walked out and shut the door behind her.

She stood on the other side of the front door, where she could see in the window without being seen, to hear what would be said about her. She heard her mom first. "I don't know what to do with her, Mom."

Maybelle spoke slowly and carefully. "Divorce is a hard thing."

"Do you think I don't know that?" Carla snapped.

"I know you do, Honey – it hasn't been easy for either of you. If there's anyone who can understand what she's going through, it's you." Maybelle held up her hand to stop her daughter before she interrupted. "And vice versa."

Carla's head dropped and then she nodded. "I know. I just…I don't know how to go from being her enemy to her ally, Mom."

"Sometimes, the quickest way to make friends with someone is to show them you care."

Carla was quiet for several seconds. "I'm sorry I snapped at you."

"You're going through a lot right now," Maybelle answered, pulling her only daughter into a hug. "I understand that."

Jessica climbed into the front seat of the car and flipped through the pages of the magazine, pretending she hadn't heard the exchange between the two older ladies. Did either of them really think they could understand what she was going through? Could she understand it herself? Half the time she felt numb, and the rest of the time she just felt angry – angry with everyone and everything. And the likelihood of her mother showing that she cared was minimal, Jessi thought. Her mom was too busy licking her own wounds and figuring out how to move forward to spend time caring about her.

Every day since the divorce, tension had been growing between Carla and Jessica. It had become especially bad since

Jessi's car had arrived. Like some final blow after a lifetime of wondering if she mattered to her parents, the impersonal gift had filled her with a hurt too deep to be expressed as anything but anger. She was angry with her dad, angry with her mom, and keeping the lid of indifference on it all, unsure that she could survive navigating the deep feelings inside her, should it all be exposed. She turned another page in the magazine.

After a few minutes, Maybelle and Carla emerged from the house, and Grandma followed them to town in her car.

"What did you think of the pictures in the living room?" Carla asked, her words purposefully upbeat.

"They're the same pictures we had in our old living room," Jessica answered, not looking up from the magazine.

"But do you like where we put them?" Carla questioned.

"The mountain scene is still over the loveseat, the waterfall is over the couch and the lily pond is over the television. It's no different."

"But the wall color and everything is different, Jess." Jessica shrugged. "Come on, Jessica, at least try to be interested!" Carla said, her voice rising.

"I'm not." The rest of the ride was quiet and tense.

They ate at the local pizza joint, and Jessica didn't say much other than to tell them what kind of pizza she *didn't* want. The ride home was even more uncomfortable than the ride into town had been, and as Carla shut the front door behind them, she grabbed Jessica's arm.

"When are you going to stop this, Jess? Hm? When?"

Jessica yanked her arm free. "Don't touch me."

Carla stared at her daughter, but Jessica didn't look at her. "When, Jess? When we move back to D.C.? Is that it?"

"Yes!" Jessica cried, her anger erupting. "I don't want to live here! What don't you understand about that?"

"You're father doesn't want us anymore, Jess! What don't you understand about *that*? We can't move back there! This is the only place we can be right now!"

Jessica knew the words her mother was saying were true. "I just want to go home! If we go home, everything will be okay!"

"Jessi, nothing will ever be okay – we *can't* go home. He's chosen a different life, Jessica, and we're not a part of it," Carla said, throwing her hands in the air, her eyes pleading with her daughter to understand.

"Well...then I hate him, Mom! I hate him!" Jessica cried, thinking back to her last conversation with her father, and kicking her shoes off with such force that they hit the wall with a thud.

"I hate him, too, Jess! I hate that he had an affair with that stupid bimbo. I hate that he betrayed me and left me alone. I hate that that woman is in our house, and I hate that he hurt you, Baby!" Tears spilled from Carla's eyes, and she wiped them away with her fingertips before she continued. "But us hating him doesn't mean we have to hate each other! We've got to stick together, Jess!" Carla turned Jessica toward her by the shoulders, and when Jessica looked at her, her young eyes were full of tears. "We're all that we've got left, Baby. Let's not lose that too, alright?"

Tears started to run down Jessica's face, and Carla pulled her into a tight hug that Jessica returned for the first time in months. She clung to her mother as if she finally realized that she was all she had left in the world. "I'm so angry with him, Mom! I just want to hurt him!" Jessica cried.

"So do I," Carla admitted, starting to sob. They stood for a long time, crying together, holding on to one another. When the tears finally subsided, the conversation continued.

"I want to hurt him like he hurt us," Jessica said quietly.

"So you cut your hair and get a tattoo? That's no way to get even, Babe!" Carla told her, brushing the dark hair out of Jessi's wet eyes.

"I know that," Jessi answered, looking her mother right in the eyes for a long moment. "I know that, I really do. I just...I thought it would feel good to make him mad."

"Did it?"

"For a second."

"Now you have to live with it, Jessi."

"My hair will grow."

"Your tattoo won't wash off."

"I know. I was just so mad."

"I'm afraid of what else you might do because you're angry," Carla admitted softly.

It was quiet for a long moment, and then Jessi cleared her throat. "You're sure we have to stay here?"

Carla nodded slowly, allowing her daughter to change the direction of the conversation. "I'm positive, but let's make it great, Jess. Let's have so much fun and be so radiant and alive that your father agonizes over the day he chose that woman over us!"

Jessica turned her face away. "I don't know, Mom."

"We can do it, Hon, we can!" Carla told her, taking her chin and turning her back toward her.

Jessica thought about it for a minute, her blue eyes wet. "Alright. Let's do it." Carla pulled her into a tight hug once again, and kissed the side of her face.

"Let's be friends again, Babe. I can lose your father, but I can't lose you." Jessica nodded, and clung to her mom, feeling like she needed to be close to her, like she never wanted to let her go again. She was the only thing she had, and Jessica was suddenly overwhelmed with the fear of losing her.

Later that night, when Jessica was in her room and Carla had gone to bed, Jessica got on her hands and knees and slid out her box of pictures. She rummaged through it until she found an old favorite. She had been around six with missing teeth and a freckled nose. Her dad had just returned from Dallas and had brought her the most beautiful doll. She had her arm around his neck, was sitting on his knee, and he was kissing her cheek.

Jessi slowly and deliberately ripped the picture in half, right down the middle, so that she was on one half and her father on the other. Then, she carefully ripped him into dozens of pieces and watched as she sprinkled them into the trash can. She put her half of the photo back into the picture box, closed it carefully, and slid it under her bed. Feeling as if her soul had been cleansed for the moment, she went to bed.

Five

The next couple of weeks went by quickly without any major happenings. Carla and Jessica's relationship improved, though it was still far from perfect. Jessica began going on long walks in the forest behind their house, enjoying the chance to get outdoors. On one of her walks, she found a giant oak and sat down at the base of it to try to think through her past, her present and her future.

It was a messy and painful task, and she soon grew weary of it. She put her head back against the trunk of the tree and stared up into the never-ending sea of leaves. It was a hot afternoon and humid enough that her dark hair was sticking to her face.

She had been sitting there for nearly an hour when she heard twigs snapping in the forest behind her. She lifted her head, but didn't have time to stand before a young man stepped through the bushes in front of her. He jumped, as he had obviously not been expecting to see her either. Jessi started to stand, but he recovered quickly and smiled.

"It's okay – don't get up. Jessica Cordel, right? We met at 7 -Eleven a few weeks ago. I'm Joe Colby, in case you don't remember."

She nodded. "I remember." How could she forget his green eyes or his charming smile? He stood, looking awkward and shy for a few moments, and then grinned.

"Mind if I join you?" She shook her head and watched as he sat down on the ground beside her, also leaning against the massive tree trunk. "I didn't expect to find you here," he said after a moment.

She was in a quiet mood, still flooded with thoughts of all that had changed in her life. "Sometimes, when I need to think, I walk. I stumbled across this tree today, and thought it would make a good place to sit and take stock of my life."

Joe looked at her. "It's a good place to do that," he agreed.

She nodded.

"What did you decide?" he asked, twirling a blade of grass between his thumb and forefinger.

"Decide about what?"

"Your life."

She shook her head. "It's a mess."

"Want to talk about it?"

"You wouldn't want to hear about it."

"Try me," he challenged.

She would never consider it. "It's not something to talk about on a beautiful summer day."

"When is a good day to talk about it?" Joe questioned, seeming curious. He watched her through inquisitive green eyes, and she felt oddly vulnerable under his gaze.

"A cold, bleak, dreary, frozen January day. The kind of day you wish you never woke up to."

She regrettably thought that her answer might make him ask more questions, but instead, with a straight face he commented, "Your use of adjectives is impressive." She couldn't hold back a small laugh, and he grinned. They settled back against the tree again and the silence stretched. "I haven't seen you around since that first day," he observed, picking another blade of grass and splitting it with his thumbnail.

"I've just been hanging out at home." She instantly regretted how boring that sounded. "We don't really know anyone yet," she added.

"That will change. School starts in a few weeks."

"True," she agreed, finding no comfort in what he said. She wasn't sure if she was more upset about leaving her old school and all of her old friends, or about coming to a new school with all new people.

It was quiet for awhile. "Are you worried about starting school here?" he asked, his voice gentle.

She held her chin higher. "No," she lied. "Why would I be?"

He shrugged. "If you want, you can hang out with me for awhile. I know pretty much everyone – you could meet a lot of people."

She felt nervous inside – this guy was genuinely nice and

his intuition was a little too close to home for comfort. She shielded her vulnerability the only way she knew how – she gave him a flirty smile. "Is that your way of asking me out? Because if it is, my answer is yes." She turned to position herself toward him, pulling her knees to her chest, knowing full-well how short her shorts were.

He looked shocked and uncomfortable at the sudden change in the conversation. He tilted his head, his eyes never leaving her face. "That's not what I was asking. This may sound weird to you, Jessica—"

"Jessi," she interrupted.

"Alright, Jessi, but I...don't date."

She frowned. "What do you mean you don't date?"

"I mean, I don't date. I've never had a girlfriend, I've never taken a girl out to dinner, I've never sat and made out with a girl at the movies." Joe seemed confident and at peace with his track record.

She studied him, then frowned. "Are you gay? I totally wouldn't have guessed you as the type." He gave her a look that told her that was the farthest thing from the truth. "Okay. Then why?"

"I'm waiting for the right girl," he said simply.

"The right girl?"

He nodded. "The girl I'll marry."

"How do you know who you'll marry if you don't date?" she questioned.

He smiled at her as if he knew a secret. "I'll know."

She shook her head and shut her eyes for a moment. "That is ridiculous. Why would you do that to yourself? This is your time to have some fun and be adventurous...why would you waste that?"

He looked at her for a long moment, as if weighing how much he should say. "I want to be pure, Jessi. I don't want to be like every other jock on the face of this planet that's been with dozens of girls. I don't want to use girls and then lose them when I see a prettier one walk by. Anybody can do that. I want to be able to give my future wife something special."

Jessica threw out her hands. "Look at you! What else could your wife ask for? You're gorgeous." She thought she saw him blush.

"I want to give her the knowledge that she's the one and only. I'll never go on a date with her and think of someone else. I'll never compare her to any other girl or long for someone else while I'm with her. I want her to know she's special. That she has my everything."

Jessica didn't know how to respond or how to comprehend what he was saying. She had never heard anything like it before, and it shocked her. "Don't you want that from your husband?" he asked.

Jessica tensed. Aside from the fact that marriage repulsed her, she had never thought about what she wanted her husband to think of when he was with her. The question made her uncomfortable, and she pushed her hand through her short hair and let it fall into her face. "Why are we even talking of husbands and wives?" she asked. "We're in *high school,* Joe Colby!"

He grinned. "But what we do now echoes in eternity. Don't you see? What we do in high school is going to affect our lives after high school."

He was so confident, so sure. She inwardly cringed as he depicted everything she wanted to be and knew she wasn't. The conversation was far too serious for her comfort. She once again fell back on what she knew, leaning forward, a small frown on her face that made her bottom lip protrude a little farther than her top. "Well, if you change your mind about the dating thing, you make sure to let me know."

He grinned at her as she stood up. "What about friends?"

She squatted down onto her heels in front of him, and rested her hand on his knee. "What kind of friends?" she asked in her best sultry voice that she had practiced in front of the mirror dozens of times.

He looked down at her hand and then up at her face, one eyebrow raised in a challenging sort of way. "The kind that can have fun together, laugh together, and," he paused and very gently removed her hand, his voice firm, "and do not have any physical contact."

Jessica considered his proposition. She did need friends – she didn't have any here. He could introduce her to everyone and, if her suspicions were correct, give her a free pass into the popular group at school. And, since she was actually going to be living in this god-forsaken town, she had plenty of time to convince him to date her. At 7-Eleven she had known that she wanted Joe Colby. He was good looking, he was a challenge, and there was something about him that was intriguing.

Her delicate face broke into a grin and she gave a quick nod. "I can handle that."

Joe grinned. "In that case, some of the guys and I are going fishing tonight. Want to come?" Jessica's eyebrows drew together. "What's wrong?" he asked, pushing himself to his feet when she did. She slid her hands into her back pockets, and pulled one side of her mouth up into a crooked smile as she glanced up at him.

"I've never fished before."

He laughed – a nice, joyful noise. "I'll teach you. I'll be by for you about eight. That's when we go because it starts to cool down around then and the fish bite."

Jessica flashed him a smile. "Okay. I'll see you at eight." With that, she left, walking along the path, the twigs crunching under her feet with every step.

~~~~~

Jessi sprayed her hair with hairspray and ran her fingers through it, pulling her bangs into a more drastic swoop. She touched up her eyeliner and lined her lips with a pink pencil, coloring them in with a gloss just a shade lighter. She pulled on a pair of tight blue jeans and a dusty green t-shirt that showed every curve. She bent to tie her tennis shoes and then straightened to rub her arms with shimmery lotion. She rolled the sleeves of her shirt up and dabbed perfume at her neck and wrists.

"Jess, what are you doing?" Carla called from the living room.

"Getting ready."

"For what?" Jessica shut off the light and left the bathroom. Carla turned from her paperwork to face her. "Where are you going?"

"Out."

Carla peered up at her from behind the rims of her glasses. "Out where?" she asked, her voice testy.

"I'm going fishing with Joe Colby and some of his friends."

Jessica's tone dared Carla to say no.

"Who's Joe?"

"Our neighbor. Remember, his mom is the one who brought over those homemade cookies last week," Jessica reminded.

"Oh, that's right. Nice lady." Jessi nodded and switched her weight from one foot to the other. "Be home by ten," Carla said, looking back at her papers.

"Are you serious? It's eight o'clock now!"

"Eleven."

"One," Jessi negotiated.

"Eleven thirty."

"Twelve thirty."

"Midnight and I'm not going any later," Carla said.

Jessi could live with that. "See you at midnight."

Carla turned on the couch, a stack of papers sliding to the ground. "Be good, Jess!" Jessica looked at her mother's pleading eyes.

"What's that supposed to mean?" Jessi questioned. Carla just shook her head and bent to pick up the papers. Jessica went out the door and sat on the porch swing. She folded one leg under her, and kept the swing moving with her foot.

She heard Joe's truck before she saw it. It rumbled up the road, causing a stir of dust. He pulled into her drive and came slowly up the lane. She stood at the bottom of the porch stairs and waited for him to stop.

"Ready?" he asked as he got out, his usual smile on his face.

"Yes. Let's go."

"Is your mom here?"

Jessi felt her eyebrows come together. "Yeah, she's inside."

Joe held up a jar of something pink and sweet looking. "My mom sent it over."

"What is it?"

"Plum jelly."

"I'll take it in," Jessi offered, but Joe strode up the stairs and knocked on the door, opening it when he heard a surprised "Come in." Jessi followed, her hands in her pockets.

Carla took her glasses off and smiled at Joe. "Well, hello!

I'm guessing you're Joe."

He nodded with another friendly smile. "Joe Colby. It's nice to finally meet you, Mrs. Cordel. It looks great in here – not a box in sight."

"We're finally getting settled in," Carla agreed, looking around.

"I like that oil," Joe said motioning to the one above the loveseat. Jessi rolled her eyes as her mom smiled.

"Me too. I found it when I was up in Montana once."

"It's nice," he paused and then held out the jar. "Hey, my mom sent over some plum jelly. She promised to give you the recipe if you like it. These woods are full of wild plum trees."

"Oh, that was so neighborly! We will certainly enjoy this, won't we, Jessi?" Carla said, accepting the jar and looking at it with a happy smile. Jessica nodded.

Joe grinned. "We'd better get going. Have a good evening, Mrs. Cordel."

"Carla," she corrected, smiling and putting her glasses back on.

Joe opened the door and held it for Jessica. Jessi was quiet as they walked to the truck, and couldn't help raising an eyebrow as he opened the pickup door for her also. Once he got in and started the engine, he shot her a grin.

"What?" she asked, crossing her arms.

"You act as if I'm an alien from another planet."

"I'm sorry, I'm just not used to guys who don't date, talk to my *mother* and open car doors. Are you sure we didn't drive back in time on our way to Glendale?"

He grinned at her and shifted gears as they turned onto the highway. "You're right. How weird!" She rolled her eyes at him. "You act as if every guy is a jerk," Joe went on, his tone still surprisingly light.

"Can you prove me wrong?"

"I can," he paused. "And I will." It was quiet for a moment. "But tell me this. If you thought I was a guy that flippantly dates, refuses to talk to your *mother*," he said, mimicking her inflection, "and expects you to open doors for yourself, why would you want to date me?"

"Uhhh…because then you'd be normal."

"Are you sure you want normal? Surely there's something better out there than normal," he pushed.

She cocked her chin at him. "I happen to like the other gender of my species. You are an imposter that only tricked me into thinking you were one."

He laughed. "I like you, Jessi Cordel." She couldn't hold back a smile.

"My air-conditioner broke," he explained, as Jessica tried to reposition the vent to hit her. He rolled down the windows and then turned on the radio, knowing there was no hope of talking with the windows down. She found her hands drumming on her knees to the beat, and realized that he had noticed, too. Grinning, he reached down and turned up the music.

He turned off of the highway onto a dirt drive that paralleled a thick line of trees. He parked behind several other cars and pickups, and jumped out. He caught the truck door as she was opening it. He raised an eyebrow at her and opened the door the rest of the way, holding it as she jumped down. He shut it. "When you're with me, I open the doors – all doors – understand?" His voice was light but she could tell the subject wasn't up for debate. She nodded and followed him to the tailgate.

He took two poles and a box with a handle out of the back of the truck. She looked at them warily. She wasn't exactly sure what they were for, but she knew that at some point they would hold a slimy, wiggling worm and possibly a cold, wet, flopping fish.

She couldn't believe what she was doing. Last summer she had lounged on her inflatable in her own swimming pool at their Washington, D.C. mansion, and now she was going fishing in the woods. The change in her life not only disgusted, but also surprised her. Still, she followed Joe down a narrow trail into the trees and came up beside him when he stopped.

There were between ten and fifteen people sitting along the bank of the river on lawn chairs, stumps, fallen tree limbs, or just on the grass, with lines stretching from their poles into the water. "Hey guys!" Joe said, announcing their arrival. Everyone turned. Joe introduced her to each person, including a pixie-faced blonde that he identified as his sister, Kara.

Kara and Jessica were the only girls present and after saying hello to everyone, Jessi took a seat in the chair beside Kara at the girl's insistent urging. Joe sat down beside her.

"Thanks for bringing the chairs, Kara," Joe told his sister, grabbing one of the two rods that were propped up against a nearby tree.

"No problem," she answered. Kara turned toward Jessica. "I'm sorry I didn't come over to meet you earlier. I wanted to, but I left for camp the day after you guys moved in and just got home."

"That's okay. We've been busy getting things unpacked."

"Are you getting settled?"

Jessica nodded. "Yeah, we finally emptied the last box and all the decorations are up."

"It looks nice," Joe told his sister, jumping into the conversation.

"That's good. We've been wondering about you guys. Mama and I were baking you a cake yesterday that we were going to bring over, but then the middle fell, so we just let Daddy and Joe eat it. Mama decided to send some jam instead," Kara said, a pleasant smile on her face.

Jessica smiled. "That was nice of you."

"Mama loves to cook and loves to share."

Jessica considered the petite blonde and decided that she liked her. She wasn't at all like her friends in D.C. She had a kind of simple beauty about her. She didn't wear makeup, and her clothes were modest and covering. But something about her made her one of the prettiest girls Jessica had ever seen. A sweet innocence seemed to have wrapped itself around her, and she exuded quiet confidence.

"Okay, Jessi, watch," Joe instructed, and Jessi turned from her thoughts about Kara to watch him. He pulled a worm out of a small plastic container that sat on the ground by Kara's feet. He ran the hook attached to the pole through the worm and it coiled and squirmed, making Jessi cringe. He looped the worm's wriggling body and stuck the hook through again before letting it go. The worm made one last attempt to escape when the hook fell to the ground, but to no avail. Joe laughed at Jessi's expression.

"It's okay, Jessi, it's just a worm," Kara offered sympathetically.

"Okay, now," Joe wiped his hands on his jeans, pulled Jessi to her feet and put the pole in her hands. Standing behind her, he helped her hold the button down, the hook behind them, and then thrust the tip of the pole forward, making the hook and the worm fly through the air and land in the calm river. "Now turn the reel once so that it clicks and that sets it – no more line can be taken out."

Jessi turned the crank. "Now what?"

"Sit and wait!" Kara answered. Jessica sat down as Joe baited his own line and threw it in. "Isn't it beautiful down here?" Kara asked, handing Jessi a soda out of the ice chest.

Jessica looked out across the wide, calm river. The banks were lined with thick trees, leafy bushes and green, rustling grasses. The water cut through the landscape like a wide silk ribbon. The sky was a pale blue, giving testament to the fast approaching twilight. Frogs were croaking and the voices of everyone along the bank were happy. "It really is."

"We've been fishing down here since we were born, I think," Joe said, holding his hand out for Kara to throw him a soda. She did, and he caught it.

"See, Brighton's dad owns the land, and our dad and his dad are cousins. They've been friends forever," Kara explained.

"What are you saying about me, Squirt?" a guy around Joe's age asked, suddenly appearing beside Kara.

"That you're a pain in the neck," Kara answered, tapping him in the forehead with the tip of her pole.

He grabbed it. "Me? I'm not the little sister who always tags along!"

She rolled her eyes. "You like me and you know it!"

"Think what you want, Kara," he told her, releasing her pole when she shook it.

He glanced curiously at Joe and then at Jessica before looking back at Joe. "So, Joe, haven't seen you around lately. What've you been up to?" Jessica smiled, catching the meaning of his seemingly innocent question.

If Joe got it, he didn't let on. "Working. This afternoon was the first time I've even had a lunch break in two weeks. It was handy, because I ran into Jessi. This morning Kara had mentioned asking her to come with us tonight, but I beat her to the punch when I came across Jessi in the woods." Jessi looked at Kara, surprised, and Kara smiled.

Brighton nodded. "Well, good thing you guys thought of it." He turned his attention to Jessica. "Bringing Jessica to introduce her to the group was a fantastic idea," he continued, smiling at her. His smile was flirty whereas Joe's was always just friendly, and Jessi found herself on familiar ground. "So, Jessica…"

"Jessi," she corrected.

Brighton smiled. "Are you from around here?"

"I actually moved down from Washington, D.C."

"What brought you to Glendale?"

"My mom was transferred." There was no need to go into the rest.

He nodded. "Do you like it here?"

She blinked slowly as a smile spread across her face. "I'm beginning to think I will." Brighton's ensuing smile matched her own.

He suddenly stood from where he had been crouched down beside Kara. "Well, I'll offer a toast to that job transfer – to bringing Jessi to Glendale," he said, raising his soda can. She smiled as she tapped hers against his when he leaned toward her, and laughing, Kara did the same. Joe joined in, too, giving Brighton a semi-annoyed look as they touched cans.

"He can be a little…obnoxious," Joe whispered to Jessi.

"*He* isn't an imposter from another planet," Jessi answered, and Joe shifted his eyes back to the river, grinning.

Brighton gave Jessica a questioning look as if asking if she and Joe were a couple. She almost smiled, inviting his attention. This was a guy she knew how to handle, and he wasn't bad looking. Still, the mysterious ways of the boy sitting beside her were too intriguing. She diverted her attention to the river, and getting the message, Brighton nodded.

~~~~~

Jessi was slowly chewing a candy bar and watching the shadows play on the far side of the riverbank, when her pole suddenly jerked. She jumped, throwing her candy bar in the air. Her sudden motion startled Kara and Joe. Her candy bar landed on the ground, the chocolate and caramel now covered with dirt.

Kara laughed at the commotion as Joe cried, "Jessi, you've caught a fish!" Jessica stood up, unsure of what to do next. "Turn the crank," Joe told her, standing up with her. She reeled and reeled. The fish fought, and she turned harder, adrenaline pumping through her veins. Joe ran down to the river with a big net and crouched beside the water. When she reeled it in close enough, he captured the thrashing fish inside the net and brought it up to her. She squealed as she saw it, and clapped her hands. Joe grinned and Kara stood to admire it.

"That's a brown trout," Joe told her, letting her take the line.

Everyone gathered around to admire her catch. The group didn't clap like they had when the first fish of the evening had been caught about ten minutes earlier, but Jessi couldn't have been prouder when Joe took it off her line and put it securely on a stringer where it would stay fresh in the water.

"Okay, boys, they're biting!" Joe said, running back up the bank to grab his own pole.

"That was a nice fish, Jessi! Get one more and you and your mom could have trout tomorrow for dinner," Kara said, holding a fat worm out to Jessi. Jessica made a face, not wanting to take it, but then she saw that Joe was watching. It was dark now, and Jessica took the squirming worm, and held up her hook.

"Sorry Fella," she told it, and then stuck it on the hook as she had seen Joe do. He watched quietly, standing above her, and when she proudly showed him her work, he looped it one more time and smiled.

"Good job," he told her. "No fish is going to be able to resist that bait."

It wasn't as tidy as his had been, but it looked alright. Jessi cast her line and tried not to show her disappointment when it didn't go as far as Joe's or Kara's. No one seemed to mind, though, so Jessica sat down.

Kara caught a fish next, and when Joe took it off the line and put it on the stringer, he determined that it was a little smaller than Jessica's – she still held the record for the nightly catch.

The night became darker and the stars shone brighter. As Jessica sat and talked with Joe and Kara and whoever else happened to wander their way, she found it easier to believe that she was sitting in a remote forest, fishing. She didn't feel the need to go find and flirt with the closest guy, which is what she and her friends would have done if she were in the city. Instead, she was able to sit and enjoy the Colby kids' friendship.

Jessica learned that Kara was fourteen, almost fifteen, and was going to be a sophomore. Joe was working for a farmer, Glendale had a football team that had made it to the state championship game four out of the last five years, Sweet Dips had the best ice cream in town and the Colbys' dad had built their house with his own two hands. She heard stories about their family, about the kids in town, and different things that had happened over the years. She found herself laughing right along with them, and the time passed quickly with fish being reeled in occasionally from the dark, inky river.

When it was nearing eleven o'clock, Joe stood and set his fishing pole down. "I think it's about time to call it quits for the night," he told the girls. He went down to the bank and pulled the stringer of fish from the river. He had caught four, and Jessi and Kara had each caught three, making a total of ten fish on the stringer. He put the fish, stringer and all, into a bucket that he filled with river water.

Kara and Jessi reeled in and stretched. Joe folded up the chairs and took the fishing poles and the bucket before telling the rest of the guys goodbye. Jessica and Kara echoed their farewells, and then Jessi carried the tackle box, while Kara carried the ice chest up to the truck. Joe put all the gear in the back and opened the door for Kara and Jessica. Kara slid into the middle before Jessica slid in beside her, and Joe shut the door. Kara explained that she had been allowed to ride out with her friend Justin, but had been told to ride home with Joe.

A comfortable silence settled over the truck during the ride home. They were all tired, but fishing had been fun. Once home, Jessi's smile was genuine as she told Kara goodbye, and hopped out of the truck as Joe held the door for her.

"I'll clean your fish and bring them over in the morning," Joe told her, shutting the door once she was out.

She nodded. "Okay," she paused, then said with a light shrug, "I had a good time tonight, Joe." She really had.

He grinned. "Good. Thanks for coming with us."

"Thanks for asking me."

He grinned at her as she started walking toward the house. "You'll get asked again."

"Good." She smiled, and then turned and jogged up to the house, stopping to wave at the door. Joe and Kara waved back and drove away.

Carla was still awake, and Jessica kissed her on the cheek. "Hey Mom!"

"You're home early," Carla commented, patting Jessi's head. "But I'm guessing by your beaming smile that you had a nice time."

"It was great!"

"Whoever would have thought that you'd like fishing?" Carla said smiling, putting her papers down and giving her daughter her full attention.

"I know. Go figure." Jessi sounded shocked.

"Or maybe you like the company?" Carla asked, her blue eyes twinkling.

Jessi felt herself almost blush. "Maybe."

"Did you catch anything?"

"Three brown trout," she answered proudly. Carla's mouth fell open, furthering Jessi's pride. She grinned at her mother like a little girl.

"Well, we'll have to have a fish fry tomorrow night. Is there enough for Grandma and Pops?"

Jessi nodded. "Easily."

"Good. We'll have to invite them. Pops will be proud to eat your fish. He's quite a fisherman himself."

Jessi smiled. She liked the thought of Pops being proud of her. "Sounds like a plan." Jessi covered a yawn with the back of her hand. "I'm going to bed."

"Night, Baby Girl."

Jessi went down the hall, brushed her teeth, washed her face and went to bed, dreaming of worms and brown trout.

Six

Jessica yawned and stretched her arms above her head. "You look comfortable," Bert commented and Jessica smiled.

"I am."

Maybelle and Carla were cleaning up the last of the dinner dishes, and dusk was just beginning to settle over the forest. Carla had fixed the trout with a special breading and had served long, crunchy green beans and wild rice on the side. It had been delicious, and Jessica was full. Now, she was stretched out on a lawn chair on the back patio with Pops in the chair next to her.

The shadows were gathering under the canopy of thick leaves just beyond the lawn, and the moss and ground cover were no longer visible. Water splashed in the creek that ran through the backyard, and birds called to each other as they settled in for the night.

"That was good fish," Bert commented, stretching back in his chair.

"Yeah, it wasn't bad."

"I didn't know you liked to fish," he went on, watching her.

"Neither did I." She watched as lightening bugs started to play hide and seek just beyond the closest tree.

"Did you know that I'm a well-known fisherman in these parts?" She turned to look at him.

"Mom said last night that you liked to fish."

He nodded, his grin smug. "Yes, ma'am. I caught a big brown trout back in '73 and held the record for fourteen years. He was a beauty."

She nodded. "Where'd you find him?"

"In the river just east of town."

Jessica decided to use some of her new knowledge, hoping her directions were right. "Out around the Bakers' place?"

Pops nodded, taking a drink of soda. "Yep. Right around there, actually," he paused. "You know the Bakers?"

"I know their son, Brighton."

56

Bert nodded. "He's a good ol' boy. As country as they come. Kinda wild, though. You'd best stay clear of him, you hear?" Jessica didn't respond. "You met your neighbors over here yet?" Bert asked, gesturing to the left of the house.

Jessica looked into the wooded land. "The Colbys?" Bert nodded. "Yeah, I've met them. Why?" Jessica asked, determined not be out questioned.

Bert was one of those men who ended every statement in a question, always trying to get more information than Jessica offered. "Seen the boy?"

"Joe?"

"Yep, that's him. Grandma says he's a little cutie. What do you think?" Jessica blinked slowly. She wasn't sure she wanted to have this conversation with her grandfather. She only shrugged. "He's a nice boy, don't you think?" Bert pushed.

"What are you saying?" Jessica asked, closing her eyes and leaning her head back.

"Oh, I don't know that I'm saying anything, just talking."

"Well, if you're not saying anything, I think I'm going to catch a quick nap." She heard the legs of his chair scrape the stone as he shifted, no doubt offended by her comment. Who cared? He was an old man – a man she hadn't seen more than once or twice a year for her entire life. Now he thought he could just waltz in and make recommendations about her love life? Hardly. Besides, she was determined to date Joe Colby with or without her grandfather's blessing.

She fell asleep and woke twenty minutes later when Carla and Grandma came out to the patio. They settled into chairs on either side of Jessica, talking over her until she couldn't sleep anymore.

"Morning Sunshine," Carla said, reaching out and brushing the short dark hair out of Jessica's eyes.

Jessica frowned at her. "You can't talk any quieter?"

Carla sent her a look. "I was just telling Grandma how proud you were of those fish."

"Who'd you go fishing with, Jessi?" Maybelle asked, crossing her legs. Jessi slapped at a mosquito on her arm and glanced at her grandfather who was pretending to be asleep.

"Joe Colby. We met his sister Kara and a lot of his friends

there."

"Joe's a nice boy. So polite," Grandma paused. "Do you know he's never dated a girl?"

Jessica's mouth grew tight. "I know."

"I was talking to his mother the other day and I was asking about her kids, and we started chitchatting about him. His parents are proud as can be. They're a good family," Grandma continued. Jessi sighed, annoyed. Her grandparents seemed determined to weigh-in on Joe.

"They sound perfect," Carla muttered. "Too bad we can't all be that perfect."

Jessica wasn't sure if the comment was directed at her or the Colbys. Grandma shot Carla a look. "I'm not comparing them to you, Carla, I'm just saying they're a nice family."

Carla gave in. "You're right. I'm sorry. We're lucky to have neighbors like them. Joe brought plum jelly by just yesterday when he came for Jessi."

Jessica didn't miss how Grandma's eyebrow went up. "Good looking *and* thoughtful," the older lady observed.

Carla nodded. "We had some on toast this morning and it was good."

Grandma looked at Jessica curiously. "Is there something going on between you two?"

"There will be," Jessi promised.

Bert opened his eyes. "You think you can make that boy date?"

Jessica gave an arrogant shrug. "I can make any boy date." Bert closed his eyes again and Maybelle settled back in her chair. Jessica couldn't understand why her grandma looked disturbed by what she had said.

"You know Heather Crebel has been trying for years, don't you?" Bert asked, his eyes still closed.

Jessica perked up as she recognized a new piece of useful information. "Has she? I wasn't aware of that."

"Have you met her?" Maybelle asked. Jessica shook her head no. "You will soon. Wherever Joe is, Heather usually is, too. She goes to his church and is just the kind of girl that is sure to turn Joe's head. His mother talks about Heather a lot. I think she hopes they'll end up together." Jessica stiffened as she felt the sting in Maybelle's words.

So her grandma didn't think she was the kind of girl that could attract Joe's attention? Fine. She would get Joe, and she'd show her grandma that no man could resist her. And, she wouldn't be so faked out by Mrs. Colby's sweetness. To think Mrs. Colby was sending over cakes and jams when she really wanted Joe to end up with Heather.

Jessi sat outside for another hour, hoping the conversation would turn back to the Colbys, and she could collect more information. When it didn't, she told them all goodnight and went in to bed. She was determined to meet Heather soon and eventually steal Joe away from her. Heather Crebel didn't stand a chance, and Jessica didn't like her already.

~~~~~

The opportunity to meet Heather came just a few days later. Kara walked over and asked Jessica if she would like to go to the lake with them that weekend as an end of summer party. Kara, Joe, Brighton, Derik, Heather and Justin were all going.

Jessi didn't give her mom the chance to say no. She told her she was going.

When the time arrived to get ready, Jessica layered a white tank top over her black bikini and pulled on cut-off shorts. She took a backpack out of her closet and set it on her bed. She debated on whether or not to pack another swimsuit. The one she wore was jet black and classy. It was a halter top that tied behind her neck, and the bottoms tied at each hip. It covered very little, and she thought it made her look sexy and womanly. She finally selected another swimsuit and held it up. It was a bright pink string bikini and had even less fabric than her black one. It looked more fun than classy and seductive, and she put it in her bag in case she would need it.

If she wanted to be dating Joe by the time school started, and make sure that Heather Crebel was not, she needed to make a big impression. She added a few more clothes and tennis shoes, slipped on her black flip flops, touched up her makeup and sprayed her hair once more with hairspray. She added her cosmetics to her bag, then went to get a bottle of water out of the refrigerator.

"Jess, think you should wear something that actually covers

up your swimsuit?" Carla asked from the couch where she was once again surrounded by piles of paperwork.

Jessica looked down. The black bikini was obvious under the white tank top. "No."

Carla considered her. "You're fifteen, Honey, not twenty-five. I don't know why you're in such a hurry to grow up."

Jessi was annoyed by Carla's comment. "By the looks of you, I don't know why I am either."

Carla physically flinched at the biting words. Then, she blew out a frustrated breath and shook her head. "Jessi, I'm begging you. Be good this weekend."

Jessica stiffened. "What is that supposed to mean?" Carla simply shook her head. "No, Mom, what do you mean?" Jessi pushed, leaning her hip against the couch and taking the lid off her bottle of water.

Carla studied her for several moments and then threw up her hands. "When you cut your hair and got a tattoo, yes, your father yelled at you, but guess who got the brunt of it. Me! The last thing I need is your father freaking out because you're fifteen and pregnant!"

Jessica screwed the lid on her water, scooped up her bag and opened the front door. "I'll be back on Sunday," she paused. "And don't worry – I packed condoms," Jessi lied. The ice in her voice was almost strong enough to freeze the August air, and she slammed the door so hard that the oil paintings rattled on the walls.

Jessica checked her watch, realized it was five 'til three, and decided to start walking. She would meet the Colbys on the road between their house and hers. She pulled her backpack onto her back and started down the drive. She met Joe at the end of her lane, and he stopped and rolled down his window. Kara wasn't with him.

"You planning on walking to the lake?" he asked grinning.

She stashed away the anger toward her mother and offered him a charming smile. "Just decided to get a head start. Thanks for letting me ride with you."

He got out of his truck and opened her door. "No problem. There might as well be two people in my truck instead of just one." Jessi climbed in and put her bag on the floor at her feet.

"Where's Kara?"

"She rode with Justin," Joe explained.

"Is there something between those two?" Jessi asked, positioning her back against the door so that she could see him. She enjoyed the chance to take in his deep tan, athletic build, and chocolate-colored hair.

"You'd think so," he answered lightly, keeping his eyes on the road in front of him.

"Well, you're her brother, you should know."

He glanced at her quickly. She was once again struck by the stunning contrast of his pale green eyes. "Let's just put it this way – Kara's not allowed to date until she's fifteen and she won't break the rules. However, her birthday is in October, and Justin is taking her out for a fancy dinner that night."

Jessica nodded. "I'm surprised your mother let her go to the lake with him."

"She trusts them both, and I'll serve as a chaperone."

Jessica thought that was foolish of Mr. and Mrs. Colby. Their son was seventeen and could surely be persuaded to look the other direction for a few hours. However, she kept her opinion to herself.

"What will we do at the lake?" Jessica asked, changing the subject after a long silence. She had never been to a lake, but she knew that Joe would be there, Heather would be there, and so would she – in her pretty bikinis.

"Swim a lot, fish some, ride around in Derik's dad's boat, have a campfire, do some waterskiing – just the normal stuff."

"Thanks so much for inviting me. It sounds like it will be a lot of fun," she said, looking up at him through her eyelashes and sending him a sweet smile.

"No problem. I hope you do have fun! It's just a little get together to say farewell to summer."

"Who all will be there?" she asked, even though she already knew.

"Let me think…of course Kara and Justin, and then Derik, Brighton, and Heather."

"Heather? I don't think I've met her."

"You'll like her." Jessica turned her head to look out the window and rolled her eyes. She didn't think so. "She's a nice girl," Joe continued. What was with everyone being judged on whether or not they were nice? Obviously, it was the only descriptive word they knew in Glendale.

"She goes to my youth group and is going to be a senior, too. She's also the head of the cheerleading squad at school, so she goes to all of the games with us," Joe continued casually. Jessica suddenly realized that she would have to become a cheerleader, something she had sworn she would never do.

"Sounds like you spend a lot of time with her."

"We're in a lot of the same activities."

"And yet you don't date?"

He gave her a small smile. "No."

"Why not? It sounds like Heather's the perfect match for you."

"I'm not sure about that."

"Why's that?" Jessica questioned, pursing her lips.

He shrugged. "I'm just not sure."

She studied him, trying to figure out why he wasn't interested in Heather, or if he really was but wasn't interested in the timing. Jessica finally decided that she was safe. If he was too interested in Heather, she wouldn't be riding with him in his truck.

"So, Joe, you play football, what else do you do?"

He grinned at her. "It's a long list."

She smiled. "We've got an hour."

He shrugged one shoulder, grinning at her. "Only about half an hour by now."

"Well, you'd best get started," she told him, grinning back.

"Well, let's see. I am the choir president, I've had the lead part in the school musical for two years in a row, I'm the president of the FCA, I'm the senior class president, I'm in FFA, FBLA, NHS, and pretty much every other club that our school has to offer. I play basketball and baseball," he paused. "Oh, and I play percussion in band."

She raised her eyebrows. "I'm impressed. And yet you still have time for homework, work, and youth group."

"And spending time with family and friends," he added with a grin.

She realized that her life would soon be getting much busier if she involved herself in everything he was doing. She also realized what her grandparents had meant when they had said he was a 'good boy.' He wasn't just good, he was golden. Like the golden, perfect child of the gods. If it were anyone but him, she would be disgusted.

"You must be a busy guy. Does anybody ever really see you?"

He laughed. "In passing. I try to set aside scheduled time for those who are really important to me – my parents and my sisters."

"Sisters?" Jessi questioned.

"Kara is my youngest. My older sister, Kimberly, is married and lives in Chicago with her husband and eight-month-old son."

"Do you see them much?"

"They come down about once a month or so."

"It's a long drive."

Joe nodded in agreement. "They want to make sure that Carson, their baby, knows his family and of course my mom eats it up – she loves him. She spends hours rocking and cooing at him."

"Sounds fun."

"It is…except sometimes she gets a *little* carried away," he said. "We all enjoy it when Kimberly and Greg come out, though. We get to see them a lot more than we get to see Kaitlynn, my oldest sister."

"And where is she?"

"Houston."

"Doing what?"

"She writes for a magazine for teenage girls. Kara gets it, and she cuts out all of Kaitlynn's articles and pins them up in her room," Joe explained, smiling fondly.

Jessica smiled, too. "Sounds ideal."

"It would be ideal if Houston was closer to Glendale."

Jessica smiled and nodded. "I can understand that."

"I had another sister, Kelsi. She was between me and Kimmy in age, but she died of cancer when we were all young," he told her.

"I'm sorry," Jessi responded, not knowing what else to say.

Joe grinned. "I was young and it's been a long time, but… I'm still sorry, too. I remember that she was a lot of fun." He paused. "What about you, Jessica Cordel? Have any brothers or sisters?"

Jessi shook her head. "I'm the one and only."

"That must have been nice, getting all of your mom and dad's attention."

Jessi dropped her pretense for a moment, and her eyes turned lonely and her voice wistful. "I always wished for a brother or a sister, just for a playmate and a friend."

Joe's expression was tender as he looked at her, and so was his voice when he spoke. "I don't blame you. I wouldn't give my sisters up for any amount of parental attention." She nodded, and then changed the subject.

Seven

Jessica and Joe arrived at the lake a few minutes after Kara and Justin pulled in. They immediately started putting up tents, and Jessica gained her first experience at bending tent poles, driving in stakes and tying grounding cords. Within half an hour, both tents were up with Kara and Jessica's bags in one and Joe and Justin's in the other.

Next, Joe and Justin made a fire ring out of stones, while Jessica and Kara looked for wood in the surrounding trees. Jessica made a face as she realized a spider was crawling up one of the sticks she was holding, and quickly dropped the load onto the growing pile of firewood.

By the time they had finished their chores, the others had still not arrived. Justin asked, "Well, do you want to go swimming?"

Jessica looked at the tall, leafy trees surrounding their little camp and the worn trail down to the lake, which sparkled blue and inviting just fifty yards away. The temperature had passed one hundred degrees, and the humidity was high.

"Yes!" Kara answered, pulling a strand of damp blonde hair off her forehead. Joe nodded in agreement and so did Jessica. "Race you to the water!" Kara exclaimed, and took off toward the lake, pulling her t-shirt off as she went. Justin ran after her. Kara stepped out of her shorts and jumped into the lake seconds before Justin.

Joe looked at Jessica when she hesitated. "You don't like to swim?" he asked, appearing concerned. "I mean…you knew we were coming to a lake and that a lake is made of *water*, right?"

She gave him an amused look. "I like to swim," she answered, but still she hesitated.

"What is it then?" he asked.

She weighed whether or not she wanted to ask the question. "Are there snakes and fish in that water?"

He grinned. "Big ones."

She tilted her head, then hiked her chin, deciding to be brave. "Then it's a good thing I'm not afraid of big snakes and fish, isn't it?"

"I guess it is," he answered, watching her as she bent to slip her shorts off.

"Will you put sunscreen on my back for me? I don't want to burn," she said, looking over her shoulder at him. He didn't say anything, but squirted some of the creamy lotion into his hands and slowly started to lather it on to her golden skin.

He lifted the back of her swimsuit to rub lotion under it, and she took it as a good sign until he turned and said, "Kara always burns there. Okay, you're done."

He had ruined the moment by talking about his little sister, Jessi thought, nearly pouting. "Want me to do you now?" she asked, bouncing back.

He peeled off his t-shirt and threw it over his tent. "Nope – no need. I never burn." She looked at the defined muscles in his chest, shoulders, stomach, back, and arms, and was disappointed that he had declined.

"Come on! Get down here!" Kara yelled from the lake where she was splashing Justin.

Jessica smiled at Joe. "Bet you can't catch me!" She took off running, and Joe followed.

He caught up to her as she splashed the first few feet into the water and gave her a gentle shove, knocking her down into the lake. She came up sputtering and laughing, crying, "Hey! No fair!" Kara and Jessica quickly formed a splashing team against Justin and Joe, and graciously the boys let the match be somewhat even.

They got out of the water, breathless and laughing, when they saw a pickup with a boat behind it pull up behind Joe's. Jessica stayed between Joe and Kara in her dripping bathing suit as she watched Derik, Brighton and then Heather climb out of the truck. Jessica knew that Heather was angry as soon as she saw her.

Heather was a pretty girl with golden blonde hair and brown eyes. She was taller than Jessica, and her shape perfect. She was beautiful, Jessi admitted with regret. Heather's beauty was marred only by the angry expression on her face. Derik and

Brighton weren't watching Heather, though; they were watching Jessica, and she sent them a charming smile.

"Guys, you remember Jessica, right?" Joe asked, not looking particularly happy.

"Yeah. How are you, Sweetie?" Brighton asked, smiling at her.

"I'm good. The water sure is nice."

"Heather, this is Jessica Cordel. Jessica, this is Heather Crebel," Joe continued after shooting Brighton a warning look.

"I like your bathing suit," Heather said with a tight smile. Her voice was snotty, and when Joe looked away, she glared at Jessica.

Jessica gave a flip of her wet hair and said, "Thanks, so do I."

"Heather, we've got the little tent, so grab your stuff and we'll get settled in," Kara said, jumping into the conversation.

"She'll drip on the tent," Heather told Kara, jabbing her thumb toward Jessica.

Joe grabbed Heather's purple bag out of the bed of the truck. "Don't worry about it," he told her. "She's coming with us to put the boat in."

Jessi shot Joe a curious look, and Heather stood open-mouthed for a moment before running after him.

"No, she can stay with us! I want to get to know her… since she's new and all! And we'll all drip in the tent at some point this weekend. I didn't mean it as anything bad," Heather said, toying with a strand of long blonde hair.

"What do you want to do, Jess?" Joe asked, dropping Heather's bag in the tent.

Jessica sent Heather a pointed look and turned to Joe. "I'll go with you guys. I've never put a boat in the water before. It will be a new experience."

Joe walked to the boat and waited for Jessi to catch up with him. His mouth drew into a tight line as he climbed in behind her and sat in the empty captain's chair as Derik pulled away from camp.

Jessica watched him as the boat traveled down the tree-lined road. "You're quiet."

"You and Heather act as if you're enemies, and you just

met," he said, shaking his head. Jessi shrugged, not denying the fact. "This is ridiculous! You don't even know each other!" Joe told her, leaning back in his seat and crossing his arms.

"I think we both want the same thing," Jessica told him, her gaze intense.

"I told you I don't date," he replied, obviously uncomfortable with her boldness.

"I didn't ask you to," she answered, still holding his eyes.

"It's not going to happen," he assured her.

She smiled. "Maybe not. But then again, maybe you will change your mind." He shook his head and looked out the windshield of the boat. "Come on. Enough of that. Tell me what these boards are," Jessi said, pointing to the long water skis.

They got to the boat ramp all too soon, and Joe stood up as Derik opened his window. "Ready to drive it off, Joe?"

"Ready!" Derik backed down the ramp, the boat going lower and lower into the water until Jessi could reach over the side and touch the lake. Jessica laughed as her body weight pushed her back against her seat with the boat at such an angle.

"I've never done anything like this, Joe," she said, and he grinned at her.

"This isn't even the good part yet."

Joe leaned over the hull to unhook the boat, and then trotted back to the steering wheel, started the engine, and drove the boat off the trailer. They puttered around on the water and pulled up to a dock.

"Grab the side, Jess," Joe instructed, and she put her hands out on the dock to hold the boat away from the wood and bolts that threatened to scratch the glittery red paint.

"What are we waiting for?" she asked over her shoulder, her arms growing tired.

"Derik is parking the truck and trailer, and then they'll get in and we'll drive the boat back to camp."

"Like, on the water?"

He gave her a suspicious look. "Have you ever ridden in a boat before, Jessica?"

She lifted her chin. "Guess I forgot to do that between manicures and shopping trips." He grinned at her, and pointed as Derik and Brighton jogged down the sidewalk and down to the end of the dock.

Derik stepped aboard first, then Brighton, his arms out for balance. He stumbled, and fell right into Jessica's lap. He laid there a second too long and she laughed as she pushed him back. "Get in your seat, Brighton."

He tugged on a piece of her hair. "I'm just playing with you, Jessi." She smiled, flirting just a little. Brighton eagerly took the bait, and smiled back. "Black is a good color on you," he observed, referring to her bikini. She saw Joe glance over at her bathing suit, too. She sent him a charming, dimpled smile as she smugly realized that Joe Colby was human after all.

Joe stood up, offering the driver's seat to Derik, and seemed quick to take the seat behind Jessica, sliding into it before Brighton could. She pushed her dark sunglasses up, and turned to the front, knowing both boys were watching her every move. She felt quite confident as the water flew by as Derik picked up speed.

The wind dried her hair and cleared her head. The mist from the water kept her cool, and the sun was warm. She put her toes up on the dashboard, closed her eyes, and leaned her head back, letting the last rays of the sun toast her face.

She sat up when Derik slowed the pace and maneuvered the boat into a cove. She was surprised to see their little camp set up on the bank. "How do you know where to go?" she asked, amazed – the lake was so large.

He smiled at her. "My family has been camping here for years. I know this lake like the back of my hand."

"Besides, we've had this back-to-school campout for three years, and we've always had the same campsite. We're pretty familiar with the way home," Joe added.

"Of course, Derik's old man was with us until just last year, so he showed us the ropes," Brighton explained, joining the conversation.

When Derik got close to shore, Brighton jumped out and Joe threw him ropes to tie to a couple of the larger trees as anchors. Then he threw a real anchor out the back of the boat and Derik killed the engine.

"We're not going for anymore rides tonight?" Jessica asked, disappointed.

Joe shook his head. "It'll be too dark soon. It's best to get a fire started and cook our dinner before the sun goes down."

"Besides, I'm hungry!" Derik said and jumped into the lake off the back of the boat where the water was deep.

Jessica watched Derik swim toward shore and hesitated to follow. "Is there a dry way off this boat?" she asked. "The sun's already gone below the trees and it might get cold."

"Come on, guys! Jump in!" Derik prompted.

"We're going to head to dry land," Joe told him, and after pulling the boat key, led Jessica up to the hull of the boat. He lowered himself into the water over the front, and stood waist deep in the lake, his swim trunks getting soaked. He reached his arms up for her.

"Oh, just jump! It's not bad!" Heather called from the bank, smiling, and shielding her eyes with her hand. Jessica smiled at her and crawled onto the front of the boat on her knees.

"Okay, Jessi, just lower yourself into my arms and I'll carry you to shore," Joe instructed.

"Are you sure?"

"It's too late to get wet," Joe told her with a friendly wink. "We wouldn't want you to get cold and you know how chilly these August evenings can be." She didn't mind that he was teasing her, especially since he was going to carry her to shore.

She hung her legs over the side and soon he was carrying her princess-style above the water.

"Joe, get out of there!" Heather suddenly shrieked. "It's a snake!"

Jessica let out a loud scream. In a combination of Joe jumping and Jessica kicking in fear, she was dropped into the water, and went all the way under, hitting the lake floor. She scrambled to her feet as Joe found her hand and pulled her up. She ran out of the lake, Joe right behind her.

Jessica was still screaming when she hit dry ground, partly because of the fright of the snake, partly because she was soaking wet, and partly because Joe wasn't carrying her anymore. Heather grinned at her deviously when Joe turned back to the water. Jessica folded her arms across her stomach and glared at Heather. That was it. This was war.

Derik popped out of the water good-naturedly, holding up a slimy stick. "This is probably what you saw, Heather!"

The blonde put her hand over her mouth and looked apologetic. "Oops. My bad. It really did look like a snake. Sorry you got wet, Jessica."

Jessi gave her a tight smile. "What can you do? You saw a snake. I'm sure I would have done the *same thing*."

Jessica turned and walked up to where Kara, Justin and Brighton were all watching, a few feet closer to the tents. Kara was laughing and she handed Jessica a towel. Jessica narrowed her eyes but decided that Kara was laughing because it was funny, not because she had schemed with Heather.

"Good thing you aren't scared of big snakes, huh?" Joe asked, his grin giving away his amusement.

"Yeah. Good thing," Jessi answered as he joined them.

"Well, we'd better start the fire," Joe said nodding up toward camp.

"We already did," Kara announced proudly.

"And we've got dinner laid out," Heather added, running up to stand beside Joe.

He nodded approvingly. "Let's eat then."

They roasted hotdogs – Jessica burnt hers – placed them in buns and added ketchup and mustard. They had chips and coleslaw that Brighton's mom had sent. Kara tossed sodas to everyone out of a huge ice chest filled with drinks. After dinner, they sat around the campfire and roasted marshmallows. They smashed their marshmallows between fudge cookies and ate the gooey dessert with lots of laughter.

Jessica sat between Joe and Kara, the place that was quickly becoming her norm, and could not remember a time when she had been so freely happy.

Jessica heard the best and the worst stories of Glendale that night. She could not remember the last time she had laughed so hard. She heard about the time that Joe and Brighton had launched a rocket right into Brighton's barn, the time that Kara had accidentally made the entire movie theatre evacuate and the fire trucks come, the time that Derik had saved a man with a two-by-four and a long piece of twine at Mossy Crick, and the time that Heather had killed three bullfrogs with her bare hands.

Jessica laughed and listened, wide-eyed, under the starry sky, the waves lapping at the shore half a football field away with the fire crackling and burning brightly. The others were just as cheerful.

As a result of Kara's presence, no words were exchanged in the tent that night, but early in the morning, when Kara left to use the bathroom (aka bushes, much to Jessica's dismay), Heather rolled over and shook Jessica until she woke. Jessi yawned and rubbed her eyes.

"What do you want?"

"I want you to stay away from Joe," Heather hissed, attempting to keep her voice quiet.

Jessica blinked at her. "Last I heard, you didn't have any papers on him."

"Stop joking around because I'm not," Heather paused. "I have waited my whole life for Joe Colby, and we'll end up together when he decides we're ready. We are totally meant for each other so don't think you can waltz into town with your skimpy bathing suits and seductive ways and steal him away from me."

"I can't steal something from you that was never yours, Heather."

The calm comment burned the blonde. "He *is* mine! He is! I am the kind of girl he is looking for. You're not. He wants a good, wholesome girl that will make a good wife. You and I both know that you aren't that type of girl."

Jessica rolled over. "This conversation is over."

"For now, but if you don't leave him alone, it won't be," Heather threatened. Jessica closed her eyes and was back asleep before Kara ducked back into the tent.

The girls woke a few hours later to so much banging that it gave Jessica an instant headache. They all jumped as they woke, and Jessica opened her eyes to see Kara sitting up, rubbing her eyes, and Heather holding her purple pillow over her ears.

Suddenly Kara shot up and yelled "Boys!" She darted out of the tent with her pillow, and Jessica watched as first Joe, then Justin, Derik and Brighton were mercilessly beaten with it. The boys laughed and shielded themselves from her shots with their arms, the cook pans they had used to create the ruckus, discarded.

Finally exhausted from her fight, Kara stood and looked at them, her hands on her hips, her pillow hanging from her fingertips. Jessica watched, shocked that the dainty, fragile-looking little blonde with a peaked face and large pale green eyes could attack with such fury.

"Just to let you boys know, I would have been perfectly happy sleeping for another hour if you hadn't made such a racket out here," Kara said.

"Ah, but it was fun, wasn't it, Sis?" Joe asked, poking her in the ribs.

She made a face at him. "Maybe for you, but you just wait and see – you're gonna get it." The guys laughed at her threat.

Jessica watched Joe as he glanced toward the tent. She smiled sleepily and gave a small wave when he smiled at her.

"Go get your swimsuit on and get the girls. The sun's up and we're going skiing," Brighton told Kara. With that, the boys were off toward the water.

Kara came back into the tent, zipped the door shut, and they all changed quickly into their bathing suits. Jessica went for the pink string suit, and she saw Heather roll her eyes as she tied it around her neck.

"Make sure you tie that tight, Jessi. Waterskiing has a way of pulling swimsuits off," Kara warned with a concerned smile.

"Like she would mind that," Heather said under her breath.

Both Jessica and Kara heard it, but neither acted as if they had. Jessica wasn't interested in fighting, and Kara was likely hoping that it hadn't offended her. Heather's swimsuit was a white two piece – skimpier than Kara's, but with much more fabric than Jessica's.

The girls emerged together and found the guys already on the boat. Brighton was standing with the two anchor ropes in hand, waiting impatiently for them.

"What about breakfast?" Kara whined.

"We have doughnuts," Justin answered.

"Well, you're going to have to wait because the girls and I are going to take a walk in the woods and brush our teeth before we step foot on that boat," Kara told him.

"Well, then make it quick," Justin instructed with one of his dimpled smiles. Jessica was thankful for Kara's leadership and hurried to be ready when the other girls were.

Joe lifted them all up to the hull of the boat where Justin

pulled them on board. Joe's hands stayed on Heather's waist just a bit too long for Jessica's comfort, but when he took a seat beside her in the hull of the boat and said, "I like the pink," she wasn't worried anymore.

She arched her back and shook out her hair. "Really? Thanks."

He looked across the lake as Derik turned the boat and headed out onto the open water. They cruised around for awhile, eating doughnuts, before Brighton tossed two skis and a rope that was connected to the back, over the side and jumped in after it. Jessica thought waterskiing looked effortless, so when all the guys and Kara had taken their turns on the skis, and Joe asked if she would like to give it a try, she was quick to agree.

She set her soda in her drink holder, stood up, pushed her sunglasses up on her nose, and took just a minute to bask in the warmth of the sun. "I don't know exactly how to do it," she said, playing damsel in distress.

"Want me to get in the water and teach you?" Joe asked.

"Would you mind?" She flashed him a smile. Joe shook his head and stood.

Jessica saw Heather's angry glare as Joe disappeared over the side of the boat. Jessica buckled on a lifejacket and then climbed up to sit on the side, her feet dangling a foot or so above the water. "Jump in!" Joe encouraged.

"There are no snakes?" she asked, swinging her feet, her question earning her a grin from the boy in the water. He reached up and grabbed her foot, pulling her in. She pushed off the side as he did to avoid hitting her head.

"Throw in the skis," Joe told Justin.

It took Jessi quite awhile to even get the skis on her feet. When she did, they kept making her feet float, and she hit her skis against her forehead. Joe grabbed the ski rope, helped her position her feet in front of her and told her how to sit in the water. He gave Derik a thumbs-up and the boat took off.

Jessica flew about ten feet, plowing water with her face all the way, before letting go of the rope. She tried it again and again. She broke a nail. Then she tried again – and again, and again and again. She was so frustrated she wanted to cry or hit something, but Joe was so patient, kind and encouraging that she managed to keep her composure.

After forty-five minutes of trying, Jessica stood up on the skis and flew across the water, a huge smile on her face. Everyone clapped and cheered, but the only one she heard was Joe, who was still in the water watching her.

"Good job, Jessi! I knew you could do it!" he called after her, his arms outstretched in the air in victory. She skied for a few minutes, then simply let go of the rope and sank down into the water as Joe had instructed her. Her legs were shaky and weak, and her arms felt as if they had been pulled out of their sockets, but she had skied and made Joe proud.

When the boat circled back around, Kara congratulated her with a beaming smile and asked if she wanted to go again. Jessi decided to get back in the boat instead. Brighton and Justin helped her in, and Derik swung the boat around to pick up Joe, who was swimming toward them. Joe skied again, since he was already in the water. When he climbed back into the boat, he gave Jessica a high five and beamed at her.

It was Heather's turn next, and as she snapped her lifejacket on, she asked, "Joe, I'm a little rusty on this – will you help me, too?"

He laughed good-naturedly and patted her on the back. "What are you talking about? You're a great skier!" She pouted as she watched Joe walk up front to sit beside Jessica, then she turned and jumped in. The frown was gone though, when she was up on the water, flying across the lake.

Jessica watched for a while, then opted just to watch the scenery that they were passing, or Joe, which were both much more pleasant to watch than Heather. She caught Joe looking at her a few times, and she would smile and flip her hair, but he always looked away. They stayed on the boat all day, and only went in for dinner and more stories around the campfire.

Every muscle in Jessica's body was sore from waterskiing, and seeing her roll her neck, Joe stood behind her lawn chair and started to massage her shoulders. "Waterskiing can be rough the first run of the season…or the first time ever in your case," he said.

She leaned her muscles into his kneading hands and closed her eyes. "You have no idea how good that feels," she told him.

"*I* would if someone would do it to me," Kara hinted from her chair beside Jessica's. Justin sprung to his feet and both girls got the soreness rubbed out of their necks and shoulders.

Jessi spent a moment feeling sorry for Heather, as she was the only girl not getting a shoulder rub from the boy she liked, but only a moment. Then Jessica just enjoyed the massage. She let out a happy sigh as Joe sat down again. She shot him a grateful smile and touched his hand for a moment, mouthing a thank-you. He nodded, grinning. Before long it was bedtime, and everyone retired to their tents.

The next day was much like Saturday had been. They water skied and swam the day away. She sat in the front with Joe, and just after noon, stretched out on her stomach with her face turned toward him. She caught him watching her a few times, but today, he didn't look away. She opened her eyes once and saw that he was missing. Seconds later, he was back with a bottle of sunscreen.

"Getting burnt?" she asked, feeling lazy.

"No, but you are." She smiled, her dimples peeking out at him. He slathered her back with sunscreen then sat back down.

"Thanks."

He smiled at her. "You're very welcome." She stretched, satisfied with their advancement. They were making progress.

"Jessi, why did you get a tattoo? The first time I saw you, you didn't have it."

She tilted her head. "You're observant."

He offered a small smile. "I grew up with three sisters, remember?" His pause was short before he asked again, "So, why?"

"What? You don't like it?"

"I didn't say that," he paused. "It's small and tasteful, I'm just curious."

She shrugged. "Guess it was just something I wanted."

"Really? Why?"

She shot him an annoyed look. "It's none of your business."

He held up his hands with a grin. "I'm sorry. I didn't mean to touch a raw nerve." He was quiet for a few seconds. "Did your mom sign for you to have it done?"

"Yes."

"She doesn't seem like she would let you get a tattoo."

"Well, she's cool like that," Jessica said.

"What did your dad say?" he pressed.

"I'm getting tired," she said, stretching, her bikini top riding up farther as she stretched her arms back. She hoped it would distract him, but he was still watching her face when she stopped. Frustrated that she had no effect on him, she snapped, "He didn't care. I'm taking a nap." She rolled over and closed her eyes, ending the conversation.

Jessica woke to Heather calling Joe's name. Joe sat up, blinking sleepily. "Joe!" Heather called again from the back of the boat, laughing. "Come here!"

When he stood, Jessica reached out and grabbed his hand. "Stay with me."

He cocked his head at her. "You're tired, remember?" He straightened and walked to the back where he sat down beside Heather, easily joining in the lively conversation taking place. Jessica leaned out to watch as Joe talked and Heather listened and laughed. She frowned up at the blue sky. Kara came up and took Joe's place. Before long, Jessi was talking and laughing again.

When the sun was low in the sky, Derik steered the boat toward camp and dropped the girls, Brighton and Justin off to start breaking camp while he went to the boat ramp with Joe to load the boat onto the trailer. By the time they came back, camp was taken down. Once everything was loaded into the right vehicles, they said their goodbyes and parted ways.

Joe and Jessi's ride back to Glendale started out tense and quiet. Finally, Joe broke the silence by talking about the crops. They talked and even laughed, but the time on the boat was never discussed.

When they drove through Glendale, Joe pulled into the ice cream shop. They went in and each got two scoops in a waffle cone. Joe insisted on paying. Once they were back in the truck, he let out a deep breath. "Jess, I'm sorry if I asked too many questions about your tattoo." He looked apologetic.

She shook her head. "I'm sorry I was angry. I just..." she sighed and blew at a piece of dark hair. "Do you want to know why I got a tattoo?" He nodded. She took a slow lick of her chocolate ice cream. "I was mad at my dad, Joe, and I just wanted to hurt him like he's hurt me and my mom. I know he hates tattoos, and I thought that if I got one, it would hurt him."

"Did it work?" Joe asked softly.

Jessi shrugged. "It made him mad."

They were both quiet as they worked on their ice cream. "Is that why you cut your hair?" She nodded. "Jess, can I offer a little advice?" She nodded again, remembering how Joe had gone to Heather when Jessica was snappy with him. "Don't change yourself for someone else, whether it's to hurt them or make them happy. You are who you are, no matter what anyone else thinks."

"You live by that," she observed thoughtfully.

"Yes, I do." He wasn't preaching at her, and he wasn't trying to tell her what to do. His voice was gentle and full of genuine concern. She wanted to reach for his hand, but instead, licked her melting ice cream.

When Joe dropped Jessica off at home, he grinned at her. "I'm glad you came, Jessica Cordel. It was fun."

She smiled at him as he leaned back against the door of his pickup. "I'm glad you asked me – it *was* fun."

"Ready for school to start?"

"Not for another two weeks," she told him, starting to walk backward toward her house.

"I'll see you soon, Jessi," he promised. She waved, and he got in his truck and drove away. That night, she called Kayly and spent two hours describing how wonderful her neighbor, Joe Colby, was.

Eight

Jessica grabbed a cart and pushed it slowly through the store. She looked at her mom's short list, and checked off the items as she put them into the grocery cart. Spaghetti sauce, tofu, macaroni and cheese, avocados, chicken breasts, soda, orange juice, and two gallons of milk went into the cart. She was about to round the cookie aisle into the canned vegetable aisle when she heard a familiar voice.

"He's never going to go for a girl like her. You should have seen her at the lake – well, you saw her Kara!" Jessica's eyebrows rose. So Heather was gossiping about her in the grocery store and Kara was with her? "She was wearing bikinis that were pretty much nothing but strings, and she was rubbing herself all over him! It was disgusting! I even saw her sneak out of our tent at two in the morning and go over to his," Heather said in a hushed tone. Jessica clenched her teeth together – she hadn't! "And also, I heard that she tried kissing him on the way to the boat dock, and he had to push her off of him."

Jessica felt her blood start to boil as Heather kept going. "She just doesn't have an ounce of self-respect or shame! If I ever had to stoop to that level to get guys' attention, I think I'd become a nun." Heather stopped for a breath as a few different girls laughed. Jessica looked at the floor, considering whether to listen to more or simply go slap her now.

"He just doesn't date, Heather." Kara sounded quiet and weak, obviously intimidated by Heather's loud opinion of Jessica.

"And when he does, I certainly don't think he would actually date *her* of all people. She's such a tramp." Heather was pouty and fishing for the others' agreement.

"No way! Don't even worry about it, Heather, you guys are perfect for each other," chimed in an unfamiliar voice. "Joe knows that." "If she was like you, you might have to be worried, but it sounds like she's not," said another.

"Oh my gosh, I would hope not! If she's like me then I

would refuse to get out of bed for the rest of my life – the world would be better off without me." Again, Heather's cruel remarks drew laughter. "I mean, she thinks she's such hot stuff just because she's from D.C., but she's not. She may think I'm less than her because I'm just the girl next door, but she's going to get a wake-up call when she realizes that Joe isn't attracted to sleazy."

She had heard enough. Jessica pushed her cart around the corner and stopped it behind Heather. Her neck and cheeks felt hot, and her heart was pounding as she confronted the group of five girls – Heather, Kara, and three others that she had never seen before.

"Joe may not be attracted to sleazy, but I doubt he's attracted to fake either," Jessica paused and took a step toward the tall blonde. "You pretend to be such a good little girl, Heather, but even I, a 'tramp' from D.C., wouldn't stand in a grocery store and lie about somebody just to make myself look better," Jessica said, her voice misleadingly calm and controlled. She swept her smoldering gaze over the group of girls before letting it land on Kara. An apology was written all over Kara's small face, but Jessica narrowed her eyes at her and turned, running out of the grocery store. No one said anything to stop her.

She got into her yellow car, her eyes burning with tears. It felt like Heather's words, true and untrue, had stabbed a hundred little needles into her flesh. She turned the key and threw the car into reverse. A quick rap came on her window and she glanced up into Joe Colby's grinning face. Her cheeks reddened in embarrassment.

He must have brought Kara into town and been waiting in his truck while she grocery shopped for their mother. Jessica's bottom lip trembled. She thought about rolling the window down and telling him what had happened, but couldn't bring herself to do it. She shook her head, looked away while she swiped at her burning tears, and then flew backward.

She zoomed out of the parking lot and out of town. She broke the speed limit on her way home and turned the radio way up to drive Heather's words out of her mind. She flew down the gravel road and gave a sharp jerk of the wheel to turn into her driveway, causing a spray of gravel. She parked the car, wiped her tears, and slammed the car door. She slipped quietly in the front door, but not quietly enough.

"Do you need help getting the groceries, Jess?" her mom asked from the kitchen.

"I didn't get them," she answered, her voice dull yet defiant.

"Why not? I need that avocado to make dinner!"

"Get it yourself."

"What happened?" Carla asked, wiping her hands on a dishtowel as she stepped into the living room.

"Nothing! I just didn't feel like getting groceries!" Jessica said, her voice rising.

"Well, where have you been?"

"It's none of your business!" Jessi yelled, and then ran down the hall and slammed her bedroom door. She threw herself onto her bed, and buried her face in a pillow. Carla knocked on the door a few minutes later.

"Stay out."

"I'm going to the store to get the groceries that you were supposed to get."

"Fine."

"Your car is blocking mine."

"Take it."

"Where are the keys?"

"By the door, Mom! Good grief, leave me alone!"

"We're talking over dinner, do you hear me? I want to know what happened in town."

"You can talk 'til you're blue in the face, I don't care."

"I'm done with this attitude, Jess! Do you hear me? I'm done! I don't deserve to be talked to like this!" Carla's voice was rising dramatically.

"Well, I don't deserve to be stuck in this stupid town! I'm out of here when I turn eighteen, Mom! I'm out! That is, if I stay that long – I might run away first!" Jessi knew that would be the end of the conversation. She heard Carla's deep breath.

"I'll be back."

"Don't hurry," Jessi said, putting her face back down into her pillow.

"Love you, too," was Carla's sarcastic response.

Jessica listened to the front door open and then close, the

car start and the engine noise grow faint only to disappear as her mother drove away. She pushed herself off her bed and unlocked her door. She needed a drink of water. She went into the kitchen, opened the cupboard above the sink, and snagged a glass.

She noticed the message on the answering machine and pushed play while she filled her glass with water. "Jessica, it's your dad. I would really like to speak with you. I feel like you're leaving me out of your life. I haven't talked to you in weeks. I'll be free to talk between nine and ten tonight. Call me." Jessica rolled her eyes and enjoyed pushing the delete button.

He acted as if she had to have an appointment to talk to him. Besides, who was he to complain that she was leaving him out of her life? Hadn't he been the one to exclude himself from it for fifteen years? Hadn't it been him who had been so busy at work that she hadn't see him for days, weeks, even a month at a time while she lived under the same roof? What a joke.

She pulled out a box of wheat crackers and munched them slowly as she sat down at the breakfast bar to look through the clothing magazine that had come in the mail. Two items were circled, both in her mom's size. There was a decent looking black dress with a silver loop neck and an adorable tan top. When that arrived, Jessica would have to raid her mother's closet. Jessi heard the car pull in, the front door open and then close.

"Interesting thing, Jess," Carla started as she set the bags on the counter.

"What's that?"

"There was an unattended cart in the canned vegetable aisle that had nearly everything on my list in it."

"Hm." Jessica flipped to the next page.

"I waited a few minutes for the customer to come back, and when no one did, I just took the cart and checked out."

"How convenient."

"What happened in the grocery store?"

"I didn't go to the grocery store," Jessi lied.

"Oh, Jessica, stop it! How many people in Glendale buy tofu? Us! That's it. You were at the store, got the groceries, left the cart, left the food, and obviously left the store. Why?"

Jessica gave a disrespectful roll of her eyes. "I guess you'll never know."

Carla put her hands on her hips and flipped her dark, shoulder-length hair over her tanned shoulder. "Fine. Then maybe I don't want to know."

Jessi shrugged. "Whatever."

"Your dad left a message for you."

"I heard it. Rich, wasn't it?"

Carla nodded. "Very. Where does he get off?"

"At the Arrogant Victim Motel, right off of Dug My Own Grave Boulevard."

Carla chuckled as she put away the groceries. "I love your sense of humor, Jess."

Jessica almost grinned before she remembered she was mad. "You should hear what I say about *you*."

"If you love me at all, you'll never tell me."

Jessi held the magazine up in front of her face to cover her smile. "I don't."

Carla messed up her hair and gave her head a gentle push. "Whatever." Jessica did smile then, and Carla wrapped her arms around Jessica's shoulders, and set her chin on Jessi's head. The rare affection startled Jessica, but Carla squeezed her. "I love you, Baby Girl."

Jessica's mouth twitched, and she patted her mom's arm awkwardly. "I love you, too." The doorbell rang, and Jessi let out a long sigh as she imagined who it might be. "But I don't love that."

"Want me to get it?" Carla asked, sounding concerned.

Jessi shook her head and stood up, walking into the living room. "Just stay in the kitchen."

"Yes, ma'am," Carla said, the sarcastic bite back in her voice.

Jessica opened the door and crossed her arms as she looked at Kara through the screen door. Kara looked pale. "Hey, Jessi. Can we talk for a little bit?" Jessica stared at her and then shrugged. She stepped out onto the front porch instead of inviting Kara in, and shut the door.

Jessica breezed past her to sit in the middle of the porch swing, leaving no spot for Kara. Kara turned and looked at her. She held out a chocolate waffle cone. "It's kind of melting – it's awfully hot today. Joe and I stopped for some, and he said you like chocolate." Jessica considered the melting ice cream cone, and finally reached out and took it. Kara smiled faintly.

"Think all can be forgotten by using ice cream as a bribe?" Jessi asked, taking her first lick.

"Not forgotten, but hopefully forgiven," Kara answered, shrugging one shoulder and shooting Jessi a hopeful smile. When there was no response, Kara took a deep breath and stepped toward the porch swing, her hand reached out imploringly.

"Please forgive me, Jessi! I shouldn't have been standing there listening. I don't know why I was. I didn't agree with her and I don't believe in gossip. I have no idea why I stayed to listen instead of getting my mom's groceries!"

"Well, if you didn't agree with her, you could have fooled me."

"I know that silence is sometimes taken as agreement, I just...."

"You just don't want to stand up for a tramp from D.C., and maybe get on Princess Heather's bad side, right? Don't worry. I get it."

Kara tipped her head. "Jessi, you are from D.C., but I'm not so sure you're a tramp, and sometimes I think you forget that, too," she paused as she regained control of her tongue. "But there's no way to reason away what I did. I was wrong, and I'm sorry. I don't blame you for being mad. What Heather said must have hurt."

Jessica looked away and shook her head. "No, not at all." She stood and looked over the porch railing.

"Heather lied. You never sneaked out of our tent, and you didn't try to kiss Joe in the boat," Kara stated.

"How do you know? Maybe I did! Don't pretend like you know me, Kara Colby," Jessi said sharply, her voice rising a notch.

"Joe told me." Jessi was quiet. Kara let out a really long sigh. "Anyway, I wanted to tell you that I am really, really sorry, and I hope you will forgive me for not standing up to Heather. And," Kara paused and bit her lip. "I want you to know that I don't agree with her."

Jessica wanted to say something mean and sarcastic, one of her normal come backs, but she looked at Kara's small, pale face, her large green eyes full of sincere regret, and she couldn't come up with one. Not one. She scuffed the toe of her tennis shoe on the porch floor. "Don't worry about it."

"I am worried about it. I sinned, and I hurt you."

Jessica let out a very small smile. "A little."

Kara swallowed. "I wish I could relive that conversation so I could do things differently."

Jessica laughed. "I've wanted to do that before, too. Unfortunately, it's never worked out."

Kara smiled and went to stand beside Jessi. "I promise that if I'm ever in that situation again, I'll stand up for the truth."

Jessica smiled. "I don't know that I would have had the courage."

"Are we okay?" Kara asked, looking hopeful.

"Chocolate does cover a multitude of sins," Jessi joked.

Kara laughed as she licked her own ice cream. "I'd have to agree with that."

"Want to stay for dinner?" It was an olive branch, and Kara smiled.

"I'd love to, but my sister is coming down for a long weekend. My mom is cooking up a storm, and I'm supposed to be helping."

Jessica nodded. "Okay."

"Sometime, though, okay? I'd love to stay for dinner sometime!"

Jessi smiled. "I'll ask you again."

"Okay. I'll hold you to that!" Kara said grinning. "I'd better get going. Have a great weekend, though!" Kara backed toward the porch stairs, as she waited for Jessi's reply.

"You too! Thanks for the ice cream."

"No problemo, Amiga!" Kara said with a grin. She turned and walked down the drive. She paused halfway down to turn and wave. "See you later!" she called and took off at a jog, cutting through the trees on a shortcut to her house.

Jessi smiled and shook her head. Kara reminded her of a young filly. Her legs were long and slender, and she still had that innocent little girl look. They were only a year apart in age, but a decade apart in innocence. For a brief moment, that fact made Jessi sad. She turned back into the house.

"What did the Colby girl want?" Carla questioned as soon as the door shut behind Jessi.

"Just to talk."

"Everything okay?"

"Perfect. She's a nice girl."

"I thought you hated that phrase."

"Only when it comes to Heather Crebel, Mom."

Carla smiled. "Ice cream. What a good idea. Do we have any drumsticks left?"

Jessi opened the freezer door. "Three."

"Let's have them for dessert."

"Fine with me."

After dinner, Jessica left the house. She walked through the trees, listening to the crunching and snapping of the twigs under her feet. The forest was calm and smelled good. She loved the musty smell of damp earth and growing vegetation. She followed the trail to the tall, tall oak tree she had found and sat at its base, her back against the trunk. She tipped her head back and allowed herself to relax.

It was quiet enough to think and solitary enough to let go. She sprawled against the warm tree, her legs straight out. She flicked an ant off her knee and slapped at a mosquito. Her cell phone rang, and she pulled it out of her pocket to check the number. It was Kayly, but she pushed the ignore button. She wasn't in the mood to talk. She just wanted to be alone. As she slipped her cell phone back into her pocket, the silence of the forest settled over her like a sheet. She closed her eyes, letting herself reorient with nature. After a few minutes, she fell asleep.

She was awakened almost an hour later by familiar whistling. She was groggy at first, and before she even had time to sit up straight, Joe had stepped into the clearing. He grinned and took a seat beside her while her hand flew to straighten her hair.

"I was hoping I'd find you here."

"I didn't expect you to come here tonight. I thought your sister was in town."

"Yeah, Kim's down, but the girls are cleaning up dinner. It will take them an hour or so with as much talking as they're doing, so I thought I'd take a walk." He leaned back against the bark and stretched his long legs out in front of him.

She glanced at him and then away, realizing she hadn't even looked in a mirror before walking out the door. She glanced back, and he was watching her. She smiled, liking the intense way he was studying her face, hoping that he was thinking of kissing her. He'd said he had hoped to find her, hadn't he? She looked up into his eyes and leaned forward just a little to give him the chance.

"I heard about the conversation in the grocery store."

Jessi cringed and quickly dropped her eyes, looking away. So much for a kiss.

"Kara told you?" she asked, her voice sounding smaller than she would have liked. He nodded. Jessica didn't take her eyes from the peaceful forest of trees as she felt her cheeks turn pink. She hoped Kara hadn't told him exactly what Heather had said.

"Anyway, about the conversation," he started.

She shrugged. "It didn't bother me at all."

He bumped her shoulder with his, and her heart fluttered. "Which is why you were crying by the time you got to your car."

"I had something in my eye." The lie sounded lame even to her own ears.

He laughed. "Sure, and I actually want to date Heather Crebel." She turned and looked at him then, and his face turned serious as he looked back at her. "Jessi, I just wanted to tell you not to worry about Heather. She means well, but sometime she judges too quickly."

"Maybe she doesn't. Maybe I am who she says I am," she challenged, raising an eyebrow.

He grinned. "Either way, I like to have my own opinions."

"Aw, an independent thinker. How special." He chuckled.

"You probably think you have me all figured out, don't you Jessi?"

"Almost," she lied. She had no idea what to think of the green-eyed boy beside her.

"Christian boy, gets straight A's, star quarterback, doesn't date – I'm so predictable – finish my story."

She let a small smile slip. "You'll grow up to be a good Christian man, marry a nice little Christian girl, play football in college, move back home to farm with your old man, and someday, watch your own kids grow up on your old stomping grounds."

He nodded, grinning and satisfied. "It sounds predictable, but maybe, just maybe, it's too early to write me off just yet." As she considered his cheerful face, she realized there was something serious in his eyes. Maybe he, like her, didn't want people to think they knew him just because of what they saw. "But what about you, Jessica Cordel? What are you going to do? Who are you going to be?"

She dragged her eyes from his, trying to collect her thoughts. Her heart was racing, her mind flying. His presence, the steady gaze of his eyes, the soft, deep sound of his voice sent her into a wild tailspin. She fell back on humor and laughed. "Not a politician like my dad, that's for sure."

"I'm serious. Tell me who you are."

"Well, I'm a spoiled little rich girl. My dad's a senator, my mom's a lawyer. I grew up alone in a beautiful house with a swimming pool, a maid, and a cook. I was voted most likely to be prom queen my eighth grade year. I'll grow up and marry someone rich, pursue a glamorous, yet unfulfilling career, and live unhappily ever after," she said, threading humor through the pitifully correct picture of her life.

"Good start, good start," he said nodding. "Now try going below the surface and telling me something I don't already know. Tell me who you really are. I really don't want to have to believe Heather's take on you," he said, teasing her.

She tilted her head and stared out at the gathering shadows. "I don't really know, I guess. I'm not sure there's anything to tell."

He bumped her shoulder again. "Whatever. I don't believe that's it."

She thought about it for several seconds and then raised her shoulders before letting them fall. "I guess I'm just a girl that's trying to find her way, you know? I'm trying to find where I belong in this world." She took a deep breath. "Sometimes, I feel like I could be someone completely different from who I am, and it's someone I want to be, but I never know who that is or how to be that girl." He was quiet.

"I know one thing, Jessica Cordel."

She loved her name when he said it. "What's that?" she asked softly, not trusting herself to look up at him.

"Right now, you're supposed to be sitting against this old oak tree with me."

She felt the smile spread warmly across her face. "You're right about that," she agreed. They sat quietly for quite awhile.

"You know what else?" he bumped her shoulder with his.

"What?" she asked.

"I think that maybe, just maybe, it's too early to write you off, too." She twirled a blade of grass between her thumb and index finger.

"Maybe we'll both surprise the world," she said softly.

"Maybe we will," he agreed. Joe tipped his head back, staring up into the rustling canopy of green. "This is my Jesus tree," he told her quietly.

"Your what?"

"My Jesus tree. Like Jesus Christ, you know? I come here when I need to pray. I feel close to Him here – like He comes down to dwell with me in these branches, or like they give my prayers a path to follow up to heaven."

"Did you come here to pray tonight?"

She watched him grin slowly and shake his head. "I came to find you. I couldn't stand the fact that the last time I saw you, you were crying. All because one of my friends had been cruel and mean and," he paused, "and wrong."

She slid her knees up to her chest and wrapped her arms around them, accidentally brushing her arm against his.

"I don't want you to think of Heather's behavior today when you think of Christians."

Jessica tilted her head and considered him for a few moments. "I don't think about Christians."

"But if you do, don't think of that. Everyone messes up, but we are *supposed* to be loving and kind."

She gave him a flirty smile. "I promise that if I think of Christians, I'll think of you."

His face flushed red. "Think of Jesus."

She shook her head, setting her chin on her knees. "I don't know Jesus."

His voice was gentle when he answered. "But Jessi, He

knows you."

As his words settled over her, she felt suddenly uncomfortable. Not with Joe, but with the thought of some mysterious God knowing her. She shook it off. She didn't believe in God. Still, a twinge of longing fluttered across her heart. Perhaps one would call it a longing for something eternal.

Joe brushed his arm against hers and she looked up at him. He grinned. "You going to be alright?"

"I'm fine."

"I'm glad you and Kara are okay."

"Your sister is a nice girl, Joe. You're lucky."

"They all are."

She nodded. "I bet."

"And I know I'm lucky. That's why I try to keep her close."

Jessica turned her head and smiled up at him. "Smart man."

He grinned. "I'd like to think so."

They sat quiet for a little longer before he pushed himself to his feet. "I'd better get back. Kimmy and Greg were going to put Carson to bed after the kitchen was cleaned up, and then we're going to play cards. I have to be there so the teams are even." She nodded. He gently kicked the sole of her shoe. "See ya, Jess."

"See ya. Have fun with your family."

"I will," he said with a grin, and then left. She took a deep breath as he walked away.

Family. It was a word she barely knew the meaning of. She sat a little longer, alone with her thoughts, then stood up to leave. She brushed the dirt off the seat of her pants, and headed back home.

Nine

"Ah. It was a nice day, wasn't it, Son?" Chris Colby said, letting out a long sigh as he dropped down beside his boy.

Joe grinned, the last rays of the summer sun hitting his face. "Yeah."

They were sitting in lawn chairs, a cold lemonade in each of their right hands. "Sure was a hot one earlier. I'm glad it cooled off."

"Yeah, I thought I was going to melt when I was fixing fences over at Cooter's," Joe agreed.

"I bet practice wasn't overly cool, either."

Joe shook his head emphatically. "It was miserable with all the equipment, but coach took it easy on us since it was so hot."

It was nearing the second week of two-a-days, and Joe couldn't be happier about that. He loved the sport, but hated two-a-days. "He's a wise man, Joe. You'll do good if you listen to his advice."

Joe looked at his dad curiously. He always listened to his coach. "I agree. I do everything he asks."

Chris was quiet for a long time and took a slow drink of lemonade. "What are you thinking about Jessica?"

Joe looked at his dad, completely confused. "What do you mean?"

"You've been talking about her a lot, and I was just wondering. Is she going to be just a friend," Chris paused. "Maybe something more?"

Joe let out a long breath and settled back in his seat. "Have you seen her, Dad?"

"Yes. I saw her in town the other day, but didn't have a chance to meet her," Chris answered.

"She's beautiful, isn't she?"

"Undeniably. How deep does that beauty run? What kind of a girl is she?"

"Bad," Joe admitted with a sigh.

"Bad?" Chris' eyebrows rose in question.

"Well, not bad, she's just used to such different things. She has such different ideas about everything."

"Including relationships, I'm guessing?"

"Relationships more than anything else," Joe said with a humorless laugh.

"What's she think about them?"

"That they're nothing. That they're just something to pass the time. A way to have some temporary pleasure."

"Hm. All relationships or just boy/girl ones?"

"I don't know, but she doesn't like her mom much and hates her dad, so I'm guessing all relationships."

"It'd be a hard way to live, wouldn't it, Son?"

Joe couldn't agree more and was overwhelmed with gratefulness for his own life. He was surrounded by a family who loved him. He had a church family that cared about him. He was one of the stars of his high school. He was well-known and highly respected in his town, and he had good, solid friends scattered across the country. He was wrapped in loving, secure arms by so many people, while Jessica was alone and fighting fiercely to survive. "That's just it. Dad, she tries to make people think she's so bad and tough, but it's just a show. Once in awhile, it's just the briefest of moments, but she lets her guard down, and she's so vulnerable and innocent and…and soft. She's so hurt Dad, so alone, so lost. I see that part of her, and I just want to care for her…protect her, you know?"

Chris didn't answer for a long time. "You have a good heart, Son."

"I think I'm going to ask her out," Joe said slowly.

"You want to start dating?" Joe couldn't miss the look of shock on his father's face.

He rubbed his forehead. "I don't know."

"You've always proven yourself to be trustworthy and you act with wisdom, so if you want to date this girl, I will respect your decision. But don't do it just to save her," Chris said, his voice gentle.

"Dad, she needs someone to love her."

"She does, but a boyfriend is not what she needs."

"I'll have more influence over her than anyone else."

"Joe, at the very heart of who you are, Son, you're an evangelist, but there are other ways to introduce her to Jesus than by dating her. If Jesus wants her saved, He can accomplish it with or without you. This is a decision you need to make apart from Jessi's spiritual needs, okay? It's not wise to mix evangelism with a dating relationship."

Joe nodded. "I understand."

"And don't forget about the girls that you've told so many times that you don't date."

Again, Joe nodded. "I know. Heather will be so mad."

"And honestly, rightfully so," Chris answered.

"Yeah," Joe said, rubbing the back of his neck. "I know."

"Well, Son, I trust your judgment, and I know that you're going to do what's best for you and Jessi, so just keep me posted, okay?" Joe nodded, his eyebrows drawn together in thought. Chris rose from his chair and stopped beside his son. Joe looked up and his dad gave his shoulder a gentle squeeze. "You're a good man, Joe."

Joe beamed. "Thanks, Dad." He sat in his chair long after his father went into the house. The shadows gathered around him, and soon he was sitting in darkness. He didn't know what to do.

He took a walk and wound up at his Jesus tree. He climbed the branches easily, having used the same footholds and branches for almost a decade. He settled high in the tree and swung his legs, looking up into the green leaves and praying. He stayed there for a long time, and when he went home, everyone was in bed.

His mom had left the under-counter lights on for him in the kitchen, and there was a glass of milk and a cookie beside a note that asked him to come tell her goodnight when he got home. He ate the cookie and drank the milk, feeling somewhat like Santa. He washed his glass out, set it in the sink with the plate, and climbed the stairs. He slipped into his parents' room after knocking, and told them goodnight before heading to bed himself.

The light in his room was on, and he found Kara lying on his bed reading her Bible.

"What are you doing, Squirt?" he asked, ruffling her hair affectionately before he pulled his t-shirt off and tossed it at the laundry hamper that sat in the corner of his room.

"I was doing my devotions tonight, and I came across some verses that I thought you might be interested in, so here." She stood and handed him a blue index card filled with writing, front and back.

He smiled at her small, neat handwriting and the verses that she had so carefully written. "Thanks, Kara."

She smiled at him, looking more pixie-ish than ever. "No problem. Goodnight, Joe."

He caught her as she went by and gave her a quick hug. "Goodnight, Sis."

She stopped at his door and looked back. "Not to sway you, but I really like Jessi. She needs someone that will care about her."

Joe gave her a sad smile. "She needs Jesus." Kara nodded, and then with one last smile, went out shutting his door softly. He sat down on the edge of his bed and began to read the verses.

*"Above all else, guard your heart, for it is the wellspring of life." -Proverbs 4:23. "Let your eyes look straight ahead, fix your gaze directly before you." -Proverbs 4:25. "Charm is deceptive, and beauty is fleeting; but a woman who fears the LORD is to be praised." -Proverbs 31:30. "Do not arouse or awaken love until it so desires." -Song of Songs 3:5. "Love is patient, love is kind. It does not envy, it does not boast, it is not proud. It is not rude, it is not self-seeking, it is not easily angered, it keeps no record of wrongs. Love does not delight in evil but rejoices with the truth. It always protects, always trusts, always hopes, always perseveres." -1 Corinthians 13:4-7. "Therefore he is able to save completely those who come to God through **him**, because he always lives to intercede for them." -Hebrews 7:25. "The goal of your faith, the salvation of your souls." -1 Peter 1:9.*

Joe sighed as he read over the verses again. He didn't know what Kara meant by them. He thought he knew the answer in the first four, but the last three confused him. And Kara's bold letters on the verse from Hebrews was nice and subtle. Why did they all think he would try to save Jessi by his own means? He thought about going to ask Kara what she thought he should do, but knew she would want him to make up his own mind, just like everyone else. He put the card down on his bedside table and turned out his lamp.

Ten

"Hello?" Jessica asked, snagging the phone from the counter.

"Hey Jessi." Joe's voice sounded warm and lazy, almost as if he had just woken up. She felt her heart flutter for a moment. This was the first time he had called her.

"Hey. It's hot today, huh?" she asked, grasping for something to say.

"Almost unbearable," he agreed. "But it's supposed to cool off tonight."

"That will be nice."

"Yeah," he paused. "I was wondering if you wanted to go fishing tonight."

"Sure," she immediately answered.

"Okay, well, if I come for you around eight again, would that work?"

"Yes."

"Okay, I'll see you then."

"Okay," she told him and they hung up. Jessi was glad that it was already four o'clock, because she could hardly wait.

"Mom, what's for dinner?" she asked, walking out onto the back patio. Her mom was sunning in her bathing suit and doing paperwork.

"Avocado salad?"

Jessi nodded. "Sounds good."

"We'll eat around five thirty. Who was that on the phone?"

"Joe."

Her mother smiled. "And?"

"He asked if I wanted to go fishing again."

"And you said yes."

"Of course."

Carla smiled, and readjusted her dark sunglasses. "Go put on your bathing suit and then come tan out here until dinner."

"Why?" Jessi asked, thinking about the air-conditioning

just a few feet away.

"Boys like sun-kissed skin. If you lie out and refresh your tan, then get a shower and put on that shimmer lotion you have, you'll glow."

Not wanting to reveal the fact that she appreciated guy tips from her mom, she suppressed a smile and simply said, "I'll be back."

In her room, she slipped into her blue eyelet bikini, and grabbing a towel out of the cupboard and her sunglasses off the kitchen counter, she took her book and went outside. She spread her towel on the concrete, and lay down on it. "Mom, would you tell me when it's been twenty minutes?"

"Mm hmm," Carla agreed, eating a pretzel stick.

Jessica slipped her sunglasses on to shield her eyes. She thought about fishing, about the last time she had been out, and about Joe. Her thoughts faded into dreams.

"Jess? *Jessica.*" She slowly woke to her mom's voice.

"What?

"It's been twenty-five minutes – turn over." Jessica turned over and instantly went back to sleep. The next time Carla woke her, she was bending over her. "I'm going to start dinner. You want to get your shower? You've been out here for about an hour now."

Jessica moved her sunglasses to rub her eyes. "It's five?"

Carla nodded. "Five fifteen."

Jessica stood and grabbed her towel, the book that still lay unopened, and her sunglasses. She went into the house, drank a glass of water, and went back to her room. With dinner only fifteen minutes away, she decided to pick out her clothes, then shower after she ate.

Once dinner was over, Jessi left the dishes for her mom and hurried back to the bathroom. She took a long, steamy shower, taking extra care with her hair and makeup. She pulled on a pair of denim shorts and a tight white tank top. It showed her tan off perfectly, and after putting on lotion, her skin really did seem to glow. She fastened a simple silver chain around her neck and the little pink jewel hung right in the dip of her collarbone. She added her watch, earrings, and perfume. She slipped her cell phone into the pocket of her shorts, tugging them down just a little farther.

"Let me see you," Carla called as Jessi opened the bathroom door. Jessi grabbed a shoulder bag and added bug spray, a baseball hat and a pack of gum. Then she went out to stand in front of her mother. Carla smiled. "The fish are going to be fighting for the right to bite your line."

Jessica rolled her eyes. "Yeah, right."

Carla laughed. "Well, at least the boy fish."

"Well then, I suppose I'll bring home enough for another fish fry," Jessica answered with a smile.

"You'll be home by eleven?"

"Mom! Last time it was twelve."

"Okay, okay. Twelve," Carla paused, "but not a minute later."

"Thank you. Besides, I was back early last time, remember?" Jessica reminded her.

"That's true."

"I'm going to go wait on the porch."

"Be good."

"Mom!"

Carla held up her hands. "Jess, I'm just saying." Jessica went out the door and took a seat on the porch swing.

When Joe pulled up, Jessica couldn't help smiling at his jeans and the white t-shirt that pulled across the muscles of his chest. She let him get the door of his truck for her. "It does seem to be cooling down," she mentioned as he shifted into reverse.

"They say it's going to rain late tonight."

She nodded, looking out at the darkening clouds to the west, and then turned back toward Joe. "So, how's work?" she asked.

"The crops are growing, the pastures are lush for the cattle – it's all going good."

"Good." It grew quiet for a few moments.

"School starts soon," he told her.

"Just a few more days," Jessi agreed, glancing his way.

"Are you ready?" he questioned.

"Ready for homework, classes and cranky teachers?" she asked. "Never. What about you?"

He shrugged. "GHS isn't so bad. Most of the teachers are pretty nice."

"I'm just not really good at school. Like not bad, but not one of those 'A' kids," Jessi told him, her expression bordering on pouty. Her father had always wanted her to get straight A's, but it had never happened. Now, she wondered if that was what drove him to Jari. She shook her head. That was ridiculous. She noticed that Joe hadn't responded. "You're one of those 'A' kids, aren't you?" she asked suspiciously.

He smiled. "Yes, ma'am."

She cocked her head. "Well, then, Mr. 'A', maybe you could help me with my homework."

"Maybe I could."

"When do two-a-days start?"

He made a face. "Two weeks ago; I died."

She shook her head, smiling. "I don't buy it. I'm sure you did fine. You certainly look like you're in good shape." He didn't look at her, but he grinned.

"What about you? Play any sports?" he asked.

She shook her head. "Not anymore. I'd rather do other things with my afternoons and evenings."

"Such as?"

"Such as other things," she answered, not sure what to say. What did she do with her time? She couldn't seem to come up with anything.

He tipped his head and looked at her. "Such as?"

She shot him an annoyed look. "Such as other things," she repeated. It suddenly became a silent battle of wills.

"What things?" His grin was quick, his green eyes sparkling with amusement.

She looked at him in complete annoyance. She had never met a boy who demanded an explanation like this. She rolled down her window and turned the radio on. He mercifully let it go as he turned onto the dirt drive where the path to the river started.

"We may not be out here long. It looks like the rain is coming in faster than predicted," Joe observed, studying the sky above the tree line. It wasn't the sky Jessica was looking at, though. There were no other cars.

She turned to Joe, surprised. "Are the others coming later?"

He parked and turned off the truck. He looked out the windshield. "It's just you and me tonight."

She cocked her head, considering his words and gave him an impressed smile. "This was unexpected."

He turned and looked at her, a smug grin on his face. "I'm telling you right now, we date on my terms or not at all. Will you agree to that?"

"What happened to you not dating?" she asked, suspiciously, expectantly.

His strong jaw worked. "I'm not really sure...but then again I think you're used to the rules changing for you, aren't you, Jessica?" Her only response was a smile.

He stepped out of the truck, and walked around to open her door. She slid out, suddenly turning on all the charm she had. They were back on her playing field. He shut the door. "Are we dating on my terms, or not at all?" he asked again as he pulled the chairs, rods, bucket, tackle box, and ice chest to the back of the tailgate. He handed her the empty bucket and tackle box. He took the rest.

"What kind of terms do you have in mind?" she asked, looking at him, slowly lowering her thick eyelashes.

"First of all, I am the only one who initiates physical contact."

She frowned. "Why?"

"Because it can't go too far, and I'm going to make sure that it doesn't," he paused. "Secondly, you can't constantly try to seduce me." She frowned again. With his stipulations, what was the point of having a girlfriend? He kicked at a clump of dirt. "That's all so far. Do you agree?"

She walked quietly down to the fishing spot. He set up the chairs while she thought. "I don't have to like you," she finally said.

"You're right."

"I could easily like any of the other guys."

"I'm not sure why you don't," Joe agreed.

"You're not the kind of guy I usually go for."

"You're definitely not the kind of girl I go for," he told her, matching her irritated comments.

"I've never seen a relationship like the one you're describing."

He finally broke into a grin. "You've never seen anyone

like me – I'm an imposter, remember?"

She grinned too, and sat down in the chair he offered her. She watched him bait her hook, considering his proposal. She stood up to cast, and when she sat down again she looked over at him. "Deal."

He grinned at his worm. "Yeah?" She nodded. "Good. Now, Jess, nothing has changed. We act like we did when we were friends, or this whole dating thing is off."

"You sound like you're threatening me," she said frowning.

He shook his head, and looked over, his eyes sincere. "I just really like the Jessica I've been hanging out with lately." She didn't know what to say to that so she didn't say anything. They just sat and fished.

Shadows started to gather and they stayed quiet. She didn't know what to do or say. She had heard countless stories from Anna and Kayly about what they did on dates, but this was a far cry from the stories she had heard. This kind of a scenario had never been discussed.

"How many other guys have you dated?" Joe's question startled Jessica.

"That's none of your business," she told him quickly.

"You're my girlfriend now, right?"

"That doesn't make it your business," she warned him.

"Why isn't it my business?" he asked, turning his head to stare at her out of those pale green eyes.

"It doesn't matter."

He let out a sharp laugh. "What do you mean it doesn't matter? Of course it matters!" She shook her head, arching her back to stretch before settling into her chair again.

"Why didn't your dad move with you?" Joe asked, suddenly switching directions.

She felt anger start to pound against her chest. "Where do you get off asking me all these personal questions?" she cried, her voice rising a few notches. "Just because we're dating doesn't give you the right to ask me every question you can think up!"

"Jessica, I just want to know you."

She surged to her feet and took a step in front of him. "Look at me! This is me! Everything you need to know is right here! Want me to twirl?" She turned slowly in a circle.

He shifted uncomfortably in his chair. "That's not what I'm talking about."

"What are you talking about?" she cried, her voice loud now. She pushed her dark hair back and blew out a short, frustrated breath. This night was nothing like what she had seen on the movies. Where were the fireworks? Where were the passionate kisses? Where were all the sparks? "I don't understand you and I don't know what you want from me!"

Suddenly, she lurched and spun as the top of her pole dunked down furiously. She gave a short yelp, braced herself, and started to reel. "Joe, this isn't a trout," she warned, having to take a step toward the river. He was instantly standing behind her, his strong hands over hers, helping her reel it in.

"Take a step back," he instructed. She did, and they reeled some more. "Jessi, I don't know what you've caught," he said, starting to laugh. They took another step back, but the fish pulled harder, and they lost some line.

They had worked at reeling the fish in for several minutes by the time Joe was finally able to let go of the pole and run down to the bank with his net. Jessica braced her feet and continued to reel, taking steps backward when able. Joe laughed and hooted as he snagged a huge catfish in the net and pulled it up onto the bank. "It's a beauty!" he hooted.

The beastly fish was thrashing wildly, and Jessica dropped her pole and ran to inspect it. She bent over Joe's shoulder to see. "That's the ugliest thing I've ever seen," she said, poking it with a stick.

"This is humongous, Jess! I'm pretty sure it would even set a record!"

"It scares me that this was in that river," she said, looking warily at the inky water.

"Aw, it can't really hurt you. Its teeth aren't sharp. If it bit you it would feel more like sandpaper."

"Well, I would prefer it not bite me at all," she said. "Are you gonna put it on the stringer?"

"No! It would pull it away. Let's put it in the bucket. ...If it'll fit." Joe dipped the bucket in the river, then lowered the massive fish into it. The fish fit, but it was bent and smashed against the sides. "When we get home I'll take a picture of you holding it up and we'll measure it."

"I don't think I can lift it," Jessi said, looking suspiciously at the big fish.

Joe grinned. "Then I'll help and someone else can take the picture."

Joe wiped his hands on his jeans and took Jessi's hands and wiped them on his pants as well, seeing that her shorts had little fabric. He didn't step back and she looked up, surprised.

His green eyes were trained on her face, and her breath caught as he captured her hands in his. After giving a wild kick, her heart thudded against her chest. She had been waiting for a moment like this all night. She looked up into his green eyes and she felt the croaking frogs, singing birds, and quiet moonlight soaking into her. She wanted to reach up and hold him, but she had promised that she would let him initiate physical contact, and even if she thought it was a stupid rule, she would rather play by his rules than not at all.

If it had been anyone else, she would have told him exactly where to put his stipulations, but Joe was different. He was probably the most gorgeous man that Jessi had ever seen, but it was more than that. He was attractive on a deeper level than Jessica could even understand. He held her mesmerized in his presence, and she shivered as his breath fluttered across her face.

This was the moment she had been waiting for ever since she had watched her first princess movie as a little girl. The moment she knew she had found her prince, he was standing right in front of her, and he knew that she was his one true love. The only thing yet to come was the kiss, and the happily ever after. Of course, everyone told her that fairytales never came true, but standing along the river in the late summer moonlight, she wondered if they might in Glendale.

The light from the moon shone across the water, the catfish was stuck in the bucket, and the river continued to move lazily along.

"Jessi, I'm glad you're going to be my girlfriend," Joe said, a smile spreading across his face.

"I'm glad you changed your mind about dating." Her comment was sincere. She wasn't only glad because she had done what everyone had said was impossible, but because she truly wanted to be close to this man. Something about him fascinated her to the point that she desperately wanted to know more.

Thunder rumbled in the distance, somehow adding something new and wild to the moment, and the next flash of lightening engraved it into their memories forever.

"We'd better go before the rain catches us," Joe said, and Jessi agreed, stepping away from him reluctantly. She grabbed the ice chest and the tackle box, and Joe juggled the chairs, poles, and the heavy bucket as they tramped up the trail.

By the time they reached the pickup, it had started to sprinkle. As Joe opened the tailgate, the clouds let loose and rain poured from the sky. Setting everything down, he ran to open the door for Jessi. She climbed in and waited in the truck, the rain pounding on the roof, while Joe put everything in the back and then joined her in the cab. They were both soaked, and the interior of the pickup smelled damp.

Jessica looked at Joe, and Joe looked at Jessica as he grinned at her. "What a night!"

She laughed as he turned the key to start the engine. "No kidding."

"It wasn't the typical first date, I guess...probably not what you were used to up in D.C."

Jessica lowered her eyes to her lap. "Whoever liked typical, anyway?" The answer was her – before she met Joe Colby. He grinned at her and with the windshield wipers going full speed, Joe turned the truck around and pulled out onto the highway.

The sky poured rain, and lightening flashed all the way back to Jessica's house. "Do you think your mom would mind taking a picture?" Joe asked.

Jessica shook her head. "Should we get out of the rain?" she asked, trying to decide where to take the picture. She wasn't sure her mom would let them bring the fish in the house.

"Why misrepresent the night?" Joe answered, grinning.

Once he parked, he ran through the rain up to the front door and knocked. Jessi saw her mom come to the door, talk with Joe for a few seconds, smile, then turn back into the house.

Joe dashed back through the rain and opened Jessica's door. She climbed out, and he shut it before jogging to the back of the pickup to get the fish. He stood on the bumper and grabbed the bucket, hoisting it over the edge of the pickup bed and stepping down with it. He hurried back to the house, Jessica walking beside him, and they stopped just outside the porch. Carla stood at the top of the stairs with the camera, opting to stay dry. Joe and Jessi were completely soaked now, and Joe reached into the bucket and pulled the giant catfish out by the gills. He pulled Jessica in front of him.

"Take this side, and I'll take the other," he instructed. Making a face, she stuck her hand in the massive gill. He let go and took the other side of the fish so that they were holding it together.

With Jessi's dark hair sticking to her face, their clothes sticking to their bodies, and water running down them in streams, Carla took their picture. Jessica knew that despite the fact that her hair and makeup were a wreck, the fish was undeniably ugly, and the night had not been marked with a kiss as she had hoped while standing along the riverbank, that picture was about to become her favorite, past, present or future.

They dropped the catfish back into the bucket. "I'll let you get out of the rain, Jess. I'll take him home and clean him, then maybe we can all get together for catfish," Joe said, backing up, grinning first at Jessica and then at Carla.

Jessica turned and held her hand up shyly. "Okay. Bye."

He waved. "See you soon." He hurried back to his pickup, hoisted the bucket inside the bed of the truck, and left, his lights seeming bright in the rain. Jessica climbed the stairs of the porch, not sure whether to hug her mother and tell her all about her night, or just go in and go to bed.

"Nice fish, Honey. I'm on the phone with Lisa, so let's talk in a few minutes," Carla told Jessi. "Why don't you take your shoes off out here so you don't drip on the carpet? You probably smell like fish." Carla returned to the house to finish her conversation.

"Well, that settles that," Jessica murmured.

Lisa was Carla's best friend in D.C. and they were probably discussing the latest gossip on Jari. A conversation like that could last for hours. Jessica was torn whether she wanted to hear the latest news or just avoid it. It didn't matter what she decided, though – Carla would surely tell her later whether she wanted to hear it or not.

None of it mattered, though. The only thing that Jessica could think of was the green-eyed neighbor boy and the night they had just shared. Jessi had a feeling tonight was the beginning of something new and unimaginably wonderful.

She kicked off her tennis shoes and opened the front door. She went into the kitchen to wash her hands, rubbing them with soap twice. She drank a glass of water and closed the shades before walking down the hall.

"Jessi?" She stopped and looked back into the living room. "Lisa says that Dad took Jari to the country club this evening. Can you believe it? She says Jari was wearing a new diamond bracelet and was hanging all over him, whispering secrets in his ear and kissing him," Carla said, holding the phone away from her mouth and making a puking motion. Jessica smiled, but she didn't care. The only thing she could think of was that maybe someday she would be whispering secrets in Joe Colby's ear and kissing him.

"I'm going to go get some dry clothes on," Jessi said. Carla nodded, and Jessi went into her room and opened the top drawer of her dresser. She pulled out another white tank top and a pair of pink, terrycloth shorts. She slipped them on, and sat down on her bed. She ran her fingers through her cropped hair, then reached forward to carefully lift her snow globe off the dresser. She shook it and watched the glitter fall around the cottage. It was a beautiful, mystical, wonderful land, and Jessica wondered again if it might be a land called Glendale.

Eleven

Jessica hurried into the store and headed straight to the film department. She had sent in the pictures from her mom's digital camera, but of course there wasn't a one-hour photo in Glendale, so she had to wait a couple of days to get them back. She paid for her pictures and almost ran out of the store. She ripped the package open and leafed through the photos to find the one she was looking for.

She stopped in the parking lot and stared at the picture of her, Joe, and the fish. She smiled and impulsively kissed it. It had been taken only two nights before, but she felt like she hadn't seen Joe in forever. She had ordered four prints of the picture, and at home she put one of them in an empty frame on her bedside table, set aside one copy to give to Joe, taped another to her bathroom mirror, and slipped the last in her folder to put up in her locker.

The start of school was only a day away, and the butterflies in her stomach already made her feel sick. It would surely be better with Joe Colby accompanying her, but the thought of starting an all new school, facing all new kids, all new teachers, all new classes and having to make it onto the cheerleading squad made her nerves raw.

The night before classes started, she felt physically ill. She tossed and turned all night, but was finally sleeping peacefully when the telephone on her bedside table rang the next morning.

"Hello?" she asked sleepily, holding it to her ear.

"Good morning, Jessi! It's the first day of school! Rise and shine!"

"Why are you so awake?" she asked, groaning.

"Why are you so asleep?" Joe countered, an audible grin in his voice.

"Because I was sleeping."

"Well, you should be awake. Want to ride to school with Kara and me?"

"I would love to," she answered.

"We'll be by in forty-five minutes."

"Forty-five minutes?" she asked, sitting up with a jolt and looking at her clock.

"We have to get into town early enough that we can go to the bakery and get doughnuts – it's a tradition. We've done it ever since kindergarten."

"Okay, well then I'm going to get a shower. See you soon."

"Bye!" he answered and she hung up, flipping the covers back and jumping out of bed.

She hurried through her shower and morning routine. She pulled on a pair of tight jeans and a sleeveless blue and white lace shirt with a blue ribbon bow tied just below her bust. She was slipping her shoes on when there was a knock on the front door. Carla was not up yet, so Jessi grabbed her bag and ran to the living room. She opened the door and smiled at Joe.

"Good morning!" he told her cheerfully.

She made a face at him. "Good morning would have been an hour later."

He laughed. "You ready?" When she nodded, he took her bag and led her to his pickup truck.

When he opened the passenger side door, Kara slid into the middle with a welcoming smile. "Are you ready for your first day of school at GHS?"

Jessica slid in. "It can't be that different," Jessi answered, giving an indifferent shrug.

Kara smiled. "Well, I'm glad you're here at GHS and not back in D.C."

Jessi smiled as Joe shut her door. "Thanks, Kara."

At the bakery, Joe paid for the doughnuts and coffee, and they ate breakfast while discussing classes, teachers, activities and the likelihood of homework on their first day.

Later, with her belly full and her hands still slightly sticky, Jessica climbed the stairs to the school between Kara and Joe, feeling small and scared. It was worse than her first day of kindergarten. They walked through the front doors, and she felt like everyone was staring at her. She lifted her chin, and pushed her dark hair back.

In a move that took a lot of courage and boldness on Joe's

part, he reached down and took her hand. In that one instant, he made the move from the popular kid who didn't date to the new girl's boyfriend. And she transitioned from the new girl to Joe Colby's girlfriend. Jessi looked up at him, relief written all over her face. She clung tightly to his hand.

"I'm this way," Kara said, stepping toward the first hall and offering Jessica a comforting smile.

"See you at lunch, Kara," Joe said, saluting his baby sister. She left them, giggling. "I'll walk you to your first class real quick," Joe told Jessica, glancing down at the paper she was holding that told her where to go. He walked her to her classroom, her hand still firmly in his. At the door, he offered her a smile. "You'll do fine, and both Kara and I will be close. I'll find you at lunch, okay?"

She nodded, trying to look cool with it all. "Sure. No problem." He grinned at her and walked away, hurrying to his own class. She lifted her head high and walked into the classroom.

She took a seat near the back and looked warily at everyone around her. They looked back, surprised by her presence. It wasn't everyday that GHS had a new student, and especially a girl from Washington, D.C.

Jessi scanned the class quickly and recognized two of the girls Heather had been talking to at the grocery store, and Justin. The numbers weren't good. One friend and two enemies in her first class alone. She took a deep breath. There was nothing she could do about it now. She sat through her morning classes without showing a sliver of emotion. She might have been scared and shaking on the inside, but on the outside, she looked as cool and calm as a still glass of water.

At lunch, Joe and Kara were waiting for her at the entrance to the cafeteria. They got into line together. Justin joined them, and they discussed their classes while waiting.

"Has it been too bad, Jessi?" Kara asked.

Jessi shook her head. "No way. It's just school." Joe grinned at her, and Jessica suddenly felt proud of herself and encouraged to press on. She saw a poster as they approached the serving counter and stopped to study it.

"Thinking of trying out for the cheerleading squad?" Kara asked, surprised.

"Yeah, I was thinking about it."

Kara nodded slowly. "You'd be good." The blonde switched from one foot to the other and back. "You realize that Heather is the team captain, right?"

Jessica tried to look surprised. "Oh really?" Kara nodded.

Jessica suddenly looked around the cafeteria for Heather. She found her standing three or four people back in line, a group of girls circled around her. She looked like she was fuming, and her eyes were aimed straight at Jessica. Jessi smiled a little, and then turned back to her own group. Jessi saw Kara watching her.

"She's a nice girl, Jessi, she really is. She just really wants to be standing where you are," Kara whispered when the line moved up and Joe started down the serving line.

"Oh, so you're on her side now?"

Kara shook her head, her big eyes serious. "Joe and Heather aren't right for each other regardless of whether or not you moved to Glendale. I just want you to understand."

Jessi looked down. "I understand."

Kara's small face brightened in a smile. "Good."

Kara turned to see what the cafeteria ladies were dishing onto Justin's plate. "Oh, yum, I love crispitos," Kara told him excitedly. Jessica looked to see what Kara was talking about. The crispitos were some kind of a crunchy Mexican food with cheesy dipping sauce. When Jessica reached the end of the counter, she grabbed a fork and napkin and then followed Kara to a table with four chairs, which Joe and Justin had just reached. Kara and Jessica sat on one side, and Justin and Joe on the other.

Lunch was light-hearted, and Jessica felt encouraged as she made her way to her next class. She could survive her years at GHS, maybe even enjoy them, if every day had a lunch like the one she had just had.

Her afternoon classes went fairly fast, and Jessica hurried out to Joe's pickup as soon as the bell rang. He dropped Kara and her off at the start of their dirt road, turned the truck around and hurried back to town for football practice. Jessica and Kara walked home slowly discussing the day, their homework and who had said what and when. They parted at Kara's driveway, and Jessica walked the rest of the way home, alone.

Carla was gone when Jessi arrived, but the note she left

said she had gone into her new office to get some work done and would be home by five.

Jessica did her reading for biology and worked her problems for algebra on the back patio to keep up her tan. When she was done with her homework, she laid her head on her arms and fell asleep, knowing her mom would wake her up when she came home at five. However, when Jessica woke up at seven o'clock, Carla still wasn't home. Jessi had a voice message from her, though, saying that she would be working late. This was more like the life Jessica had been used to before Glendale. This felt normal.

Jessi rummaged through the fridge and found the makings for an avocado and alfalfa sprout sandwich on rye bread. She poured herself a large glass of water and sat down to eat. Her phone rang seconds later, and it was Kayly. She spent two hours on the phone with her, listening to Kayly's stories from her first day of school. After hanging up, Jessi watched a program on television and went to bed, knowing that Joe's call would come early the next morning.

Twelve

The next morning, Joe called to wake her up, and day two started. Jessica got up, showered, dressed, grabbed a breakfast bar and left, her mother presumably still asleep in her room. Kara scooted into the middle, Joe shut her door, and they were off to another day of school. Jessica handed in her homework in biology and sat down close to the back, trying to ignore everyone around her. She pulled out a purple notebook and opened it to a clean page to take notes.

"Oh, how sweet. You have a purple notebook and a matching purple pen, Jessica."

Jessi looked up into the face of the pretty speaker, whom she had never met, and smiled. "You must be on the cheerleading squad."

"Co-captain. How did you know? You've seen me with Heather?" the girl asked, standing above her.

"You have the same sweet disposition," Jessica answered with a tight smile. The girl put her hands on her hips. Jessica lifted her chin and continued to smile. She wouldn't be intimidated by Heather and her little group of followers.

The girl squatted down in front of Jessica, until she was at eye level. "Don't try out for the squad."

Jessica tilted her head. "I think I can if I want to."

The girl shook her head. "Don't even waste your time. The girls and I don't want you ruining Heather's year any more than you already have. Find something else to be interested in."

Jessica gave a tight smile. "Class is starting, Blondie." The girl glared at her, straightened, and walked to the front of the class where one of her friends was saving her a seat.

"Don't worry about Monica. She'll be nice after awhile." Jessica looked over at the girl who had spoken. She was a pretty girl with red curls, brown eyes and a beautiful tan. She occupied the desk to Jessi's right.

"I actually wasn't worried about her," Jessi said, her voice indifferent. The girl considered her for several moments.

"I'm Tacy Cambil. I moved in from Texas a couple of years ago. It will take a few months, but eventually you'll be accepted as part of the group," Tacy paused. "Although, with Joe Colby as your boyfriend, it probably won't take you so long with most... and much longer with others." The redhead gestured up to Monica and the other cheerleader.

"I don't care about being accepted," Jessica lied.

Tacy turned to her biology book. "Fine. So it won't be a problem for you." Jessi shook her head, looking bored with the whole conversation. "Well, that's a relief. I was considering taking pity on you and being a friendly face in the crowd."

Jessica shrugged. "I've already got the only friendly face I need."

"Joe?" Jessi nodded. "Well, good. I didn't really have time to be friendly anyway," Tacy told her. Jessica shrugged, and the girl turned back to the teacher.

Jessica didn't talk to Tacy or Monica anymore, but wrote a long letter to Anna, instead. She took a few notes in biology, but the teacher only gave about five minutes worth of useful information. She went to algebra and social studies. She ate with Joe, Kara, Justin and Derik, then went to gym. As Jessi walked into the gymnasium, she saw Monica down on her knees bracing another girl as the girl tried to bend over Monica's hands backward, then kick over in a back walkover. The simple gymnastic move wasn't going well.

"They say that Natalie will make the squad if she can just do a little tumbling."

Jessica looked over at Tacy. "So, what?"

"I can help you learn to tumble, too."

"I told you, I don't need a friend," Jessica said, putting her hands on her hips and lifting her chin.

"I wasn't offering friendship, Smarty. You want to be a cheerleader, I can teach you what you need to know to get on the squad."

"Oh, and I suppose you know how to tumble?" Jessi gave her a disbelieving look.

"I'm a cheerleader."

"You're kidding."

Tacy shot Jessi a knowing glance. "Do I like Heather? Yes. She's a nice girl. Do I dislike you because she does? No. You deserve a fair shot."

"You're brave," Jessi paused, "or stupid to be seen talking to me twice in one day. You may lose your spot on the team."

Tacy shook her head and suddenly did a standing back flip. "I'm the best tumbler they have. They won't kick me off, and I can deal with Heather." Tacy studied Jessica for a few moments. "She really is a nice girl."

Jessi gave a tight smile. "So I've heard."

"You would know if you weren't dating Joe."

"Then I guess I'll never know." Jessica turned away, running past Monica and Natalie, joining in the soccer game that was taking place.

"The word is that you and Joe officially hooked up," Brighton said as he tried to steal the ball from Jessica.

She looked up, surprised to see him in her class. "I didn't know you were a year younger than him."

"I'm not. I started kindergarten a year later because my birthday didn't make the cut-off." He paused and she nodded. "So, is it true?"

"Maybe." She broke away and started to run across the gym with the ball. People were yelling that they were open, but instead, she went for the goal. Despite the valiant dive by the goalie, the ball hit its mark. Brighton ran up alongside her, put his hands on his knees and bent over, catching his breath. "Nice shot."

"Thanks."

"Is it true?" he asked again.

"Yes."

"I'm surprised. Don't get me wrong. You're super good-looking, but Heather isn't so bad, either, and..." he paused. "She's a nice girl." Jessica rolled her eyes and wiped her face on her tank top. "They're just...better suited," he continued.

"What are you saying? That I'm not good enough for him? That since I'm not blonde and perfect, we shouldn't be together?" She reached up and shoved him, causing him to stumble backward. "I'm sick and tired of hearing how nice and perfect and beautiful Heather is!" she finished. With that, Jessi took off, stole the ball and made another goal.

When gym was over, she pulled her tank top off in the locker room and took a quick, cold shower before dressing. She hurried to choir where she sat with the other altos, her chin up, glaring at the wall.

"What's up, Jess?" Joe asked, suddenly beside her. He turned and tossed his bag up to his seat in the bass section.

She tried to smile. "Nothing."

He gave her a knowing look. "Yeah, right. You look mad."

She gave a dry laugh, but there was a bite to her tone. "What? I don't seem blonde and perfect and angelic and like the perfect girlfriend and the perfect cheerleader and the perfect match for you anymore?" He was quiet, and she stole a glance to see his expression. Her eyes met his, and she suddenly felt the same butterflies she had at the river after catching the monstrous catfish.

He leaned close to her and his words were quiet. "If I wanted to date Heather, I would date Heather, but guess what."

"What?"

"I'm dating you." A small smile lifted her lips and she felt reassured. "But I suppose her name does come up quite a bit," he went on. She nodded, her head hanging for just a moment. The choir teacher walked into the room. Joe started to stand, but then leaned back down. "Want to have dinner with me tonight? At six?" She nodded, and he left. She heard him joke and laugh with the other guys as he took his seat.

She opened her folder full of music and looked over it. Too bad she had no clue how to read music. Or sing, for that matter. The teacher seemed nice though, and Jessi could sit and glance at Joe every once in awhile, so choir passed quickly.

History was next, like a light at the end of the tunnel, then, at three o'clock on the dot, the bell rang. Jessica grabbed her stuff and raced out to Joe's truck. She arrived first. Kara came about a minute later, then Joe came jogging through the parking lot. Once they were all in, Joe drove to the dirt road, opened their door, and they both slid out. A cloud of dust rose as he turned his truck around and headed back to town for football practice.

"So, how was your second day, Jessi Cordel?" Kara asked, swinging her backpack by its strap as they started walking. Jessi shrugged. Kara tilted her small chin and tucked her hair behind her slightly pointed ears.

"I talked to Brighton," Kara said. Jessi shrugged one shoulder. "See, everyone always thought that Joe and Heather would be together someday. It's just going to take awhile for everyone to change their thinking, that's all," Kara explained.

Jessi shrugged again. "I don't care what they think."

Kara smiled. "Okay."

"When are you and Justin going to start going out?" Jessi asked, changing the subject. Kara shrugged her dainty shoulders.

"I don't know if we will. I'm not allowed to date until I turn fifteen, which is in a couple of months. We haven't really talked about it. We're just really good friends." Kara paused and smiled. "We always have been."

Jessica smiled at her and shook her head. "He likes you."

Kara's expression turned hopeful. "You think?"

Jessi nodded. "Totally. It's so obvious." Kara's smile made her whole little face light up.

Jessi suddenly noticed how very small Kara was. She was just a year younger than Jessica, but Jessica was 5'7" and Kara had to be around five feet. She was dainty all over, and still looked like a little girl. Her pointed ears made her look like a little pixie. She was wearing capris and a polo shirt that was buttoned just below her neck. Jessi began to wonder if her parents forgot to feed her when she was little, but then decided that even if Kara had been denied food as a child, the petite factor worked for her.

"Jessi, want to come in and have cookies and do our homework together?" Kara asked when they came to her drive. "I know you and Joe are going to dinner, but Joe won't be back from football practice until five thirty. Then he can take a shower and you guys can go."

Jessica considered Kara's offer, then thought about going home to the empty cottage and doing her homework alone. "Sure. Your mom won't mind?"

"Not at all!" Kara assured, then led the way.

Jessica had never been inside the Colby house before, and she looked around curiously as she followed Kara in the door. It wasn't as large as her home in D.C., and it was a different style for sure, but it was beautiful. It was classy and country all at the same time, and a large open stairway with a curving wooden railing opened up right inside the front entry. Straight ahead was a large, open family room with a ceiling that rose up two stories. To the right was a formal dining room, and a large kitchen was just beyond that, visible through an archway on the far wall of the dining room.

Hannah Colby was standing at the sink peeling vegetables for dinner, when Kara and Jessi entered the kitchen. Kara kissed her mother on the cheek, then told her Jessi was with her.

Hannah's face was one big smile as she turned and squeezed Jessica's arm. "Hi! It's so good to have you here! How's school going for you, Honey?"

Jessica nodded, wary of Hannah. Grandma and Pops had said that she wanted Joe and Heather to end up together. "Good."

Hannah leaned her hip against the counter. "So, you're getting settled okay?"

Jessica nodded, lifting her chin. "I don't mind new places or meeting new people."

Hannah smiled. "Well, that's good! That will serve you well in life. I'm sure the kids here are glad to have you. I know Kara and Joe are!"

Kara nodded as she poured two glasses of milk. Jessica felt her defenses against this warm lady weaken and she gave a small smile. "Hopefully."

Hannah smiled and patted her arm. "I'm sure they are." The Colby mom turned to arrange cookies on a plate. "How's your mom doing?"

"Good."

"I'm glad to hear it. Is she getting her office all set up? I saw her working there yesterday."

Jessica shrugged. "I don't know. I haven't talked to her."

"Well, when you see her tonight, tell her I said hello and to stop by anytime she'd like."

Jessica nodded. "I will."

"We're going to do our homework, Mom," Kara said, putting her arm around her mother's waist. "We'll be down after a bit." Hannah nodded, and kissed Kara's hair.

Kara carried the milk, and Jessi followed with the plate of

large, homemade chocolate chip cookies. Kara led her up the stairway, through a living room with a computer, couch and bean-bags, down a short little hallway into a room decorated in pink and white checks. She set the milk down and turned, her cheeks pink. "It's kind of little girlish."

Jessica shrugged. "There's nothing wrong with pink."

Kara grinned and flopped across her bed. "Nope. I guess not." In the corner between the two big windows was a white desk with a laptop on it. The desk had a small white chair. "I'll do my homework on the bed, and I can move my laptop if you want to do yours at the desk," Kara offered.

Jessi shook her head. "I can just do mine on the floor." Kara agreed. They both ate a cookie and drank some milk before stretching out to start their homework. Kara finished her home-work first, took a book off her nightstand and started to read. When Jessica shut her last textbook, Kara stood up and stretched. Jessica slid her books into her backpack and did the same.

"What do you want to be someday, Jessi?" Kara asked, sit-ting back down on the bed, swinging her legs back and forth.

Jessica climbed up to sit beside her. "I don't know."

"You have no idea?" Kara asked.

Jessi shook her head. "No, but I know I want it to be big, and important and interesting."

"Politics?" Kara asked, testing the waters.

"No! Absolutely not." Jessi traced the pink checkered com-forter. "What about you?"

"I've always wanted to be a pediatric physical therapist."

Jessica smiled, surprised by Kara's plans. "Why?"

Kara tilted her head and pulled her feet up under her. She helped herself to another cookie. "There were complications when I was born. I was in intensive care for over two months. It took me longer to walk and run. I couldn't even ride a bike with-out training wheels until I was eight."

"You seem fine now."

Kara nodded. "I am. I was in physical therapy for four years and it helped me a lot. Since then, I've wanted to be a thera-pist to help kids with disabilities feel like they're as good as other kids."

Jessica nodded. "I can understand that." It was quiet for a

few minutes. "Once, I wanted to be the girl on the flying trapeze at the circus," Jessi offered. "My dad was going to be my partner."

Kara giggled. "What changed your mind?"

"I saw a girl's partner drop her. My dad said it was a fluke accident, that he would never drop me," Jessi paused, continuing to trace the checkers in the comforter with her finger. "But then he met Jari." Jessi sighed and looked up at the ceiling. "He didn't accidentally drop me. He just let go. He didn't even want to hang on anymore."

Kara swallowed and looked up at the ceiling, too. "Did it hurt?"

Jessi pressed her lips together. "Getting dropped always does."

"I can't imagine."

"Don't try."

"What's she like? Jari, I mean," Kara asked.

Jessica shrugged. "I've never spoken to her."

Kara studied her face. "Are you very angry with her?"

Jessica nodded. "I hate them both."

"That's understandable," Kara said slowly.

A slow smile spread across Jessi's face. She really thought that maybe Kara did understand, or at least she was trying to. No one had ever really asked her about the divorce or how it made her feel. She had listened when Carla had expressed her anger, when Anna and Kayly had whined about how much they would miss her, and even to her dad when he had explained that he had to follow his heart – but no one had ever asked how she felt about it. "I wish he had never met her."

"How did they meet?"

"She was his secretary. I'm not sure when their affair started, but it had been going on for awhile when mom and I found out about it," Jessi explained, her voice numb.

"It kept escalating until they couldn't stop it," Kara said, nodding with understanding.

"It was his choice," Jessica pointed out quickly.

"Of course. It's always a conscious decision, but once you start sticking your toe in to test the water, then your foot will go in, your leg, and before you know it, you're doing a cannon ball into the deepest end," Kara responded.

Jessi was quiet for a moment. "What hurt the worst was that he never even attempted to put an end to it," she finally said. "It was just hello Jari, so long Carla and Jessica."

Kara bit her lip. "Someday he'll feel bad," she told her.

"I don't just want him to feel bad someday," Jessica admitted. "I want him to squirm and writhe and realize that he lost everything he holds dear. I want him to suffer just like we're suffering. He destroyed our family, and he doesn't even care."

Kara offered Jessica another cookie. "Stepping out of God's will and protection usually results in that – destruction. The devil is here to kill, steal, and destroy." Jessica didn't respond other than to shrug. She took a big bite of her cookie just as Hannah opened the door.

"You girls have your homework done yet?"

Kara nodded. "Yeah, we're just chatting."

"Mind if I join you?" Hannah asked.

Kara shook her head and held out her hand. "Have a seat." Jessica felt her eyebrows draw together. How did two teenagers chat with an adult in the room? It was too censored, too formal.

Hannah curled up in the pink butterfly chair in the corner. "What are you talking about?"

"Jessica's parents' divorce." Jessica cringed at Kara's honesty.

"I'm sure that has been really hard for you," Hannah said, her voice gentle and kind. Jessi shrugged. "I'm sorry."

Hannah's simple apology for something she had nothing to do with was strangely comforting to Jessi. It was quiet for several moments. "Would you like to stay for dinner, Jessica?" Hannah asked after a stretch of silence.

"I think Joe and I are going out."

Hannah raised her eyebrows. "Oh." Hannah's surprise dissolved into a smile. "Well, that will be fun for you two! Promise me that sometime, though, you'll come for dinner."

Jessi thought about it – it was a whole meal with Joe's parents, but it was a whole meal guaranteed with Joe. "Alright."

"Next Monday?"

"Sure."

The conversation turned to one of Kara's teachers, and before long, Joe stuck his head in the doorway. His face lit up in a grin when he saw all three women sitting and talking, before announcing that he was going to take a shower. Fifteen minutes later, he came back. Jessi stood, grabbed her bag and told Kara and Hannah goodbye. Kara and Hannah continued to sit in Kara's room and talk, even as Jessi left. Jessi couldn't help thinking it a bit strange.

The mother and daughter were soon forgotten, though, as she followed Joe to the front door. His blue jeans and bright green t-shirt looked amazing against his tanned skin and dark chocolate hair. He opened the large front door for her, then jogged to open the truck door. She slid in and crossed her legs as he went around to climb in the driver's side. They made small talk about school, classes, people and life in general on their way into town.

He took her to a small Italian restaurant that was decorated in grapes, grape vines, and lattice. It was pretty, and for a moment she wasn't sure if she was in D.C. or Glendale. The food was outstanding. He clinked his water glass against hers and said, "Here's to our first dinner out together."

"I'll toast to that," she answered with a smile.

His free hand was resting on the table, and she reached across and softly rubbed it. "Joe, I like you."

He grinned at her. "I like you, too." In a move that surprised her, he captured her hand and kissed the back of it softly before setting it on the table, patting it twice.

They finished their meal, Joe paid the bill, and he opened the door for her as they left. The ride home was full of comfortable silence. He walked her to her front door, his hands in his front jean pockets. They stood on her porch, and she waited for him to stop beating around the bush and kiss her goodnight. He finally smiled and took a cautious step forward. He gave her a quick hug and kissed her forehead before stepping back. "I enjoyed having dinner with you tonight. Can we do it again soon?"

"Anytime you want, Joe Colby," she answered.

He gazed down into her face, his eyes warm, and grinned, tugging on a piece of her hair. "Goodnight."

She rested her back against the front door as he turned. "Goodnight," she answered, sounding completely smitten.

"I'll call you in the morning," he promised, walking backward toward his truck. She nodded and gave a little wave.

Thirteen

Jessi felt strangely nervous all day on Monday. It wasn't a big deal to eat dinner with Joe and Kara, but she was going to be around their parents. She could care less what her parents thought of Joe, but she knew he was different. His parents' opinions mattered to him. She had to make a good impression.

Jessi did her homework and then fussed with her hair in front of her bathroom mirror. She lined her lips and put on a frosty shade of lip gloss. She peeled off her shorts and tight shirt and tossed them in the hamper. Jessica stood in front of her closet for quite awhile and finally decided on a cute white dress with embroidered black flowers scattered across the bottom. It was cap sleeved, and probably one of the most modest summer outfits she owned. Fluffing her hair again, she added earrings and black dress shoes, then sprayed herself with perfume and put on lotion.

She hopped in her car and started it up. Backing down the lane, she drove less than a mile east before pulling into the Colbys' drive. She parked beside Joe's truck and had butterflies in her stomach as she approached the house. After knocking, she tucked her hair behind her ear.

The door opened, and Joe was standing in a blue button-up shirt and khaki pants. She was glad that she had not misjudged the formality of the meal. His pale green eyes lit up as he grinned at her. "You look beautiful," he told her, stepping out onto the porch. She looked away in a moment of uncharacteristic shyness.

"You look good, too," she said, turning a smile up at him.

He tilted his head, grinning. "Are you hungry?"

"Sure," she answered, so nervous that she couldn't think of food. He took her hand, distracting her from her nerves. She wished he had kissed her instead.

They had been going out for well over a week, and he had yet to kiss her or do anything else she had been expecting. While being mildly disappointed and incredibly confused, she felt mostly intrigued and curious. Now, she was spending an evening with the Colby family, and she had the sense that tonight would influence her and Joe's relationship greatly. That made her even more nervous, as she was acutely aware of how much she didn't want anything to come between them.

He was so incredibly good-looking, and whatever had drawn her to him that first day at 7-Eleven, was even stronger now. She was determined to make a perfect impression on his parents.

"My mom made lasagna," he told her.

She smiled. "That sounds amazing." He shot her a grin, and led the way into the house. Kara was just coming down the stairway, and she gave Jessi a quick hug.

"Mom made lasagna because you were coming over," Kara told her, then paused. "You should come way more often. I love lasagna!" Jessica laughed.

Hannah met them at the kitchen door, wiping her hands on a towel. "Jessica! I'm so glad it worked for you to come over tonight." She stepped forward and gave Jessi a warm hug. Jessica saw her notice that they were holding hands, but when Jessi quickly tried to release Joe's hand, he held on. Hannah smiled. "Come into the kitchen. Would you like something to drink?"

"Joe, would you give me a hand with this?" Chris asked, coming out of the kitchen, gesturing with his head to the pan of lasagna he held.

Jessi had never met Chris Colby and was surprised to see that Joe's dad had the same pale eyes, the same thick, dark hair and the same tan. He was still a very handsome man, even as he pushed fifty.

"I'm guessing you must be the infamous Jessica I've been hearing so much about," Chris said, grinning at Jessi. She nodded, instantly put at ease by the friendly man who was so like Joe.

"Yeah, Jess, this is my dad, Chris," Joe offered.

Jessi smiled. "It's nice to meet you."

"You too, Jessi. We sure are glad to have you tonight." Chris sent her a friendly wink and then shifted his attention. "Now Son, if you don't mind, this pan is getting a mite hot."

Joe released Jessica's hand to grab some hot pads and follow Chris to the dining room table.

"Is that lasagna done, Chris?" Hannah called after them.

"Looks like it to me," he answered.

She turned to Jessica and waved her farther into the kitchen. "What can I get you to drink? We have lemonade, water, tea, soda and milk." Hannah waited for her answer, her pretty blue eyes fixed on Jessi.

"Lemonade would be great."

"Okay. What do you want, Sweetie?" Hannah asked, turning to Kara.

"Milk, please." Hannah poured their drinks.

"Would you mind asking the guys what they want, Jessi?" Hannah asked, and Jessi immediately headed for the dining room.

"What would you guys like to drink?" she asked, stopping beside Joe.

"What are the options?" Joe asked.

"Lemonade, water, soda, milk and tea, I think," she answered, trying to remember everything Hannah had listed.

Chris winked at her. "Sounds about right."

"I'll take milk," Joe said as he stuck a spatula in the lasagna.

She turned. "What would you like, Mr. Colby?"

He shook his head. "Call me Chris, and I will take milk, also." She nodded and smiled, going back to the kitchen. What was it about this family and milk? And with lasagna? She thought the combination sounded gross.

Keeping her thoughts to herself, she relayed the information to Hannah and helped Kara carry the full glasses into the dining room. She was surprised to see Chris tossing a salad and adding dressing to it when she returned to the kitchen. She barely remembered a time when her dad had sat down to a meal with them, and yet here Chris was, not only obviously planning to join them for dinner, but helping to get the meal on the table! However, after raising a son that opened doors and pulled out chairs for girls, why wouldn't Chris Colby help in the kitchen?

"We have berry cheesecake for dessert, Jessica," Hannah mentioned, carrying a basket of garlic bread past her.

"That sounds wonderful."

"Good. I thought so, too."

"Okay, it's ready, everyone come sit down!" Chris announced, carrying the salad into the dining room, gesturing for

Jessi to go ahead of him.

Chris held Hannah's chair, then Kara's, and Joe held Jessica's for her. It appeared so natural that Jessi felt sure that it was a normal occurrence in the Colby household. Jessica joined hands with Joe and Kara when they held their hands out, and Chris blessed the food. Chris served everyone, filling the plates and passing them around. They all began to eat.

"How was practice tonight, Son?" Chris questioned once he swallowed his first bite. "This is phenomenal, Dear," he added quickly, patting Hannah's hand.

"Great. I think we have a chance of going to the playoffs again this year," Joe answered.

"Is Derik's knee still hurting him?" Hannah questioned, seeming concerned.

"He's doing better – he can punt again at least," Joe told her.

"Derik had a crazy accident last year in track. He twisted his knee when he was running the 4x4, and the doctor said without major physical therapy, he'd never play football again," Kara explained between bites of lasagna. Jessica nodded, grateful for Kara's quiet explanation.

"Do you play sports, Jessi?" Hannah asked, pushing her light-brown hair behind her ear.

"I'm going to try out for the cheerleading squad." She thought she saw a funny look cross Hannah's face, but it was gone before Jessica could verify it.

"That would be great if you made the team. It's such a fun sport and a great way to meet other kids," Hannah answered.

"And she would have to come to all of my games," Joe added, looking happy about that.

"Yes, she would," Hannah agreed with a smile.

"Mama was a cheerleader," Kara added, taking a sip of milk.

Hannah laughed. "Yes I was, but that was a long time ago."

"Here at GHS?" Jessi asked, putting effort into seeming interested.

"No, I graduated from Baltimore West."

Jessi looked up quickly. "You grew up in Baltimore?"

Hannah smiled. "I did."

"I met this pretty little thing in college," Chris explained, grinning. His wife softly hit at his arm, obviously embarrassed.

"When are tryouts, Jessica?" Hannah asked.

"Friday."

"Well, I'll be praying for you," Hannah said, smiling. "You'll have to let us know how they go.

Jessi offered a small smile back. "Thanks. I will."

"So, you two were officially going out as of the night of the giant catfish, right?" Chris asked the question after taking a long drink of milk. Jessi had a hard time swallowing her lasagna – here it was. The dreaded conversation.

Joe turned to Jessica. "That's right. I still have that fish in the freezer. You guys should come over sometime and we can eat it." Jessi nodded at Joe, and he turned to answer his dad's question. "Yeah, that's right."

"That makes it just about two weeks," Chris commented, and Jessi wondered what he was getting at. Joe didn't seem worried. He continued to eat his food, looking as if he didn't have a care in the world. Suddenly, Chris shook his head. "That fish was a big one. I would have liked to reel him in."

Joe grinned. "Dad, it was crazy! He fought so hard that I honestly didn't know if the line would hold."

Chris whistled and shook his head again. "Have any plans for Saturday, Son?" Now it was Joe's turn to shake his head. "What would you say to going down to the river and trying our hand at catching his brother?"

Joe grinned. "Sounds good."

"I'll pack you a picnic lunch," Hannah offered.

"I'm going, too, so you'll have to pack an extra sandwich," Kara piped in, talking with her mouth full.

"Do you want to come too, Hon? What about you, Jessi? We could all go!" Chris said, looking at his wife and then at Jessica.

Hannah smiled. "Sounds like fun. I haven't fished in quite awhile – I'm not even sure if I remember how anymore."

"Well then, it's settled. It's just up to you now, Jessica," Chris said with a wink.

Jessica didn't think that spending her Saturday with adults seemed very appealing, but she looked at Joe's hopeful face and realized that she would get a day with him. "I don't have anything going on."

Chris clapped his hands together. "Good! It will be a family fishing trip. I'll pack up some sodas and candy bars and get the poles ready. Honey, you can pack us a lunch, and we will head out at about nine on Saturday morning." Jessica's heart softened as Chris's words settled over her – a family fishing trip...and she was included.

"Sounds like a winning plan," Joe added, his forkful of lasagna already halfway to his mouth.

Everyone grew quiet as they ate and thought of the weekend to come. Jessica noticed Joe smiling at her, and she smiled back.

"So, Jessi, how often have you been back to Glendale over the years?"

Jessi finished chewing before she answered Chris. "Only about once a year," she paused. "If that. My dad didn't like it here, and my mom preferred her country club and spas to coming back to visit."

"So, why did you move here?" Joe asked curiously.

"I guess my mom felt like it was the only place she could go – like someone was here to watch her back." Everyone around the table nodded.

"It must have been hard to be part of such a public divorce," Hannah said, and Kara nodded in agreement.

Jessica nodded, then shrugged, feigning indifference. "Isn't every divorce hard?"

"You've got a point there," Chris agreed. "Sweetheart, this lasagna is wonderful," he said again, sneaking another compliment for his wife into the conversation.

"It really is. Dad, can you get me another piece?" Kara asked, passing him her plate. He dished her seconds on lasagna and handed it back.

"Thanks. It's the same as always," Hannah said, obviously pleased with the compliments.

"Well, it's the best lasagna I've ever had," Jessi commented honestly, and Joe nodded his agreement, passing his plate to his dad for thirds.

"Want any more, Jessi?" Chris asked, and Jessica shook her

head no.

"I'm so full, but thank you." She was proud of the manners she could pull out when she had to.

"Around here you get seconds whether you like it or not. Plus, it's lasagna," Joe said, winking at her before grabbing her plate and passing it to Chris. She nearly protested, then thought otherwise. She wasn't quite stuffed yet, and the lasagna was delicious. Besides, she didn't want to offend Joe's mom. Chris mercifully gave her a small piece, and Joe put her plate back in front of her.

"So, Honey, do you think those tomatoes that survived the rot are okay to eat?" Chris asked, the conversation switching direction again.

Hannah shrugged. "They're beautiful. I just picked some this morning, but you never know."

"Mom's tomatoes had some kind of a black fungus on them this spring," Kara explained. Jessi nodded her understanding. The conversation continued with the family bouncing from subject to subject. Jessi had the odd feeling that this was what a normal evening looked like at the Colby house, and as foreign as it felt, she liked it.

When the meal was finished, Jessi helped Kara and Hannah with the dishes while the guys pulled out a deck of cards and dealt them out. Jessica sat beside Joe and leaned against his arm as they shared a hand of cards while he taught her how to play hearts. When the night was over, there were goodbye hugs from Hannah, Kara, and even from Chris. They made her promise to come for dinner again soon.

When Joe walked her to her car, he intertwined his fingers with hers. She leaned against the side of her car, and he stood close, looking down at her with a pleased smile. "Thanks for coming tonight. It's really important to me that you know and like my family and that they know and like you."

"If they're anything like you, I think I want to know them," she answered. He laughed softly.

She thought about kissing him, but then thought of his stipulations. "You should kiss me, Joe Colby."

He grinned, amused. "Why's that?"

"Because I think I would like it," she told him, flirting with her eyes. He kissed her forehead and then stepped away.

"Your mom is going to be wondering where you are if you don't get home soon."

"No!" she groaned and stomped her foot as he opened her car door for her.

He leaned over the top and grinned. "I don't want you to get in trouble." She shut her door, pouting, and backed her car up the drive.

She had endured an entire night with his parents for nothing but a little peck on the forehead and a few seconds of holding hands and being close. She went home and went to bed, frustrated by his lack of affection. She desperately wanted to know what it felt like to kiss the boy she was quickly becoming enamored with, yet he seemed satisfied with friendly hugs and disarming winks.

Fourteen

Jessica walked out of the locker room in a tank top, spandex shorts and tennis shoes. She thought Heather was going to kill her dead with the glare she shot her. The fuming blonde met her halfway to the little group. "Oh no, you're not! You are not trying out to be a cheerleader!"

"Actually, I am," Jessi responded, collected and calm.

"You won't make the team!" Heather threatened, watching Jessi's back as she walked away.

"You never know." When the cheerleading coach turned in Jessica's direction, Jessica ran, did a round-off back handspring, back flip across the mats that were laid out and stuck the landing. She watched the coach's eyebrows go up and all the girls' shocked reactions.

"Where did you learn to tumble like that?" the coach asked, approaching Jessica.

"I did gymnastics in D.C. I competed at level seven before quitting," Jessi answered confidently.

"You sneaky little gymnast – you should have told me," Tacy said, appearing at Jessi's elbow, obviously impressed.

"Can you do a front handspring?" the coach asked, after sending Tacy a smile. Jessica nodded. "What about your splits?" Jessica turned and did a front handspring into her middle splits.

"Or did you mean my left or right?" Jessica went into each split, all the way down.

"Wow," Tacy breathed, impressed.

Standing in a little circle of girls ten feet away, Heather didn't look happy. "What a show off," Heather said, her voice dripping with jealousy.

"No kidding," Monica agreed, standing with her arms folded across her chest, just like Heather.

The coach ignored the two girls and stood back. "Let me see your jumps – straddle, tuck, pike, and split." Jessica went through them all.

The coach sent Heather an apologetic glance and then turned back to Jessica with a smile. "Jessi, I'm Jill Scott. Welcome to the cheerleading squad. We'll finish tryouts today and start practice next week." Jessica nodded and turned, heading back the direction she had come. She gave Heather a haughty smile and walked into the locker room to get her bag.

She heard Heather trying to talk the coach out of her decision, but Jessi knew it was in vain. A small school like Glendale would not pass up a gymnast for its cheerleading squad. She flung her backpack over her shoulder and didn't change her clothes before making her way to the football field.

She had missed her opportunity for Joe to take her home, so she sat on the bleachers and did her homework, spending more time watching him than focusing on her algebra. When she was done with her homework, she pulled her knees up to her chest and just watched. She noticed that many of the guys were shooting her looks, but she only had eyes for Joe.

When practice was over, he pulled his helmet off and ran across the field, jumping up into the bleachers. She wanted a kiss, but settled for him taking her hand and leading her to his pickup, laughing and talking. He congratulated her when she told him about making the squad, and they started making plans for the season. He drove her home and walked her to her door, pecking her on the cheek before getting back in his truck and heading home with a promise to see her in the morning.

Carla wasn't home again. Jessi hadn't seen her more than two or three times in the past two weeks. She worked late and didn't get up until Jessi had already left for school. Jessica wandered around the house for a few minutes and decided that she was hungry. There were no leftovers, so she cooked herself a box of macaroni and cheese.

She sat on the back patio to eat, catching the last rays of the sun. The air was cooling off, and there was a slight breeze ruffling the leaves around the house.

~~~~~

Saturday passed quickly as Jessica spent nearly the entire day down at the river, fishing with the Colbys. They talked, laughed, had a picnic, and caught fish. The weather was hot and the humidity high, but the shade from the tall trees was a welcome solace. A breeze floated down the river, cooling them off.

Jessi felt absorbed into their family and more at home than she was at her own house. Their light teasing and genuine caring touched a nerve deep down inside her that she hadn't even known she had. For the first time, she felt like she wasn't alone – like she was part of something.

When Hannah congratulated her on making the cheerleading squad and squeezed her hand, Jessi actually felt a jolt of pride – as if it were an accomplishment to be proud of and excited about, not just something that had to be done to spite Heather and spend time with Joe. When Kara asked questions about her latest math assignment, and Jessi was able to explain it in a way that Kara understood, Jessi felt like an older sister – something she had never been.

Late in the afternoon, when Chris announced that it was time to head home, Jessi was ready for their hugs, and even reciprocated them. Whether or not Chris and Hannah Colby had been secretly dreaming about Joe marrying Heather someday, Jessi felt something from them that she wasn't used to – acceptance and love. It covered up all the preconceived ideas she had about them.

Joe drove her home, walked with her up the porch stairs, and steered her toward the porch swing. "Is your mom home?" he asked, looking out at the driveway. Jessi's yellow car was alone.

"Doesn't look like it."

"Where is she?" he asked.

Jessi shrugged. "Work, probably. I don't know. I haven't seen her in awhile to ask."

Joe's eyes looked troubled, and he reached out and tucked her hair behind her ear. "You looked like you were having fun out there today."

A smile spread across Jessi's face. "I did have fun."

"Even with parents present?" Joe teased.

"Even with," Jessi paused. "Joe, I feel like your parents care about me, and, well, that makes me feel…happy, I guess, inside." She was instantly embarrassed by how cheesy her words sounded.

Joe didn't seem to mind. Instead, he wrapped his arm snugly around her shoulders and tucked her in close against him. "They do care about you," he agreed. It was quiet for a moment.

"It's just funny, you know," Jessi paused, and when she spoke again, her voice was raw with pain. "Your parents, they love you and you spend time together – as a family. They ask you about details in your life, and you laugh together. I haven't seen my mom in days, my dad in months. When we do talk, if they actually ask me something about my life, they don't know enough to ask the details. It's always 'how's school?' because it's the only thing they know that I do."

"Sweetheart," he said softly, turning and drawing her fully into his arms for the first time. His first pet name felt like cool water to her parched heart, a drop of affection in a desert place void of love, and she wrapped her arms around him and held on.

"I feel more loved in your family after being with you two times, than I do with my own parents after an entire lifetime," Jessi continued, the truth spilling out at the urging of his affection.

"Jessi, you are loved. You are. By my parents and my sister and…by me. We love having you around. You're part of the family now."

"Why? How? I just met you all."

"Why? Because when you're a part of our family, you're loved. And how are you part of our family? Because you're my girlfriend and that makes you part of us."

"I don't feel like your girlfriend," Jessi said, her face against his chest, soaking up every word he said.

"You don't? Why?"

"You don't treat me like I thought a girlfriend would be treated."

He sat back, disturbed by her words. "I don't? How? I'm sorry, Jess. How can I treat you better?"

"You don't…well, you don't kiss me," she said softly. She felt embarrassed to bring up the subject, but she didn't understand. Was it something that was wrong with her?

~~~~~

His look of concern melted into a smile. "Well, is that all?" She nodded and when she looked up at him, her eyes held the haunted look of an orphan. He framed her face with his hands. "I've been waiting to do that for a long time."

"You have?"

This Jessica, this soft and vulnerable girl, was not the girl that Joe was used to, and the look in her eyes was breaking his heart. She looked so hurt, so deprived of love. This was the real girl that he had known was inside her all along, and this was the girl that he wanted to reach, to touch and to love.

Everyone deserved to be loved by somebody, and although her mom and dad likely had good intentions, to him it seemed like she was utterly alone. He felt himself getting drawn into her emotion, and wanted to make it better. This girl who felt deeply, was real, genuine, honest, and open – was incredibly attractive to him. He couldn't believe she looked so surprised that he wanted to kiss her.

"Yes," he answered softly. "Jessi, may I kiss you?" he asked, studying her beautiful face. A smile spread across her lips, across her face, and up into her pain-filled eyes, chasing away the shadows and replacing them with warmth.

"Yes, you may."

Nervous and excited all at the same time, he touched his lips to hers once, twice and then again. She brought her hands up and linked them around his neck, and he held her close. Kissing Jessica was a glorious feeling, and he wanted to continue, but slowly pulled away. He smiled down into her face and brushed his thumb across her cheek.

"That was my first kiss," he told her, his green eyes locked on to hers. He saw the blush start to rise in her cheeks.

"Mine too," she confessed.

"No kidding?" he asked, shocked, and she nodded. That was definitely something he hadn't expected. And it made the kiss even sweeter. He studied her face, watched her crystal blue eyes, and continued to rub his thumb across the smooth skin of her cheek. She was beautiful. He wanted to kiss her again. "I should go," he said, forcing himself to stand.

"Okay," she agreed, standing up, too.

He touched her cheek again and shot her a charming smile. "I'll talk to you tomorrow," he promised. She nodded, bit her lip, and smiled as he walked backward off the porch.

～～～～～

When his truck was out of view, Jessi turned back to the house thinking about their kiss. He was the best kisser she could imagine. His kisses made her knees weak and her insides warm. He tasted warm, rich and like summer. They had just shared their first kiss and it had been perfect.

Granted, it was a little more awkward than what she had seen in the movies, but it was their first, and it was with Joe Colby, so the awkwardness didn't matter. She touched her fingers softly to her lips and then went inside smiling.

~~~~~

A few days later, Jessica was sitting on her bed doing her homework when her door flew open. She jumped and then rolled her eyes when her mom bounced in. "Did you ever hear of knocking?"

"Sorry, Jess, I just wanted to surprise you."

"Actually seeing you was surprise enough. Do you know you haven't been home for dinner in a week and a half?"

Carla tipped her head. "What are you? My mother?" her tone was biting.

Jessica gave a tight grimace. "No, but you're supposed to be mine."

A glimmer of guilt shadowed Carla's pretty face, but she recovered quickly. "I know! Which is why I want to have a girls' night tonight. Joe said you don't have plans, so don't try to get out of it. I brought home popcorn, your favorite ice cream, and that new chick flick that Kayly was talking about on the answering machine."

Jessica was quiet, stunned by her mom's behavior. They hadn't had a girls' night since she was a little girl, and even then it had been rare.

"I'll make chicken parmesan for dinner with steamed asparagus, and then we can watch the movie. How does that sound?" Carla's excitement was contagious, and Jessi felt it seeping into her.

"Good."

"Okay, how much longer do you have on your homework?"

Jessi considered the book. "An hour."

Carla smiled and turned, her dark hair swinging over her shoulder. "I'll have dinner ready!"

Jessi hurried through her homework and was in the kitchen a few minutes early. Carla put the meal on the table, and they sat down to eat. "How's Joe?" Carla asked immediately.

"Great," Jessi paused. "Amazing, smart, insanely gorgeous…"

"Perfect, adorable, strong, and the list goes on and on, right?" Carla asked, leaning forward. "Have you kissed him yet?"

"Mom!" Jessi cried, her cheeks turning pink.

Carla grinned smugly. "Is he a good kisser?"

Jessi took a drink of water, regaining her composure. "Yes, he actually is an amazing kisser."

"That's good. How far down do you feel it?" Carla asked, cutting her chicken.

Jessi smiled. "Down to my toes."

"He's a keeper," Carla announced, chewing. Jessica nodded as she stuck an asparagus stick.

"How's work?"

"Going very, very well. My office is settled, my clients are handling the change well, and my boss is very pleased with my productivity."

Jessica nodded. "That's good."

"Yes, it is. That reminds me, I have to go to Chicago next week."

"Really?"

"Yes. Would you like to come? We could do some shopping, some sightseeing, get some pizza…."

Jessica shook her head. "Our first football game is a week from Friday. I can't miss practice. And I have my first biology test next Wednesday. I really can't get away."

Carla considered her answer, and then nodded. "You'll be alright by yourself?"

"Of course. This is Glendale, Mom, remember?"

Carla nodded. "Point taken."

After dinner, Jessi microwaved the popcorn while Carla did the dishes. They sat down together and watched the movie, pausing it in the middle to get bowls of ice cream. When the movie was over, they both just sat there for an extra minute, and Jessi looked at Carla and smiled. "Thanks for planning a girls' night, Mom."

Carla looked taken aback by Jessi's comment, and she shrugged. "I just thought it would be fun, you know?"

Jessi nodded. "It actually was." Jessi looked down at her empty bowl and realized their evening was probably something that Kara and Hannah would do together often, and here she was doing it with her mother. Although it felt odd, it felt nice, and she went to bed a few minutes later feeling warm and happy inside.

She sent Joe a text. "My mom and I had a girls' night tonight. It was actually fun."

His reply came seconds later. "I know. I'm glad you enjoyed it."

She frowned. Surely Joe hadn't suggested the idea to her mom, had he? Hadn't Carla said something about him earlier? Jessi felt annoyance start to set in at the thought, but then let it go – either way, she had enjoyed the night. It had been nice not to spend another evening alone.

Fifteen

Joe pulled on a t-shirt, rubbed gel into his hair and used a little of the cologne Kara had given him for Christmas the year before. He was in a hurry, but making sure to cover all his bases. Jessica's mom had gone to Chicago for work, and Jessi had invited him over for a movie. It was the first time he was going over to her house for a date, and he was oddly nervous.

He ran down the stairs and popped into the kitchen to tell his mom he was leaving. She was still washing the dinner dishes, and Kara was scooping the leftovers into a small container to put in the fridge. "You're headed out?" Hannah asked him, a pleasant smile on her face.

"Yep. I won't be late getting back."

"Okay. When will Carla be back?"

"I'm not sure. Sometime tonight." Joe thought he saw a flicker of concern cloud his mother's face for just a moment, but then it was gone.

"Well, have a good time, and tell Jessi we say hello!"

"And tell her that next time I want to be invited over for a movie, too!" Kara said, still pouting about the fact that she hadn't been included.

"Kara," Hannah warned kindly.

Joe grinned at his little sister. He knew she had been struggling all evening with the fact that she was being left out. "I will," he promised. With that, he was out the door and headed for a break in the trees, which served as a shortcut to Jessi's. There was no reason to drive when it would take him five minutes to walk. And the walk would give him time to think.

He was aware of the trust his parents were placing in him by allowing him to go tonight, and he deeply appreciated it. He knew it wasn't easy for them to let him go to his girlfriend's house when her mother was out of town. It would be just the two of them, but his parents trusted him, and he would be sure to uphold that trust.

Still, he was more excited for the evening than he was completely sure he ought to be. And he knew why – he was actually beginning to fall for Jessi. He had thought she was beautiful, liked hanging out with her, and had been intrigued by her when he had first asked her out. But the majority of his reasoning then was that he wanted to be someone who cared, someone she trusted. He expected to eventually have the opportunity to introduce her to the One her soul longed to know.

However, in the past week he had felt his emotions start to get involved. On Saturday, when she opened up to him, and when he sat and held her and eventually they shared their first kiss, he realized he was actually falling for her. He still wanted to witness to her, but now he had other interests as well. He liked her. He liked her sense of humor, her stubbornness, how she smelled, how her hair fell across her face, how her eyes were a vibrant blue, and how her hand felt so delicate in his. When she was truly open and vulnerable, he felt like she was innocent and new. And he liked how it felt to kiss her.

At first, the realization that he liked her scared him. He had used the better part of Sunday spending time with God, being open and honest, telling Him every thought he was having concerning the dark-haired neighbor girl. With his motives becoming more complicated, he thought about calling the whole thing off. That was before he realized two things – the harm it could cause, and the fact that he didn't want to.

He felt as if God had been just as honest with him, and he felt a warning deep down in his spirit. Yet it was a warning laced with grace, as if it was right to continue moving forward, but necessary to walk very carefully as danger lurked around every bend. Joe had spent a long time listening for a strategy to build a Godly relationship and lead Jessi to the Lord at the same time, and came up with three things that were imperative. He needed to keep his eyes and his priority on Jesus, flee temptation, and guard his purity and hers with a fiery passion.

He had written the three steps and a verse on an index card and propped it up on the end table beside his bed. Even now the verse *'The thief comes only to steal and kill and destroy,'* ran through his mind. Not that Jessi was the enemy by any means, but Joe knew that the enemy would use her in whatever way he could to cause him (and her) to fall.

Still, when he stepped into the clearing surrounding the Cordels' cottage and saw Jessi sitting on the front porch waiting for him, he jogged the last few hundred feet. When he reached her, he pulled her close and kissed her.

The scent of her perfume wafted up and enveloped him and her kiss was sweet and minty. Her swooped bangs brushed against his face, and her shirt felt soft under his hands. When she reached up and put her arms around his neck, pulling him closer, kissing him again, he didn't pull away.

They had kissed several times since Saturday, and each time the kisses were longer. Now, her kiss was more intense and demanding than it had been yet, and he felt a warmth start to grow in his belly and spread through his limbs.

The kiss didn't end, and he couldn't breathe. It was not so much from a lack of oxygen as from the effects of her being so near.

She pulled back and smiled, whispering a greeting. "Hi," he answered, barely able to catch his breath. He was glad that she had pulled away, as he wasn't sure he could have.

"Come on in! I have the movie all ready to watch, and my mom is gone. She won't be back until the early morning hours, so we have plenty of time."

Joe felt a hint of danger in her comment and told himself no more kissing – it's not that he thought anything would happen, but he wanted to keep the slate perfectly clean. Thankfully, Jessica was playing by his rules and not initiating physical contact, so he was certain that if he kept things light and comfortable during the movie, she would as well.

He followed her up the porch stairs and into the house, closing the door behind himself. A bowl of popcorn and two sodas sat on the stylish coffee table. "I also have ice cream in the freezer if you want any of that later," Jessi told him, seeing the direction of his gaze.

"Sounds great."

"Um, okay, go ahead and sit down, and I'll push play," Jessi said, tucking her hair behind her ear. He realized that she was also nervous about the night.

"You know, I've never seen your whole house," Joe said,

stalling on the movie for a few minutes.

She looked surprised at the change of direction. "Okay, I'll show you around." Joe held her hand as she showed him from room to room, hoping that both of their nerves would calm down, and they could just have a good time as normal.

In her room, he paused and tapped her biology book. "How did your test go today?"

She made a face. "I need a tutor."

He laughed. "I happen to be a great tutor."

Her face lit up. "Are you? What would you say to helping me out?"

"Deal." She smiled up at him, and he smiled back. He let his eyes wander around her room and took in the paintings on the wall, the plush looking bed, the fashionable furniture and their picture on the bedside table. "You have great decorating taste, Jess."

"I'd like to think I have great taste in more than just interior decorating," she told him, her tone flirty.

"Oh yeah? Like what?" he asked, taking the bait, enjoying the chance to flirt with her over something harmless.

"Oh…like food, clothes, perfume," she stepped close enough to him that her shirt brushed his, "and men…"

The atmosphere was suddenly electric, and Joe felt a pang of terror as he realized that being alone with Jessica in her house, in her room, was more of a temptation than he had thought it would be. There was something about being alone with her that felt mysterious and exciting, like anything could happen. He laughed and stepped back, his nerves active again, taking her hand and leading her out of her room. "I would say that's true. Especially the last one."

Getting back to the safety of the living room, he plopped down onto the deep couch and reached for the popcorn. Jessi grabbed the remote and sat down beside him, hitting play. They munched on popcorn as the opening credits rolled across the screen, and Joe reached out and opened first his can of soda and then hers, handing it to her so she could take a drink. As the movie played he began to relax, the mood changing from electric to comfortable, and for that he was thankful. His nerves smoothed out, and he began to breathe easier.

"Want ice cream?" Jessi whispered halfway through the movie. Setting the empty popcorn bowl on the table, he nodded. "I'll get it," she told him, quickly standing up. A couple of minutes later, she was back with brownie sundaes complete with cherries on top.

"Did you make these brownies yourself?" he asked after taking his first bite.

"No...but I put the ice cream on top myself!" she said, and he laughed.

"Well, they're amazing!" They ate the rest of their dessert in silence, and once they were done, Jessi got up to take the bowls to the kitchen. As she passed through the living room she said, "I'll be right back."

"Want me to pause the movie?" Joe asked, turning and watching her walk down the hallway.

"No. I'll just be a few minutes, and I've seen it before," she answered before disappearing into her room.

An unexpected warning started going off in his heart, and Joe shifted in his seat. "LORD, what's going on?" he asked aloud, responding to the alarms sounding within him. The shadows were gathering in the corners of the room, and in five minutes it would be completely dark. *"Flee temptation, Son,"* were the words quietly whispered across the surface of his understanding, and he narrowed his eyes, trying to make sense of it.

Temptation? Of the whole evening, this was the least tempting time – Jessi wasn't even in the room, and he made sure and reminded the LORD of that. Again, he heard the gentle, yet concrete warning. Joe looked down the hall and then at the movie. He couldn't leave while she was in her room. She would surely wonder where he had gone. It would be rude.

"I'll go when it's over," Joe promised, spending a moment focusing on the movie to gauge how long was left. There weren't more than ten minutes remaining, and by then Jessi should be out. He could tell her goodbye and head home.

"Go now." It was fainter than '*flee temptation*' had been and Joe tried to listen harder, wondering if it was God speaking, or if it was simply his imagination. He thought he heard the command again. He continued to debate on whether to leave right away or to wait until Jessi came out and the movie was over. Fi-

nally, as everything within his heart quieted, he decided to stay to watch the end of the movie and tell Jessi goodbye. Then he would go home. Right away.

~~~~~

Jessi slipped into a lacy black bra and panties. She pulled her black silk robe on and tied it loose enough that it hung open to show her choice of clothing. She looked at herself in the mirror, added a frosty lip gloss and sprayed herself with perfume. She smoothed her hand over the butterflies in her stomach, and lit candles around her room. She stopped to stare at herself in the mirror, her hands spread over her chest.

She couldn't believe that in a few hours, she wouldn't be a virgin anymore. She would finally be grown-up. After tonight, there was no turning back. The thought scared her, but she felt more excitement than fear. She pressed down her nerves, told herself again that Joe would thank her for being bold, slipped silently down the hall, and walked into the dark living room.

~~~~~

He heard her steps. "Jess, you missed the end of the movie!"

"Stay there," she told him, her voice sultry. She started lighting candles one by one until her shape came into focus and then the shortness of her robe, the tanned smoothness of her legs, and the perfect way her hair fell.

"What are you doing?" he asked, uneasy.

"Lighting candles," she said simply, shooting him a dimpled smile over her shoulder.

Joe didn't understand. She turned toward him, and his mouth fell open. "That's your robe," he stated, his voice dull.

"Yes, it is," she answered as she crossed the floor to him, her blue eyes intense.

Joe's mind was screaming at him. Jessica was the essence of beauty. She was intelligent, funny, he was really beginning to care for her, she was standing in front of him in a silk robe and she was willing. What man wouldn't be ecstatic? Yet, he pushed himself to his feet.

She came to him and kissed him. He stayed perfectly still, his hands stiff at his sides. "Joe, tonight I'm going to let you have a little fun," she told him. Emotions warred for control. His human desire begged and raged at him to take her up on her offer, but his conscience was screaming that it was wrong. A familiar, soft voice in his heart pulled at him, even in the midst of such inner conflict.

He shook his head weakly. "No." She kissed him again. Her kiss was sweet and intoxicating and his thoughts were growing fuzzy.

Three quiet words settled upon his mind. *Flee from temptation.* "Oh my God," he groaned deep in his throat, and then, quicker than a flash of lightening, he broke off their kiss, pushed her away, and rushed to the front door.

"What are you doing?" she cried in shock.

"What am *I* doing? What are *you* doing?"

"You know you want to!" she countered.

"Of course I want to!" he answered huskily. "Which is exactly why I'm leaving now, and should have half an hour ago." With that, he turned and left, slamming the door behind him.

~~~~~

Jessica stood in complete shock, then ran and flung open the front door. He couldn't seriously be leaving! But he was nowhere in sight. She turned, her eyes huge, and shut the heavy front door. She leaned back against it, her lip starting to quiver. The house had never felt so empty.

Self-doubt and confusion filled her, and she looked down at herself. She wrapped her arms around her middle and dug her fingers into her skin. She wasn't good enough. Giving a strange cry, she dropped her hands, leaving ten red lines scratched across her body. Very slowly, she sank to the floor where she stood and started to cry. This was not how the night was supposed to end.

She had wanted Joe to accept her gift with great delight. She had wanted him to take control of the night, to show her the way, to give her a night to remember forever and treasure as her first time. She wanted him to tell her how beautiful and perfect she was, to show her the most intense beauty of love. Instead, he had denied her, refused her, and ran away like she repulsed him; and she didn't know why.

Joe was her boyfriend, a teenage boy with raging hormones. Jessi thought she had looked the part. She had spent an hour and a half in the lingerie shop, picking out just the right outfit. She had paid over fifteen dollars for the perfect kind of lip gloss, had shaved twice, and had put on multiple coats of lotion just to make the night perfect. She thought that she would have been desirable or at least satisfactory.

She sank over her knees, her tears falling on the carpet. This never would have happened to Anna or Kayly. A new thought occurred to her. It wasn't because she was selective that she was still a virgin. It was because she wasn't desirable.

She hadn't been enough emotionally to keep her dad, and now she wasn't enough physically to keep a boyfriend. If she wasn't enough emotionally or physically, she had nothing left to offer.

Her breathing was ragged, and the muscles in her abdomen hurt from sobbing. Finally, she pulled her fingertips under her eyes, wiping off her running mascara. She stood and went to bed, dejected, her eyes burning, her heart bleeding.

~~~~~

Joe took off at a jog through the forest. He needed to be alone. His heart was still pounding, his mind racing. His hands were shaking, and her kiss burned on his lips. Beyond all the effects of Jessica, one feeling stood out above all the rest. Shame.

He put his hands out and fell hard against the oak tree, resting his head on the bark. He hadn't left when he should have. When he had first heard the warning, he should have run out of there. But he hadn't. He had let his reasoning override what he knew was right, and had very nearly fallen into the trap of sexual immorality.

"Jesus, I know better! I knew I should have left! I know better than to put myself in that position!" Joe held his hands up and watched them shake. "LORD, she's too dangerous for me. She's like a river that pulls me to a spot in the current that's too strong for me to stay on my feet," Joe admitted into the night air.

Other than the crickets and the quiet croaking of frogs, he didn't hear any response. The stars shone bright, and the wind rustled the leaves. He sighed and rested his head against the bark. "I'm sorry, Jesus. I'm sorry. I let sin entangle me in front of the very girl that You've called me to witness to. I failed her tonight, and I failed You. She deserves better than that, just as You do."

Joe looked up at the sky and felt a quiet peace settle over

him like a warm, soft blanket. With his sins confessed and forgiven, he walked home and read from his Bible before going to bed.

His slate had been wiped clean before God, but before Jessica, it was still marked up. And despite the fact that he was forgiven, he had to deal with the immediate consequences from his disobedience, decisions and actions.

The next morning, he called to wake Jessica up as normal, but she didn't answer. He worried as he got ready and barely said a word to Kara on their way to Jessi's. She wasn't waiting outside on the porch like she usually was, and it took three loud knocks before someone answered the door. Carla looked sleepy, a white robe tied tight around her, a cup of steaming coffee in her hands. "Good morning, Joe," she said with a smile.

He smiled back. "Good morning! You made it home." She nodded, a lopsided smile propping up one side of her face.

"Yes, but very late last night."

"Sorry to wake you. Is Jessi ready?"

"Well, when I heard you knock, I went in to check on her. She's not feeling well this morning and isn't going to school," Carla answered, looking concerned.

Joe's heart sank. So, that was what she was going to do? Just avoid him? That was her way of dealing with what had happened? "What's wrong with her?" he pushed.

"She said her stomach isn't feeling well."

Joe tipped his head and let out a frustrated sigh. "I'll pick up her schoolwork for her and bring it by later."

Carla nodded and smiled warmly. "Thank you, Joe. You're such a good guy."

He let out a deep breath, having to push away the guilt her comment stirred up and remind himself that he had already been forgiven. "No problem. We'd better get to school."

"Have a good day."

"You too," he said, turning.

He jogged back to his pickup and relayed the news to Kara, who looked suspicious. "How was your movie last night?" she asked, watching him closely.

He nodded. "Fine."

"Really?"

"Yes." She watched him, her eyes narrowing, but he kept his eyes on the road. She turned away and took a drink from her travel mug of milk.

"You should get her flowers."

"I plan on it."

"What did you do to upset her?" she questioned, her suspicions confirmed.

"Nothing good, that's for sure."

"Want to tell me about it?"

He shot her a sideways grin. "No."

She shrugged. "Okay, just thought I'd give you the chance to get it off your chest."

"It's already gone."

She offered him a drink of her milk. He took it and grinned when she said, "Ruth's Floral has a good deal on roses right now. They advertised it in the newspaper."

~~~~~

When Joe stopped by with Jessica's schoolwork after football practice, she was waiting on the front porch. Jessi had spent the morning lying in her bed with a box of chocolates, feeling sorry for herself, and the afternoon thinking about how Heather might cash in on this tension in their relationship.

She had been waiting on the front step for an hour by the time she spotted Joe's truck. She jumped up and ran to him, waiting for him to put the vehicle in park. He got out of his truck, and they both stood there awkwardly for a moment. "Want to take a walk?" he finally asked.

She shook her head, stepped close, and threw her arms around his neck. "I want you, Joe! I'm sorry. I shouldn't have done what I did last night. I just wanted you to be happy, and I thought that was what you would want. Please just tell me you aren't going to break up with me!" She clung to him like a little child, and after his initial shock subsided, he wrapped his arms securely around her back.

He reached back into his truck and pulled out a dozen red roses. "These are for you."

She stared at them. "What do they mean?"

"They mean we need to talk," he said, grinning at her. "But definitely not about breaking up."

She let out a deep sigh of relief. "Joe, I'm sorry." He took her by the hand, and swinging it, they started out on a well-worn path.

"Jessica, we're expecting different things from this relationship and from each other."

"What are you expecting?" she asked, looking at her roses.

"I'm expecting someone I can share my time with, someone I can care about, and someone that can respect where I come from. What are you expecting?" She shrugged. "No, come up with something," he urged her.

"Well, fine. I expected you to want what I offered last night. My friend Anna said I would lose you if I didn't give you the chance. She knows a lot about relationships."

He tipped his head, and she thought she saw him blush. "Okay, so you explained what you expected out of last night. What do you expect out of me?"

"I...I don't know."

"Jess, think about it...what do you want from me?"

"I want someone to do things with," she paused, her voice growing faint. "I want someone that cares, someone that makes me feel loved."

He let out a small smile. "I can be all of that...it just might look differently than you would think."

"I didn't feel loved last night," she said dully, and he could hear the pain in her voice. For the first time, he considered how it must have made her feel when he left.

He stopped and turned her toward him by the shoulders. "Jessica, I really like you and I like going out with you, but before you ever appeared on the scene, I was a Christian and I made a promise to Jesus to be pure. I'm waiting until I'm married and that's why I left last night. It had nothing to do with you." She didn't look at him. "If doing that sort of thing is something that is really important to you, we may not be able to be together," he went on slowly.

She stared at him, hurt, her blue eyes full of confusion. "I like you," she told him.

"And I'm glad because I like you, too, but you have to know this. Either we break up, or we can continue going out with you understanding that I will not do any of that until I'm married.

If you choose that option, I need you to promise that you'll respect my decision and not make it more difficult for me than it has to be."

She let out a small smile. "Like wearing my robe?" she teased lightly.

He tipped his head back and blew out a short breath. "Yes. Like wearing your robe. Not a good idea." It was quiet for a long time. "Which option will you choose?"

"I don't know. It kind of ticks me off that you don't find me attractive enough," she said, tossing her head. "I mean, why would you even want me as your girlfriend?"

He shook his head and framed her face with his hands. His tenderness made her go instantly still. "Jess, it's not that at all." He gave a small, uncomfortable laugh. "Trust me, it's not. I won't do that with anyone until I get married. It has nothing to do with how attracted I am to you; it has everything to do with a previous commitment."

She smiled, then looked at the ground, her smile fading. He put his finger under her chin and tipped her face back up. "Why does it have to be like this?" she asked sadly. "I know kids that go to youth group, and they...well, they do the normal things that couples do."

"Normal things?" Joe asked incredulously. "Normal for married couples, yes, but it shouldn't be normal for couples who aren't married!"

"But it *is* normal, Joe! It really is! Why do you pretend that it isn't? Everyone does it!"

Joe shut his eyes, his chin dropping to his chest. *Oh Jesus, how do I answer her questions? Give me the words and give her the ears to hear!*

"Jessi, do you see a ring on my finger?" he asked softly.

"No," she answered, startled by his question.

"Do you see one on yours?" She shook her head. "Then I can't tell you yes. I like you a lot, Jessica. And I get that other kids do it, I really do. And we could, too, but all it is to you is sex!"

"As opposed to?" she asked, not understanding.

"Love, Jess! It's supposed to be making love! It's supposed to be saved for the sanctity of the marriage bed, for the love of husband and wife. It's supposed to be an act of love that you enjoy with the same person for your entire life. It's supposed to be beautiful and good and sacred. Whether you understand it or not, I made a promise, and the Man I promised has not forgotten!"

"Joe, he won't blame you!" she told him, searching his pale green eyes.

"Yes, He will! Jessi, He's going to honor my sacrifice and my self-control."

"How?" she challenged.

"By making it beautiful when I'm married." He couldn't believe he was discussing the subject so openly.

"I can make it beautiful for you now, Joe!" she cried, and he saw with despair that she didn't understand.

"Trust me, Jessi, you don't want this as bad as you think you do," he said, not sure how to make her see the truth.

"I do want it, Joe! I want it! I am almost sixteen and still a virgin!"

An acute sense of relief flooded him, and he softly murmured, "Thank God!" He closed his eyes for just a second and then continued. "God says that it's best within marriage, Jessi. Don't you want the best?"

She looked up into his green eyes and felt a sense of despair. "I want it now."

"Won't it make it so much sweeter if you have to wait for it?"

"I *have* waited for it. I waited when all of my friends didn't," she complained.

"Why did you wait?" he asked curiously. She was quiet for a moment.

"Because I want it to be special. I want it to be with someone I actually care about," she finally said.

"Then think how exciting that night will be when it's your husband." He saw that he had finally proven his point. "Jessi, I can't explain to you just how important this is to me. I can't explain how necessary my morals are to my life and to my faith. It's part of who I am," he said. "I haven't always been a good example of Jesus for you, Jessi, and I ask for your forgiveness."

"Why should you ask for my forgiveness? I don't even believe in your Jesus."

"Because my witness has been weakened. Obliterated, actually. I want you to look at me and see a man of strength and conviction, not a man easily given to temptation."

She stared up at him, her eyes sincere. "I see the strongest man I've ever known," she told him softly.

"Then you haven't seen many men, Jessi," he told her, feeling the weight of her words.

She was quiet for a long time. "I felt so worthless last night, but then this morning, Joe, when I thought you might get angry and break up with me, I realized that the only thing worse than not making love to you would be not having you at all." She fell quiet, letting that settle as she looked at the ground. Then she raised her eyes and looked up at him from under her dark eyelashes. "So I think I choose option number two."

He pressed his lips against hers for a brief moment. "I'm glad that's what you decided," he told her. "Jessi, I'm sorry I made you feel worthless. You are worth *much*." She smiled.

"So now that we've had this talk, do we still have stipulations? Can I initiate kisses yet?" she asked, her voice hopeful.

He nodded. "Yes. But nothing else. And you have to do it with your clothes on." She laughed, choosing to see the humor in his comment. "Deal?" he asked.

"Deal."

He grinned at her, and she smelled her roses. "They're beautiful. Thank you," she told him, smiling.

He took her hand, and they continued to walk. "I thought you might like them."

"You ready for your first game?" she asked, moving the conversation to an easier subject.

"Absolutely. I can't wait! Are you ready to cheer?"

She squeezed his hand. "I'm ready to cheer for *you*!"

"How's it going with Heather?"

Jessi shrugged. "We just don't see eye to eye."

He nodded. "Just so long as you guys are working on it."

Jessi tried to smother a sarcastic smile. "Yeah, we are."

They continued to walk, and he dropped her off at her front door. He squeezed her hand and walked away. She went in to put her roses in a vase of water, then carried it into her room to make it the centerpiece on her dresser, right beside her snow globe.

Sixteen

The first football game of the season was a home game. It seemed as if the entire town of Glendale turned out to watch it. The night was hot and muggy, and insects swarmed around the big stadium lights. Little kids laughed and ran, tossing footballs behind the concession stands, and the bleachers were so packed that people were standing along the fence. More people were streaming in with their black and gold blankets to sit on, nachos in their hands, and small flags to wave when the Pirates scored.

The student section was in the middle of the stands and extended seven rows up from the bottom. Most of the girls were dressed in black tank tops and had written the boys' numbers on them with gold paint. Some of the guys had their faces painted, and all of the students had newspapers to hold up in front of their faces when the opposing teams' starting line-up was read. A group of young boys stood right outside the locker room, determined to be the first to see the team's first appearance of the year.

Jessi stood on the track with the other cheerleaders in her short, pleated, black and gold skirt and sleeveless black top, edged in gold. Her pompoms were shiny black and gold. "GHS! GHS!" the cheerleaders chanted, clapping their hands. The crowd was fully participating in the cheer, and the players had not even entered the stadium yet.

"Spirit line!" Heather instructed, checking her watch. The cheerleaders all headed to the edge of the field. Jessi let out a deep breath and shook her head as she ran. She was tired of Heather's bossiness. It was bad enough during practice, but she had a feeling that during the game, it was going to be even worse.

The last few weeks of cheerleading practice had been tense and unpleasant for Jessica, although some of it was self-inflicted. Tacy had repeatedly offered friendship, but Jessi had always declined it. She didn't need friends – she had Anna and Kayly, Kara, and most importantly, Joe.

Dozens of fans spilled down onto the field to join the spirit line. They joined the cheerleaders, and Jessi found herself being jostled by people on all sides. She bit her lip and cast an annoyed glance over her shoulder at the laughing students around her.

"Shake your pompoms, Jess!" Kara bubbled, pushing through the crowd to stand beside her. Kara's cheeks were flushed and her eyes were sparkling.

Jessi smiled. "I'm glad to see that you're having fun."

"Aren't you?" Kara asked. "I love football!"

Jessi grinned at Kara's enthusiasm as the players burst out of the locker room doors. "Me too!" she answered.

"This is so exciting, Jessi! I love the first game!" Jessica looked around Kara to see Hannah and smiled. Their excitement was infectious.

The crowd put their arms up, cheering and yelling as the Glendale Pirates ran through the line of waving hands and took the field. Jessica cheered along with the rest of them, then ran back to her post with the rest of the cheerleaders. She clapped, yelled, jumped, and on occasion, wowed the crowd with a back-handspring or flip, just as they had practiced. The first half went fast, and it was obvious that it was going to be a blow-out.

"There's no way they're going to come back from thirty-five zip and win the game, eh, Jessi? I'd say the season opener is in the bag for the Pirates!" Jessica turned around to see Kara leaning over the railing, grinning, her blonde hair falling around her face.

Jessica nodded her agreement. "Definitely."

"They're certainly not going to with the way your brother can throw the ball!" Heather added, pushing her way into the conversation. Jessica gave her a disdainful look.

"Do either of you girls want something? I'm going to the concessions stand," Kara said, straightening.

"I'm okay, Kara, but thanks. You're so sweet," Heather said, smiling up at Kara.

"Save me a couple of your nachos," Jessica told her and Kara nodded.

"Will do. Have fun girls!" Kara left and when Jessica turned, Heather was glaring at her, her eyes flashing.

"What?" Jessica asked, blinking slowly.

"The Colbys are nice to everyone – even people like you –

so don't feel special."

Jessi gave a tight smile. "That's what I assumed, considering they put up with you."

"I'm a saint compared to you," Heather said, her voice quiet and low.

Jessica leveled her eyes at the blonde. "And humble enough to admit it."

The barb hit its mark, and a twinge of guilt crossed Heather's pretty face. She tossed her blonde ponytail and turned back to the other cheerleaders. "Okay, girls, let's start another cheer." Jessica rolled her eyes. Putting up with Heather and her self-righteous attitude all year was going to be hard to swallow.

Fifteen minutes later, the players came back onto the field. After two more quarters, Kara's prediction was officially true. The Pirates won forty-nine to three – a great beginning to their season. Jessi went out for ice cream with Joe and his family after the game and wrapped her hands snuggly around her milkshake while listening to the easy family banter.

"I was sure you were going to miss Justin with that fifteen-yard pass in the third," Kara said, licking caramel off her spoon.

"He wasn't looking over his shoulder," Joe countered.

"Don't blame him! You were off and you know it!" Kara accused, defending the absent Justin.

Joe grinned. "If you hadn't been screaming so loud, I wouldn't have overthrown the ball. You distracted me."

"That was totally Mom, not me," Kara said, holding her hands up.

"Whatever! I heard your squeaky voice say 'Throw it, Joe, throw it!'" The whole family laughed at Joe's light-hearted rendition of his sister. Kara made a face at him.

"In your sister's defense, your mother did make her voice hoarse," Chris said, joining in.

Hannah agreed with her husband, putting her hand to her throat. "It just gets me so anxious, but ah, this ice cream helps."

Joe laughed. "I'm glad, Mom, I'm glad."

"What did you think of your first GHS football game, Jess?" Joe asked, turning to the girl beside him.

She looked right into his eyes and smiled. "You were amazing."

"Oh, Jessi, don't say that," Chris groaned. "You're going to blow his head up like a balloon. He's going to start thinking he's a one-man-team!"

Joe shook his head. "Whatever. I'm nothing without my offensive line."

"You'd still be amazing, Son," Hannah countered, her face glowing with pride. He shook his head, and turned back toward Jessica, his eyes shining into hers as he smiled at her.

"Don't believe a word she says," he told Jessi. Hannah hit him on the arm.

~~~~~

It was exactly one week after the season opener that the football team had their first away game. Jessica was hot and tired by the time school let out. Waiting outside for the bus to arrive was a welcome relief before spending two hours in a hot vehicle on their way to the game. The month of September had yet to produce any relief from the heat and the buses didn't have air-conditioning.

She was lying in line, her head on her duffel bag, her eyes closed. "Jess, you know we can't sit together right?" Joe asked, leaning toward her. He was sitting beside her, but had been talking to friends on the other side of him.

She opened one eye and looked up at him. "What?"

"Yeah, school policy – boys can't sit with girls," he told her.

She shrugged, trying not to let him see how disappointed she was. "Okay."

He grinned at her and turned back to his teammates. She closed her eyes against the sun and retreated back to her quiet place.

"Jessica, when are you going to change into your uniform?" Heather's testy voice came from somewhere close by, and Jessica groaned, opening her eyes.

"Soon."

"Well, you'd better do it before the bus shows up," Heather paused. "Unless you're planning to change on the bus."

"Do it!" Dawson, a defensive lineman, called from his spot against the trunk of a tree. Color filled Heather's face as Joe glanced distastefully at Dawson, then up at Heather.

"I just thought I'd remind you," Heather said and hurried away to go sit with her friends as if she was the queen of the school.

Jessica sighed and pushed herself to her feet.

"Don't worry about Heather, Jess. She just wishes she looked that good in your clothes," Dawson called out, tipping his cap down over his face.

Heather shot him a dirty look. "I would never wear something like that," she told him.

"I wouldn't want you to," he joked. Heather didn't find the humor in his teasing.

As Jessica walked toward the school with her duffel bag to change, she realized that there was a lot of truth in Dawson's statement. Heather was watching her with an expression that fit somewhere between wistful and green with jealousy. Jessica looked down at her tight denim jeans and tight, layered spaghetti strap shirts in lime green and watermelon pink. They looked as if they had been painted on instead of pulled over her head. Maybe Heather thought that if she was allowed to wear tight clothes like Jessica, Joe would notice her. But Jessi didn't truly know why Heather was jealous, and she didn't care. She dismissed the thought as she changed into her cheerleading uniform.

When she went back to the curb, everyone was in the bus waiting for her. She felt color rise in her cheeks as the bus driver gave her an annoyed look, shutting the door after she climbed aboard.

"What took you so long, Jessi?" Monica asked, flipping her long hair over her shoulder, a sweet smile plastered on her face.

"I thought I saw your head in the toilet, and I was thinking of how to get you out," Jessi paused. "But then I realized that someone had just forgotten to flush." A few of the guys chuckled quietly, others coughed into their arms. Not many of them had the gall to laugh aloud. Heaven forbid you upset Heather Crebel or one of her perfect-haired followers.

Jessi ruefully admitted to herself that if it hadn't been for Joe, she probably would have been one of them. As it was, a friendship with Heather would never be possible. Jessica breezed past Monica, then realized that all of the seats were full. Joe looked at her out of concerned eyes, his expression sympathetic.

"Looks like there's no room, Jessi," Heather said, faking disappointment in the seat behind Joe.

"Want to share my seat?" The voice was familiar, and it annoyed Jessi. Why was it that the harder she tried to stay away from Tacy, the more time she had to spend with her? Why didn't the girl understand that she didn't need a friend? But the bus driver was getting impatient and Jessi was desperate. She dropped onto the bench seat as Tacy slid over.

"Thanks," she mumbled.

Tacy shrugged. "I want to get this show on the road just like everyone else, and we couldn't go with you standing there in the middle of the aisle." Jessica accidentally let a small smile slip before putting on headphones and turning on her music.

Tacy pulled the speaker out of Jessi's ear a few minutes later. "Good song – I love this band." Jessi nodded, replaced the speaker, and closed her eyes. She planned to sleep all the way to the football game, but woke when Tacy jabbed her in the ribs. "Do you get this?"

Jessi looked groggily at their biology homework. "Ask Joe. He gets it."

"Really?" Tacy's voice brightened a little too much for Jessica's comfort, and she woke up more fully.

"Fine. I can help you." Jessica spent the next fifteen minutes wading through the lesson.

"I like Au," Tacy said with a smile.

"That's chemistry, Tacy, but yes, especially if it's on your finger with a lot of precious stones set into it," Jessi agreed.

"Whatever," Tacy answered. "Someday I'll have two rings for every finger. Real of course," the red-head promised, holding her hand out as if to imagine the rings that would one day sparkle on it.

Jessi glanced over her shoulder at the pale-eyed, olive-skinned boy a few rows back. "I'll have at least one." As soon as the words left her mouth, she regretted them. As if she was thinking their relationship was actually going to last...or that she wanted it to.

"You like him a lot?"

Jessi wrinkled up her nose and shook her head, lying. "No, he's just cool to chill with right now." Jessi traced one of the pleats in her skirt before continuing. "He's just so different. I've never known anyone like him."

"And you never will. Trust me, there's only one Joe Colby in the world. Pity there aren't more. I'd take one for myself." Jessi laughed uneasily. "But don't worry, you're safe with me. I would never steal another girl's boyfriend. It's just wrong," Tacy paused. "Even if it is Joe Colby."

Both girls warily looked back at the blonde sitting behind the boy in question. Neither said anything. The way that Heather was flipping her hair and laughing right into Joe's eyes, was saying it all. Heather didn't care that Joe was already in a relationship.

Jessica turned around and scooted farther down in her seat, disgusted. "Her charm won't work on him, Jessi," Tacy said, scooting down, too.

"It better not."

Tacy shook her head and opened a granola bar. "It won't."

"What makes you so sure?" Jessi asked, pouting. *She* wanted to be sitting behind Joe. *She* wanted to be laughing and flirting.

"Other than the fact that he's a totally loyal guy with a keen sense of right and wrong?" Jessica nodded. "She's been trying for years and until you, he's never dated," Tacy reasoned. That made Jessica feel a tiny bit better, and she turned around to peek at Joe again. He was flipping through a history book now, only half-interested in the conversation his seatmate was engaged in with Heather.

"Want half?" Tacy asked.

Jessi accepted part of the granola bar. "Thanks."

"Do you like to go shopping, Jessi?" Tacy asked, pulling her part of the bar apart with her fingers before eating it.

"Do you like breathing?"

Tacy smiled. "Want to go with me next Saturday?"

Jessi's eyes grew excited. "You're going somewhere outside of Glendale?"

"Up to the city. My older sister, Jillian, is taking me and said I could ask you to come."

"Count me in!"

Tacy and Jessica chatted off and on all the way to the game.

Jessi hurt her ankle a little during one of her jumps in the second quarter, but shook it off. Joe played excellently, and the Pirates had their second win of the season.

Joe and Jessi rode home with Chris, Hannah, and Kara, who had driven up to watch the game. After a quick stop at a fast food restaurant, Jessi slept against Joe's shoulder all the way back to Glendale. He fell asleep too, his head bouncing against the window. Kara fell asleep against Jessi. It was a domino line of sleepers, and despite the fact that Joe elbowed her once, and Kara was accidentally drooling a little on her shoulder, Jessica had never felt more comfortable as she slept.

Seventeen

"Joe, I don't think this relationship is a good idea." Joe was sitting across the table from Rob Caiten, a tall soda sitting in front of each of them.

Joe shook his head. "I know how it sounds, but Rob, she needs Jesus. You should see how she needs Him." Joe had just finished telling his friend and mentor what had happened the Wednesday Carla was out of town.

Rob shook his head. "That doesn't mean you have to date her."

"I can do this, Rob."

"I know you can – you have more faith than I've seen anyone your age have, but this isn't a question of faith. It isn't your job to save her."

"But I have access," Joe told the older man.

"To what?" Joe tipped his head at his youth group leader's dry response, getting his not-so-subtle meaning. Rob shook his head. "I'm sorry, I just don't want to see you stumble."

"I know," Joe paused. "But I think I need to take this opportunity to witness to her."

"Bring her to youth group."

"She's not ready."

Rob steepled his fingers and looked at Joe seriously. "Are there other reasons you're dating her? Besides wanting to introduce her to Jesus?"

A sheepish smile spread across Joe's face. "Not necessarily at first, but now…I like her, Rob." Joe could see the battle going on inside his mentor. Joe knew Rob wasn't sure whether to be relieved that Joe wasn't dating Jessi just to witness to her, or concerned that Joe actually liked this girl who seemed to be the most unnatural choice for him.

"Fine, but Buddy, be on guard. Don't give the devil the opportunity to get to you. You know he'll take the chance in whatever form he can."

Joe nodded. "As my mentor and my friend, will you pray for me?"

Rob grinned and nodded his head. "You don't even need to ask." Joe grinned back.

When Rob Caiten and his wife Katie, both in their late twenties, had moved to Glendale three years earlier, Joe had found not only a friend, but a man who would help direct him in his walk with God and hold him accountable. He had been grateful for Rob's influence in his life ever since.

"How's Katie?"

Rob's eyes softened at the mention of his wife. "Ready for the baby to be out!"

Joe nodded. "I'm sure. It's soon now – just two more weeks, right?"

Rob nodded his head and let out a deep breath. "Boy am I ready! If I have to make one more run to the supermarket at three in the morning for pickles or orange juice, or whatever it is that we don't have and she's craving, I think I'm going to go nuts." Rob talked big, but Joe knew he was kidding. Rob adored his wife and secretly enjoyed playing her hero every time her hormones kicked in, and she *needed* something.

"Have you decided on a name yet?" Joe asked, taking a long drink of his soda.

Rob nodded. "Got it narrowed down to a couple."

"Which ones?"

"Haven Joy or Rachel Rose."

Joe nodded. "They're both nice."

"I told Katie she could choose between the two since we like both of them. She said she wanted to see which would fit."

"Makes sense."

"I told her she gets the final decision on the girls if I can have dibs on the boys."

Joe shook his head. "Your daughters will wrap you around their little fingers like your sons never will."

"Oh no. My sons and I, we're going to bond."

"Of course you'll bond. You'll be close. But your daughters will smile up at you, batting their eyelashes, and you won't be able to tell them no. Just ask my dad," Joe told him.

"Don't sound so happy about it," Rob said with a laugh.

"No, its fine, I just wish I possessed half the power and charm over my parents that my sisters have. There's not a thing they couldn't get if they really wanted it."

Rob scooted his glass around in the moisture it had made on the table. "I guess if my daughter has eyes like Katie's, you might be right."

"I am – you wait until she's born. You'll see."

Rob dipped his head in surrender. "Katie's mom is coming down next week."

"How long is she staying?"

"Hopefully at least a few weeks after the baby comes. I know Katie is going to need help while she recovers." Rob had the utmost respect for his mother-in-law.

"Are we going to cancel youth group for a couple of weeks?"

"No." Rob brushed the question away. "No way. Unless Katie is in labor, we'll have it."

"Are you sure?"

"It's only two hours a week."

"What about our study?" Joe asked, referring to the Bible study he did with Rob every Thursday night.

After being the youth group leader for only two months, Rob saw that Joe was craving more depth and intensity than the other kids were ready for. That's when Rob had started mentoring Joe. They met for an intensive Bible study weekly and usually squeezed in soda or pizza a few times every month, just to check in.

"Let's see how it goes. I may have to cancel one week."

"No problem. I completely understand."

"So, how's football going?" Rob asked, changing the subject.

Joe settled back in his seat and pulled his pant legs down. "Not to boast, but its going good."

Rob grinned. "Good! I'm glad. You'll play ball in college yet, watch and see. It could pay your way."

Joe grinned. "I hope so."

"Well, I'll tell you what, I sure enjoyed that last game! You guys were great."

"The defense was amazing," Joe conceded.

Rob smiled, and bumped Joe's elbow as he took a drink. "It wasn't just the defense." Joe modestly bobbed his head but didn't say anything.

"When are you going to give that Hail Mary a try in a game?"

"Soon! Maybe this week or next. We've run that play in practice several times and I've completed six of the passes. Coach loves it. He says we're going to run it at least once every game."

"Too bad you're not a show-off. You could really have some fun with your arm." Joe grinned. Rob's expression turned serious. "With Jessi being as pretty as she is, and having the season that you are, make sure you watch your pride. Being the star quarterback, dating the most sought-after girl in school, and being such a 'good boy' could go to your head. Guard against it." Joe took the warning in the way it was intended – genuine concern.

"I will."

Rob smiled at him. "And bring Jessi over sometime. I want to meet her."

"I will. That could be fun."

"Let's talk about it more after the baby's born."

"Sounds good. Katie may not be up for entertaining for the next couple of weeks, huh?"

Rob shook his head before checking his wristwatch and grabbing his drink. "I promised Katie I'd be home by nine."

Joe also stood. "Yeah, I should get going, too."

"It was good talking to you, Son." Rob said, pushing the café door open.

"You too, Rob. Take care."

"You do the same. I'll be praying for you."

"I appreciate it. I'll do the same for you, Katie, and the baby."

"Thanks. And Joe, remember what I said."

Joe nodded. "I always do." Rob saluted Joe and Joe grinned, returning the sign, getting in his truck and driving home.

Eighteen

Carla looked ruefully at the ringing telephone, but extended her arm to take it off the cushion. "This is Carla."

"Carla, it's me." She sat up straighter.

"Hello, Bill."

"Hello." There was an awkward silence.

"So, how are things going?" he asked, obviously uncomfortable.

"Stop beating around the bush – what do you want?" Carla asked, lifting her glasses and pinching the bridge of her nose. Nothing could give her a headache faster than talking to her ex-husband.

"I was wondering if I could talk to Jessica."

"Call her cell phone."

"She won't answer."

"Well, then she's probably busy."

"Come on, Carla, just have her talk to me." Bill sounded like he was becoming frustrated.

"Well, she's not here."

"Where is she?" Carla licked her finger and turned the page of the file she was looking at.

"Out."

"Out? With who?"

"Friends. Probably Joe – those two are always together."

"Yes, I've been meaning to speak with you about that. Do you think that's healthy? Spending so much time with one friend?"

"They're not just friends, Bill, they're dating."

He was silent for a moment. "Why didn't I know about that?" Now Carla knew he was angry.

"Maybe because you don't talk to your daughter."

"I try! She won't talk to me! She hasn't answered her phone for almost two months. And I never gave permission for her to date!"

"I did." Carla's firm reply made him grow quiet for a few moments. She mentally noted that she had never actually given permission for Jessi to date, nor had she been asked, but she was permitting it, so surely it was the same thing.

"Well, Wonder-Mom, where is your daughter now?"

"Probably in town or down by the river."

"What would she be doing down by the river?"

"Probably fishing, I don't know!"

"Well, why don't you know?" Bill questioned.

"What do you want from me, Bill? I'm not her babysitter!" Carla cried, standing up to pace the living room.

"No, you're not – you're her mother!" Bill almost yelled back. He calmed himself. "She is a sixteen-year-old girl who is out of control and looking for some boundaries. You need to set some for her."

"You don't know anything about her. And for the record, she's still fifteen," Carla told him.

"I know that she has chopped her hair off, injected ink into her skin, been out past midnight on school nights, spends every free minute with this Joe Colby, and that her mother has no idea where she is for hours at a time! You need to get control of her," Bill spat back, ignoring his mistake on her age.

"Don't tell me how to parent my daughter!" Carla yelled, stomping to the kitchen and pulling a bottle of wine out of the bottom cupboard.

"Our daughter, Carla! She is *our* daughter!"

"Funny. This summer you seemed to have forgotten that. Well, since you think you're such a perfect father, maybe you should help with her," Carla shot back.

"Well, maybe I should. Maybe I should go back before the judge and request custody."

"Don't be a jerk, Bill."

He let out a deep breath. "I didn't call to fight with you, Carla," Bill said, showing effort to even out his voice.

"Well, then why did you call?"

"I'm concerned for her."

She gave a sarcastic laugh. "Well, that's a first."

"Stop it. I know she's angry with me, and I know that she's doing things to get back at me."

"Well, you do pull yourself away from your new girlfriend

long enough to actually notice a few things, don't you? Bravo. It's a little late as it has been going on for months, but better late than never."

Bill cleared his throat, and his voice was gruff when he answered. "It was actually Jari who pointed it out to me, and she's worried that—"

"Oh that's rich! So now Jari, the big-boobed, big-haired girl who ruined our family, is now *worried* about *our* daughter. That's priceless, Bill, really, it is."

"Stop speaking of her like that! And, for your information, Jari knows what Jessica is going through."

"Oh, this is good, keep talking."

"Carla, I'm serious. When Jari's parents divorced, she went a little wild to make them angry. She dyed her hair, got a tattoo, started drinking—"

"That's when she got her implants, too, I suppose," Carla interrupted.

"And slept with men she didn't even like, just to make her dad angry," Bill continued as if he hadn't heard.

"So, that's how you two met!"

"Carla, *knock it off.* This is a serious matter. Jari's worried that Jessica will revert to that when nothing else gets us back together."

"Jessi's not stupid, and she's not Jari," Carla said, falling into a somber mood and taking a drink of the wine she had poured.

"Is she on birth control?"

"It would only make it worse, Bill, we've discussed this before."

"We can't live in a bubble, Carla. She's a beautiful girl, and boys out there in Glendale must have noticed that!"

"Well, encouraging it with the protection of birth control isn't going to help matters at all. I'd rather have a virgin daughter than one who was having safe sex, wouldn't you?"

"You know I would, I'm just saying."

"Well, whatever you're saying is ridiculous!"

"Oh, Carla, always so naïve," Bill said, his voice full of pity. Carla seethed.

Pressing her hand to her forehead, she forced herself to remember that the conversation was about their daughter, not either of them. "Bill, I don't want you to say anything bad about Joe Colby to her, do you hear me?"

"Why?"

"He's a good boy, and I've never seen a kid with the morals that he has. There is no one safer for Jessi to be with than him, and he is the best protection we could ask for in her teenage years."

"He looks out for her?"

"Better than either of us ever have."

"And he doesn't encourage drinking or partying?"

"He encourages fishing and studying. Sometimes he's so good, it almost bores *me*!"

Bill actually chuckled. "Well, you always did like yours a little on the wild side."

"And then I married you," she answered dryly. It was quiet.

"Well, fine, she can date." Carla let out a huff – as if it was his decision. "But Carla, please, just set down some boundaries for her and make her follow some rules. That's all I'm asking," Bill continued.

Carla sighed. "What Jessi wants, Jessi gets. She doesn't like boundaries."

"She doesn't have to like them. You're her parent, not her friend."

"Well, if you're so good at this, why don't you give it a try?" Carla spat at him, offended again.

"Maybe I will," he said, getting flustered.

"Well, maybe you should."

"I bet Jari and I could do a better job than you."

She hung up and hurled the phone at the carpet, where the battery fell out, and it bounced. She wiped a tear off her cheek, finished her glass of wine, sat down on the couch and went back to her paperwork. After seventeen years of marriage, two months of being separated, and three months of being divorced, William Cordel could make her angrier than anyone else on earth.

~~~~~

"Where have you been?" Jessica jumped. The house was dark and quiet. She hadn't noticed her mom lying on the couch, a washcloth over her eyes.

"Out."

"Doing what? With who?"

Jessica blinked, crossing her arms, offended by the onslaught.

"Friends."

"Joe?" Carla asked expectantly.

"No, it's Wednesday. He has youth group on Wednesday nights."

"So, who were you with?"

"A friend."

"What friend?" Carla pressed.

Jessica sighed and rubbed her eyes. "Tacy. We went out for dinner after cheerleading and then went back to her place to finish our biology." Jessi's voice was prickly. "Why do you care?"

"I care, Jessica, I care! I'm your mother, and I deserve to know where you are! I would appreciate it if you'd call me if you're going to be out late. What time is it anyway?"

"Ten-thirty."

"Ten-thirty? You stayed out until ten-thirty on a school night?"

"I get it – Dad called," Jessica replied dryly.

"Yes, and I got a long lecture because you didn't have the common decency to tell me where you were going."

"Hey, don't blame this on me. You didn't ask!"

"Well, I shouldn't have to," Carla snapped.

"Mom, you haven't been home while I was awake in days. When was I supposed to tell you my schedule? Since when do you care? And you don't bother to let me know yours," Jessica pointed out, preparing for a fight. Carla ignored her.

"He says I need to set down rules. He says you're out of control, you want boundaries, and that you need to be on birth control."

"He also said he would love you until death did you part," Jessi reminded.

Carla was quiet and then started to sniff. "I know. I didn't believe a word of it anyway."

"I'm going to bed, Mom," Jessi said, suddenly weary. Her mom and dad's fights drained her.

"Okay, Sweetie. Did you get your homework done?"

"Yes."

"Okay. I'll see you tomorrow night."

Jessica went back to her room and locked her door, dropping her book bag on the floor. She was ready to go to bed and forget the entire conversation that she had just had with her mother.

Nineteen

"Jessi?"

"Hi Mom." Jessica repositioned the home phone against her shoulder. She was cooking fish sticks and peas for dinner, and steam was roiling up from the pan of boiling green vegetables.

"Honey, I wanted to let you know that I have to stay late at the office tonight." Jessica felt a pang of loneliness shoot through her. She hadn't seen her mom in three days. They hadn't shared a meal in over a week. Tonight she was supposed to be home for dinner. "Jess, Honey, are you there?" Carla asked when Jessi was quiet.

"Yeah."

"Oh, you're upset. Jessi, I'm sorry, but I have this hearing tomorrow, and I have all this work to do beforehand. I just can't get home early tonight. I want to, I do, but I just can't swing it."

Jessica shoved her hands into her jean pockets. Her jeans were tight, her long-sleeved tee close-fitting and brown. "Sure. Whatever," she answered.

"You know what, Jess, never mind. I'll just juggle some things around and—"

"No, Mom, seriously, I want you to stay," Jessi said, flipping her hair back and resting her hip against the counter. "I have plans anyway."

"What plans?"

"Plans. With Joe."

"I should have guessed. You guys are pretty much inseparable these days."

"Pretty much," Jessi answered, and turned the peas off.

This was pathetic. She was making up plans with her boyfriend. If only he didn't have youth group on Wednesdays, she wouldn't have to fabricate anything. For once, Jessi was glad her mom never paid attention to her schedule. If she did, Carla would have caught her in the lie.

"Okay, well, I'll let you go. I'll be home late. Don't wait

up."

"I won't."

"I'll see you tomorrow."

"Sure," Jessi answered and hung up. She stared at the oven timer and waited for the fish to be done. When the timer went off, she pulled the pan out of the oven and set it on the stove. She arranged four fish sticks each on two plates and added small mountains of peas. She poured two glasses of cold water and set the table.

She sat down in her chair and looked at her mom's untouched plate. Jessi ate quietly, pretending that she wasn't the only one at the table. She had been doing this since she was small. She hated eating alone, and two plates seemed much less lonely than one. When she was finished, she dumped her mom's food in the trash, poured out her water, and put the dishes in the dishwasher. Five minutes later she was out the door, not being able to stand the silence any longer.

She got in her car and just drove for over an hour. She filled it up with gas, bought a candy bar and a soda, and then went to Joe's. He was just getting home from youth group. She wanted him to hold her and kiss her. She wanted him to make all the sadness inside of her go away. Instead, they sat on the hood of her car, leaned against the windshield, and looked at the stars until Joe said it was time for them to go to bed. He squeezed her hand and waved as she drove away.

She parked outside of her dark house, her car alone in the driveway. She went in and went to bed without turning a light on.

~~~~~

Jessica frowned as she listened to Joe's plans for the weekend. When he paused, she jumped in. "Joe, we were supposed to spend Saturday together."

"Well, my dad and I are going to the city to look for a tube to pull behind the boat next summer."

"I know. I heard you say that the first time, but you said on Wednesday that we had to make cookies this weekend! I bought the ingredients and found a recipe," she cried, hurt that he had dismissed their plans so easily.

"So, save them for next weekend."

"Joe, I told Tacy that I couldn't go shopping with her this

weekend because you wanted to spend time together!"

"Well, now you can go shopping, Jess! It will be fun." Jessica pressed her hand to her forehead, too angry to speak for a moment. He wasn't getting it.

"No, they left yesterday after school – I can't go anymore." There was a pause.

"I'm sorry, Hon." He sounded genuinely apologetic, but with her weekend plans in rubbish, it wasn't enough.

"No, Joe, I don't want an apology, I want you to tell your dad that you can't go with him tomorrow and come make cookies with me."

"And how am I supposed to tell him that?" he asked, his own voice becoming testy.

"By telling him that you already had plans!"

"What, Jessi? I'm supposed to say, 'I'm going to go bake with Jessica, so I can't go with you even though we haven't hung out for a couple of months?' Why would I do that, Jess? We can bake anytime!"

"Because first of all, it was your stupid idea to bake, and secondly, I'm your girlfriend!"

"He's my dad!"

"And?" she cried, pushing herself to a standing position, too hurt to stay sitting.

Her textbook fell to the floor and landed on her toe. She kicked it violently against the wall, stifling a cry of pain.

"And...my family comes first, Jess. Every time," Joe shot back angrily.

"I'm glad to know how much you care about me, Joe," she answered sarcastically. She heard him let out a frustrated breath.

"Jessi, I didn't mean it like that," he started. She clicked the off button and flung the phone on to her bed. There was only one way that could have been meant, and it wasn't in her favor.

She stood, shaking with anger, tears pricking her eyes. She waited for him to call back. He didn't. After fifteen minutes, she suddenly sank down onto the bed, her head in her hands, and began to sob. It was over. That was it.

She didn't hear from Joe all night and after doing her homework, half-heartedly, she pulled out a quart of ice cream. She turned the air-conditioner on to make the house cold, curled up on the couch with a blanket and watched her old movies where all the princesses lived happily ever after. She slept there that night and didn't wake up until two in the afternoon on Saturday. She watched more movies and ate more ice cream. Carla was once again gone on business and only called once to check up on her.

When Jessi opened the door to a knock on Sunday evening, she expected to see Grandma and Pops. She almost fell over when she saw Joe. Her mind raced over her pink shorts, lime green t-shirt and messy ponytail. Her cheeks flushed red. She thought about just shutting the door in his face, but his pale green eyes looked so apologetic that she couldn't. She hoped her own weren't still red from crying.

"What do you want?" she asked, her voice hard and void of emotion.

He shifted, his t-shirt pulling tight across his chest. "Can I come in for a minute?"

"No."

He gave her a crooked smile. "Then do you want to step outside, and we can sit on the porch swing and talk?"

"No," she answered, lifting her chin.

He took the dark green baseball cap from his head and held it in both of his hands. "Jessi, I'm sorry. Everything I said Friday came out all wrong." His apology made her uncomfortable and that made her angry.

"Oh, I think it came out all right. You meant it, and you know it," she snapped.

"I did," he said calmly, his eyes sincere.

"Well then, why don't you go back to them?" she asked and slammed the door in his face.

She turned her back to the door and balled her hands into fists. He had deserted her, ignored her, backed out on the weekend that *he* had planned for them, and had come to rub it in her face. She saw in his eyes that he would do it again if he had the chance.

She felt as if he had stabbed her in the back. She wanted to scream at him that she never would have done that to him – that he came first every time. She never would have chosen anybody over him. She wanted to yell that she should be his first choice, too. She had thought that, for the first time in her life, maybe she was someone's number one. She'd thought he wouldn't choose another over her. She had thought he cared. Obviously she had thought wrong. Again.

He knocked loudly on the door, and her anger boiled. She wouldn't let him torture her anymore! "Go to hell, Joe!" she yelled, kicking the door as hard as she could. She covered her face with her hands, her anger dissolving into tears.

~~~~~

All of the color drained out of Joe's face at her words. No one had ever said anything so harsh to him before, and it shook him down to the core. He wanted to leave, to run away from such harshness, but he forced himself to stay.

What he had said to her on Friday had been true, but completely unnecessary. There had been a much better way to help her understand the importance of the trip, but instead, he had blurted out the first thing that came to mind, not bothering to consider if it was kind or not. He had worried all weekend about having to apologize. He knew now that all his worrying had been for good cause.

He stood quiet, waiting and wondering what to do, and his heart dropped right out the bottom of his shoes because of the sounds he heard. They weren't mean words, more yelling, or more kicking, but the soft, secret sound of her crying on the other side of the door.

He normally would have left as she requested, letting her have her space, and then approach her the next day with another apology. But he had seen how his words had crushed her before her eyes had started to snap and smolder, and now the sound of her crying gripped his heart. So, instead of leaving, he put his hand on the doorknob and turned it, slipping through the door with an odd ache filling his chest. She looked up, shocked to see him inside her house, and his heart flopped at the sight of her tear -stained cheeks. He took her by the shoulders and pulled her to him.

"Your touch is not going to make this better, Joe!" she cried, trying to hide her tears, fighting against him. He held her close and buried his face in her hair.

"What about my heart, Jess? Can that make it better?" He

felt the tension drain out of her, and her hands wrapped in his t-shirt. She pressed her face against his chest. He enveloped her in his arms and smoothed her hair, comforting her as he would have comforted Kara.

Her crying picked up at first, but then slowly quieted as he held her. When he finally tipped her face up with a finger under her chin, her tears had stopped. He pushed wet tendrils of dark hair out of her eyes and wiped her wet cheeks with a tender hand.

"I messed up. I'm sorry. I should have explained, Jessi. I've been with my family for seventeen years, and my loyalty has to belong to them first. However, I should have asked my dad if we could go a different weekend or discussed it with you before making any decisions."

He saw how his gentle words gripped her heart. She buried her hands deeper in his t-shirt and looked up at him out of clear blue eyes. "Are we going to break up?"

His stomach tightened and a small jab of fear pricked his heart. He wanted to tell her absolutely not, but his conscience forced him to give her the option. "Not unless you want to."

She took in his pale green eyes, the masculine line of his tanned jaw, the chocolate shine of his hair, and the strong curve of his mouth. She closed her eyes and thought about the past few days, when she had done nothing but wallow in self-pity and her broken heart. She swallowed hard and shook her head, even though her heart screamed for her to break it off while she still could. He grinned at her and framed her face with his hands.

The difference between how he felt about her and how he felt about any other girl in the world had never seemed wider than it did right then. At that moment, all he could think about was the way he had hurt her and how badly he wanted to make it better. Without feeling any pressure from her, he lowered his head and brushed his lips across hers. He felt her pulse speed up under his thumb. Joe smiled and slid his hand around to cup the back of her neck.

She gave an innocent sigh of relief as he kissed her again, and the sound made his heart drum. His experienced, worldly, cold little Jessica was, in actuality, innocent and sweet. He pulled her close and deepened the kiss. She relaxed against him, and he held her tight. He broke it off to let her breathe, stroking her hair.

"I'm sorry I made you cry."

She gave a slight shrug of her shoulders. "You aren't the first," she answered softly, no condemnation or self-pity in her voice. His conscience pricked at her wordless, simple forgiveness, and his heart ached for her again. She really was such a sweet girl.

"I'm sorry about that, also." He ran his hands down her arms to take her hands in his. "Jessica, would you do me the honor of making cookies with me?"

Her eyes shone at him as she smiled. She offered him her hand as she turned. "It would be my pleasure, good sir."

~~~~~

When Carla arrived home, two hours later, she walked into a house that was full of laughter. Flour covered the counters and was sprinkled across the floor. Jessica's face was smudged with cookie dough, and Joe's green t-shirt had a white handprint on it that looked exactly Jessi's size. Two dozen cookies were cooling on wax paper on the dining room table, and two dozen were still in the oven.

"It's not my fault it's getting late. If you hadn't dumped the entire bottle of salt in, we wouldn't have had to make two batches!" Jessi was telling Joe, laughter bubbling out of her. Carla stayed where she was, just peeking around the corner to watch Joe and her daughter.

"Well, if you had told me two teaspoons instead of two tablespoons, I wouldn't have put too much salt in," Joe teased back.

"Well," Jessi started. "How was I supposed to know that a little 't' meant teaspoon?" Joe gave a hearty laugh and drew Jessi into his arms, planting a quick kiss on her forehead.

"You're adorable and," he wiped at the smudge on her cheek. "So dirty!"

Jessi purposely planted another hand on his chest, making a new flour print. "So are you!" Joe released Jessi as the timer went off.

Carla tiptoed over and opened and shut the front door, more loudly this time. "I'm home!" she called. Jessi and Joe came around the corner to greet her, Jessi offering her one of the warm cookies. "Yummy! Thanks, Sweetheart!" she said, kissing Jessi's cheek. "How was your weekend?"

"Terrible," Jessica admitted. "But tonight has been great," she finished, beaming up at Joe.

It took the three of them almost half an hour to put the kitchen back in order, and Jessica sent Joe home with a plateful of cookies for his family. After telling them both goodnight and squeezing Jessi's hand, Joe left. Not long after that, Jessi went to bed.

Carla shut the door to her room, sat down on her bed and dialed Lisa's number. Her friend sounded groggy. "Lisa, remember me telling you about Jessi's boyfriend, Joe?" Her friend took a long minute to answer.

"Vaguely. Why?"

"He is the best thing that has ever happened to her. You should have heard her laughing tonight. I haven't seen her this happy since she was a little girl."

Twenty

"Is it still rewinding?" Tacy asked as she walked down the stairs with popcorn.

Jessica looked at the old-school VCR and nodded. "It's going so slow."

"Yeah, that thing is a piece of junk. We need a new one, but Dad's too cheap." Tacy folded her legs under her as she sank into the cushions of the couch and handed one of the big bowls that was overflowing with the salty snack, to Jessi. She kept the other in her lap.

The popcorn was warm and buttery, and Jessi popped a handful into her mouth. "Yum. Good popcorn, Tace."

"Thanks." The girls were sitting in Tacy's basement, blankets and pillows spread out on the ground, the small refrigerator against the wall stocked with all sorts of soft drinks and snacks.

Tacy's father worked for the city, and her mom was the receptionist at the elementary school, so the house was nice but not fancy. It was the last Saturday night in October, and it was chilly outside. The leaves had turned to bright yellows, oranges and reds, and were now gathering in yards and gutters.

"I love this movie," Jessi said, yawning and stretching out on the couch, laying her head on one of the oversized pillows.

"I know. It's my favorite," Tacy agreed. Jessi and Tacy had already watched the movie together a handful of times since they had become friends. It had quickly become a sleepover tradition. Jessi had come over for dinner, stayed to do some homework, and decided to spend the night when Tacy asked. So far they had painted their nails and done a rejuvenating mask on their faces. The plan for the rest of the night was popcorn, movie, truth or dare and bed.

"Tacy!"

"What Mom?" Tacy called, clearly annoyed by the interruption.

"You have a phone call!"

"I hate it when she stands at the top of the stairs and yells," Tacy complained to Jessi, rolling her eyes. "Who is it?"

"Dawson."

"Tell him I'm busy!"

"Are you?"

"Yes!" Tacy cried, irritated by her mom's gentle question. "We're starting a movie down here, all right?"

"I'll tell him," her mom answered.

Tacy shook her head and then looked at Jessi. "They can just be so annoying, you know?"

"Completely," Jessi agreed and Tacy sighed.

"I'm surprised you didn't talk to Dawson. Didn't you just go out with him last night?"

"Only to make Carter jealous."

"Did it work?"

Tacy nodded, grinning. "He was at Sweet Dips when we got there, and you should have seen his face! They don't get along at all, and I could tell Carter was mad."

"That's good, right?" Jessi asked.

Tacy shrugged. "I hope so. I knew I had to do something extreme to get his attention."

"Carter seems like a pretty cool guy."

Tacy nodded. "And if he didn't have his head buried in that stupid guitar all the time, he might actually realize that there's another gender on this planet."

"Well, it sounds like you got his attention last night," Jessi said with a smile.

"Yeah, I hope. We'll see on Monday at school, I guess." Tacy had been chasing Carter since school started, and the tall senior had yet to notice.

"So, what was it like going out with Dawson?"

"Terrible! That boy is such a player."

"He seems like it."

"As soon as we left Sweet Dips, I made him bring me right home."

"Good thinking," Jessi said.

The movie finally finished rewinding. "Did you get your biology homework done?" Tacy asked as she grabbed the remote.

"Not yet. I'm going to finish tomorrow."

"Me too. There's so much reading it's ridiculous! I'm not going to spend my entire weekend reading about the body of a cow! I'll read the chapter on the heart, because everyone knows that's most important, then I'm done."

"Me too," Jessi said, making up her mind to follow Tacy's lead. Surely there was no need to read the rest.

Tacy turned the movie on, and they both fell quiet as the familiar characters played out the familiar scenes. Both girls let out a happy sigh as the two stars kissed.

Jessi's popcorn was only half gone when she fell asleep, and Tacy only lasted a few minutes longer. When the movie was over at one in the morning, no one was awake to turn the TV off, so the screen stayed blue until late the next morning.

~~~~~

"So, your senior year of football is almost over. How do you feel?"

Joe's face lit up at Rob's question. "I feel like we might win state. I feel good about that," Joe answered.

Rob stroked his chin with his finger and thumb, thoughtfully nodding. "You might. I think you have a good chance of it."

Joe kicked back in the recliner. Rob's house felt like his own – warm, friendly and homey. Rob expected him to continue talking about football. Instead, Joe turned the conversation to what was occupying his mind. "Did you see Jessi cheer at our last game? She did back handsprings down the track at half time. She's a great tumbler."

"I did. And yes, she's very talented."

Joe looked thoughtful. "She's still having problems with Heather. They just cannot get along."

Rob settled back in his own recliner and folded his hands over his chest. "How's that going?"

"What? Heather and Jessi?"

"No. Your relationship with Jessi."

"Great. She's amazing!" Joe answered easily.

"How are you doing emotionally? You aren't getting too attached, are you?"

Joe shot Rob an annoyed look. "What's that supposed to mean? A few months ago you were saying 'make sure you're dating her for the right reasons – don't date just to witness to her –

you're playing with her heart.' And now, when I really care about her, you say, don't get too attached?"

"I didn't mean it like that," Rob said calmly.

"Well, what did you mean?"

Rob picked his words carefully. "I'm just saying that you don't know that you both want the same thing out of this relationship."

"She wants someone to love. Someone who loves her."

"She wants purpose, meaning, and *Love* – a love you can't give her. She wants God, Joe, she just doesn't know it."

"I know and we're getting there. I'm finding all kinds of ways to witness to her through our conversations."

The young man's eyes were so hopeful. Rob again measured his words carefully. "Be careful that you don't become her god."

"That won't happen. I'm constantly pointing her to Jesus."

"That's good," Rob said slowly.

"Why do you say it like that?"

"Don't get so defensive, Joe. That's good. Really, it is. How's it going physically?"

Joe darted his eyes away for a brief moment. "Fine."

"Really?" Rob pressed.

"Why do you ask these questions all the time? Don't you trust me?"

Joe's accusation told Rob all he needed to know. "In the beginning you asked me to hold you accountable, remember?" Rob asked, just a little irritated by the teenager's change of attitude. That silenced Joe, and he was quiet and thoughtful for quite awhile.

"You're right. I'm sorry. We haven't done anything bad, just kissing, but sometimes…well, Rob, sometimes my thoughts aren't as pure as they probably should be."

"Every man struggles with that, Joe. It's the battle we all have to fight," Rob paused. "Just make sure you fight it."

Joe raked his hands through his hair. "Sometimes when we kiss, well, sometimes I wish I didn't have to live by all these rules. She's just so…." Joe's voice faded off.

"She's beautiful, desirable and willing. It's a dangerous combination," Rob said, taking a drink of his soda.

Joe let out a long breath. "Tell me about it. And sometimes when she touches me...." Again, he didn't finish his sentence.

"She makes your blood boil."

"Yeah." Joe's head dropped in shame.

"I've been there, my friend. Still get there on a daily basis."

"But you're married."

Rob grunted. "Thank God."

"What did you do before you were married?"

"We put limits on our physical affection and how much alone time we spent together. You can't very well go too far in a crowd."

Joe nodded thoughtfully. "That's true. At least not physically."

"Mental purity is something that you're going to have to fight for, Buddy."

"It's a cause worth fighting," Joe said.

"Agreed. Being like Jesus is always worth the fight."

"I wish I could have lived when he lived, Rob."

Rob took another drink of soda and stretched back in his chair. This was the reason he was a youth pastor. This was the reason he invited kids into his home even on nights when all he wanted was to spend time with his wife and daughter. This was why he devoted every Thursday night to the mentoring of one young man – for Jesus Christ. He wanted to spread the gospel to young people, help them find a faith that would carry into eternity, encourage them on their walk through life, and help them truly know the One who longed for relationship with them. Because He was so completely worth it – no matter the sacrifice.

"So do I, Joe, but He wanted both of us to walk the earth now. Not then."

"I know, but I just want to be able to be with Him and know Him. To sit across the table from Him, see Him, talk to Him, and hear Him speak."

"He gave you His Spirit so that you can."

"But it's not the same."

Rob nodded. "I know. I've often wished the same thing. Or that one of His original disciples was still here to encourage us and tell us what Jesus was really like."

"I guess they knew we would feel that way – they did write

it all down," Joe said, holding up his Bible with a grin.

Rob nodded. "True. I'm glad they did."

"Me too."

"What do you think God wants you to be doing right now that was important enough for you to live in this moment of history?" Rob questioned curiously.

Joe's answer was quick and sure, yet it made Rob cringe inwardly. "Save Jessi."

"What else?"

Joe shook his head. "Right now all I know is that I'm supposed to be saving Jessi."

Rob sat forward in his chair, fitting the tips of his fingers together. "Saving her from what?"

Joe looked at him as if he were nuts. "Herself...from sin... from death."

Rob tilted his head at him. "And can you do that?"

"Well, Jesus can!" Joe said, realizing the mistake in what he was saying.

"Yes." Rob sat back and let out a deep breath. "Joe, you're not going to be the one to lead Jessica to Christ."

Joe jerked back as if Rob had punched him. A crestfallen look fell across his young face, making him look like no more than a boy. "Why would you say that?"

Rob's face gentled in compassion, but the feeling in his heart was no less intense. "God may be using you to plant seeds, but you will not be the one to harvest her soul, my friend."

"No! That's stupid! No one has a better chance of reaching Jessi than I do."

"His ways aren't our ways."

"No, Rob, you don't understand." Rob didn't say anything, and Joe sat forward, frustrated. "You don't understand, Rob," he repeated. "I have more influence over that girl than anyone else – she does whatever I tell her."

Warning lights went off inside of Rob, and his eyes darkened in concern. "If that's true, proceed with caution. That's a huge responsibility for someone who's seventeen."

Joe shook his head and looked down as if he was disappointed in Rob for not understanding. The older man let out a long sigh. His friend wouldn't like the next thing he had to say any better. "Maybe God doesn't want Jessi coming to Him out of love and obedience to you, but out of love and obedience to Him."

~~~~~

Jessica stared at the sky as she gently swung back and forth. The hammock was soft beneath her, and she floated a couple of feet above the ground.

"It's my favorite spot back here," Pops commented. Jessi didn't say anything. Her mom might have made her spend her Saturday with her grandparents, but that didn't mean she had to interact any more than necessary.

Jessica stayed quiet for a long time. Pops kicked at a clump of snow that was still hanging around from the last cold spell. "It's warming up a little. That's nice – too early in the winter for it to be this cold and snowy," he observed. Jessica set the hammock swinging again with her foot. "You know, it's okay to talk to me. I may be old, but my brain still works on occasion," Pops said, his voice gruff.

"I don't have anything to talk about," she answered slowly.

"Oh, I bet you do. I can just see the wheels turning behind those blue eyes." When she was quiet, he asked, "Don't you have any questions for me? Isn't there anything you would like to know?"

She was quiet, but then suddenly she turned her head to look at him. "Hey, Pops, what did you think when Mom and Dad got married?"

He lowered himself into a lawn chair. They were in his backyard, the fence hiding them from the surrounding houses. They were both bundled up to ward off the cold, but enjoying the little bit of sunshine and a chance to get some fresh air.

"I thought I was losing my little girl."

"And did you?"

He looked at her seriously. "Yes. We hardly saw you guys when you were up in D.C. and now…well, now she's different."

"She's bitter now, huh?"

Pops nodded sadly. "Divorce does that to a girl."

"She's not a little girl anymore, Pops."

"She's still mine, Jessi." Jessica smiled, hearing the defensiveness in her grandfather's voice.

"What was she like when she was young?"

"She was like you," Pops said with a tender smile. "She thought we were too old to understand anything about her. She was wild and rebellious, and didn't tell us anything more than what we insisted on knowing." Jessica absorbed the way Pops summed her up, feeling a little sad, but then noticed the wink he sent her, and felt better. "She wore nice clothes and was the most popular girl in school. She was headed for big things, that girl was," he continued.

"She changed boyfriends like she changed her socks, and we were worried when she went off to college," he went on. "She brought a different boy with her every time she came home, so when she brought Bill Cordel home for a weekend, we didn't expect it to last. I think it was only when he slipped the ring on her finger that we first considered that it might."

"It sounds like she caused you a lot of worry," Jessi observed, watching her grandfather curiously.

Pops grinned at Jessica, and rubbed his forehead. "She was a pain in the neck, your mom was, but I love her all the more for it. That's just who she is. She was born to break the rules." Jessica let that settle.

"What did you think when they got a divorce?" she asked.

Pops pushed back in his seat and settled down a little more. "They'd been living separate lives for a long time. She was immersed in her work, breaking the path for change, and he was involved in a totally different sphere of influence. He didn't make time for her, and she didn't make time for him. Their marriage was on the rocks before you were born. You were an attempt to right what was wrong between them, and you were the glue that held them together for as long as they were."

Pops stopped and popped the tab on a can of soda. "Your grandma and I have seen it coming for a long time," he paused. "Not that we like it, and not that we didn't try to stop it, but we've seen it coming."

"Well, yeah," she agreed as if it were a no-brainer. "They never used to do anything together. They were both so busy, sometimes they'd go a week or more without even seeing each other."

"Where did that leave you, Jessi?" Pops asked.

She gave a sardonic smile. "Alone."

"What do you think of them being divorced?" he asked.

"Two people that selfish can't possibly exist together under the same roof for too long – it was inevitable."

"They aren't all bad, Honey. You'll understand someday."

She gave a dry laugh. "I'll understand why I found my dad having an affair with his secretary one day when I went to his office to ask if he would take me to summer camp because Mom was too busy at work? Or why Mom missed almost every one of my gymnastics meets because 'they needed her at the office?' Is that something I can ever understand, Pops?"

He grimaced. "Understand, yes. Recover from, maybe not." They were both quiet.

"Mom's trying now," Jessi finally told him. "She came to Joe's game the other night to watch me cheer. We've had a couple of girls' nights."

"She does love you."

Jessi nodded. "I know." She really did. Love just looked differently to her mom than it did to her.

"So does your dad," Pops added.

"Not as much as he loves Jari."

Pops propped one foot up on his opposite knee. "Love isn't lust, Jessi. Love is a deep, quiet lake; lust is a shallow, muddy puddle."

Jessica shook her head. "Whatever."

Again the silence stretched. "Jessi?"

"What?" she asked cautiously.

"Will you invite your grandma next time you have a girls' night? It would mean a lot to her."

Jessica thought about it. "Sure, if I remember."

"Try hard to remember, okay?"

She nodded. "Okay."

"That boyfriend of yours has an arm that just doesn't quit, doesn't he?" Pops said, changing the subject.

Jessi grinned with pride. "He's a star."

"Best GHS has seen in quite a few years...maybe ever," Pops agreed.

"You were at the last home game?"

"Been to every home game so far," Pops told her proudly. "I think they may go all the way this year. It looked iffy in the middle of the season when the defense wasn't holding up, but the boys have really pulled it together."

"They have districts this week," Jessi told him.

"I think they'll win."

"Me too," Jessi agreed with a smile.

"You're quite an asset to that cheerleading squad, too, Jessi. You sure know how to wow a crowd with your tumbling. How are you getting on with that Crebel girl?"

"Heather?"

"Yeah, she's the one."

Jessica shrugged. "She's a snot."

Pops chuckled. "It's a generational dislike. Your mother and her mother never got along either."

Jessi turned to look at him. "Are you serious?"

"Oh yeah! Deborah and your mom fought like cats and dogs all through school. See, the problem was that they both fancied that they ruled the school – and a little school like GHS can't have two queen bees."

Jessica stared up into the cloudless blue sky. "Hm."

"Don't let Heather give you any smack, you hear me? You may be dating her wanna-be-boyfriend, but he chose you and not her. If it comes down to it, don't let her forget that."

Jessica grinned. "I won't, Pops."

He stood, gave her hammock a push, and turned. "It's too cold out here for my old bones. I'm going in."

"Call me when it's time for dinner."

"You'll freeze if you stay out here much longer," he answered.

"I like the peace and quiet."

"I do, too. I'll make you some hot cocoa," he offered with a tender smile.

"With the little marshmallows?" Jessi's voice was hopeful.

"You bet ya. I'll put extra in yours and mine. Grandma can't handle too many, but I say, who the heck cares about all that sugar and cholesterol garbage?" Another wink.

Jessica smiled. "Thanks, Pops."

He went in the sliding glass door, and she was left alone with the odd realization that she had just spent half an hour having a conversation with her grandfather – and she had enjoyed it.

Twenty-One

The seconds were passing quickly, and GHS was three points behind. It was the championship game of Joe's senior year. Jessi was with the other cheerleaders on the sideline, and he could hear her cheering for him wildly.

A college recruiter was in the stands, and Joe knew that this was the play that really counted. This play could be the deal-maker or breaker for a college scholarship.

It was the last play of the game, and Joe had never felt so nervous in his entire life as he did when he called for his men to line up. This was his last chance. This was the culmination of his high school football career.

The ball was snapped and landed perfectly in his hands. He looked to his wide receivers and found them covered. He looked to his running backs and realized neither was free. The opposing defense was good, and two linebackers were charging straight at him. There was a small hole to his right. It was a risk, but he only needed five yards to win the game. Joe dodged and ran and jumped, closing his eyes tight, afraid to look, stretching his arms out, his fingers digging into the ball. As he landed, he heard Justin let out a whoop and a holler, and he heard the junior that had made the tackle swear and hit the grass beside him. Joe opened his eyes and realized that the ball and his arms had landed across the goal line.

The crowd was on its feet cheering, screaming and clapping. Jessica was jumping up and down on the sidelines, her pom-poms glittering and sparkling under the big lights. Joe jumped up and held the football high above his head in victory, pointing up at the sky as he ran to the new line of scrimmage. He jumped up and down, praising God for the opportunity to win the championship game his senior year.

He jogged to his position, his teammates pounding on his helmet and back, yelling as he went. The ball was snapped, Joe caught and held it, and Derik kicked it spiraling through the goal posts. The announcer's voice boomed out of the big speakers, declaring Glendale High School the state champions and reading the final score.

Joe's teammates all began jumping, hugging and huddling at once, yelling, cheering, and shouting joyfully. Someone poured the sports drink on the coaches, and they didn't mind at all. They, as well as the players on the sidelines, barreled onto the field, joining into the celebrating mass of men.

The crowd was going nuts. The stadium was shaking with the noise of their cheering, stomping and screaming. Joe saw his mom jumping up and down, hugging his dad. Kara was screaming, her hands cupped to her mouth. He pulled his helmet off, his face stretched in a huge grin. He waved at them jubilantly and turned as he heard Jessi shouting his name from somewhere close by.

She wiggled her way between players, her eyes shining. Reaching him, she threw her arms around his neck and kissed him passionately. He heard a few whistles and hoots as she did, and he playfully pushed one of the guys closest to him. She buried her hands in his sweaty hair and kissed him again. When she finally pulled back, he cried, "Jess, did you see that?"

She grinned at him. "Oh my gosh, of course I saw it! I am so proud of you! You sneaked it in!" She kissed him once more, then hugged his arm and did a little dance beside him. He reveled in her excitement and pride in him and dropped his helmet onto her head. She wore it proudly as they made their way through the crowd. Other players were slapping him on the back, and his coaches shook his hand, leaning close as they exchanged a few words of congratulations.

Jessi chattered like a magpie as they walked toward where all the fans were streaming down onto the field. She released him as he jogged the last few feet to give his mom and dad hugs. He embraced Kara and Kimberly, and shook Greg's hand. Then, he pulled Jessi close again. She wrapped her arms around his waist and smiled at everyone as they all began talking about the game, the last play and what that meant for the team. Glendale High School had won the state championship for the third straight year. The small school was proving to be a force to be reckoned with.

Kara excused herself and came back with Justin a few minutes later. Her face was shining, her hand in his. They had officially become a couple after Kara's birthday, and Joe and Jessi hung out with them often, along with Carter and Tacy, who had been going out for several weeks now.

Justin and Joe embraced and beat each other's backs, and everyone laughed. Then, everyone congratulated Justin. Soon Pops and Grandma joined them, shaking Joe's hand and hugging Jessi. Pops was beaming as he squeezed Jessi's arm and said, "I told you your boyfriend had quite an arm, didn't I? I told you they would go all the way, didn't I?" Jessi was laughing and agreed.

Carla had made it to the game, too, and was just a couple of seconds behind Pops and Grandma as she had stopped to say hello to someone. Joe gave her a hug as she congratulated him. Then, the college recruiter approached Joe, and everyone was quiet. He extended his hand, breaking out in a grin. "Well done, Son! We'll be in touch soon. Have fun celebrating with your family...after a game like that, you certainly have it coming."

Joe thanked him, elated, and Chris grabbed his son's shoulder and squeezed it hard as if realizing all those hours of playing catch in the backyard, football practice, and driving to games had finally paid off.

For the next hour, community members, extended family members and other players kept stopping to say a few words and shake Joe's hand. Jessi felt ready to burst with pride.

Eventually, after staying on the field for a long time, they all went out for ice cream. Jessica sat and hung on Joe's every word, looking up at him adoringly, leaving the majority of their hot fudge sundae for him. She talked a little to Kara, Kimberly, Pops and Grandma, but she mostly sat transfixed by Joe's every move and word.

That night, when he turned off the truck in front of her house, he didn't move to open her door and neither did she. She scooted toward him, and he met her in the middle, stretching his long legs past the gear shift and into her foot space. She ran her fingers up into his hair, and he pulled her close to kiss her.

Suddenly, his face screwed up in pain. "What is it?" she asked, concerned.

"A leg cramp." She sat back and instantly started massaging his calf.

He relaxed after a few minutes, and she moved back up to kiss him. "Want to make out?" she offered with a smile, her eyes twinkling. He kissed her softly, laughing low in his throat. Then he reached out and, on the fog that had collected on the inside of his windshield, wrote, "I love Jessica Cordel." She didn't move for a couple of seconds, and he held his breath. Then she reached out and wrote, "I love Joe Colby." He grinned and gave her a lingering kiss.

He tried to hide his disappointment when he noticed the light in her kitchen turn on. He opened her door and carefully turned her and pushed her out of it. "Your mom is probably wondering where you are – it's been hours since the game ended." He walked her to the front door, his arm circling her waist. Despite the freezing temperatures and the fact that she was still in her cheerleading uniform, her bare legs exposed to the biting cold, she stood outside her door and kissed him for awhile longer.

"You're going to catch a cold," he finally told her, feeling the chill of her skin under his hands. She shook her head, kissing him again. He shot her a grin as he opened her front door and gently pushed her into the warmth of her house. "I'll call you in the morning, Jess."

Sighing, she leaned against her door and smiled softly at him. "I'll be waiting for your call." He tweaked her nose, then turned and left. He started his truck and went home, where he sat up for hours with his dad, talking through and reliving every play of the game.

~~~~~

For the first time ever, Jessica, Carla and Maybelle made Christmas goodies together. Football season was over, basketball had started, school was out for Christmas break, and Jessica had almost three weeks at home.

The week before Christmas, Grandma and Pops came out every day, and they all made frosted sugar cookies, fudge, peanut brittle, caramels, taffy, chocolate covered cherries, popcorn strands for the Christmas tree, popcorn balls, little cheese crispies, and every other dessert or snack they had the recipe for.

On Christmas Eve Day, they made a gingerbread house. Grandma made the gingerbread, Pops piped on the frosting, and the four of them added gumdrops, raisins, granulated sugar, licorice, dyed-green coconut covered pretzel sticks, and cocoa for the dirt path. They had Christmas Eve dinner and opened their presents.

The Colby's invited all of them over for Christmas Day, and by eleven o'clock in the morning, they were ringing the Colby's doorbell. "Merry Christmas!" Joe said as he swung the door open wide.

"Merry Christmas!" the four of them answered in unison. Joe gave Carla and Grandma quick hugs and shook Pop's hand. He directed them into the living room, then turned to Jessica and pulled her into his arms for a short, sweet kiss.

"Merry Christmas, Love."

She smiled at him and toyed with his hair. "Merry Christmas."

"You look gorgeous as always." She was wearing black slacks with a burgundy sweater and smiled at his compliment.

"Thank you. And you dressed up for the occasion. I like it," she said, smoothing the front of his dress shirt.

He made a face and pulled at his tie. "We just got back from church, and Mom says I have to wear it until dinner's over."

She kissed him again. "You look nice."

"You should have gone to church with us."

She smiled. "I slept instead and then sipped hot cocoa in my pajamas while checking what Santa brought me."

"And what did he bring you?" Joe asked.

"Not what I really wanted."

He grinned, confidently. "Me?" She nodded and leaned forward to press a kiss against his masculine chin.

"Yes, you," she answered. He took her hand and twirled her on his finger, brushed a piece of hair tenderly behind her ear, then pulled her into the house and down the hall.

"Come meet Kaitlynn!" he told her, making a beeline for the kitchen where Kara and Hannah were cooking with Joe's older sisters. "Kaitlynn, I'd like to introduce you to a very special girl." All four women turned, and Hannah gave Jessi a knowing smile as she stepped forward for a hug.

"Merry Christmas, Honey," Hannah told her.

Jessi smiled and returned the hug. "Merry Christmas."

Kara's hug was next.

"Stop! Guys, I want to introduce her," Joe whined, and Kara shot him an annoyed look as she stepped back before saying her greeting.

"Who says you get to introduce her?" Kara challenged, folding her arms across her chest. Joe shot her another look and then grinned at his other sisters. Kimberly gave Jessica a small wave, not daring to interrupt after Kara was scolded.

"Kaitlynn, this is Jessi. Jessi, this is my oldest sister, Kaitlynn," Joe said, beaming.

The oldest Colby girl, Kaitlynn, looked almost identical to Kara, only older and a little taller. Kimberly, who Jessi had met at the state championship game, looked more like Joe. All their eyes were the same pale green. "It's nice to meet you," Jessica said politely, smiling at Kaitlynn. The older girl smiled back, the same Colby smile that Joe, Kara, and Kimberly had.

"It's nice to meet you, too," Kaitlynn paused. "I've heard so much about you. Every time I get on the phone to my brother, all I hear is Jessi this, Jessi that."

Jessica felt herself blush. "I hope it's good."

"It is. So good, it's almost sickening!" Kaitlynn answered, laughing. Kimberly gave an exaggerated nod of agreement. "He makes you sound so sweet and perfect that sometimes I'm not sure if he's talking about a girl or a hot fudge sundae," Kaitlynn continued.

"Okay, okay. That's enough, Kait," Joe cut in, giving his sister a playful shove and grinning. He snagged a cookie from a tray. "Want one, Jessi?" She shook her head no. "Yes, you do. They're delicious," he told her, getting one for her anyway.

"No, I'm fine," she protested. She had already eaten so many cookies in the last twenty-four hours that she felt sick. Ignoring her protest, he held the cookie out to her.

"Joe, she doesn't want one, leave the poor girl alone!" Kim said, setting one hand on her growing belly and the other on her slender hip.

"Kait, I'll have to send some of these goodies home with you," Hannah said, the conversation taking a turn to Texas. "Otherwise, we'll be eating them until Easter."

While the girls settled back into conversation, Joe continued to hold the cookie out to Jessi. She gave in and took a bite. He smiled at her. "Good, isn't it?" She nodded and ate the rest of the cookie to make him happy. He shot her a victorious grin.

"Jessi, this morning when I was talking with Kimmy, the baby kicked, and I felt it." Kara had slipped her arm around her older sister and was smiling at her growing belly adoringly.

Jessi gave a small smile. "Cool."

"Have you ever felt a baby kick, Jessi?" Jessica shook her head as Kara continued. "I just can't believe there's actually a little life in there! Like, a real person!"

"I never thought about it like that," Jessi said looking away, thinking about the time she had gone to an abortion clinic with Anna.

"I know, I hadn't really either until Kimmy gave birth to Carson," Kara agreed.

Jessi noticed how wistfully Kaitlynn was watching Kimberly. She wondered if anyone else noticed how much Kaitlynn wanted to be a mother, just like her younger sister.

Christmas dinner was huge with all the fixings. Jessica ate until she was stuffed, sitting comfortably between Pops and Joe. The conversation was lively and fun, and it held her attention throughout the entire meal. After everyone was through eating, the women cleaned up. They had just finished when the men announced it was time to open presents.

Little Carson, his brown hair baby-thin and pale green eyes so like his uncle's, sat in front of the tree and clapped his hands, laughing in delight. The tree was decorated beautifully, and Grandma commented on it several times.

The presents were doled out, and Jessi was glad that Hannah and Chris liked the oil painting that Carla had picked up for them on one of her business trips. Kara was excited about her gift card to one of Jessi's favorite stores and the shopping trip it insured. Jessi wasn't sure what to say when she unwrapped the soft-cover silver devotional Bible that Hannah and Kara had picked out for her. She glanced at Joe quickly before thanking them and flipping through the silver-edged pages.

After gifts were opened, Grandma and Carla helped Hannah serve dessert. Shadows fell over the merry household early as the wintry day came to a close. Everyone was starting to break off into little clusters to eat leftovers when Joe sneaked Jessi out through the back door. The air was biting cold, and heavy drifts of snow lay over the patio and yard.

"It's cold out here, Joe," Jessi said, looking longingly at the warm light streaming from the windows. He was quiet and she looked at him curiously, waiting for him to tell her why they were standing out in the lightly falling snow.

He stepped close to her and drew her into his arms. He put his cheek against the side of her head. "I appreciate this, Jessi."

"What?"

"You being here today. I need for you to know my family," he told her. She closed her eyes and breathed deeply, shivering from his nearness.

"I like them. I do. You know that," she answered. He didn't seem to hear her.

"I also need you to know why we celebrate Christmas." She tilted her head in confusion. Were the Colbys so special that they didn't celebrate Christmas for the normal reasons? "Later tonight, after everyone finishes eating, we'll all gather in the living room. My dad will open his old Bible, and he will read us the Story. He'll read about God sending His Son to earth, Jesus' life, His miracles, His sacrificial crucifixion, and His resurrection. It's the gospel story, and it's why we celebrate Christmas." She suddenly felt uncomfortable in his arms, and he cringed as she stiffened. "I want you to listen closely, Jessi." He put his fingers under her chin and forced her to look at him. "It's important to me."

He felt her melt and once again felt a stab of fear as he realized the control he had over her. If he stumbled just once, he was a danger to her – whatever he asked of her, she would do. As he looked down into her pretty face, he saw the vulnerability in her eyes. It kept him from giving her a kiss.

She pretended to be so strong and aloof, so untouchable, but he saw inside of her where she was grasping around for someone to hold on to. She just wanted someone to love her. He kissed her cheek, framing her face with his hands. "Promise me you'll listen, Love." She shivered and leaned her face into his hand.

"I promise."

Jessi kept her promise, but she also used the time to study those in the room. She could tell that this family felt deeply as they listened to the words of the story. It was like the words from the old book stirred up strong emotions within them, as if they were hearing a story of a loved one's life. As Jessi watched them, she almost yearned to feel the same emotions. What would it be like to feel so deeply? To believe that something so ambiguous, was so concrete? And if they believed so strongly, the one question Jessi couldn't get out of her mind the rest of the night was – *what if they were right?*

When Carla said it was time to go an hour or so later, there seemed to be never-ending hugs, goodbyes, and promises to get together again soon. When Jessi had finally made her way down the line, she pulled Joe out onto the porch for a private goodbye. Their breath hung in the cold Christmas air, and after laughing about pretending to blow smoke, she pressed her lips against his.

He smiled at her and broke off the kiss, stepping back. "Merry Christmas, Jess. I'll be by tomorrow with your present. It's still okay if we exchange gifts tomorrow, isn't it?" She nodded, frustrated by his lack of affection.

The door opened, and her family came out before she could say anything else. He patted her back and stood on the porch to watch her walk out to the car. Their first Christmas together was over, and despite the fact that she had been hoping for more alone time with Joe at the end, she couldn't think of a single Christmas in her entire life that had been better.

Twenty-Two

It was the middle of January when Jessi opened the heavy front door to find Joe on her porch. He looked serious as she pulled him into the house and out of the cold. He had only dropped her off from school an hour before, and she was surprised to see him.

"What's up?" she asked. He pressed his lips together and then let out a long sigh.

"We need to talk, Jess." She felt her heart begin to pound as he led her to the couch.

"About what?" she asked once they were seated. He pulled a letter out of his coat pocket and put it in her hands. It was dated the middle of December, and as she quickly read it, she wasn't sure how to feel.

"I was accepted, Jessi, and they're giving me a scholarship to play football." She put it down.

"It's a great opportunity," she said slowly.

She knew that the Division I school had been scouting him, but she hadn't heard about it since state championships. She had wishfully told herself that they hadn't offered him anything. The school was too far away for him to come home except on four-day weekends or breaks.

"It's far away," he said slowly. She nodded, her eyes on the letter in her lap. She took a deep breath, mustering up all the strength she had, and smiled at him.

"Well, we'll just have to make this spring and summer special. And then in the fall...." She let her sentence dangle.

He reached out and grabbed her hand. "This is what I've always wanted, Jessi. I've always dreamt of going to college and playing football. This is the exact school, too. And, when I get done there, I'll be in a perfect position to go to seminary." She had heard about his dream to be a pastor before, but still she cringed. "But things are different now," he continued. "This is a long ways away from Glendale...away from *you*." She shook her head.

"You have to follow your dreams. I won't keep you from them." She tossed her hair, pushed down her true emotions and laughed. "I mean, what? Did we really think this was going to last? We're in high school, Joe. People don't marry the people they date in high school."

His face fell for a moment before he realized it was all an act, and he reached out to take her hand. "But I want to marry you, Jessi. I *do* think it's going to last." Sheer terror and fireworks of joy warred for control over her.

She had promised herself she would never marry. What she had grown up knowing of marriage had been anything but good, and she wanted nothing to do with it. Still, his raw confession tore at her heart, and something within her that had long been denied suddenly seemed to burn again. And to be married to Joe Colby! Regardless of what marriage had been like for her parents, she knew that marriage with Joe would be completely different.

He quickly continued. "That's not a proposal. I'm not asking. Not here, not now. But I am saying that I do want this to continue. This isn't a fling for me, Jessi. I expect to be with you for a long, long time. And I want to make this decision together." His words touched her, and she felt her heart melting a little more. Just that he would consult her was huge.

She had known that he would likely go off to school next fall, but when she hadn't heard much about it, she thought he was making his plans, setting his course and next fall, well, that would be that. So long Glendale, so long Jessi. It was huge to her that he was including her in this decision and casting a longer vision for them than the end of summer. His retraction of anything that may have sounded like a proposal calmed her nerves.

"You have to go. This is a great opportunity," she said firmly. He nodded.

"Will you be here waiting for me when I come back?" She didn't even have to think about it. She knew that she would always be waiting for Joe Colby, no matter how old she was or where she was in life. He had captivated her, and she would never get over him.

"Yes."

"Do you promise?" She nodded, watching his face.

"I promise," she told him. He leaned forward and kissed her soundly.

"Okay, then I'll go, but I'll come home as much as I can. Maybe you can come visit me too, and after you graduate, maybe you can also go to school there."

Jessi hadn't given any thought to her plans after high school. She had no idea what she wanted to do or be, but she was suddenly sure where she would be attending college. She would follow Joe anywhere. "I'll apply tomorrow."

He grinned at her and pulled her to him, giving her a long hug. "Thank you for letting me go. This is huge, Jessi! It's what I've always wanted! But I can really enjoy it now, knowing that I can have it *and* you! I got this letter back in December, just a week or so after the big game, but have been stressing out about it. I didn't know what you would say."

"I want you to have everything you've ever wanted, Joe," she said softly.

He grinned at her and then stood up. "I have to go – Mom said I have to be back for dinner, I just…well, I had to talk to you about this." He reached down and pulled her to her feet. He kissed her forehead. "I love you, Jessi."

She nestled her face in his shirt. "I love you too, Joe."

He left a few minutes later, and she stood in the doorway watching him back up the drive. She gave a short wave when he waved at her, and she bit her lip, not being able to hold back a smile.

Maybe it really wasn't a fling. Maybe this was something real, something lasting, like he said. And maybe she wanted it to be. Maybe, she thought as she shut the heavy front door, maybe this love, maybe Joe Colby, was like her religion. This was something she could believe in.

~~~~~

"Jessi, your dad's on the phone for you." Jessica looked up from her dinner plate, her mouth full of spaghetti.

"Tell him I'm eating."

"I did. He said it's important and he needs to talk to you now."

Jessi uncurled her legs from under her, stood up and went to take the phone from her mom. She watched with regret as

Carla took her seat and began to eat again. They hadn't shared a dinner in a month, and now that they were, her dad had called and interrupted it. How had he known?

"Hello?"

"Hey Sweetheart, it's Daddy!" His greeting immediately set her on edge, and she sat down on the couch, wondering what he wanted. Whatever it was, she knew she wasn't going to like it.

"Hello."

"How are you doing?" he asked.

"Fine."

"Just fine?"

"Yes." It was quiet, and she sighed, giving in. "How are you?"

"Great!"

"Great?" she asked, her eyebrows raising in question. What was the cause of all this paternal joy? She hadn't heard him this excited in a long time.

"Well, Jessi, I need to talk to you about something very important, so I need you to go into a room all by yourself and listen to me, okay?" A list of possibilities ran through Jessica's mind, and she cringed.

"Can we do this later?" she asked dryly. "I'm in the middle of dinner."

"No. I won't be able to talk later, but I have to talk to you tonight." She sighed, looked at Carla, and rolled her eyes.

"Okay, fine. I'm in a room by myself."

"Okay. Good!" There was a long pause. Her dread grew with every passing second. "Jessica, I asked Jari to be my wife, and she said yes!"

"You what?" Jessi cried, standing up. Wasn't it bad enough that he had chosen that woman over them? Now he was going to marry her? Despite her disapproval, though, she had been somewhat expecting this. She reminded herself of that while taking deep breaths.

"We're getting married, Jessica! Isn't that good news? And that means she'll be your—"

"Don't even say it," she warned, interrupting him. He wisely left his sentence unfinished.

"Jari and I looked over our schedules, and we have decided

to get married two weeks from Saturday. It's far enough before the election that a wedding won't interfere and, well, it's just the perfect time. I want you here, Jessica, and I knew you would need some notice. That's why I had to speak with you tonight."

Two weeks? They were getting married in *two weeks*? "Is Jari pregnant?" Jessi immediately questioned. At the table, Carla snorted.

"Jessica! No, she is not pregnant!" Bill scolded, sounding shocked.

"Well, why so soon?" At least if the wedding was a couple of years down the road he might come to his senses...or Jari might.

"We're not willing to wait any longer."

"Why not? You're already living together – how different could marriage be?" Jessi asked, feeling sick to her stomach.

"Don't judge me," Bill warned, and she tensed at his tone of voice.

"Why do you want to marry her?"

"I love her, Jessica."

"Like you loved Mom? You do realize that those huge boobs of hers will sag someday, right?"

"I don't love her because of her looks," Bill snarled.

"That's right. It was her sunny personality that caused you to hire her that first day when she came in for her interview in a miniskirt, wasn't it?"

"Well, it certainly isn't yours that caused me to call tonight," he shot back.

"I'm not coming to your stupid wedding," she answered in response. If he wanted to talk dirty, so could she.

"Jessica, this is a very important day for me, and I want you, *my daughter*, there for it."

"I won't come."

"Yes, you will," he told her, his voice sickeningly pleasant and controlled.

"Make me."

"Don't think I won't, Jessica Nicole." She forced herself to take a long breath and turned her voice sweet.

"Okay, Daddy, I'll come." There was a slight pause, and she knew she had surprised him.

"Good. I'm glad to hear you agree so eas—"

"And I will make it the *worst* day of Jari's life," she continued.

It was deadly quiet on the other end of the line. Finally, he spoke. "You wouldn't."

"I would. I figure two weeks will give me a good amount of time to plot my destruction," Jessi assured him.

"You wouldn't do that to Jari. She's never been married before and she's so excited about this wedding."

"I don't care at all about Jari," Jessi said, her fuse lit. "Don't you understand that? If she didn't care how we felt when she ruined our family, why should I care about her?"

There was another long pause. "Jessi, don't. You know what? Bring Joe. Joe can come with you. You can have a nice weekend just the two of you. I'll get you a hotel room and you can order room service or whatever – I'll pay for the whole thing."

What had seemed like an enjoyable bribe seconds earlier turned sour as Jessi realized her dad was simply worried about appearances. His marriage to his young secretary would look better if his daughter was there – like a stamp of approval in the eye of the press.

"Joe and I won't be coming. We'll be spending that weekend with *family*."

Her barb was sharp, and she knew it hit its mark when he said, "I'm your father, Jessica."

"Have you ever stopped to ask yourself *why* she's marrying you? Do you really think she *loves* you? Do you think she's *attracted* to you? She's just a few years older than I am, Dad! You're old enough to be her father!" she said, unleashing on him.

"That's enough, Jessica," her dad ordered in white fury.

"Fine. I'll stop, but just do me a favor and sign a prenup. And don't come whining to me when she leaves you for someone her own age. Because she will. Young pretty women don't stay married to old men for long, and I would still like to have an inheritance when she gets done with you. So, sign a prenup. And let me go on the record saying – I warned you."

"If you're going to act like this, young lady, we don't want you at our wedding."

"Well, this is how I'm going to act."

"Then consider yourself uninvited." Jessica raised an eyebrow.

"Thank you," she told him, and pushed the off button when she heard the click of him hanging up on her. She took a deep breath, ran her hand through her hair, and took her seat at the table. Carla looked up at her.

"I can't believe he fights with you like that. It's hard to tell which one of you is the teenager."

Jessi nodded, but found that she couldn't swallow another bite of pasta. Her appetite was gone, and her throat felt too tight to swallow anything. Despite the fact that she didn't want to go to her dad's stupid wedding, she was both hurt and troubled by their fight. Her dad was mad at her, and while she didn't *really* care... she kind of did.

She was pushing the food around on her plate with her fork when Carla reached across the table and tipped Jessi's chin up. Carla searched her daughter's blue eyes intently. "What's happened to you, Honey? You used to be that cruel and worse, then come back and finish your dinner without blinking an eye." Jessi dropped her eyes that were beginning to fill with tears and toyed with the lace tablecloth.

Carla released her, shocked. "You're so tender." Jessi didn't think that was supposed to be a compliment. Still, she couldn't muster up any defenses or raise any walls of indifference.

"I just hate hating him, Mom, and I hate that he hates me. I hear it in his voice. He does. I just want to stop fighting with him and have him leave me alone!"

"He doesn't hate you, Hon," Carla said, coming around the table to kneel beside Jessica. She pushed a piece of hair behind her daughter's ear as the young woman kept her eyes downcast. "He doesn't. He just doesn't know how to show you that he loves you." Jessi tried to smile.

"Yeah, Mom. Maybe," she agreed, but she didn't buy her mom's lies for a minute.

Carla released a long sigh and pulled Jessi into her arms in a tight hug. "I know we aren't good parents, but we really do love you, Jess."

"I know you do, Mom. I love you, too." Jessi said, wrapping her arms around her mother's back, hugging her hard.

"And your dad?" Carla asked, concerned. She may be bitter and angry toward her ex, but she didn't want to see those same feelings eating at Jessica.

Jessi pressed her lips together and met her eyes. "I don't know. I just want it to be over."

"Oh, Sweetie!" Carla said, pulling her into another hug. She smoothed Jessi's hair and kissed her temple, rocking her back and forth like she had when Jessi was a baby. Jessi let her, and that made Carla's heart swell. They cleaned dinner up together, then watched a movie while sharing a blanket and a bowl of popcorn on the couch. For the first time in a month, Carla and Jessi spent more than twenty minutes together in one day.

The day of Bill's wedding, Carla encouraged Jessi to go shopping with Tacy and Kara. She wanted Jessica out of the house, because she knew when she opened her eyes and realized the boy she had fallen in love with as a young girl was marrying another, it would take an act of God to keep her from the wine bottle.

She was right. She drank the day away, going through one bottle of wine after another. Finally, she fell into a deep slumber and slept until it was pitch black outside.

When she woke with a splitting headache, she reached for the nearest bottle and poured herself another glass to ease the pain pounding behind her eyes. She began to hiccup and put her hand to her mouth.

Any other crisis, and she would have just gone to the office to bury herself in work, but her husband had married another woman. His betrayal had never felt so deep. She wanted to drink the day away in solitude.

By the time Jessi came home at a little past midnight, Carla was so drunk that she was singing loudly. Jessi could hear the off-tune melody before she even opened the front door. She stood perfectly still for a moment, not knowing what to do.

She knew why her mom was drinking. One look at Carla that morning and there was no doubt she would pull the wine out to numb the pain of Bill's marriage. Jessi took a step toward her mom's room, wanting to help. Instead, she turned and went to her own bedroom. There was nothing she could do or say. She tuned out her mother's drunken melodies with her own music and went to bed.

She pulled the covers over her head and tried not to think about her family. Thinking of her dad made her feel an uncomfortable mix of sadness and anger. Thinking of her mom sent her into a deep sorrow. Her dad was married to the lover he had forsaken them for, and her mom was drinking herself to sleep in her bedroom. What a lovely family she had.

And to think of all those years in D.C. that people had envied their family. Others had wanted to be like them. They had wondered what it would be like to be a Cordel. Well, Jessi could tell them – it was awful. As if working all the time, always trying to be perfect, loneliness and pretending weren't enough, add betrayal, guilt, grief, sorrow and revenge. She sighed. Squeezing her eyes shut tight, she tried to force herself to sleep.

When sleep finally came, she dreamt of Jari in a white dress and her dad in a tux. Her dad was telling her that she wasn't invited, that he wanted her to leave. Jessi was trying to convince him she had changed her mind, that she would be nice. During the whole fight, she watched Jari standing in the background and actually saw the heart in her chest breaking. In her dream, Jessi felt so bad for Jari that she wanted to run and comfort her.

When Jessi woke up, she felt even more confused and distraught than she had the night before. "As if Jari feels the least bit bad," she told herself as she climbed out of bed. Still, the dream made her uncomfortable for the rest of the day.

Twenty-Three

The phone rang, making Jessi jump. She released a deep breath and shook her head as she reached for the phone. "What's up?" she answered.

"Jessi, what are you doing right now?" Jessi frowned, trying to place the voice. It was so like Kara's, but it wasn't.

"Uh…" she started, concentrating as she dragged the nail polish over her thumbnail. "Eating a lollipop and painting my nails."

"Well, what are you wearing?" Jessi frowned again, still not sure who had called.

"Is this Kara?"

"Nope! Guess again!" Jessi heard quiet giggling in the background.

"Hannah?"

"Go fish."

"Kimberly?"

"Jessi, I'm so hurt! Am I here so little that you would guess all of the women in my family before me?"

"Kaitlynn?" Jessica asked, surprised.

"Yes! You are finally right! So, what are you wearing?"

"I just changed into my pajamas. Why?"

"Well, change back into your clothes because you're going to a movie with us."

"Us?"

"Mom, Kara, and me!"

"Where's Joe?"

"It doesn't matter, Silly, because you're coming with us. You'd better hurry – we're already on our way." Jessi didn't even consider saying no, as she likely would have a year before. She didn't even hesitate.

"Okay," she agreed quickly, and hung up.

She twisted the lid on her pink polish and hurried into her room. She threw on a pair of jeans and a fitted white sweater, careful not to touch her nails. Then she slipped on her black heels.

Her mom was gone, so she didn't have to check before going out. She pulled on her coat and walked out the door as Kara ran up the porch stairs. Kaitlynn gave a short wave from the front seat of the car, as did Hannah.

"Hey Jess! Come on! Get in," Kara said, turning to run back to the car. She got in one side, while Jessi slid in the other. "Brrr! It's cold tonight!" Kara said, one last shiver shaking her before she settled into the car's warmth.

"Hey Jessi! How are you tonight?" Hannah asked, starting to back the car up the drive.

"I just can't believe you guessed me last! *Last!* That wounded me, Jessi!" Kaitlynn said, turning in her seat to look at the dark-haired teenager.

"I'm sorry. I just hadn't heard you were coming."

"I know!" Kaitlynn grinned. "It was a surprise visit."

"Hm. Is there a reason?" Jessi questioned.

"That's what I asked," Hannah said, reaching back and squeezing Jessi's knee.

"She won't tell, just smiles *that* infuriating smile," Kara added, shaking her head at her older sister's grin.

"Where's your mom tonight, Sweetie?" Jessi shrugged her shoulders at Hannah's question.

"I don't know. At work probably."

"She works late a lot, huh?" Kara asked, holding her hands in front of the heater vent.

"Yeah, I guess," Jessi answered, glancing back at her dark, lonely house as Hannah turned off her lane. She was glad to be in the car with the Colby women.

"Can you believe it's almost March, and it's still this cold?" Kara asked, finally content with the temperature of her hands as she laid them back in her lap.

"It is pretty late in the spring for these temperatures," Hannah agreed.

"In Texas it's already eighty degrees," Kaitlynn bragged. "The grass is green, the trees are flowering and last week I went to the beach with some of my girls."

"Ugh. That makes me sick, Kait," Kara said.

"Well, then maybe when you graduate, you should just move to Texas with me, and you can live in the sunshine, also."

"Oh, no!" Hannah interrupted. "It's bad enough having one of my daughters clear down in Texas! I won't have two."

"Mom, maybe you and Daddy should just come visit more! You've only been down to my place six times," Kaitlynn whined.

"Kait, you've only lived there two years!" Hannah protested.

"Yeah, that means you've only come three times a year!"

"It's a miracle I could get your dad away those three times."

"Well, if he's the holdup I'll just bat my eyelashes and ask him nicely," Kaitlynn said with a laugh.

"You always were the best at buttering up Daddy," Kara accused, grinning.

"Oh, whatever! That's not true!" Kaitlynn protested.

"Yes, it is! You're the oldest – his first daughter."

"Kara, don't even start with me. You're the best, and you know it – you're the baby!"

"I don't get treated like the baby," Kara argued.

"Yeah, just like my name isn't Kaitlynn."

"Girls!" Hannah interrupted. "Your father treats you all equally. And you all have him wrapped around your finger. It doesn't matter which one of you is batting the eyelashes and asking please – it works for you all."

Jessi settled back in her seat, smiling, enjoying the chance to listen to the easy banter going on between the three Colbys. She had never seen their teasing be hurtful or mean. It was always done in love and humor.

"If only I could get my way that easily," Hannah finished under her breath. Kaitlynn waved her hands dramatically in the air, and Kara leaned up into the front seat as both girls protested.

"Hold on! Hold on! What was that, Mom? You'd better wait just a minute! Daddy would change his name if you asked him to," Kaitlynn said, starting to laugh.

"If only he would take out the trash," Hannah said with a dramatic sigh.

"Mom, Daddy always takes out the trash! You're just whining!" Kara answered, giggling as she leaned up to hook her mother's hair behind her ear so that she could see her face. Hannah broke into a grin.

"You girls are right. Your father is so good to me. I'm probably more spoiled than either of you," she gushed.

"That's better, Mom," Kaitlynn said, settling back in her seat. "Cheesy...but better." Hannah hit her daughter's arm. "Jessi, you haven't seen this movie yet, have you?" Kaitlynn asked, the conversation shifting again.

"No, she hasn't. When we drove by the theater the other day she said she wanted to see it," Kara answered for Jessica.

"What movie are we going to see? The new Gwen Phyllips one?" Jessi asked. Kara nodded, grinning.

"I'm so excited. I've been waiting all year for this movie to come out!" Kaitlynn said, and Hannah nodded her agreement.

The joyful conversation continued all the way into town. When Hannah parked in front of the theater, they all hurried out of the car. Hannah insisted on buying all the tickets, popcorn and soda. By the time they took their seats in front of the big screen, all four girls were laughing.

The movie was touching, and Jessi sighed contentedly as the star actor kissed the actress. In the next frame, the girl was tragically killed in a car accident. As the rest of the movie played out, it thoroughly tugged on her heartstrings.

She didn't notice that Kara was crying until the small blonde whispered, "Jessi, you're heartless!" When Jessi looked around, she found that Kaitlynn was also crying quietly and Hannah's face was shiny with tears.

"I should have brought something to wipe up this mess!" Hannah said, laughing at herself. Jessi wished she had tissues to offer the Colby women, but had none. When she offered to go get some, they told her they didn't want her to miss the movie.

Kara put her arm through Jessi's and snuggled in close as the movie continued. Jessi smiled. She had often dreamt of watching a movie while cuddling with her boyfriend, but she had never quite thought she would be getting hugged by her boyfriend's little sister during a movie. It made her feel loved, like she belonged.

When the credits rolled across the screen and the aisle lights came on, Hannah was the only one still crying. She laughed as she tried to remove the tears with her fingertips.

"It ended happy!" Jessi said, putting her hand on Hannah's arm, confused by the continuing tears.

"Oh, she's done for, Jessi. Every time Mom starts to cry, she cries until she gets distracted," Kaitlynn said, getting up.

"It's true," Kara agreed.

"Well, thanks, girls," Hannah said, making a face at her daughters before turning to Kaitlynn. "Do I have mascara all over my eyes?"

Kaitlynn wiped at her mom's smeared makeup while raising her voice to make her announcement heard. "Well, I just happen to have the perfect distraction. Let's go to Sweet Dips and get some ice cream. I'm buying," Kaitlynn announced.

At the ice cream shop, Jessi allowed Kaitlynn to pay for her double dip chocolate waffle cone and sat down with Hannah and Kara. When Kaitlynn took her seat, she was beaming, but she took two slow licks of ice cream before she said anything.

"Spit it out, Kait!" Hannah finally said, tugging on a piece of Kaitlynn's straight blonde hair. Kaitlynn laughed.

"Okay, well, the reason I asked you here – Mom, Sis, and Jessi – is because I have something to tell you." Kaitlynn took a moment to enjoy the anxious expressions. "Jake and I are getting married!" she finally cried. After a short second of shocked silence, Kara squealed.

"Kait, Kait, you're getting married?"

"When did you decide this?" Hannah cried at the same time, clapping her hands and laughing.

"How did he ask you?" Jessi asked, leaning forward for the story. Kaitlynn laughed and held up her hands for quiet.

"Well, he asked Daddy a couple of weeks ago for his permission." Hannah made a face, and pounded her fist softly into her hand.

"I can't believe him! I can't believe he didn't tell me! What a wretched little traitor!"

"No, Mommy, I wanted to be the one to tell you, and Daddy knew that!" Hannah gave a consenting look.

"Go on!" Kara urged.

"Okay, well, once he got permission, he planned this elaborate date. It all started with a videotape that he sent by a delivery boy to my apartment. When I got it, I plugged it in, and it was him telling me where to go for my first clue."

"A treasure hunt!" Jessi breathed, her eyes big. Kara took her hand under the table and squeezed it, her eyes shining, just as involved in the story as Jessi.

"It started out at the church where we met," Kaitlynn continued.

"Oh, that's perfect!" Kara squealed. Kaitlynn beamed.

"I know. He's just like that. He's so thoughtful. Anyway, the next clue took me to the place we went for coffee on our first date."

"Now was he with you through all of this?" Hannah interrupted.

"No. I was by myself. The clues led me all around town to places that are important to us or where we have a history together, until I finally found him in front of the fountains at the park where we always walk. He was down on one knee with a velvet box in his hand. He opened it, smiled up at me, read me this beautiful poem he had written, and asked me to marry him." Kaitlynn paused for effect, and Kara gave a happy sigh.

"What did you say?" Hannah asked, her eyes shining.

"Nothing! I was crying so hard that I couldn't answer – it was just all so beautiful!"

"Oh, that's my girl!" Hannah exclaimed, pulling Kaitlynn into a hug. Kaitlynn grinned and returned the embrace.

"When I pulled myself together enough to talk, I said yes," Kaitlynn finished, still grinning.

"I'm so excited for you, Kait! When's the wedding?" Kara asked.

"Well, we're still debating, because Jake has to leave at the end of May to go on another deployment."

"You'll have to wait until he gets back. You won't have time to plan a wedding in three months," Jessi observed.

Kaitlynn nodded. "Exactly. I don't want my only wedding to be rushed. So, what we're thinking is to wait until he gets back, which will be the winter after next, and get married then."

"So long?" Hannah asked, her face falling just a little.

Kaitlynn nodded again. "I know. I'm not sure how I feel about it either, but it's what makes sense."

Kara's smile brightened the moment. "Kait, we're going to have so much fun this next year planning your wedding! We'll make the time go fast with all of our plotting and scheming," Kara comforted. Kaitlynn nodded, excited again.

"I know! I want you all to help me! And I mean *all* of you!" Kaitlynn said, smiling warmly at Jessica.

Jessi smiled back shyly, then turned her attention back to her ice cream. She had never helped plan a wedding before and knew she would be of very little help. Still, it felt nice to be included.

They finished their ice cream in excited leisure, then talked all the way home. The lights were still off when Hannah pulled up in front of Jessi's house. They offered to walk her in, but she told them she would be fine – this was normal for her.

She gave them all quick hugs goodbye, then hurried into the house and out of the cold. As she put away her fingernail polish that was still sitting on the counter, she felt happy and warm.

She had never been part of a family like this before. And that's exactly what she felt like she was – a Colby. She changed back into her pajamas and went to bed, curling up on her side and burying her head in her pillow. She fell asleep with a smile pulling up the corners of her lips.

Twenty-Four

Jessica slid her notebook away, glad for the interruption, and picked up her cell phone. She made a face when she saw her dad's number. She thought about ignoring it, but knew he was bound to get demanding soon. She hadn't answered his calls since before the wedding. "Hello?" she answered warily.

"Hello Sweetheart." She swallowed the hurtful reply that came to mind. "How are you? I haven't talked to you in awhile," he went on. Bill's voice was already a little edgy.

"I'm fine. How are you?" she asked, going through the necessary motions.

"I'm glad to hear that. I'm doing well." There was a brief silence. "How's school?"

"It's school." He laughed.

"I always felt that way, too." She wanted to tell him not to liken himself to her, but bit her tongue in hopes of keeping some semblance of peace.

When the silence stretched again, he asked, "Has your mother told you not to talk to me?" Jessi jolted at the sudden subject change.

"No."

"It would be just like her to do something like that." Jessica rolled her eyes.

"Actually, Dad, we don't talk about you. At all."

"Is she seeing anyone lately?" he asked.

"Why don't you ask her?"

"You know she would never tell me!" Bill said, anger sneaking into his voice.

"I'm not your informant, *Dad*," Jessica answered, her tone turning icy.

He sighed. "I didn't call to fight with you, Jessica."

"Why did you call?" she asked, having lost all interest in the phone call.

"I want you to come up here."

211

"To D.C.?" Jessica felt her heartbeat quicken.

"Yes. I know you miss it up here, Sweetheart."

"No!" she cried. "I mean, no, I'm happy here, Dad."

"I haven't seen you in nine months, Jessica."

"And your point is?"

"A girl needs to be with her father," he replied.

"No, she doesn't. This girl is just fine where she is."

"You need a steady male influence in your life," he told her.

"Pops is here!"

"I did say steady, didn't I?" She felt her anger toward him seethe. She nearly said what came to mind, but again bit her tongue.

"Dad, this is ridiculous. I have Joe and Pops, and I am doing just fine."

"How is Joe? Been spending much time with him lately?" She glared at the far wall, hating how her father could ask the meanest questions in the most diplomatic voice. He had always been able to lay expert traps with his questions.

"More than I ever spent with you," she spat at him.

"Jessica, I want to meet this boy."

"No!"

"No? Jessica, you are a minor and my daughter. I have the right to meet him."

"You relinquished every right you had when you abandoned our family," she almost yelled, feeling like her dad was threatening to shut off her air supply.

"Would you stop saying that? I didn't abandon anyone!" he bellowed. He paused and when he continued, his voice was calm and smooth again. "Jessica, either you bring your young man up here for a weekend, or I will pursue full custody." Fear shot through her.

"You wouldn't dare."

"Jessica, I'm just asking you to come up for one weekend," he said with a sigh. It would be one weekend too many. Bill sounded pleased with the corner he had her backed into, and she covered her eyes with her hand feeling a sick sense of dread.

"Meet us halfway, and we'll have lunch. No more," Jessi answered. It was quiet for a moment, but she knew he would agree. They were used to negotiating.

"Deal. Next Saturday," he said.

"I'll check with Joe."

"Next Saturday," he repeated.

"Fine." Jessi hung up feeling sick.

~~~~~

Jessica sat looking quietly out the car window at the passing countryside. She felt nervous and filled with dread as she thought about the impending lunch they were on their way to. The last thing she wanted was for Joe to have to meet her dad or Jari. She hated them both, and she loved him. Was there any way that could turn out well?

Joe reached over and took her hand in his, rubbing his thumb across the back of it. "You're so quiet," he said. "It's going to be okay." She forced a small smile.

"Maybe," she answered.

He kissed her hand, and shook his head. "It will be. Jesus has a plan for today."

She laughed. "Right."

"Jessi, regardless of whether or not you believe it, God loves you, and He has a plan for your life. He's got this day all orchestrated."

"Well, then hopefully He's a magical composer, because there is no way that this is going to be pleasant." Joe was quiet, knowing she was in no mood to talk religion. So instead, he prayed.

Half an hour went by in silence. "It's a pretty drive," he finally said.

"If only it wasn't ending in a cage of wolves," she muttered. He laughed.

"You're so pessimistic! Cheer up! It's your dad and his wife."

"Exactly," she agreed gloomily. His face grew serious.

"It's one lunch, Jess. And then we'll go home."

"If he doesn't eat us for dinner first," she answered.

"Hey. Look at me." He waited until she did. "Have I ever let any harm come to you?" She shook her head, looking down. This was different. "And I won't today, either. We'll make it fun, okay? We have an entire day all to ourselves." His words only added to her guilt. He was telling her that he would protect her, and she was feeding him to the lions.

Joe made pleasant conversation the rest of the way to the restaurant, but she barely talked. When they parked, he opened her door for her, his customary grin in place.

He was so innocent. She had a feeling he had never encountered the type of man he was about to have lunch with. A strong desire to protect him rose up within her. "Okay, talk about golf and rainfall, and avoid presidential candidates at all costs," Jessi suddenly said, trying to prepare him in some way. "If the conversation gets really awful, ask him how his campaign is going. Elections are next year. It's huge for him. Also, ask—" Joe patted her hand and put it in the crook of his arm.

"It's going to be all right, Love," he assured her. She swallowed back the flood of words that filled her mouth.

"I doubt it," she muttered under her breath.

When the waitress led them to their table, Jessi's stomach churned. It had been a long time since she had seen her dad, but here he was in his suit and tie, as real and living as could be. He hadn't changed a bit. Jari sat beside him, blonde, beautiful, and voluptuous, wearing a large diamond on her finger and an elegant, yet simple, black dress.

Jessi immediately felt like her burgundy dress was too casual. She was proud of how Joe looked in his suit though, and clung to his arm as they came to the table. Bill and Jari stood, and Bill pulled Jessi into a quick, stiff hug. He rubbed her arms briskly.

"It's good to see you, Jessica. You've grown."

"It happens." He gave a tight smile.

"I suppose it does. Jessica, you remember Jari, don't you?" Jessi couldn't even fake a smile at the large-chested husband-stealer.

"Of course." She didn't make it sound like a pleasant memory. "Hello *step-mother*." Joe put his arm around her in a warning. She glanced up at him. His eyes were not condemning, simply beseeching. She took a deep breath and decided she would be nice for his sake.

"Hi Jessi," Jari answered, trying too hard to be cheerful. Jessi wanted to tell her that she could call her Jessica, but didn't when Joe rubbed her shoulder with his thumb. Instead, she offered Jari a tight smile.

"Dad, Jari, this is my boyfriend, Joe," Jessi said, her voice softening.

Bill put his hand out, his eyes narrowing. "It's nice to meet you, Joe."

Joe grinned. "You too, Mr. Cordel. I've heard a lot about you."

"None of it good, I'm sure," Bill replied, waving his hand as they all sat.

"Not much of it," Joe responded honestly, holding Jessi's chair for her. Bill shot a frown at his daughter.

"I'm glad to hear you've been missing me as much as I've missed you, Jessica," Bill replied dryly. She gave him a half-smile, and then clutched Joe's hand under the table for support.

Bill ordered his drink and Jari's when the waitress came, then gestured to Joe and Jessica. They ordered their drinks and opened their menus, which he promptly took from their hands to hand to the waitress. "There's no need to look. You'll love the special."

Jessi reached for her menu, her eyes snapping, but diverted her hand to her glass of water when Joe said, "Okay. We'll both take the special then." The waitress left, and Jessi slumped, knowing that now was when the real onslaught would begin.

"Jessica, don't slouch," her dad said casually, and she sat straight, wincing. She had forgotten how he was constantly commenting on her posture.

"So, Joseph," Bill started.

"Here we go," Jessi muttered under her breath.

"What is it that your father does out in Glendale?"

"He's a businessman, sir. And a good one."

"Yes, I'm sure he is." Bill's voice sounded anything but sure. "And what kind of business is he in?"

"Actually, he's involved in many different kinds of business."

"Ah, jack-of-all-trades, master of none," Bill replied, smiling a diplomatic smile.

Joe hesitated and then smiled. "Actually, sir, he just enjoys being active in a variety of things."

"Such as?"

"He works in real estate."

"How so?"

"He's a broker and also has several rental properties throughout the state."

"Interesting. Anything else?"

"He's on the city council and is an assistant basketball coach at my high school."

"How nice that he's involved in your life," Bill said, his tone biting. Jessica shot her dad a dirty look. Joe smiled, not seeming rattled in the least.

"It's great. He also owns a small ranching and farming operation."

"Ah. So, you're a farm boy. How ironic," Bill said, smiling pointedly at Jessica. She glared at him, and he held his hands up. "What? I just find it interesting that you would be attracted to a boy cut from farm cloth. In the past your tastes have always been a bit...finer."

Jessi had never noticed before how deep her dad's jabs really were. Now, she was painfully aware of each one as she felt Joe flinch.

"Well, I am. Very much so," she answered quickly. Joe rubbed his thumb over her hand. "Joe's dad is very respected in Glendale," she went on. "And by his family," she finished pointedly, watching her dad absorb her own jab and then recover.

"Ah, Glendale. Good old little Glendale." She bristled.

"His father is a hundred times the man in Glendale that you will ever be in D.C.," she shot back. Bill's face took on a shocked expression, then a smooth smile slid into place.

"I'm sure you're right, Dear."

His pacifying response rubbed on Jessica's already raw nerves.

"Stand down, Soldier," Joe whispered, winking at her. Despite her dad's behavior, she couldn't be angry when Joe winked. For the first time since they entered the restaurant, she felt the urge to smile.

"Jessica, I love your dress. Where did you find it?" Jari asked, her smile a little too bright. Jessica's response came out too quick for her to stop it.

"Oh thank you, Jari. I got it at Annie's Dress Shop, but um, they don't do custom tailoring to increase the bust size." Jari's face fell, and Bill started to say something as Joe cleared his throat.

"That's okay, Bill, Jessi's just trying to be helpful," Jari said patting Bill's hand. Jessi forced a sweet smile as she sat back in her chair.

"Jessica, don't slump," Bill snapped. Jessi sat up straight with a tight smile and tilted her head as she took a deep breath.

Joe squeezed her hand under the table, and when she looked at him, the sorrow in his eyes was so deep that it made her feel ashamed. It was her father and step-mom in front of them, his family they were attacking, and she was the one who couldn't hold her tongue. He was sitting as controlled and gentle as ever, and it made her feel weak.

"Daddy, how's your campaign going?" she asked, turning back, determined to resist going back to the girl she used to be.

"It's going well. The polls say I'm five points ahead of my opponent," Bill said.

That's good news!" Joe said, grinning. "Congratulations!"

"Don't congratulate me yet, Joseph," Bill responded quickly, his expression hard. "Politics is an unsteady business to be in. The mob loves you one day and hates you the next."

"Bill has been working so hard on this campaign. We've been all over the state raising support. He's such a people person," Jari said, smiling up at her husband. He smiled back.

"And Jari is always the adoring one," Bill responded. "She's so innocent. She has no idea what people can be like." Jessi wanted to question Jari's innocence, but thought better of it. Conversation was actually pleasant at the moment. The campaign talk continued until their food came.

Jessi could barely eat as the conversation turned back to Glendale, Carla, Grandma and Pops, and Joe and his family. But Joe answered every question gently and refused to take offense. Jessi was able to follow his lead, and they successfully made it on to other subjects.

Jessica learned that Bill's golf game was improving, the next presidential election was damned, because neither candidate was worthy of the title, and that Jari was the leader of a spinning class. A retort sprung quickly to Jessica's lips, but she stuffed her mouth full of green beans instead.

"Take smaller bites, Jessica. You're supposed to be a lady, remember?" Bill corrected. He put his napkin on his plate and started talking about their honeymoon in Europe.

Jessi could feel herself growing green with envy as he talked of the Swiss Alps, the canals of Venice, the ancient ruins in Greece, the castles in England, and the theatres in Vienna. She grew even more jealous as Jari joyfully added that she had bought the dress she now wore, in Paris.

"It sounds like it was an amazing trip. Maybe we should get their route and follow it someday, Jessi. What do you think? Wouldn't you love to see Europe?" Joe asked, pulling her back from her dark feelings. She pictured traveling Europe with Joe, and all the jealousy drained out of her. It would surely be exponentially better than anything her dad and Jari had experienced. She smiled up at him.

"Yes," Jessi answered simply, gazing adoringly up into Joe's face. "Yes, I would."

"Then we'll go someday, Jess. I promise."

Bill cleared his throat. "We can discuss the likelihood of that at a later date. We won't cross that bridge until we come to it." Jessi barely heard him as she scooted her chair closer to Joe's, tucking her hand into the crook of his arm. After all, her dad's objection amounted to nothing compared to Joe's promise. She let out a happy sigh, thinking about what a wonderful trip it would be. When she glanced up, she saw that Jari was smiling at her almost affectionately. It made her uncomfortable and she looked away.

They all had dessert, and Jari graciously steered the conversation to a discussion of a new bill that was causing a huge fuss in the House of Representatives. Bill turned his attention to that, and Jessi was amazed when Joe challenged him on one of his claims. Bill seemed just as shocked, and asked Joe to support his view. Joe did, quite concisely, then sat quietly waiting for Bill's response.

Bill dismissed the issue without addressing any of Joe's points. Still, Jessi was proud of Joe's knowledge and even prouder of his courage. Joe let it go, following Bill's conversation, fanning it slightly to keep it alive but never pursuing anything to the point of an argument.

Before Jessi knew it, dessert was over, and politeness called for them to leave the restaurant. Joe scooted Jessi's chair out for her and helped her into her jacket. They walked out to Jessi's car with Bill and Jari. Jessi stayed protectively by Joe's side, wrapping her arms around his waist as they stood in the chilly spring air, talking awhile longer. He put his arms around her back to keep her warm and continued following Bill's lead in the conversation.

Finally, Jari tugged on Bill's sleeve and said she was cold. Bill shook Joe's hand and then embraced Jessi, again rather stiffly.

"It was good to see you, Jessica." She smiled.

"You too," she answered, realizing that she wasn't completely lying. Bill and Jari walked away. Joe rubbed her arm as he opened her door and waited as she attempted to gracefully slide into her seat. She slipped her heels off as he shut her door. Once they were both shut into the car, he leaned on the center console and brushed her dark hair out of her eyes.

Now that wasn't that bad, was it?" he asked.

"You were amazing. I can't believe you stayed as cool as you did."

"His words can't affect my peace, Jess."

"Where do you find that peace?" she asked, leaning her face into his hand. He smiled.

"The only place peace can come from." She gave him a lopsided grin.

"And where is that?"

"Jesus." She weighed his answer thoughtfully.

"If Jesus can give that kind of peace, He just may be worth believing in." Joe grinned, excited.

"He is, Jessi, He really is."

"Maybe, but do you know who I believe in?"

"Who?"

"You," she said softly, hoping he could see the love she felt for him shining in her eyes.

"Jessi, I'm not—"

"I know," she said, smiling. "You're not God. But I am

incredibly proud of you! I can't believe you can hold your tongue like that. Sometimes I say mean things before I even know I'm going to."

Joe tried to cover his disappointment as he realized she wasn't seriously considering believing in Jesus, and he reminded himself that if nothing else, he had planted another seed. "But you did a good job today," he encouraged. "You slipped a couple of times, but you pulled it back together."

"Joe, I'm just not good like you. He makes me so mad."

Joe grinned as he turned the car on. "I can see why." She laughed and took his hand as he backed out.

"You understand my concern now, don't you?"

"He is one of the most diplomatically mean people I have ever met," he conceded.

"I know! He can say something that is technically okay, and mean it in the cruelest way!" Jessi said, finally able to laugh about her father's hurtful ways. Joe laughed too, and squeezed her hand.

"No wonder you thought you were feeding me to a pack of wolves – I seriously wondered if he wasn't about to rip me to shreds a few times," he told her, grinning. She nodded.

"He's vicious."

"That's true. Although," he paused, "I'm not sure I agree with your assessment of Jari. She seems nice, and I don't think she likes all the fighting." Jessi's eyes narrowed.

"Her body made you overlook her faults, Joe."

"Don't even think that," he told her, tipping his head toward her with an amused look. "I never even looked below her face."

"That's impossible," she told him. He shook his head.

"I'm serious, Jess. I didn't. You know why?"

"Why?"

"Because I didn't want you to be able to say, 'her body made you overlook her faults.'" She made a face at him. "And besides, I don't need to look at any other woman – I'm already taken." His words made her give him a grudging smile, and she leaned over and kissed his cheek softly.

"Don't forget that," she told him.

He took her chin in his hand and glanced at her, taking his

eyes from the road for only a second. "I'll tell you what, though. If you ever turn that tongue on me, I think I'll run for cover." She groaned.

"I know. But I did hold back occasionally. I thought of a lot of things that would have felt good to say, but I tested them against whether they were true, kind and necessary, and decided against it." He ran his thumb over her delicate chin.

"I'm proud of you," he said. She smiled shyly, his words warming her heart.

She was quiet for a moment and then said, "Joe, I'm sorry he criticized your dad. You know I love your dad, don't you?" He grinned.

"You'd better be careful with what you say, Jess – you're going to make me jealous," he teased. She pulled on his tie and he chuckled before turning serious. "Don't worry about it. I know that my dad is great, and no matter what, no one could ever change my mind." She tipped her head and kissed the palm of his hand, then settled his hand between both of hers and held it as he drove.

When it was dark and he was getting tired, they stopped for ice cream and ate their hot fudge sundaes as they went down the road. Their conversation became less frequent as the night wore on, but they sat in pleasant silence, enjoying the level of comfort they shared.

When he stopped in front of his house, he got out, and she climbed into the driver's seat to drive home. He stood there, looking down at her. She smiled. "Thank you, Joe." Even though she wasn't close to her dad, she was glad Joe had met him. It meant a lot to her.

"You're welcome." His pale green eyes locked with hers, and she felt his smile warm her up inside.

"Are you going to church in the morning?" she asked.

"Of course."

"I hope you can get up for it."

"I will," he promised.

"Well, I'd better let you get to bed then. Goodnight, Joe." He bent down and pressed his lips against hers.

"Goodnight, Jessi." He smiled at her and shut her door. She backed out of his driveway and drove home.

Twenty-Five

Jessica fastened her necklace as she walked into the kitchen to grab a breakfast bar. Joe and Kara would pull up in front of her house in less than five minutes, and she just needed to put her shoes on. Glancing up, she dropped her backpack as her mouth fell open.

"Mom!" Jessi yelled and the sleepy-eyed man put his finger to his lips.

"She's still sleeping. She had," he paused to chuckle, "quite a night." The look on Jessi's face said she wasn't amused. He cleared his throat and became serious again. "You must be Jessi. She's told me a lot about you."

"I'm sure she did. There's a lot of time to talk on the way home from the bar," Jessi said, putting her hand on her hip and smiling a sarcastically sweet smile.

"We didn't meet at the bar. I'm from her—"

"I don't care where you met," she snapped. "And it's Jessica to you." He nodded and blinked slowly.

"Fair enough."

She glared at him. "What are you doing here?" she asked, her mind reeling. Had he been there all night? Had he just come for breakfast? Why did he look sleepy and rumpled? Had her mom known him for long? Were they dating? Why hadn't she ever said anything?

He hesitated, watching her closely with his dark eyes. "Your mother, Jessica, is a very attractive woman." She felt sick at what his answer implied.

"Then what the heck is she doing with *you*?" Jessica paused for effect. She watched as her words hit home, both wounding and offending him.

"You certainly are a polite young lady," he said, his tone dry.

"And you are trespassing. If I ever see you on this property again, I'll call the cops and have you arrested." He leveled his gaze to hers.

"You don't have the authority to do that."

She took a step forward and gripped his chin with a deceiving tenderness. "I will make your life hell if I ever see you again." She saw the dull spark of fear deep in his dark eyes. She released his chin. "And don't eat my breakfast bars." She took the open box from the counter, plucked the unopened bar out of his hand and spun on her heel, catching her bag and her shoes up in her hand.

She slammed the front door so hard the windows shook in their panes and saw with relief that Joe was driving up the lane. She jogged up the driveway in her socks and pulled the door open after Joe slammed on his brakes to avoid running over her.

"Jessi, I would have opened that for you if you had given me the chance," Joe told her as she climbed in. His grin faded as the look on her face registered. "What's wrong?" he asked. She slammed the truck door, took a breakfast bar, then stuffed the rest in her backpack.

"Nothing," she muttered. He raised an eyebrow at her, then at Kara. Kara sat quietly, watching Jessica with concern, compassion already beginning to fill her small face. She reached out and laid her slender hand carefully on Jessi's arm. Jessica's blue eyes looked tortured as she looked up at them. "Let's get out of here."

Joe put the truck in reverse and backed out. Jessi glared out the windshield as her mom came running out of the house yelling, still tying her robe. Joe thought about stopping the truck, but handed Jessi his coffee and continued to back up the drive instead. By the way Carla was yelling and Jessi was glaring, it seemed as if both women needed some space.

"Whose car is that?" he asked quietly. Jessi took a sip of the steaming coffee.

"You should ask my mother." The Colby kids exchanged a look as understanding dawned on them.

Joe cleared his throat. "A friend?"

"Right. A *friend*," Jessi answered sarcastically. It was quiet the rest of the way to school, but Kara kept her gentle hand on Jessi's arm. Jessica could feel Kara's peaceful concern flowing through her touch. When Joe came around to let Kara and Jessi slide out after parking in front of the school, he caught Jessi's arm and kept her beside the truck. Kara gave Jessi's shoulder a gentle squeeze and ran off across the parking lot to where Justin was waiting for her by his car.

Joe watched Kara go, then turned and drew Jessica into his arms in a firm, comforting hug. She shrugged her shoulders, her entire body stiff against him. "Carla has a right to a love life, too, Joe," she told him, her voice dull.

He held her at arm's length and forced her chin up so that he could see her eyes. "She's your mother, Jess."

"I know," she said, her expression decidedly indifferent.

"Say it. Say you're angry with her. Say you're angry that your mom brought a man into your home that is not your father." Jessi tossed her head, her dark hair flying.

"She has the right to have a sleepover with anyone she wants. She's a grown woman."

Joe gave her a gentle shake. "Jessica! Look at me!" She was surprised by his abrupt action and brought her eyes up to meet his. She felt her resistance melt and her walls fall. This wasn't another enemy trying to hurt her. This was Joe. Her Joe.

Her eyes smoldered, even as tears pricked them. "Okay, fine. I'm mad! I'm so mad that I'd like to go home and slap her! She's such a hypocrite – abstinence, abstinence, abstinence, Jessica, abstinence is the only way, and then she goes and brings home Fred Flintstone!"

"I haven't seen a car like that in Bedrock," Joe mentioned. Jessi looked like she might slap him, so Joe quickly hid his slight amusement. "You're completely right, Love, but we all make mistakes. Your mom and Fred might have made love but—"

"That's not making love, Joe, that's having sex!" Jessica cried, throwing her hands out toward him. Joe's face broke into a beaming grin, as he heard his own words repeated back to him. She finally got it. "That couldn't have been anything more than a one night stand – I have never even heard of him! This, what we have, this is love!" she said and closed the distance between them, throwing her arms around him.

"There's a difference?" he asked, his eyes shining.

"Like night and day," she whispered, tears continuing to gather in her eyes. "I wish my mom could know this kind of love."

He brushed a kiss against her hair. She took a deep breath, savoring the peace and joy that he gave her, and rested her head against his shoulder. He wrapped her in his arms and held her for several seconds. "God has a plan for her, just like he has a plan for you, Jessi." She ignored his comment.

"Thank you for teaching me the difference," she told him, looking up into his eyes. He felt his mouth go dry with emotion. He gave her a weak smile and kissed her forehead.

"I'm sorry about your morning, Jess." She nestled her face against his shirt.

"I don't know what is wrong with her lately," she told him.

"Loneliness. It can make people do stupid things."

"I couldn't believe it when I saw him sitting there," she went on. Joe gently smoothed her hair.

"I bet it gave you a shock."

She nodded, then regretfully checked her watch. "The bell will ring soon."

"Are you going to be okay?" he asked, his voice deep and concerned. She smiled and nodded.

"Until three o'clock, I'll be fine."

He smiled, took her hand, and they jogged up to the door together. He twirled her once they were on the cement, and she laughed. As he held the door open for her, he asked, "Will you go to the river with me after track practice?"

"I'll catch the biggest fish again," she teased.

"Will you?" The bell rang, and they both started to run. "Jess? Should I plan on it?"

"You know I will!" she told him, grinning, and waving over her shoulder.

"Don't run in the halls, Jessica," one of the teachers called, but she was already headed to class.

School passed slowly, but after one pop quiz, five hours of boring lecture, two experiments gone bad, one hour of trying to find the right pitch and a mildly hard track practice, Jessica met Joe back in the parking lot.

Kara was riding home with Justin, so Joe gave Jessi a soft kiss before boosting her into the truck. He shut her door and went around, getting in. She slid across the bench seat as he started the engine and sat arm to arm beside him. She told him about her day and asked about his. After remembering that they were supposed to go to Pops and Grandma's for dinner, they rain-checked on fishing. Joe turned the truck around and headed back into town.

"So, was he nice?" Joe asked as they sat licking their chocolate ice cream cones in a booth at Sweet Dips later that night. Jessica licked slowly.

"He wasn't bad," she answered. "He didn't seem like the normal one night stand. He was clean shaven, seemingly intelligent, handsome."

"Hey," Joe objected, shooting her a jealous look. She smiled and bumped him with her arm.

"Not anywhere as handsome as you."

"Where did they meet?"

"I don't know," she answered.

"What's his name?" he asked.

"Fred, remember?" Joe grinned and Jessi continued. "I have no idea what his name is, but he tried to eat my breakfast bars." Jessi took a bite of her ice cream.

"The nerve!" She shot Joe a glare for his not so subtle tease, and he held up his hands in surrender. "What are you going to do when you get home?"

"Sneak in my window and hope my mom took up permanent residence at her office." He laughed.

"As likely as that is, you're going to have to face her eventually." She made a face.

"I know. But I don't want to. I may slap her."

"She may slap you." Jessi's eyebrows rose dramatically.

"And why is that?" she questioned.

"You were rude to her guest."

"I was mad!"

"What purpose did it serve?" he asked thoughtfully.

"Communication!" He grinned.

"How do you think that made your mom feel?"

"I didn't know I was supposed to care!" she said, taking offense at his gentle words.

"You should."

"Why?"

"Because she's your mother, Jess."

"And?"

"And whether you realize it right now or not, someday you're going to want a relationship with her."

"That's never going to happen," she told him defiantly, the memory of the morning still fresh. He put his finger beneath her chin and forced her to meet his eyes.

"What about at our wedding? Don't you want her to put the veil over your face and kiss your cheek before you walk down the aisle? What about when we have babies? Aren't you going to want your mother there at the hospital with you? Aren't you going to want her to hold them close to her heart, just like she did you? What about when our firstborn learns to walk? Aren't you going to want to call her and tell her all about it?" Tears sprang unbidden to Jessi's eyes, and Joe gently wiped them from her cheek with his thumb. "That's what I thought," he told her.

"She should put more effort into our relationship – she's the mother!"

"Maybe so, but right now, you're the one who needs to forgive." He paused and laid his hand against her cheek. "Will you?"

She watched his eyes and saw how they begged for her to say yes. "If you come talk to her with me."

"This is between the two of you, Jessi."

"I can't forgive without you there!" He smiled right into her eyes, filling her with warmth.

"Then wouldn't it really be me that was forgiving and you being an extension of me?" Jessi's eyebrows drew together in a frown.

"I don't know how to forgive."

Joe laughed and released her chin. "You forgive almost better than anyone I know! I've messed up so many times over the past year, and you go on as if it never even happened."

"But that's different – that's you." He wrapped his arm snuggly around her shoulders and pressed his lips against hers.

"And this is your mother. You love her too, whether you admit it or not." Jessi looked down at her ice cream cone and licked it before it dripped.

"She hasn't asked for forgiveness."

"It doesn't matter. Forgiveness is something that takes place in your heart, regardless of the other person's behavior."

Jessi sat and thought about that as she finished her ice

cream cone. She wasn't very good at that kind of forgiveness.

That night, Jessica softly shut the front door behind her. The living room was quiet and dark. Jessi looked on the couches, but her mom wasn't there. She went back to her room, kicked off her shoes and threw her book bag on the ground. Then she went out to the kitchen. It was dark and quiet, but Carla's car was outside so Jessi knew she was home.

She stood outside Carla's bedroom door for a long moment, looking toward the kitchen where the unfamiliar man had been that morning. How was she supposed to forgive? She had come out for breakfast to find a man she didn't know sitting in her kitchen. Wasn't it bad enough that her dad had cheated on her mom? Did her mom really have to stoop to his level? Jessi sighed as she realized they weren't married anymore. Why should Bill get to be with Jari, and Carla have to live alone?

Jessica knocked on the closed door, almost afraid of what, or who, was on the other side. However, when Carla opened the door it was only her, looking tired and older than Jessi had ever seen her look. "Jessica, thank God. I thought you probably ran away from home." Jessica immediately took offense at her mom's tone. She sounded anything but thankful.

"You thought or you wished?" Jessi regretted how snotty her own tone was as soon as the words left her mouth. Carla took a moment to coolly meet her eyes.

"Good question."

"Where's your boyfriend?" Jessi asked. Carla sighed.

"He left. As soon as you did. He didn't come into work today." Her tone was defensive.

"What's his name?"

"What do you care?" Carla paused then sighed. "Judson."

"It sounds like a kind of tractor."

"Jessica!"

"Okay, I'm sorry. I just came in here to tell you that," Jessi paused, the words feeling thick in her mouth. She didn't want to say them. "I'm sorry."

Carla seemed confused. "You were rude!" she finally accused. Jessi nodded.

"I know. Will you forgive me?" Carla frowned.

"You told him you would make his life hell!"

"And at the time, I meant it. Will you forgive me for saying it though?"

"And you…you…" Carla paused and then suddenly dissolved into tears, slumping heavily against Jessica. "And I promised to be faithful to your father for the rest of my life, and my promise means nothing anymore."

Jessica put her arms around her mom and awkwardly patted her back. "It's okay, Mom."

"No, it's not okay, Jessica. I just…I just started thinking about your dad. I felt so lonely and I was so mad, Jessi. So mad that he had chosen another over me. I wanted to prove that I was still desirable – that I'm not old, worn out, and only fit to be traded in on a younger model."

Jessica didn't know what to do with her mom's confession, but her heart stirred with compassion. First forgiveness, then compassion – all in one day. What kind of a person was she turning into? Pushing the disquieting thoughts aside, she squeezed her mom's shoulder.

"I think you're…beautiful," Jessi said, the words feeling foreign on her tongue. Carla looked surprised, and rightfully so. Jessi was fairly certain she had never said anything so nice to her mom before. "Mom, just because dad's with Jari, you don't have to sleep with Fred."

Carla acted as if she hadn't heard Jessi's slip of the name; she only seemed to remember why she had brought him home. She looked around, her eyes suddenly desperate. "I have some work I need to do. We'll talk about this later." Jessi shook her head and caught her mom's arm.

"No you don't. We need to talk about this now."

"Don't you have homework?" Carla asked. Jessi knew it was the end of the conversation. Carla was not ready to ask for forgiveness, but as usual, she was ready to bury the issue under work.

"Yes, Mom, I do. I'll see you in the morning. Sleep well." Jessica kissed Carla's cheek and slowly turned away, her feet dragging as she walked to her room. She felt more defeated and weary than if everything had blown up in a big fight. However, an unfamiliar peace washed over her that gave her new energy as she picked up her book bag. She had forgiven her mom.

Twenty-Six

March passed quickly without any major happenings except for Kaitlynn's engagement and the lunch with Bill and Jari. Jessi took track and thought she was dying the first two weeks. She ran sprints and found that she was in the top three more often than not.

Pops came to every track meet, rain or shine, home or away, and timed her. No matter how she did, he took her and Joe out for ice cream after the meet. Joe also came to the track meets, and sat in the stands with Pops, carrying on easy conversations while watching the events. The two men became friends and regularly had a good time together teasing Jessica.

Jessi enjoyed the track meets immensely. She joked with Pops and lounged in the bleachers with Joe, as she got a tan between races. Oftentimes, Grandma came along and brought snacks for everyone. Kara came to share the day as often as she could. Hannah and Chris made it to all of the home track meets to cheer Jessi on, and Carla made it to almost half of them. They all sat together in the stands like a family, and Jessi had never felt so loved.

Joe had more time that spring, since football and basketball were over, and he spent it hanging out with Jessi. Carla worked long hours, but every few weeks she came home and surprised Jessica with a girls' night. Jessi kept her promise to Pops and invited Grandma. All three of them enjoyed the special nights of bonding and laughter. Once, they even had a girls' weekend, and the three of them went into the city together, stayed in a hotel, went shopping, and attended an opera. It was fun, and Pops told Jessi later that Grandma had the time of her life.

The first day of April, Jessi was sitting on her bed doing homework when she heard the front door open and close. "Jessi?" Jessica looked at her clock, surprised. She hadn't expected her mom to be home for hours. Her unexpected arrival and frantic cry drove Jessi to stand and meet her in the hall. "Jessi!" Carla grabbed Jessica and hugged her hard.

"What's wrong, Mom?" Jessi asked cautiously, anxiety filling her.

"It's Pops. He's in the hospital," Carla said, tears gathering in her eyes.

Without hesitating, Jessi grabbed Carla's arm and started for the front door. "What happened?" she asked, alarmed, as they rushed out of the house.

"He's had a heart attack, Sweetie."

Jessi's heart skipped a beat. "When?" she asked, running down the porch stairs to Carla's car. When they were both in, Carla sped down the driveway, and broke the speed limit as she turned toward town. "When did it happen?" Jessi asked again, trying to make sense of what her mom had just said. He had been at her track meet just the day before and he had looked perfectly fine.

"Just a few minutes ago. I was out running an errand when Grandma called. She was getting the mail, and when she went back into the house, he was lying on the floor by his chair. It was a good thing she found him when she did, or the paramedics said he wouldn't have made it." Carla's voice was shaky.

"So, she called the ambulance?" Jessi questioned.

"Immediately. He was being transported to the hospital when I spoke with her. I'm sure he's there by now."

Jessi was staring at her mom out of wide blue eyes. "Will he be okay?" The question came out in a whisper.

"I hope so." The fear in Carla's voice caused a lump to form in Jessi's throat. She turned her eyes to look out the window at the passing town and told herself over and over that everything would be okay.

When they arrived at the hospital, Jessi was first out of the car. She ran all the way to the information desk and was already asking about him when her mom caught up. "He's in surgery, Miss Cordel. However, I believe Mrs. Hill is in the second floor waiting room and is expecting you," the nurse told Jessi. Jessica nodded and ran to the elevator.

Pops had to make it. He couldn't die. He might be an old man that she had barely known a year ago, but things were different now – she needed him. He really tried. He put forth the effort to know her. He put forth effort to love her. And he did it well. For one of the first times in her entire life, she felt loved and accepted. She knew that Pops was proud of her. And she had learned to love him.

Grandma caught her in a hug as soon as she appeared in the doorway of the waiting room, a hug that Carla was absorbed into when she entered seconds later. The three of them stood hugging, Grandma crying.

"How is he?" Carla asked, her voice fearful.

"The doctor said that he doesn't look good, Baby," Grandma told Carla. "His skin was so ashen. He was clutching his chest when I found him, and...." The older woman dissolved into tears, and Carla held her mom's face to her shoulder, trying to calm her. Jessi softly rubbed her Grandma's back and bit her lip, trying to hold back her own tears.

"It'll be okay, Grandma," she offered quietly. It had to be.

A man cleared his throat behind them, and they all turned to look at the doctor in scrubs. His face was serious. He pressed his thin lips together, then slightly shook his head. "He passed away on the operating table. I'm so sorry, Mrs. Hill, Ms. Cordel, Jessica." Jessica stared at the doctor. His daughter was in her class, and she had always thought he seemed like a nice enough man, until this very moment. Now, she wanted to slap him for what he had said.

"Oh!" Grandma moaned and sank to the floor very slowly, her head in her hands.

"Mom!" Carla cried, sinking to her knees as well and wrapping her arms around her mother.

"What do you mean he passed away?" Jessi questioned, angrily.

"He died, Jessica," the doctor said gently, nodding slightly.

"No! Obviously you weren't treating him as you should have been! Can't you bring him back? This is the twenty-first century! People don't die from heart attacks when they live two minutes from a hospital! Why weren't you helping him? Do something for him! *Do something for him!*" Jessi cried, tears stinging her eyes.

"Jess, don't, Honey!" Carla begged from the floor, her upturned eyes watery.

Jessi looked from her mom to the doctor, then back to her mom. She gave a strangled cry and ran from the room. She ran down the stairs and out the front door. She ran down the street and down the highway. Sheer adrenaline and grief kept her going. She ran down the county road, then cut through the forest. She finally collapsed, exhausted, against the trunk of Joe's Jesus tree. She fell to the ground and wrapped her arms around her knees, rocking herself gently.

~~~~~

Hours later, Joe quietly walked up and stood above her. She was a welcome sight as darkness had fallen hours before and still there had been no sign of Jessica. He knew she had heard him approach, but she hadn't looked up. "I'm glad I found you. Your mom is really worried, Jess," he told her, his voice gentle.

"He died," she whimpered, starting to rock herself again. He let out a deep breath and sat down beside her, pulling her into his arms. "I know, Babe, I know." Her head snapped up and she pulled back.

"You don't know!" she cried, standing up. He stood up, too.

"Jessi," he started, pulling her into his embrace. Her lips were blue from the cold, her cheeks were red and tear-streaked, and her eyes had a wild look to them. He wasn't letting her run again.

"No!" she cried. She tried to pull away, but he held her arm tightly. He startled as she swung back toward him and started to beat her fists against his chest, yet he didn't release her. She finally collapsed against him, holding him as tight as she could, sobbing. He breathed in a breath of relief and held her close, stroking her hair, knowing that, for the moment, the worst had passed.

"I know, Sweetheart. I know," he murmured softly, trying to absorb her grief. If he could take it on himself, he would in an instant.

"Joe," she started.

"What, Love?" he asked gently.

"He loved me," she whispered. "He really loved me." He closed his eyes against the raw pain in her words and nodded his head.

"Yes, he did."

"He was always there in the bleachers, cheering for me."

"He was one of the loudest," Joe agreed.

"He always timed my sprints and argued with the officials."

"He always had the correct time," Joe answered softly.

"He always remarked about how good the fish was," she said, starting to whimper again.

"He always could appreciate a nice fish," Joe agreed.

"He always winked at me when I was upset."

"He had a knack for making people smile."

"He made me feel wanted when I was all alone," she whispered brokenly. Joe pushed her hair back from her face and pressed a gentle kiss against her temple. Her face crumpled as she began to cry harder again. "He really loved me, Joe, and now he's gone."

Three days later, Joe sat with Jessi at Bert Hill's funeral. He held her in one arm and held her hand with his other. He was as close as physically possible, offering warmth and strength, yet her skin was as cold as ice, and she trembled like a leaf in the wind.

She didn't cry during the service like her grandma and mom, but Joe felt her tension steadily increase. After the service, when he went to help Carla out of the car at the cemetery, Jessi clutched his hand.

"Don't leave me!" she begged, and he consented, tightening his arm around her.

As the casket was lowered into the ground, Jessi's grandma tossed a single red rose down on top of it with a strangled cry. There was hardly a dry eye in the three hundred people that surrounded the grave. Bert Hill had been a well-liked and well-respected man in Glendale, living there his entire life, and his numerous friends and family members had turned out to pay their final respects.

After the graveside service, Joe stood back as his family approached. Hannah gave Jessi a long hug and he watched with a tender smile as his girlfriend clung to his mother. "Come over sometime soon, will you, Jessi? We can talk if you'd like." Jessi nodded and held on to Hannah. Hannah smiled as she smoothed Jessi's hair back and kissed the girl's forehead. The older lady reluctantly gave way to her daughter.

When Kara hugged Jessi, Joe wondered if he would ever get her back. Kara hugged her for a long time, whispering comforting words to her until Joe could see Jessi's back relax and her shoulders slump. Kara moved on to hug Carla with one last concerned smile for Jessi. Then Chris pulled the thin girl into his arms and gave her a steadying hug before carefully directing her back to Joe. Jessi looked up at Chris tearfully and said, "Thanks for coming." Chris squeezed her shoulder.

"We wouldn't have missed it, Jessi. We loved Pops, too."

Lemonade and cookies were served back at the church, and Joe held Jessi on his lap as she pretended to nibble at a cookie while talking in hushed tones to Tacy and Kara. He tugged one side of her black skirt down over her nylons to make the hem even, then traced the vertical lines of her black sweater. He rested his forehead against her shoulder and just sat with her, offering comfort and support as she needed it.

That night, once everything was finally over, he took her to her grandma's house. She kicked off her black heels and sat with him on the old couch. He asked if she wanted to watch a movie, but she didn't. He asked if she wanted to watch TV, but she didn't. He asked if she wanted ice cream, but she didn't. She just wanted to sit.

He could tell she was exhausted, and when he dimmed the lamp and prompted her to lie down in his lap, she was asleep within minutes. When Carla and Maybelle came in from quietly discussing the funeral in the kitchen, they spent a few minutes watching the sleeping girl.

Maybelle pushed Jessi's dark hair back with a trembling hand and allowed herself to smile at her granddaughter. "Bert really loved her."

Joe touched the back of Maybelle's hand gently. "It was mutual." Maybelle smiled through fresh tears.

"I'm glad she's able to sleep," Carla said.

"Me too. She hasn't been sleeping well," Maybelle agreed softly. Carla shook her head, then smiled at Joe.

"Joe always makes Jessi comfortable. He can convince her to do anything he wants," she said.

Joe grinned and stretched his arms above his head before putting them back around Jessi. Maybelle ruffled his hair.

"You're a good boy, Joe."

"Thanks, Maybelle," he said gently. "I am truly sorry for your loss."

Her old blue eyes were still watery, as they had been for the past three days, and she held a hand to her mouth as she nodded. "I still can't believe he's gone," she admitted. She paused, collecting herself. "But I'm glad you've been there for Jessica. She has needed someone. She's taken this hard."

He nodded solemnly. After a few more minutes, he woke Jessi and told her he was going home. She walked him to the door and hugged him tightly, thanking him softly for all he had done. He left her reluctantly and drove home, his heart heavy.

Jessi drank some water and went in to bed. She was sleeping with her mom and grandma in the spare room. Although it was tight, it felt good to be so close to family – to people who were experiencing the same pain. They all fell asleep cuddled against each other and slept soundly through the night, glad that the funeral was finally over.

The next week was touch and go. Maybelle and Carla cried a lot, and Jessi tried to lose herself in catching up on the school work she had missed. Once Carla and Jessi went home, Jessi went to sleep with her radio on every night, trying to drown out the sound of her mom crying and singing in her bedroom. What had started the day of Bill's wedding had only continued since then, and Bert's death had escalated it again.

The empty wine bottles piled up in Carla's trash, and when Jessi begged her to stop one night, Carla tearfully agreed. But the next morning there was a newly emptied bottle in the garbage. Jessi went to school frustrated and scared. Joe tried to comfort her, but as he watched her life falling to pieces around her, he felt as if his hands were tied. He had nothing to offer her other than his own strength, because Jessi wouldn't accept the strength of the only One who could truly help her.

Joe spent almost all of his free time in prayer, lifting Jessica and her family up to the LORD, but he didn't see anything changing. He grew frustrated as weeks dragged by, and Jessi became increasingly frightened and sad while Carla dove deeper into the alcohol. He offered words of encouragement and told Jessi that God had a plan, but as he watched the situation become worse, his words started to sound a little empty, even to his own ears.

Slowly, Jessi pulled herself up and started to live again. She stopped over at her grandma's often, and twice a week Joe went over with her for dinner. It became a habit to take fresh flowers to Pops' grave every Tuesday afternoon.

Jessi finished out the track season running faster than ever. She took her timecards and laid them on Pops' grave, along with the flowers. Carla didn't come to any more track meets, saying the memory was too painful, and Maybelle came only to a few, looking more fragile and sad each time. Chris and Hannah came to every meet, but Joe still missed Bert in the stands, and Jessi was constantly aware of his absence.

Slowly the sad memories faded, though. By the middle of May, Joe almost found himself forgetting that Jessi's family had gone through such a dark time. The only reminder was Bert's absence and Carla's increased drinking.

Twenty-Seven

"I can't believe you're making me do this," Jessica pouted as she stared disbelievingly at the plain square building.

"You never know – you might enjoy it." She gave Joe a look. She didn't need to say a thing – he understood and grinned. "We'll go shopping for a dress for graduation tomorrow," he reminded.

"We'd better, or else I never would have come." He tried to keep his smile to himself, and handed her the t-shirt he had brought for her. "What's this?" she asked, holding it up. "You don't like what I'm wearing?" He glanced at her pale peach lace shirt, the way it set off her bronzed coloring and how the fabric clung to her girlish body.

"No, you look great," he paused and gave her a pointed look. "Which is why you're wearing my t-shirt." She smiled, comforted by his compliment, and after holding his shirt to her nose and breathing deeply, she slipped it on over her head. "It's a little big," he observed. She smelled it again, and smiled at him.

"It'll work," she answered.

He took the ponytail holder off the dash and put it around his wrist. "C'mere."

She turned to face away from him, and he carefully pulled her hair up into a ponytail. He smoothed the bumps out with his fingers, then wrapped the elastic band around it tightly, admiring his work with pride. She leaned back on her elbows and tipped her head back to look at him.

"Are you sure we have to go in?" she asked, her large eyes pleading with him. He tipped her head back a little farther and kissed her forehead.

"I'm positive."

"What if I hate it?" she asked. He grinned and smoothed the frown off her forehead with his hand.

"It's only one day," he answered. She made a face at him, and he kissed her forehead again and came around to open the door for her. "You'll be fine," he promised as he took her hand, then pulled her out of the truck and across the parking lot.

"What's he doing?" Jessica asked, looking disgustedly at a man sitting outside the door. His clothes were dirty, his shoes ragged, his hair was greasy and his beard was stained yellow. He had an old backpack by his feet with a bed mat rolled up and tied to the top.

"Waiting for lunch," Joe answered simply. He deliberately stepped around Jessica to put himself between her and the homeless man, but he smiled and said, "Hello." Jessica didn't say anything, but went through the door when Joe opened it for her. He led her down a quiet, dim hallway and pushed through a stainless steel, swinging door. Jessica was surprised to see that there were over a dozen people in the large kitchen, all bustling around, preparing food, and getting things ready for lunch.

"Oh my Lord, it's my baby boy Joe! You've brought him back to me once more! Thank you Jesus!" Jessica was startled at the words that rose up above all the other ruckus. She searched the workers, trying to decide who had just sent up the loud praise. She didn't have to wonder for long. A large black woman with an apron and a hair cap came running out of the group, catching Joe into a big hug, her smile lighting up her whole face. She squeezed him, praising God, and Joe laughed as he returned the embrace.

When she stepped back, Joe instantly said, "Helda, I'd like you to meet my girlfriend, Jessi. Jessi, this is Helda – an old friend."

"Who you callin' old, Boy?" Helda asked, shooting Joe a dirty look and hitting his arm. He laughed, and so did she. "It's nice to meet you, Miss Jessi. I've heard a lot about you." Jessica smiled politely, but shot Joe a curious look

"It's a pleasure to meet you, too," she said.

Helda beamed at Jessica, then at Joe. "It sure is nice to have you two here!" She looked at Joe. "I've missed you lately." He looked at the ground for a moment, then up at her and smiled.

"I know. I've been kind of busy."

She gave him a knowing smile. "So I hear." He grinned and reached down to hold Jessica's hand. Helda stood and smiled at the couple for another moment before springing back into action. "Well, there will be time to chitchat later. Right now I've got work for both of you. Jackson's waitin' for you over there, Joe." Helda pointed, and Jessica noticed a man that waved. Joe waved back.

"I'll check on you in a bit, Jess," he said, shooting her an encouraging smile as he walked away. Jessica watched him, her eyes wide. He hadn't told her they would split up.

Helda took her by the arm. "You're gonna serve the mashed potatoes, Baby. Here's your spot right here. If you need more, you just call for Eliza," Helda paused and looked around, as if to point the woman out. "Oh, I don't see her right this minute, but she's around here. You just call out 'n' she'll come with more." Helda handed a big ice cream scoop to Jessica, and Jessica took it, suspiciously, wondering if it was dirty. "You gonna be just fine, Sugar," Helda encouraged, patting her shoulder. Then she hustled away, leaving Jessi alone.

Jessica looked at her big tray of mashed potatoes and blinked slowly. It would take forever to scoop all those potatoes, and Helda had said she might need more. Her heart sank.

She looked out past the serving counter at a dining room with an outdated color scheme. One half of the big room was filled with tables and chairs. The other half was separated by screens and was filled with cots. Jessica realized that dozens of people, mostly dirty and in little more than rags, were already lining up at the end of the counter. She cringed. Didn't they have anything better to do with their time? Like...get a job?

"This is the most disgusting, degrading thing I have *ever* done," she whispered to herself.

"Don't worry. I thought that very same thing when I came for the first time, thirty years ago." Jessi jumped, startled by the close proximity of the classy looking speaker who was watching her with a knowing smile. "I'm sorry, I didn't catch your name, Dear."

"Jessica Cordel," Jessi paused. "Jessi for short."

"I'm Elizabeth Jefferies," the lady said before pausing with a smile. "Eliza for short."

"You're the governor's wife," Jessi responded, surprised. "You support that new legislation about making late-term abortions against the law, and you're a child's advocate."

"And you pay attention to politics," Eliza said with a wink.

"I try not to," Jessica answered, drawing a laugh from Eliza.

"I understand completely! Sometimes I get so tired of all the games that I just want to forget that I know anything about the subject."

"Me too," Jessica agreed, almost under her breath.

"And why do you know so much about it?" Eliza questioned.

"My dad is a senator."

"Not our senator," Eliza pointed out as if she had known all along. "So, what are you doing here?"

"My mom and I are starting a new life in Glendale. My boyfriend um…asked me to come with him. We're going shopping tomorrow." Eliza smiled.

"It's your first time volunteering here?" Jessi nodded. "And your man had to drag you, kicking and screaming, all the way?"

Jessi took a moment trying to formulate a polite response.

"Pretty much," she finally conceded.

"And he bribed you with a shopping trip?"

"Yes," Jessica admitted. Eliza nodded.

"Same reason I came to begin with. It's okay, Jessi, it'll change." Jessica looked at her doubtfully, then out at all the grungy people.

"Somehow, I don't think so."

"Oh, you'll go awhile thinking they're disgusting, that you'd give anything to be somewhere else, that you can't wait to leave. Then one person will come through," Eliza paused, "and you'll look into their eyes, and your very heart will change."

"I doubt it. Look at them – they're gross. They probably haven't showered in months…maybe years!" Jessi judged, unashamed.

"You're probably right, but Jessi, they're real people, just like you and me. They have real needs, real emotions, real experiences. They're doing their best to survive. They're searching for hope. They're looking for someone who will show them a little of the love and mercy that they're craving. These poor people are searching for our loving God, and they don't even know it," Eliza paused again. "People in high places who shower regularly are searching for the same thing. Do you know anyone like that?"

Jessi looked down and slowly shook her head. "Nope."

"Hm." Eliza looked out at all the people.

"You're a Christian?" Jessi asked cautiously. Eliza nodded.

"Yes, ma'am. How about you?"

"No," Jessica paused. "Joe is."

Eliza nodded. "I see." There was no condemnation from this lady, and Jessi relaxed. Eliza took a breath to say something else, but just then Helda bustled out to the middle of the dining room.

"Hello Babies! How ya'll doing today?" Helda went on to give directions, then the people started coming. Eliza slipped away to check on the lady serving the meatloaf, and Jessi was left by herself. She was amazed at how busy the mashed potatoes kept her.

As the line moved along in front of her, the smell became almost unbearable, and she tried hard not to look at anyone. It would just be better for everyone if she didn't make eye contact. She scooped and plopped the potatoes, keeping her eyes on the white food. Some mumbled thanks as they moved on, but she didn't answer. Her hand grew tired, and all she could think about was getting done.

She glanced up to check the progress of the line and saw that it still went out the door. Dismal questions filled her mind. Would it ever be over? Would the stream of people ever end? Why would all those people choose such a life? What in the world made it desirable?

Jessica gritted her teeth and plopped a pile of potatoes on a plate, but the tray didn't move. She cautiously glanced up and found the man that had been outside the building, staring at her. He smiled to reveal gross, rotting, yellow teeth as he looked her up and down. "You sure are a purty little gal."

"Move on, Sugar – can't hold up the line." Helda was instantly beside Jessica, and the man grudgingly moved on.

"Thank you," Jessi whispered, her stomach churning.

"You're welcome. If I hadn't said something, he would'a," Helda said, shooting her a bright smile and gesturing over her shoulder. Jessica quickly glanced behind her and realized that Joe was about ten feet away, warily watching the man with the yellow teeth. After watching just a moment longer to make sure the man kept moving, Joe turned back to his own assignment. Knowing he was near and watching out for her, helped Jessi finish out the lunch.

Once she was done serving, Helda kept her busy was various tasks as the volunteers started to put the kitchen and dining room back in order. After a couple of hours, most people had cleared the building, and those remaining were resting on cots in the back. "How are you?" Jessi jumped – Eliza had startled her once again.

"Glad it's over."

"I know, Jessi, but you did good. Only a few more hours, dinner, and you're done. You will get a few hours of sleep, then go shopping tomorrow."

Jessi smiled, thankful for Eliza's encouraging reminder. "You're right."

"Think you have the grit to go on?" Eliza asked. Jessi raised an eyebrow, thinking about the next several hours.

"Maybe."

"I think you do." Eliza gave her an encouraging smile and left.

"Hey Sugar, could you take this rag and go wipe down those tables?" Jessica reluctantly took the rag Helda offered her and set out on her newest job. After she had every table wiped down, she had the option of washing water pitchers and glasses or sweeping the floor. Choosing to wash dishes, she stood next to five other women at a long counter of sinks. Behind her, more women were standing over sinks.

Yellow rubber gloves went all the way up to Jessica's elbows, and a stray piece of hair was hanging right in her face. She blew at it, but it continued to tickle her nose. Her back and neck ached terribly, and she had a headache that pounded right between her eyes.

The washer behind her lost control of her sprayer and soaked the back of Jessica's shirt and jeans. The lady laughed through an apology, and Jessica waved the problem away through gritted teeth. The two women on either side of her were chatting a mile a minute, and it was driving her crazy. If she had only chosen the sweeping job, she could have smacked them both over the head with a broom!

She was just about ready to scream and stomp out of the place when tanned arms came around her stomach and soft lips planted a gentle kiss against the back of her neck. She relaxed against a strong chest, and tipped her head up. She had never been so glad to see chocolate hair and pale green eyes. "Joe," she moaned, letting him absorb her weariness.

"I'm so proud of you, Jessi." She smiled, the whole day suddenly okay – Joe was proud of her. "Are you holding up?"

"I'll be fine." She wished the day was already over. She wished they could go out to his truck, drive through city traffic to a hotel, grab their stuff and go inside. They would go swimming, get some sleep and then go shopping. But they couldn't leave yet – dishes still needed to be washed, and dinner needed to be served.

Joe rubbed her shoulders and her neck, taking away every ache and hurt. She let her head drop and closed her eyes, not seeing the women around her smiling at Joe's thoughtfulness. When he stopped, she rolled her neck, and he pulled the offending piece of hair back out of her face. "Feel better?" he asked, resting his chin on her slender shoulder.

"Yes! A lot better. Thanks, Joe." She turned her head and pressed her lips against the side of his face. "You are the sweetest guy ever!" she whispered for his ears alone. He laughed and kissed her forehead.

"You just keep thinking that." She smiled.

"Don't worry. I will."

"Hey, you missed a spot," he said, pointing. She made a face at him as she dunked the glass into the dishwater again and scrubbed it clean.

"Joe, do you know in my entire life I have never washed dishes for this long before?" she asked. He laughed.

"Are you sure this isn't the first time you've washed dishes?" She paused in her scrubbing.

"I resent that comment, and no! I have washed plenty of dishes."

"I bet I've washed way more dishes than you," he told her, a smug, challenging expression on his face. Her mouth fell open, and she blinked at him slowly.

"I didn't realize it was a competition. I happen to be very

proud of my accomplishments today."

"Honey, I am, too – especially because you don't do this wifey kind of thing very often," he answered, not able to resist teasing her a little more. She narrowed her eyes at him slightly, grabbed the sprayer and pulled the handle. He jumped back, sputtering. She shut it off, raising her eyebrows at him.

"What were you saying?" she asked. He stared at her, a grin threatening to give away his amusement.

"You soaked me."

"You insulted me," she countered, turning back to her glasses and water pitchers. He may be teasing, but she wasn't. He paused, letting the silence stretch.

"I'm sorry, Jess. I was just joking. I didn't mean to offend you." He brushed back her dark hair. "I really am proud of you." She leaned her head into his hand with a quiet sigh.

"Thanks. It's okay. I guess I'm just a little cranky." He wisely didn't comment.

"I'd better get back to work – I see Jackson looking for me," he said. Joe gave the back of her neck an encouraging squeeze. "Keep up the good work, Jessi." She nodded, and he walked away. She watched him go, then looked down at the dishes that still filled her sink.

She *had* washed dishes before. Of course not much, but she had done it. She knew he hadn't meant anything hurtful by his teasing, yet she felt hurt. He didn't think she had the skills it took to be a good wife. He had basically said as much. The thought made her scrub with a vengeance, pouting.

Twenty-Eight

Jessi took a sip of her ice water as she walked back to the serving counter.

"Jessi, Baby, you're Miss Mac and Cheese. Plant those little feet right here," Helda said cheerfully, motioning to Jessica's spot. "Here's your scooper. And 'member, give them babies an extra scoopful. They've got some growing to do and need the extra sustenance. Besides, macaroni and cheese is their favorite mosta the time," Helda paused and gave Jessi an affectionate smile. "It used to be Joe's favorite, too. I used to make it for him." Jessi tilted her head, interested.

"Was it?" she asked. Helda nodded, turning to place her large backside against the edge of the counter. She stared at the far kitchen wall, going back through the years in her mind.

"I took care of him every day for months when he was just a little guy. His mama got real sick when Kara was born, and Kelsi was already fighting cancer. With three little ones and an infant at home and one sick little girl in the hospital, Hannah needed help. Jackson and I weren't married yet, and all I had was a goldfish – Galls. His bowl moved real easy, so we just moved in with the Colbys. Hannah and I were real good friends."

Sorrow shadowed Helda's expression. "It was a sad time. Once the funeral was over, I moved back home and just came over couple times a week to take care of Joe and the girls, givin' Hannah some time to heal. Joe was my baby, though. We had a special bond. Until we moved, he'd come over after school for a snack every Tuesday and Thursday. I'd feed him chocolate pudding," Helda mused with a smile.

"He likes chocolate pudding? That's good to know," Jessi replied. Helda laughed.

"You pump him full of it, Sugar – he has to have some way to keep that hair of his so chocolaty brown!" Jessi smiled, and Helda went on. "I always knew if that boy had a bad day – he'd be over right around when I started dinner, just hanging

246

around, asking what I was making. I'd make him homemade mac 'n' cheese, and we'd carry it out to the tree house and eat up in the leaves." Helda stopped to reflect on the memory, smiling.

Jessi felt a twinge of jealousy. Helda, like so many others, had been there for Joe. Jessica's childhood had been so different than his, and she felt it again acutely. Joe had been surrounded by loving people who constantly offered their help and support. Jessica had been given everything she had ever wanted, except that which she really needed – love and attention. There had never been chocolate pudding, long talks, or mac 'n' cheese up in the leaves for her. The little girl hurts still echoed in her heart.

"I used to spoil that boy something awful. Everyone said I'd ruin him, but I just couldn't say no to those green eyes and that charming smile," Helda continued, obviously enjoying her trip down memory lane.

Jessi smiled. "That makes two of us." Helda smiled, but there was a look of concern in her eyes.

"Sometimes it's best to say no, Sugar." Helda glanced up at the clock. "Oh, it's time to feed them. Let's get started people!" she announced loudly, clapping her hands above her head to get everyone's attention.

The workers prepared to serve the food while Helda went out to announce dinner. The line started to form and shuffle through.

"Let me fix this for you." Eliza stopped beside Jessica and tucked a loose piece of hair up into the plastic cap where it belonged.

"Thanks."

"You're welcome. Still holding up okay?"

"Almost done," Jessi answered.

"You're glad."

"Ecstatic doesn't even begin to describe it." Eliza laughed and patted Jessi's back.

"Jessica, I'd like to invite you and Joe to come spend the night at my house. I have plenty of extra rooms, and there's no need for you two to stay at a hotel when my beds are sitting empty." Eliza smiled. "I'll even feed you breakfast. The governor makes a mean pancake." Jessi laughed at her wink. "And then you can keep the money you'll save for the mall tomorrow," Eliza pointed out.

Jessi considered that new incentive, then Eliza's wistful look. The kind lady wanted her to accept.

Reality set in. It would create havoc if her father found out. A democrat senator's daughter staying the night at a republican governor's house. That would make quite the story for the press. Jessi shrugged off the thought. Who cared about her father? She didn't.

"That sounds good," she answered. Eliza squeezed her shoulder.

"Good. I'll find you after the line goes through."

"Okay." The line started moving. Jessica held her full scooper, ready for the first person. The faster she fed them, she figured, the faster they would move on and the faster she would be done. The first person through was an older lady, her face looking weathered, her front teeth gone. The next was a skuzzy, bearded man. Ew. He moved on, and Jessica breathed a sigh of relief as she plopped scoop after scoop of mac and cheese, growing more excited with every scoop she gave away, knowing she was that much closer to freedom.

"Two scoops, please. It's my favorite." The voice was sweet, high, and had a lisp.

"Mine, too." There was no head to either voice, just two trays moving along the high counter. Jessi leaned over to see the little girls.

They were young, maybe three and four. Their brown hair was matted and tangled. The oldest girl had a bruised cheek, and the other had a bloody scratch on her forehead. Their clothes were nothing but rags tied together. Four brown eyes stared back at her – pure, innocent, searching, pleading, hurting.

Jessica just stood there, looking at them. They were so little. The right front tooth of the first was missing, the gap making her all the cuter. They stood very still as Jessi stared at them, just staring back.

"Whose children are these? Whose are they?" Both girls jumped at her sudden, demanding questions. Who dared to take such care of two beautiful little girls? Who dared to dress them in rags and make them march shamefully through a food line at a homeless shelter?

No one claimed them at first. The people in line just watched. Finally, the woman behind them stepped forward, sighing wearily. "I found 'em 'bout a block away 'round some dumpsters all alone, so I brought 'em in." Jessica stared at her. They had been all alone eating out of dumpsters? She shifted her eyes back to the girls.

"Where's your mother?" Jessica asked them. The small one's lip trembled, and her eyes grew wet and shiny. The oldest pressed her lips together, and rubbed her nose.

"We don't know. She just wasn't there when we woke up 'while back."

"You're all alone?" Jessi questioned. They both nodded. "Who takes care of you?" The littlest girl pointed to the oldest.

"What's holding up the line, Sugar?" Helda asked, bustling in. Jessi dragged her eyes from the girls to turn them to Helda for just a second.

"These girls are all alone here. They have no parents," Jessi answered. Helda peered over the counter just as Jessi had.

"Okay, you just give them double scoopfuls," Helda said. "Babies, you stay right there. Helda's comin'." The big lady hurried out of the kitchen, through the dining room and struggled through the line to get to the girls. Jessi scooped the biggest spoonfuls that she could onto their plates, and they told her thank you. They stared at her as Helda moved them on, and Jessica stared back.

Something about them ripped at her heart. Maybe it was that they were all alone. Maybe it was how small they were. Maybe it was that in some small, pitiful way, they reminded her of herself. Whatever it was, she could hardly take her eyes from them.

Helda slid their trays down the counter, and they moved past the ham to the green beans. The line moved on. Jessica scooped mac and cheese, the look in their sad little eyes still in her mind. They were hurting and alone. Just as she had been.

She looked up at the person in front of her. It was a girl who was probably close to twenty. Her nails were dirty, her clothes suggestive. Her hair looked oily, and her dirty face was painted thick with make-up. Jessica shivered when she looked up into the girl's eyes. They looked dead and lifeless; so cold and empty that Jessica couldn't detect a speck of life in them. The girl moved on.

The next person was a man, and Jessica quickly looked up into his eyes, wanting to see what they held. Pain. Intense pain. He moved on. Another man came – he was weary. He was weary of life itself – a kind of weariness that no amount of sleep could cure. The next woman's eyes revealed anger – unchecked, uncontrollable, empty anger. It was directed at nothing, just there, waiting for someone to direct it at. She didn't offer any thanks for her scoop of macaroni and cheese.

Jessica spent the rest of the time intently watching the eyes of the hungry. They were all different, and yet alike. They were all searching, unfulfilled. As soon as the line was gone, and the seconds line had been served, Jessi tried to search out the girls. She didn't see them at first, and that was okay. She had something she wanted to do before she found them.

Abandoning her scooper and the macaroni, she went in search of Joe. She found him with Jackson, already starting to wash some of the large serving dishes with a hose. She grabbed his arm. "Joe, can you take me somewhere?"

"Where?" he asked, looking up, surprised to see her.

"Somewhere really important!"

"Where?" he asked again, giving her a suspicious look.

"To the store! Come on, please?"

"Jess, we'll be done soon," he said, sighing heavily, as if he was on to her scheme. "I have work I need to finish."

"You can finish when we get back." He raised an eyebrow at her.

"We're coming back?"

"Yes, come on. We have to go before they leave," she said, trying to pull him toward the door.

Joe shot her a confused look and was about to ask her to explain herself, when Jackson slapped him on the back. "Take the girl to the store already. We'll finish when you get back." Joe nodded at Jackson and allowed Jessi to pull him through the building.

"Where are you going, Jessi?" Eliza called after them.

"To the store! We'll be back!" Jessi promised, and Eliza nodded with a knowing smile. She had seen the teenager talking to the two girls. Eliza allowed herself a small smile after the young couple left – she had been praying for those little girls or somebody like them, to come through the door all day.

Jessica jumped into the truck as soon as Joe opened the door for her, and he hurried around to get in, laughing at her urgency. "Where are we going?" he asked, turning the key.

"The closest clothing store. I don't care which one it is, just go fast." He shot her another suspicious look as he pulled out of the parking lot.

"Are you sure you're not just trying to sneak in a little early shopping?"

"No, Joe I'm serious about this," she told him, frustrated, turning toward him in her seat. "When I was serving mac and cheese there were these two little girls. They were dirty and small, and I got so mad I asked whose children they were. Someone said they had found them by some dumpsters and brought them in. *Dumpsters,* Joe! They were all alone – they don't know where their mother is. They never said a word about their father, and they've just been toughing it out all by themselves. They are so small, and their clothes are barely there. I have to get them some new clothes so they'll be warm. And I want to pick up a brush for their pretty brown hair and a couple of dolls for them to hold." He slowly reached over and took her hand, unsure what kind of answer would be appropriate.

"Joe, I just have to do my part to make sure those little girls are okay." He kissed the back of Jessi's hand, still quiet, and searched the surrounding stores and buildings until he turned into a well-lit parking lot.

He parked and opened Jessica's door for her, faithfully pushing a cart through the store behind her as she made a beeline for the little girls' section. Four pairs of jeans, eight shirts, two dresses, two packs of panties, two packages of socks, two belts, two windbreakers, two sweatshirts, four pairs of pajamas, two pairs of tennis shoes, two pairs of flip flops, two backpacks, three books, two dolls, a package of pink ponytails, and one pink glitter brush later, Jessica pulled out her credit card that Bill Cordel paid the bill on.

"Think you should do that?" Joe asked, offering her a gentle smile.

"Finally, the tax payers' money will go to a good cause and get returned to the people who need it most," she told him quickly, as she finished the transaction. Joe nodded, pleased with her answer.

She pulled Joe out of the store just as quickly as they had entered, and she sat with the bags on her lap and around her feet as Joe drove back to the shelter. "I hope they're still there."

"If not, you can give your purchases to Helda, and she'll get them to the girls."

"I know, but I want to give them everything."

Joe smiled. "I know you do." He pulled into his previous parking place at the shelter.

She didn't wait for him to open her door, but he reached for the bags before she had the chance to grab them. "Let me carry these, Jess." She nodded, only taking the one that was in her hand. She ran for the door, and he ran to catch up. He grabbed the door handle, out of breath. "Want me to come with you?" he asked as he swung it open for her.

"You promised Jackson that you'd be back."

"True. You'll be okay?"

"Without a doubt," she told him with a firm nod. He handed her the sacks, and left for the swinging door to the kitchen. Carrying the bags, she wandered through the tables full of people, looking for the two small girls. She wanted to give them their new belongings and see them smile. She wanted to help.

She walked by the man with the pain-filled eyes. His tray sat in front of him, hardly touched. Two worn canvas bags sat at his feet, his ankles through the straps as if he thought they might get stolen. A cardboard sign rested against his knee and Jessi moved her eyes to read it. In large black letters it read, '**Car Accident. Lost Son and Wife. Unable to Go On.**' The words resonated inside of Jessi. There was no mention of money or of food. He wasn't listing a need. He didn't want charity. He just wanted others to know what had happened to him. He wanted them to know his pain and understand why he was the way that he was — why he couldn't go on.

Without hesitating, Jessica reached out and pressed her clean, smooth hand over the top of his dirty, rough one. He smelled bad and was grungy, but she didn't notice as he turned to her with slow, stiff movements. He looked up at her with eyes full of a pain that was so intense it hurt her. A tiny glimmer of gratitude flickered in his face when she squeezed his hand, then he turned his head to continue eating. No smile, no words, but she knew that he understood her loud and clear. She moved on – there was nothing more she could do for him.

She wandered through the people. Seeing the girl with cold, empty eyes, she took the seat beside her. The girl looked over at her, her mouth full, then started to quickly shovel food into her mouth again. She looked as if she hadn't eaten for days. Her bones stuck out, and her face was gaunt.

Jessica thought back to all the dinners she had complained about – the way she had complained about the brownies being dry only the night before. She thought about the lobster feast that her mother had cooked earlier in the week and the meal her grandma had made her Tuesday night, full of all her favorite foods. She hadn't appreciated it all nearly enough.

"Hi," she paused, her voice suddenly soft. "I'm Jessi." The girl didn't look up.

"I'm Angel," she answered, continuing to eat. Her voice was as lifeless as her eyes, and it gave Jessica a chill. Angel still had several bites of food left when a nasty looking man suddenly took her arm. Angel pulled it away instantly. "I want to finish." He grabbed her arm again, clenching his fingers into her skin. His lips pulled back in an ugly snarl.

"We had a deal." She winced, and her head dropped.

"Okay, okay." Angel glanced at Jessica, still without a visible stir of life within her. "Excuse me, ma'am – I've gotta work for my food, just like everyone else." Her voice was almost mocking. She walked away with the man, not even flinching when he jerked her roughly toward the door. Angel slid her tray into the tray return, then turned to look at Jessica. For just a moment there was a spark of life in her eyes, a look that begged Jessi to help her. Jessi stood, but the girl turned and walked away, the nasty man still directing her with rough jerks of her arm.

The realization that she was a prostitute settled heavily over Jessica. Angel sold her body to men, and had obviously sold a little piece of her heart and soul each time as well, which was why her eyes looked so empty. There was nothing left.

With a sick feeling settling in the pit of her stomach, Jessica realized that Angel was paying for something that was free. The shelter didn't charge for a meal. It was a free gift held out for anyone who wanted it, yet Angel would pay out of her own flesh for something she didn't owe. If only she had known.

Jessica slowly pushed away from the table, the sorrow of the people settling into her bones. She searched with more focus this time and finally spotted the little girls. Jessica ran to them, the bags hitting against her legs. They were standing against the wall, watching everyone mill about. Jessica dropped to her knees in front of them.

"What are your names?" she asked. The girls looked scared and tired. The little one put her finger in her mouth but neither said a word. "My name is Jessica. You can call me Jessi." She thought that they still weren't going to answer, but finally the oldest spoke.

"Jessi," she repeated. Jessica smiled brightly.

"Yeah! That's right! Good job. What's your name?"

"Morgan."

"That's pretty."

The little girl blushed and pulled her sister in front of her, wrapping her arm around the littlest one's shoulders and chest. "This is Montana. I call her Tani. She's four, I'm five." Jessi had been a year off when she guessed how old they were. They were small for their ages. The little one, Montana, peeked into Jessi's full bags, curious.

"Come with me, girls." Jessi took their hands and went in search of a quiet, semi-private corner. When she found one, Jessica sat down on the floor, no thought given to her expensive jeans. The girls copied her. "First, I got you clothes." The girls oohed and ahhed as Jessi pulled things out of the bags, one after another, and laid them in their laps. They fingered the smooth, strong fabric, and pretty colors.

Twenty-Nine

Joe stood still, watching. Twenty feet away, in a corner, Jessica sat with two little girls. New shoes were on their feet, looking out of place against the rags they still wore. Two piles of clothes sat beside them on the floor. The littlest was curled up on Jessi's lap, fast asleep. Jessi was running her hand through the sleeping girl's hair and over her face. She had her arm around the oldest girl, who was cuddled against her side. Jessi had a book in her hand and was reading quietly. The oldest girl was struggling to keep her eyes open, but finally they closed as she lost the battle. Jessi set the book down and smiled. Both girls were cuddling their new dolls against their chests.

"LORD." It was the only word Joe could think or choke out. All of his emotions were rolled into it. He loved her. He had loved her before today, he would have loved her after today, but he would no longer have the chance. The girl he had brought with him to the homeless shelter no longer existed. This new Jessi that he saw – the Jessi that was sitting on a dirty floor in a homeless shelter, cuddling two dirty, smelly, poor, little orphans against her expensive clothes, hugging them and reading to them – brought forth a new depth of love that Joe hadn't known existed.

This new Jessica, this woman who held her hand out to the poor and the hurting, was a woman he had never known before. Joe felt an awestruck wonder fill him as he watched the LORD continue to change her heart as she sat there.

A slender hand slid onto his shoulder.

"The caseworker will be here soon. In less than ten minutes." Joe looked over into a classy, pretty face.

"This isn't her, Eliza."

"Or maybe this really is." Joe let that settle, his heart about to burst with pride and joy in his beautiful girl. "She won't want to give them up," Eliza commented, thinking aloud. Joe shook his head. "You're staying at my house tonight," she continued, changing the subject. He gave her an amused look.

255

"You never cease to amaze me."

"Oh, it wasn't hard, Joe. She's a sweet girl." He nodded.

"I know. How are we going to get her to church?"

"Just ask her," Eliza paused. "That girl will do anything you want her to." Joe smiled, but Eliza's expression was serious. "Which reminds me, what were you thinking when you planned on the two of you staying alone in a hotel room?" Eliza straightened his collar as he sighed. "Don't play with fire, Honey."

"I'm strong," he muttered, sounding anything but.

"Of course you are, but a teenage boy and a beautiful girl, whom he loves, all alone in a hotel room overnight is not a good idea. Ever." His shoulders slumped.

"I know, but I had to bring her here."

"I know you did. I can see why. But you should have called. You know we always love to have you," Eliza said, squeezing his shoulder. Jessi looked up, saw them, and carefully motioned them over.

"I see you've met Eliza," Jessi whispered with a tender smile. Joe grinned and shot the older woman an amused look.

"She didn't tell you that she's my aunt." It was a statement more than a question. Jessica's mouth fell open.

"And see, she liked me even when I was just Eliza Jefferies. Don't have such a big head. She can like people who aren't related to you," Eliza teased, tweaking her nephew's ear.

"She just liked you because we look alike," Joe answered, rising to the occasion. Eliza laughed.

"You goose! I married into your family." Joe grinned.

"Joe, Eliza, I want to introduce you to some very special girls. This is Morgan and this little one is Montana," Jessi said, centering the conversation on the girls she held. Joe's smile was filled with tenderness as he knelt beside them.

"They're beautiful." He ran his hand over Morgan's hair. "Jessi, the caseworker will be here soon." He saw the argument in Jessica's eyes before she ever opened her mouth, and softly shook his head. She searched his face for a moment, then nodded.

"Let me hold them until she arrives," she said. He brushed a dark piece of hair out of her face and smiled.

"Deal."

Eliza quietly excused herself, and Joe carefully eased himself down onto the floor at Jessi's free side. He wrapped his arm around her shoulders and looked at the small girls. "Aren't they beautiful?" she sighed, brushing back Montana's matted hair. Joe nodded.

"Poor little girls," he said softly.

"Look how young they are, Joe! They're just babies, and they're so alone. They need so much – food, playtime, love, happiness, birthday cakes and presents, an education, adoring parents, pretty dresses, goodnight hugs and kisses."

"I wonder if they'll ever get that," he questioned, and she leaned her head against his.

"I hope they do."

"I *pray* they do," he countered.

"I think I would take the time to pray if God would help these girls." Joe smiled.

"Maybe you should take the time, and see if He does. What would it hurt?"

"I'll probably never know," she reasoned.

"They will." She was quiet for a few seconds.

"Joe, I want to help them." He picked up the empty sacks.

"You already have." She shook her head.

"More. Joe, someday, can we do foster care? Can we be the home they bring these beautiful girls to?"

He didn't answer flippantly. "Yes, Jess, we can," he answered, serious about what he was committing to. The caseworker appeared in the dining room with Eliza and Helda.

"Promise?" Jessi asked, searching Joe's eyes, her bottom lip trembling as she realized she would have to give the girls up very soon. He smiled at her, his gaze steady.

"I promise."

The caseworker approached them, and Jessica carefully shook Morgan's shoulders. "Hey, Baby Girl. Wake up, Honey. The lady is here to take you to a nice family." Morgan sat up, her eyes wide and scared. She reached for Montana and pulled her little sister into a close embrace, as if she could protect her under her skinny little arms.

The caseworker knelt in front of them and nodded to Joe and Jessica. "Hello Sweethearts," she said to the girls.

"We'll be together?" Morgan asked, glancing between the

adults as Montana pulled herself from her fuzzy dreams. The caseworker cleared her throat.

"Not tonight. We couldn't find room for both of you at the same home, but by tomorrow you'll be together."

Morgan looked at Jessica, scared and confused. Jessica offered her an encouraging smile. Morgan stood when the caseworker asked her to, and Jessica set Montana carefully on her feet. Then, she scrambled to her own feet to follow the girls out. Joe stuffed the clothes into the backpacks and followed, jogging to catch up with them.

When the caseworker had both girls stowed away in her car, she thanked Eliza, then Helda, then Jessica and Joe. Jessica gave her the backpacks and then stared into the girls' window. She held Morgan's scared brown eyes and kept them until the car pulled away. Then, taking a deep, steadying breath, Jessica walked back in to finish up her work and tell Helda goodbye.

There were big hugs and promises to see each other again soon. Joe intertwined his fingers with Jessi's as they walked out to his truck. He opened her door and shut it once she slid inside. She was quiet as they pulled out of the parking lot.

"How do you feel, Jess?" Joe asked, reaching out to hold her hand.

"Like I might cry," she whispered, looking at him out of large, sad eyes.

"You did good, Love." He wasn't surprised when big tears slipped down her cheeks. She cried softly as he drove through the city. He cleared security at his aunt and uncle's and parked in front of the governor's house.

He killed the engine of his truck and wrapped her snuggly in his arms. With big, gentle hands, he wiped away every tear. He didn't say anything, knowing there was nothing to say, but continued to hold her.

"I love you, Sweet Girl. I really, really do," he told her, his cheek resting against her head. She smiled at him.

"I love you, too."

"And I am so proud of what you did today." Her heart warmed at his tender praise.

"Thanks for making me come."

"I knew that you would eventually be glad you did."

"You know me, Joe Colby, like the back of your hand." He gave her a faint smile.

"I want to know you more." She soaked his words into her thirsty heart, like water being poured on to a dry sponge.

Feeling as if he was on a string she held, he leaned down and kissed her softly. "I'm glad we didn't try to stay alone in a hotel tonight, Jess," he whispered. He kissed her once more, then sat back.

He pulled her out of the truck and they headed up the stairs of the front porch. The front door opened and his uncle stood in the doorway. "Joe! I thought I heard you pull in! How are you, Son?" Joe released Jessica and bounded up the stairs, his hand out, a grin on his face. His uncle pulled him into a hug, and Jessica smiled.

"I'm doing good. How about you?" Joe answered.

"I'm doing just fine myself. Come on in." Jessica followed Joe into the big house as the governor stepped back. "Who is this pretty young lady?" Jessica smiled at the friendly man, and he winked at her good-naturedly.

"Alan, this is my girlfriend, Jessica Cordel."

She saw the mischievous glitter in his eyes as her name registered. "Good to meet you, Miss Cordel." She let her eyes sparkle back.

"It's a pleasure to make your acquaintance, Governor, but please," she paused. "Call me Jessi." He chuckled.

"Jessi, call me Alan, and you may have forgotten, but we have met." She remembered. It had been several years back, and Alan had been arguing with her dad at a benefit dinner. She couldn't remember what about now, but she remembered that the jolly governor had winked at her and slipped her his piece of chocolate cake after seeing her devour her own.

"So we have."

"Does Senator Cordel know you are here?" Jessica smiled.

"He soon will, won't he?" Alan's expression grew serious.

"Your father may find out, but it won't be from me." Jessica smiled again.

"If he does, it won't be the end of the world. Maybe he can spin it into some kind of positive press – extending an olive branch to the enemy camp," she said. Alan chuckled.

"Bipartisan cooperation," he agreed as he led them into a spacious and formal living room.

Joe pulled Jessica down onto a plush loveseat, where he tucked her in against his side. Alan sat in a tall wing chair, a glass of water on the table beside him.

"It's been awhile since I've seen you, Joe."

"Yeah, it's been several months. You've been awfully busy this term," Joe agreed, pointing out the obvious.

"Yes, well, that will soon be over."

"Less than a year left," Jessi observed, including herself in the conversation.

Eliza arrived home and, with Jessica's help, brought everyone tall glasses of iced tea. Eliza settled into the wing chair beside her husband.

The conversation flowed from subject to subject, some deep and tense, some light and fun. After a couple of hours, Jessi pulled her feet up onto the couch and rested her head against Joe's chest. He smoothed her hair and rubbed her face as the conversation continued.

After a while, Eliza led Jessi up to a spare room and showed her where to find everything she might need. The room was large, much like Jessica's room in D.C. The four-poster bed had three layers of thick, fluffy pillows. Joe carried Jessica's bag up to her room, and after a quick kiss goodnight, he left.

She changed into her pajamas and took a few minutes to look around the room, taking in the rich, luxurious feel, before jumping onto the soft bed. Lying under the covers a few minutes later, she stared at the ceiling and offered up a short, quick prayer for Morgan and Montana. When she was finished, she let out a deep sigh and said, "Well, I hope it was worth it." She went to sleep and didn't wake until her alarm went off the next morning.

Joe came for her seconds later, and she had no choice but to pad down to the breakfast table in her tank top, pajama pants and bare feet. Her hair was a mess and she had not yet brushed her teeth. They ate breakfast earlier than Jessica had ever eaten breakfast on a Sunday before, and Eliza had been right – the governor really knew how to make pancakes. They were delicious.

Jessi had eaten all she could hold and was sipping orange juice when Joe said, "Well, you'd better run up and shower.

Church starts in an hour." Jessica almost choked on her juice, but didn't say anything. Joe's eyes pleaded with her, so she grudgingly ran up and quickly got ready.

When he came to check how she was doing, she was just slipping on her shoes and zipping her bag. "That was sneaky of you," she told him.

"What was?" he questioned, though he already looked guilty.

"Telling me to bring a skirt to shop in when you really meant for church." He groaned and pulled her close.

"Going to church is something I do, Jess. It's important to me to go every Sunday, and since we're going to be together anyway, I really want you to come with me." She considered his words, feeling her irritation simmer down. "Will you come?" he asked, twisting a piece of her hair around his finger and looking into her blue eyes. "Please?" She wanted to tell him no, but her will faltered.

"I'll do anything you ask me to," she whispered, her heart vulnerable as she looked up at him.

"Don't tell me that," he whispered back, the mood suddenly serious.

"It's true."

Clearing his throat, he stepped back. "You look beautiful, Jessi," he told her, taking in her white skirt and sleeveless pink blouse, changing the subject. Her pink shoes matched perfectly, and her swooped bangs fell across her face just right. He twirled her on his finger to get the whole effect and then led her down to the front door where Alan and Eliza joined them just minutes later.

The church was huge, and the singing good, however Jessica soon lost interest in the sermon. It was all about God and Jesus, getting saved, resisting sin and a whole bunch of other religious stuff. However, she learned that if she crossed her legs and leaned over them, setting her elbow on her knee and her chin on her fist, Joe would rub her back. She sat through most of the service like that. After a few more songs, they were dismissed. As they walked out, Jessica congratulated herself on making it through her first church service. If Joe was going to be a pastor, many more were sure to follow.

After church, they went out to eat with Eliza and Alan, then after goodbyes, they went to the mall. Joe followed her into countless stores, a good-natured smile on his face the entire time. He ended up buying her a cute top and a new dress for his graduation. He received his just reward when they got to share a milkshake and eat hamburgers with fries for dinner.

She talked to keep him awake on their way back to Glendale, and it was late when he pulled up to her house. The front lights were on, as well as the living room lights – a sure sign that Carla was home. He opened the door for her and watched in adoration as she covered a yawn as she slid out of his truck.

At her front door, she turned and kissed him goodnight. The kiss wasn't long, but delicate and sweet. He wanted more, but settled for tugging on a piece of her hair. "See you in the morning. Sleep well," he said. She opened the door.

"Goodnight," she told him softly, smiling at him until the door shut. He jogged to his truck and drove the short distance home.

He told his parents he was back, assured them that Eliza and Alan were doing great, as were Helda and Jackson, and went to bed. His dreams were full of his beautiful, *merciful* Jessi and what the future might hold for them.

Thirty

Jessi pushed a small pack of tissues into her purse and zipped it shut – Hannah would need them. She paused in front of her mirror and fixed a piece of hair that was out of place. She smoothed her hand over her knee-length black dress. It had a strip of tight, decorative white trim around the strapless top and a wide white ribbon around the fitted waist. She wore a delicate, black choker necklace and matching earrings. She sprayed on an excess of perfume and hurried out of her room.

"Mom! Are you ready?" she called, slipping her heels on as she went. Carla was waiting by the front door, and they rode to the high school together. When they had pressed their way through the mass of people to get into the gym, she searched the crowd for several minutes without locating the Colbys. Kara had been watching for them, though, and stood up and waved until she caught Jessi's attention. Jessi and Carla hurried down the stairs and pushed their way past a full row of nicely dressed people.

Graduation day was a big event in Glendale. Almost everyone knew someone who was graduating. The gym was already getting hot, and people were using their bulletins as fans. The janitor was opening the exit doors, hoping for a breeze. Jessi dropped into the empty seat beside Kara.

"Hello, ladies!" Kara said in greeting. Carla and Jessi both returned the greeting, smiling at the pixie-faced blonde.

Jessica leaned around Kara as Kaitlynn cried, "Jessi! How are you, Hon?" Kaitlynn's fiancé, Jake, stood as Kaitlynn leaned across Kara's lap to embrace Jessica. Jake shook Jessi's hand and offered a smile.

"Jessica, you look stunning! I love your dress!" Kimberly said from her seat on the other side of Jake. She was holding Carson on her lap. Greg was holding their new baby, Samuel. The infant's skin was still red and wrinkled. Jessi smiled.

"Thanks. I like yours, too. You look great! How are the

kids?" Jessi asked.

Kimmy ran her hand over Samuel's tiny head and smiled. "Growing like bad weeds!" Carson grinned, showing his new white teeth.

"Hello, Sweetie!" Hannah called out from the other end of the line of family. Jessi waved, and Chris winked at her.

The band began to play, and everyone settled down, a hush falling over the crowd. The graduates marched in to traditional music, and cameras flashed. Jessi took pictures, zooming in on the most handsome boy in the group. Joe was all grins in his black cap and gown. His tassel was gold, and it dangled off the side of his cap. He looked up at his family and smiled at them as they took his picture. The graduates sat, and Joe went forward to give his valedictorian speech. It was an amazing speech and instantly brought tears to Hannah's eyes.

"Well, Mom made it almost five minutes," Kara whispered to Jessi with a smile. Jessi pulled the tissues from her purse, and they passed them down the line. Hannah accepted them with a grateful sniff, then leaned out to mouth a thank-you to Jessi.

When Joe finished his speech, the entire crowd burst into applause. Greg let out a shrill whistle, and Kimmy clapped Carson's hands, bouncing the little boy on her knee. Joe took his seat, and the awarded scholarships were read.

Next, the salutatorian gave her speech. She had a nice speech too, but Jessi didn't think it was anything like Joe's. The band played another song. Then, a small group of honor choir students sang a song. It sounded beautiful but was slightly marred for Jessi as Heather was sharing music with Joe. She felt a small twinge of jealousy, but forgot about it when Joe took his seat.

When he crossed the stage to receive his diploma from the superintendent, Jessi was so proud she felt as if she might explode with joy. Hannah and Kaitlynn used up her package of tissues. Kimmy used her nursing blanket to wipe her tears, and Kara used the back of her hand. Jessica couldn't stop smiling. He was amazing. He was handsome, gentle, honest, committed to excellence, and intelligent. She couldn't ask for anything more.

The family moved as a group when they went to find Joe after the ceremony. When they found him, he hugged every member of his family and kissed the girls on the cheek. A grin stretched across his face as he hugged Jessi, lifting her off her feet, giving her a quick twirl. She laughed.

"You did it, Joseph Colby! You graduated!" she said. He gave her a quick kiss, his green eyes shining into hers.

The graduation party was fun and crazy. Jessi was pulled in what seemed like a hundred different directions by friends, Joe, and Joe's immediate family. Many of the Colbys' extended family and friends were in town for the graduation, and Jessi was being introduced every time she turned around.

She helped Kaitlynn serve cake until she was pulled away as Hannah introduced her to great-aunt Thelma. When she escaped from that conversation, she served punch with Kara until Kimmy came to introduce her to family friends, Janice and Larry. Joe pulled her from that conversation to introduce her to his cousin, Garrett. Eliza and Alan were there, and Jessi finally settled down at a table with them, thankful to have a chance to eat her chocolate cake with white frosting while discussing the latest bill that Alan signed.

Joe and Jessi were both exhausted as he swung her hand and walked her to her front door that night. The party had lasted until after eight, and Jessi had stayed to help clean up. Joe had driven her home, but the ride was quiet, both of them talked out.

Joe steered her toward the porch swing and they sat. She kicked off her heels and curled up against his side. He draped his arm across her shoulders and rocked the swing with his foot. They just sat there for a long time.

"I'm proud of you. So proud," Jessi finally said, resting her hand against his chest and looking up at him. His head was tipped back, his eyes closed, but he grinned.

"It was a fun day – one that I've looked forward to my entire life." Jessi ran her hand down the side of his face.

"Your speech was amazing."

"I stuttered a little in the middle."

"It wasn't even noticeable," she assured. He opened his eyes and kissed her.

"You're so perfect, Jess," he told her. "I love how encouraging you are." She smiled at him.

"I'm only telling you the truth," she answered adoringly. He pulled her close and was about to say something else when his cell phone rang.

It was his mom. Kim and Greg wanted him to open gifts before they had to leave, and they were leaving first thing in the morning. He hung up.

"Want to come, Love?" he asked. Jessi thought about it and shook her head.

"I think I'll stay here and maybe go to bed. I just got really sleepy."

"Are you sure?" he asked, tracing the line of her eyebrow. She nodded. He kissed the tip of her nose.

"Okay. Goodnight, then."

"Goodnight," she answered. He stood up to leave. "Joe?" He turned. "Congratulations," she told him with a sleepy smile.

He grinned. "Thanks." He left, and she uncurled her legs and picked up her shoes. She went into the house and checked on her mom. She was sleeping soundly in her bed. Jessi got a drink of water and went to bed as well. Graduation was over, and her boyfriend was no longer in high school.

Thirty-One

On the first day of summer vacation, Joe took Jessi to a swimming hole at the river. He came for her early, and they hiked to the spot. With the warm late May sun shining down on them, Joe set aside the picnic he had packed, and they went swimming, jumping in from a rock that stood several feet above the water.

Jessica swam through the quiet cove and came up when she could touch. As the water became shallower, she found herself in more of a current.

The main river bubbled over a shallow granite riverbed, sounding like music as it flowed downhill. The current was strong right in the middle, and that is where she stood, the water no deeper than the middle of her shins, watching the glistening stream part as it went around her legs. Although the deep swimming hole was shady, the sun shone bright over the main river channel.

She watched the water sparkle as it passed and little minnows glint silver as they swam closer to the bank. Water splashed rapidly from a ten-foot waterfall, adding its lovely cadence to the serenity of the place. The trees on the banks were tall, and their new leaves were fresh and green. Small purple flowers sprinkled the banks of the river, and the water cooled the air. It was quiet and calm, and Jessi closed her eyes, breathing deeply. The forest around her smelled moist and earthy, the warm scent seeming to linger in her airways.

Joe stood off to the side, watching, his arms crossed over his chest. She was beautiful. Beads of water glistened on her skin, and the spray of the waterfall sent dancing rainbows down around her, making her look like some princess of the forest. He smiled tenderly as he tried to memorize the picture.

The look of pure innocence and peace that filled her face was something so precious that if he were a painter, he would spend a lifetime trying to capture it on canvas. But he wasn't a painter, just a common farm boy, so he stood and attempted to commit it to memory.

She stood still and quiet for a long time, and Joe took the opportunity to pray. His prayer was full of praise. He praised God for the life He had given him, for the place he called home, for the river that watered the land, for the beauty that encompassed it, for the beautiful day, and for the girl who stood shin-deep in the water. His prayer subtly shifted from one of praise to pleading. He prayed for faith, for self-control, for the strength to flee temptation, but mostly for Jessi.

In any other setting, in any other place than this river, she was in turmoil. He saw her struggle every day. He saw her fight for peace, love, and belonging. He saw her grasp after things of the world when what she deeply desired was something unearthly. It made him hurt for her. She was so unhappy and as much as he tried to offer her a solution, he secretly knew he wasn't getting anywhere. He told his parents, Rob and his friends that he thought she was getting closer to making a commitment to follow Christ and denied it when they said that the only thing she was learning to worship was him. But deep down, he knew it was true. It made him feel desperate to get through to her.

He was Joe Colby. He was the devoted one of his youth group. He was going to be a pastor. He should know how to help her. He had been to evangelism conferences, had done a study on how to reach the unsaved and yet, when he needed it most – when it was his own *girlfriend* – he was unsuccessful at showing her Jesus.

He just needed more time. Just a little more time. And so that was what he prayed for most of all. More time with Jessi. He had to hold on to her just a little longer. Soon, she would come to Jesus and then they could get married. She could work alongside him, and they could truly become one. It would all happen, he just needed more time.

~~~~~

As the summer went on, Bill Cordel became more and more insistent that Jessi come home to D.C. Weary of the fighting and assuming there was no way she could hire someone who could actually contend with Bill's attorney, Carla withdrew. Instead of fighting, she drank wine.

Jessi didn't blame her. Up against Bill, Carla was powerless

– there was nothing she could do. Her extensive knowledge of environmental law would be useless in a custody battle. Still, Jessi clung to the hope that it would all blow over, that her dad would realize he would much rather have his life with Jari and leave Jessica alone.

On June twentieth, the very thing she feared most, happened. When she checked her voicemail after returning from swimming with Tacy and Kara, she heard the words she had been dreading. "Jessica, it's Dad. I'm calling to let you know that I went back before the judge today. Your mother is no longer a suitable caregiver for you, so I petitioned for custody. He granted me full custody of you starting July first. You're coming home, Sweetheart. Call me when you get this exciting news!"

Jessica dropped the phone as the message ended, her eyes wide, her stomach churning. She closed her eyes slowly and sat perfectly still for a moment.

Could he be serious? He must have pulled some strings. There was no logical reason her mother should have been deemed an unsuitable caregiver.

She retrieved her phone from the floor and punched in a number. "Hello?"

"Joe, you need to come over right now."

There was no hesitation. "I'll be there in a minute." She met him at the front door, and he lifted her off her feet and into his arms. He pressed a hard kiss against her lips. "You scared me. I thought something was wrong," he told her with a tender smile.

"Something is wrong." Her pupils were dilated, and her face pale. His eyebrows drew together.

"What?" She dialed her voicemail and held the phone out to him. She watched his expression change throughout the message. "Jessi," he said softly, as he hung up and hooked a piece of dark hair behind her ear.

"What are we going to do?" she asked, biting her lip.

"Call your dad." She nodded and dialed.

Joe led her to the couch and drew her down beside him. The phone rang four times before Bill answered. "Hello?"

"Dad?"

"Jessica, did you get my message?"

"Yes."

"What do you think, Honey?" Bill asked, sounding jubilant. Joe squeezed her hand.

"Dad, that's not going to work for me."

"What do you mean that's not going to work for you?"

"I mean it is not going to work. I have a life here, Dad. A good one – a life that I don't want to leave."

"Well, you can have a life here."

"I have to finish school."

"You can finish school here."

"Dad, all of my friends are here."

"You can make new friends here," he answered, his voice smooth.

"I can't leave!" she cried, her voice rising.

"Isn't this really about Joe, Jessica?" he asked, his tone condescending.

"Yes, it is. I'm not leaving him!" Jessi vowed. Joe rested his forehead against her shoulder as his mind raced, trying to make sense of what was happening.

"Actually, you are. I have a court order."

"Dad, you can't make me do this."

"I can, and I will. End of discussion. Now I have a meeting to attend. I expect to see you on July first. I'll email you your plane ticket."

"Dad, no. We're not done!" Bill hung up, and Jessi sat dumbfounded for a moment. Silence settled over the house, and Jessi's chin dropped to rest against her chest.

"Any chance he would let me marry you right now?" Joe asked, hopeful.

"None."

Joe shrugged. "Okay, I'll just switch schools."

"No! Joe, you have a full ride at the University!"

"I don't care. I want to be close to you." Jessi shook her head.

"You would be spending thousands of dollars to be close to me for a year. Probably more. You can't do that! We're going to need that money when we get married. We could use it for a down payment on a house," she reasoned. She didn't want him changing his plans for her. Her reasoning hit its mark.

"Do you think he would reconsider?"

"No," Jessi whispered, her voice sounding hopeless. If her dad had convinced the judge, there was nothing left to do other than to go. "If worst comes to worst, it will only be for a year. We'll be together as soon as I'm eighteen," she told Joe, running her hand up through his hair.

He shook his head. "A year is too long. I'll die without you." She kissed him softly.

That night, Joe and Jessi told Carla the news together. She cried, she ranted and she raved. She called Bill and yelled obscenities at him. And when nothing worked, she poured herself a glass of wine and downed it in one swallow. The next day, Joe called and asked for Jessi's hand in marriage. Bill said no.

Carla drank, Jessi cried, and Joe prayed. The first day of July grew closer and closer. Jessi called and fought with her dad every day. Joe attempted to plead her case more than once. Carla yelled at Bill every night. Jessi received her e-ticket.

The day before she was to leave, a hard knock came on the front door. Jessi climbed off of her bed and stretched her arms above her head. She had just gotten home from swimming with Kara, and she felt warm and lazy. The knock came again, and she abandoned her book to walk down the hall. The knock came a third time, and she called, "I'm coming, hold on!"

She opened the door, and Joe stepped in as she did. His green eyes were dark and smoldering. The air around him sizzled as he pulled her to him and kissed her hard. She touched her lips softly when he drew back and looked at him questioningly.

"Come on, let's go," he said, taking her hand.

"Go where?" she asked as he pulled her out the front door. He pulled the door shut and stayed a step ahead of her all the way to his truck. The truck was on, in reverse, and backing down the drive before she could ask any more questions. "What's the hurry?" she asked as he turned onto the gravel road.

"Your flight is supposed to leave in sixteen hours." She grew quiet and her eyes fell to her lap.

"Yeah." He reached over and grabbed her hand, intertwining his fingers with hers.

"You won't be on it."

"Joe, we've been over this so many times – I have no choice. We've exhausted all our options. If I don't take this flight, he'll just get mad and book another one. I'll be forced to go – he has a court order." Jessi's voice was weary and empty. She didn't have the strength to come up with any more plans.

Joe was quiet, but his eyes were filled with fiery intensity. "He can't take you from me." She let out a bitter laugh.

"Actually, he can, and he's bound and determined that he will."

Joe turned onto the dirt road leading to the river, taking the corner a little fast. She braced herself with her hand on the dash. Dust rolled up around the pickup, and the clouds in the west were dark.

"Think there will be rain tonight?" she asked, changing the subject, considering the billowing storm clouds.

"We'll see," he answered, his voice distant.

"What's the blanket for?" she asked, noticing the item that sat on the seat between them.

"You'll see," he answered firmly.

She fell quiet, thinking about his distance and the plane ticket she had printed out. In twenty-four hours she would be in her old house with her dad and Jari. She would be facing an entire year without her mom, Grandma, Kara, Tacy, Chris, Hannah, and most importantly, Joe. The coming year seemed like an eternity. Why was he being so distant and aloof now, on their very last night together?

He parked and killed the engine.

"Are we going fishing?" she asked. He grabbed the blanket and carefully pulled her across the seat and out his door. He took her hand and walked down the trail to the place where they usually put their chairs to fish. It was where they had stood on their first date, the same river rushing along with its magical silver sound, the same tall trees, the same fragile, small purple flowers. It was then, in that spot, that she realized the force that made his eyes smolder was determination mixed with passion. The result could be dangerous.

She stood back as he shook out the blanket and let it settle on the ground. He came to her and slipped his hands beneath her shirt.

"Joe, what are you doing?" she asked, studying his face.

"I have an idea," he told her, and pulled her shirt over her head.

"What's your idea?" she asked, covering her chest with her arms modestly. He let her shirt fall to the ground, peeled his own off over his head, and dropped it on top of hers. He smiled curiously as he gently pulled her arms away. She struggled against his strong hands. "Joe, you don't want to do this."

"If you're pregnant, your dad can't separate us." Her face fell.

"Joe, no." Her protest drew a frown. "What about your dream?" she continued, not wanting to displease him. He shook his head.

"We'll be a family, Jess – you, me, and the baby. We'll worry about dreams and school and jobs later, but the important thing is, we'll be together." She shook her head.

"I can't let you do this. What about your faith?" Anger snapped in his eyes.

"I don't care," he told her and kissed her hard. "I love you, Jessica Nicole Cordel, and I won't let anyone take you away from me, not even God."

The cool breeze sifted over their bare backs, causing them both to shiver. "I'll be okay," she said weakly in a last ditch effort to save him from himself. His eyes fastened on hers, and she saw down into his soul where he was desperate and in pain. A lone tear slipped down his cheek.

"I won't be."

Her lip quivered as she kissed his tear away.

"Let me love you," he begged. "I want to do this. I need to do this," he told her, his voice imploring. She wanted to give in, but she couldn't. Not yet.

"Joe?" He didn't answer. "Joe?"

"Hm?" he finally asked, trailing kisses down her neck.

"Joe?" she asked again, waiting for his full attention.

"What?"

"Are you sure?" she asked just once more.

He took her face in his hands and looked deep into her blue eyes. "I'm sure I can't live without you." Her resolve faltered, and she buried her hands in his hair.

"Okay," she whispered softly.

Thirty-Two

Jessi woke up abruptly, and her eyes flew open. She looked around her room where the darkness still made shadows in the corners, then out the window where she could see color peeking out above the trees, a sure sign that the morning sun was coming. Stretching, her eyes fell on the sleeping boy beside her. The memories of the night before came back sweetly.

Her heart warmed and softened at the sight of Joe sleeping beside her, and some emotion deeper and stronger than she had ever felt, surged through her. She smiled as she recognized it as love. She loved him. She really did.

"Then leave." It was the quietest voice she had ever heard, and she wasn't even sure she had heard it. It was more like the words had just been heard by her heart. She dismissed it as a crazy thought.

Why would she leave? She loved Joe, and he loved her. Things felt more perfect to her than they ever had before. Still, when she closed her eyes, she saw his face as it had been last night. For the briefest of instances, when he had given in to pleasure, she had seen a look in his eyes that would haunt her forever – intense guilt and pain. It had only lasted a moment, and then his eyes had filled with adoration, joy and great excitement once again. But she was unable to shake the memory of that look now, not even when she cuddled close to him, trying to remember the wonderful events of the night. Her mind started to race.

What if Joe was right? What if she was pregnant? What if she wasn't? He would marry her, she knew he would. Then he would be trying to get through college and play football with a wife and maybe a baby. When he went to seminary and studied to be a pastor, would people put together the birth of their first child and how long they had been married? Would they let him be a pastor when he had fathered a child out of wedlock? Would she end up keeping him from achieving all that he desired? Would she end up holding him back? Would she become chains around his ankles? Would he be happy? Is that the kind of life he wanted? He would never complain,

274

she knew he wouldn't, but the thought of holding him back, of being a source of discontentment in his life, was something she couldn't bear.

She started thinking about Joe's God. Joe loved Him. She knew he did. More than he loved anything or anyone else...or at least it had started that way. She had seen that powerful love when she first met him, and it had been a challenge to her. She hadn't understood it, and had been determined to become the object of such passionate devotion.

Now, as she watched him sleep peacefully in her bed, she had a thought that filled her with an indescribable sorrow. Had she won? Had he sacrificed his morals, his convictions – the very core of who he was – for her? It had been happening for weeks, for months, and she knew it. There had been so many moments that she had seen him hesitate. At first, she had pushed him to make a decision that she wanted. Over the summer, she realized that she was no longer pressuring him to make decisions that were against what he believed in. He was making those choices himself in hopes of pleasing her, of winning her.

It had culminated last night. Even when she had protested, hoping to save him from himself, he had pressed on until he had done the one thing he had promised not to do until his wedding night.

She thought she would have been happy that she had become the center of Joe's universe, the one he sacrificed all for. Instead, she felt so heavy and full of pain that it was a real, physical thing. She had a hard time even filling her lungs with air.

Joe had made a declaration last night of where he stood, of whom he served, and Jessi was filled with unexpected dread. Would the One whom he had loved so passionately, now forever scorn Joe? Would He turn His back? Would He reject him? Would He refuse him all of his hopes and dreams? Did Joe have anything left? Did he still love the One he called the Lover of his soul, or would Jessi remain at the center of his life – his reason for living? Pressure swelled within her chest until she could barely drag in a breath.

She let out a soft, strangled cry as the pain overwhelmed her, and she covered her mouth with her hand to keep from waking Joe. She knew what she had to do. Perhaps it was that strong love that filled her every time she looked at him or thought about him. Perhaps it was the fear that she had ruined everything for him – that she had taken everything he held dear. Or perhaps it had been that quiet voice that had come from nowhere and seemed to have no source. Whatever drove her to the conclusion, she knew without a doubt that, as hard as it would be, because she loved him, she had to leave.

The realization terrified her. She didn't know if she could live without Joe Colby. She snuggled in closer to him and let his body warm her.

Over the last year, he had changed her. He had become her everything. She remembered days by what she had done with him. She counted success by his smile. She motivated herself with a promise of him. Now, with the reality of her coming departure settling over her, her life stretched out bleak and lifeless before her. Without Joe Colby, all the hope, all the joy she had only begun to let herself feel, would be gone.

Suddenly, she felt wetness on her face and realized she was crying. Though she desperately tried to tell herself that it wouldn't be forever, she knew that this was goodbye.

About an hour later, when the sky was lit up with brilliant strokes of orange and pink, as if a painter had been sitting before a blank canvas and had erupted with a beautiful picture, she climbed carefully out of bed and showered and dressed. She quietly packed the few clothes she had left out and her snow globe, zipped her suitcase and took it out to the car. When she came back in, her mom was standing at the kitchen counter making coffee.

Jessi motioned to her to be quiet, and Carla tilted her head and studied her with hard eyes. "Why is Joe's truck here?"

"He stayed the night," Jessi replied quietly.

Carla stared at her for a long moment. "Did you guys sleep together last night?"

Jessi couldn't tell if her mom was angry or just sad. Jessi let out a deep breath. "Mom, can you put your coffee in a to-go mug? I need you to take me to the airport." Now the look on Carla's face was undeniable – pure shock.

"You're going? Just like that? No fighting, no pouting, no trying to get out of it?" Jessi's eyes filled with tears again, and she drew in a deep breath.

"No. I have to go."

Carla's eyes filled with tears, too, and she quickly nodded and turned away. "You're right. You'll never win against your dad long-distance. It's better to go and argue in person." Jessi nodded, but she knew that even if Bill Cordel changed his mind, she couldn't come back.

While Carla got her coffee ready and dressed, Jessi sat down at the table and wrote a note.

My amazing Joseph,

I don't know what to say to you other than you've changed me in every way that a girl can be changed. You've made me feel alive, like life is something to be cherished, not endured. You've made me realize that love is beautiful and sweet and strong and rare and un-selfish.

Be a pastor, Joe. Be the best pastor in the whole world – you have the ability to change people and change hearts – don't let anything mess up your opportunity!

I have to go, and even if you don't understand it now, you will. This has been the best year of my life.

Goodbye, Joe.

All of my love,
Jessi

When she finished, she read it again and then again. Suddenly, she picked it up and tore it into pieces. If she left that, he would come after her. He would never let her go. It had to be a clean break. Whatever he thought of her, whatever he thought her reason for leaving, she couldn't leave that note.

Again, she was filled with sorrow, knowing that he wouldn't understand, thinking of what he might assume about her reason for leaving. She quietly stepped down the hall and cracked her bedroom door just enough to look at him. She hoped that somehow he would know how he had changed her, what he had taught her. She hoped he would know how he had taught her to love, how he had made that very word change from something ugly into something beautiful. She hoped he would know how he had changed her entire life. She hoped he would know how much she truly loved him. She turned and walked down the hallway and out the front door to her mom's car without looking back.

Jessi didn't say a word, but cried silently as they backed down the drive. She watched the little cottage grow distant and felt her heart breaking. Lying inside of it in the back bedroom was the man that her entire world had revolved around for a year – the best year of her life – the year that had changed her entire existence. And she was driving away.

"You okay?" Carla asked, reaching out and holding Jessi's cold hand. Jessica looked at her, her eyes full of so much pain that Carla felt as if they were ripping her heart out.

"No. No, Mom, I'm not." Carla kissed the back of her hand.

"I'm sorry, Baby. I really am. I don't know what to do." Carla started to cry softly.

"There's nothing you can do," Jessi answered.

"It's only for a year, Jess – just remember that. In a year you can go wherever you want. You'll have the freedom you've always wanted."

Jessi thought about the freedom she had always wanted, and realized she didn't want it anymore. She wanted roots. She wanted love. She wanted belonging. She wanted people in her life who cared enough about her to have expectations and boundaries. But what she wanted didn't matter. Not before, not now.

Except now the reasons were different. Before, no one had cared what she wanted; now, she cared so much for another that her own wants paled in comparison to his needs.

Jessi stared out the window, her face set. She looked longingly at the Colbys' house as they drove by. She stared down the road that led to the river. She watched as they passed all of the small businesses as they went through town. She stared at GHS and the football field. She turned and stared at Grandma's house. She watched the 'Come Back Soon' sign as they drove past it. Her heart sank. She would never be coming back.

They were both quiet all the way to the airport. Carla parked, and together they lugged Jessi's two bags to the check-in desk.

"I'll send the rest of your boxes through the mail," Carla offered. Jessi nodded.

The airline worker checked her bags, and her mom walked her through the small airport, holding her hand as if Jessi was still a little girl. Not wanting to say goodbye yet, Carla and Jessi sought out a quiet table at an airport restaurant for breakfast. Neither of them ate a bite or said a word.

Finally, Jessi broke the silence. "Well, I'd better go; it's time to board."

Carla threw their untouched breakfast in the trash, then took Jessi's hand again and walked her to her gate. They were just in time.

Carla put her hands on Jessi's shoulders and searched her face. "Jess," she paused as if she couldn't get out what she wanted to say. She finally took a deep breath. "I wrote you a letter." Jessica took the envelope in surprise. She ran her fingertip over the beautiful handwriting on the front. "Promise me you won't read it until you're alone in your room tonight." Jessi nodded, her throat too tight to talk.

A few tears rolled down Carla's cheeks, and she said, "Come here." She pressed her lips into a tight line and pulled Jessi into a hug. Jessica clung to her, burying her face in her mom's hair. The stewardess announced the last call to board, and Jessi had to go.

"I love you, Mom," she said, tears running down her cheeks. Carla pressed her lips together, and nodded until she had enough control to speak.

"I love you too, Baby Girl." She kissed Jessica's cheek and gave her one last hug. She walked Jessi to the gate, then tapped her on the behind as she went through. "Tell Kayly and Anna hello for me." Jessi just nodded, and walked down the tunnel, her vision blurred with tears, each step feeling like a struggle she wasn't nearly strong enough to take.

She scooted past two older men into her window seat and closed her eyes. She opened them as they started to taxi away from the airport. Her hands flew to the small window, and she stared in disbelief as she watched Joe run up to her mom, ask something, then look at the plane.

She could see his heart sink, even from a distance. He looked like a balloon that had been deflated. He ran and almost bounced off the glass of the airport window, his palms flat against it. As the plane backed up, he started to beat on the window with his fists, and Jessi watched, sobbing, as she saw her mom try to comfort him. Joe stopped pounding on the glass, but kept his hands against it, staring at the plane. The sun sparkled on his tears, and she watched, tears running off her own face, until she couldn't see him anymore.

The man beside her handed her a tissue, and she took it without a word. She brought her knees up to her chest, buried her face against them, and didn't stop crying until they were landing.

In D.C., she stood, stiff and cool, and walked off the plane. She didn't speak to her dad or Jari, and when her dad tried to give her a hug, she held her arm out straight to stop him. He stood and stared at her for a long moment, and Jari glanced between the two of them nervously.

Jessica met Bill's eyes, and with a cold, hard voice she said, "You ripped my heart out today and dropped it from an airplane. Don't expect me to be glad to see you." With that, she walked to baggage claim, grabbed her suitcases and carried them herself to the car that was waiting for them.

She didn't say anything all the way home. Upon arriving, she went straight to her old room where she shut and locked the door. She dropped her bags on the floor and sat in her egg chair to read her mom's letter.

My sweet daughter,

If anyone had told me I was going to address you like that a year ago, I never would have believed them. But now, with the lady you have become, I can't call you anything else.

You have changed in a way I can't even start to describe, Jessi. I am so proud of you. I want to tell you that I am so glad for this past year in Glendale – I feel as if I've gotten to know you. I will never forget the dinners, the sun bathing, the fishing trip, the fair, the holidays, the late-night movies, or anything else about it. Those memories bring a joy to my heart that will make it glow for centuries. I may not always be perfect, Jess, but I love you, and you are the most important thing in the world to me.

Baby Girl, I ask you now not to hate your father. Your heart is too soft to let it fill with that again. He has done horrible things and you have every right to hate him, but don't do it. It will eat you alive – as it is eating me. You're better than that, Jess, stronger than that. Don't let your heart grow hard again.

And I ask that you return to me soon. I love you and I miss you. You have become the reason that I breathe, the reason that I eat, the reason that I get out of bed, the reason that I go to bed in the first place. You are my motivation, and I can't wait to see how you grow and change in the years to come.

After so many years, I finally feel as if I know fully what people mean when they talk about the strength of a mother's love.

I look forward to your high school graduation, your college years, your wedding, the birth of your first child, and all of the beautiful moments that follow. And even though we can't be together right now, know that no matter where I am or where you are, I am with you in heart and spirit.

Remember what you've learned in the past year, remember who you are, and don't be afraid to let people see it. You are truly an amazing girl with incredible potential. I love you and I miss you. I'll see you soon.

Loving you always,
Mom

Jessica held her hand to her mouth to keep a sob in and read the letter again. The emotion that had been poured into her mom's words made her heart ache and tears stream from her eyes.

The last time she had been in her bedroom, she never would have imagined she could feel so deeply while reading a letter from her mom. But now, all she wanted to do was run back to Glendale and leap into her mother's arms.

She heard her cell phone ringing in the living room and was thankful that her dad had taken it away – it was Joe's ring. She opened her suitcase to get out a pair of pajamas. She wasn't in the mood to do anything but go to bed and try to escape the pain pressing in against her.

The first thing she noticed was that her clothes were wet. She pulled back the first few shirts, and let out a short sobbing breath as she uncovered the source. The glass of her snow globe had broken. The sparkles and the glass lay in little piles on her damp clothing.

It was painfully fitting. As she stared at it, she saw herself in that globe – her dreams, her life, her heart – they were shattered and lying empty and exposed, in a hundred jagged pieces – pieces that could never be put back together. She crawled onto her bed, pulled a blanket over herself, curled up, and cried herself to sleep.

Thirty-Three

Hannah heard the front door slam, and she cringed. She had spent half the night and the entire morning hoping that what she thought had happened, hadn't. When her only son walked into the kitchen, she knew it had.

Joe's face was red and had tear marks on it, looking much like it had when he was a child. In his green eyes was a raw mix of intense anger and deep shame.

He threw up his hands. "She's gone."

"Jessica?" she asked. He nodded and slumped into a chair, putting his head in his hands.

"I don't understand why she left. Why would she leave? Why would she do this? I had a plan all figured out! I told her how she could stay, and she didn't choose to!" He looked up at Hannah, his whole face angry now. "No, you know what, Mom? She wanted to go. She wanted to! She got what she wanted – what she had always wanted – and now there was no reason to stay. It's exactly what I thought. I was a game to her – a challenge. She won and that's that."

Hannah put her hand out to touch his arm, but he shrugged it off and stood up. He slammed the chair against the table as he pushed it in.

"I was so stupid. What was I thinking? I knew I shouldn't have dated her. She was exactly what everyone said she was."

"Joe!" Hannah said, shocked to hear her tender son speak so harshly of someone else – especially Jessi.

He turned and stalked out of the room without another word, and Hannah slowly sank into a chair and began to cry. She couldn't sort out which tears were for Jessi, and which tears were for her only son.

When he had not come home, she had stayed up most of the night calling him and praying. She had feared that he had made a decision that was against everything he knew was right, yet she had expected one of two things. She had expected that either Joe would come home with a perfectly legitimate excuse and they would talk about keeping her better informed next time, or that he had indeed stayed the night with Jessi, and he would come home broken, ashamed and repentant. But neither scenario was true. He had definitely spent the night with Jessi, but he was neither ashamed nor repentant – only angry.

As a mother, her heart broke – both for Joe and for Jessi. Hannah knew Jessi. She knew her heart and how much she loved Joe. In D.C. there was a young girl whose heart was broken – of that she was sure. Joe was too blinded by his own anger to realize that Jessi had likely left in hopes of saving him from himself.

Hannah had seen the path they were taking leading to disaster for a long time, but as parents, she and Chris had done all they could to offer their advice, direction and wise council to their son. In the end, he had to make his own decisions. Unfortunately, he had made a very bad one, and her heart ached for him. Maybe he didn't realize it now, but down the road, she was confident that he would regret that one night like he would never regret anything else. Not only had he lost his girlfriend, but he had also lost something he could never get back – his innocence.

She would call Chris later and give him the update she knew he had been dreading all morning, but for now, all she could do was let her forehead sink to the table and pray – pray for Jessi, pray for Joe, pray for their family, pray for open eyes and repentant hearts. She prayed that the very act that had taken Jessi away from Joe, wouldn't take Joe away from Jesus.

~~~~~

Over the next month, Joe slowly started to improve. He carried on with youth group and his other summer activities. He prepared to go off to college, and he worked during the week. On the outside everything looked fine, but Hannah was worried about him. He was lack-luster. All of his spunk, all of his spirit, was gone. Underneath his calm exterior, he was still angry; he didn't understand.

She hadn't seen him pick up his Bible or have quiet time since before Jessi left. Whether or not things looked okay, whether or not anyone but her, Chris and Joe knew the truth, she knew that things were far from being alright. She spent her time in constant prayer for him, imploring the LORD to pursue him and bring him to the cross once again.

Joe called Jessi constantly, and his frustration, anger, and despair grew every time he reached her voicemail. It was after one of those times that Hannah cleared her throat and went somewhere she hadn't yet had the courage to go.

"Maybe the fault was not all hers, Dear." Joe looked up at his mom after he closed his cell phone.

"I never said it was."

"You say that you serve God, but you have forsaken Him for another."

"No, I would never do that."

"Joe, don't you see? You made her your goddess – you worshipped the ground she walked on, Son. You still do," she said as gently as she could.

"That's not true!"

"Isn't it?" she asked softly, laying her dishcloth down on the counter.

"No! It's not!" he told her, his reply quick and angry. Hannah rested her hip against the counter and smiled sadly at him.

"I make dinner for your dad and you kids every night. It's something I promised your father I would do a long time ago – that I would serve him by putting a meal on the table every night," she only paused to toss her dishcloth into the sink. "What if I went into the house of another man and I began to put all of my energy into serving him and his children. Would I still be serving my husband?"

"Why are you saying this to me?" Joe demanded, his face screwed up in pain.

Hannah felt her heart ripping as she watched her son. He was in so much pain, enough that it was clouding the judgment and wisdom that he had always possessed.

"Jessi isn't the only one who needs to come to Jesus, Joe."

"I don't need this lecture right now, okay?" he said, his voice angry. She shook her head sadly, but pressed on.

"I know that you are hurting, Son, but remember your first love. It wasn't a blue-eyed girl, it was a nail-torn man." Joe turned and stalked out of the kitchen, knocking a chair over as he did. Hannah wiped at her unwelcome tears and offered up another silent plea as she went to right the chair.

~~~~~

Joe stormed out of the house, slamming the back door behind him. He decided to walk out his frustration and kicked at the forest floor as he went. Eventually, he found himself at his Jesus tree – a place he hadn't been in weeks.

He paced back and forth in front of it, talking out the whole situation, words of anger pouring out of his mouth – anger at Jessi, at himself, at God. He paced back and forth, back and forth, his steps heavy. So many emotions were raging within him that he felt like he would erupt.

Finally, he stopped and stood absolutely still, breathing fast and staring at the tree. It was as steady and faithful as the first day he had found it. He stared at the place he had so often sat with Jessi, stared at the initials carved into the trunk, stared up into the big green canopy of leaves.

"God, why?" he suddenly shouted, kicking at the ground, making dirt spray. "Why take her away? Were you so mad at me for having sex with her that You took her away? Was that Your judgment, Your consequence for what I did? Why did You even bring her here? Why put her in my life? Why make me love her? Why give us this year together if you were only going to rip her away? You knew what would happen! Was it all to test me? I failed! Is that what You want me to say? I failed! I wasn't strong enough! And now You ripped her away, because I wasn't strong enough! Is that it?" Joe balled his fists, his eyes squeezed shut, unable to say anything more.

For the first time since the day Jessica left, tears came and they ran down his face, hot on his cheeks, falling to the ground one after another.

In the silence that followed, as he stood in the hot forest crying, he heard a quiet, still voice that he hadn't heard in months, yet the words were crystal clear as they washed over his heart. *"You shall have no other gods before me."*

"God!" Joe sank to the ground, his chest so full of pain that he could no longer stand. "I always pointed her to you. I never let her worship me. I never became her god."

After the briefest of silences, words came that were like an arrow to his heart. *"No, but Son, she became yours."*

All the air went out of Joe as if he had been hit hard in the back, and he sank down until his forehead rested on the forest floor. In the stillness that followed, he knew that the LORD was right.

As busy as he had been pointing Jessi to Jesus, he had put her on a pedestal and placed her above all other things. He had been willing to sacrifice everything for her – his hopes, his dreams, his convictions, his beliefs, his purity, even his relationship with Jesus. How long had it been since he had stopped to spend any time with the One his soul loved? The answer was, even long before that fateful night at the river.

He wept as the realization sunk in. He could finally see how far he had fallen. The dirt under his face turned to mud, and still he could not stop. His heart was breaking all over again. Not for a blue-eyed girl this time, but for a nail-torn man. A man whom he had let down. A man whom he had turned from. A man whom he had deliberately disobeyed.

"Oh God, my God! How far I've strayed from You! Bring me back! Bring me back to the companionship we used to have!" Joe cried, his hands grasping handfuls of earth. "I used to desire only You, but I've turned. I've neglected You for another! Forgive me, Father! Forgive me! Bring me back! Remind me of my first love!" Joe prayed.

Suddenly, he saw Jesus standing before him with an outstretched arm, offering His hand. He saw Him, and yet he could not respond. He did not feel worthy. Joe felt the need to wallow in his sorrow, in his shame, to pay penance. He was certain that he would have to go through at least a shameful 'time out,' that is, if the LORD would even allow him to come back at some point. But, despite the ashamed thoughts and voices that kept trying to convince him that there was no way Jesus could forgive him and welcome him back so quickly, the Jewish man still stood there, His hand outstretched, a gentle, longing expression on his face. *"Come. Take my hand. Accept my forgiveness,"* He was saying. He stood there as a Man who still loved Joe and was offering forgiveness all over again. Just like that. There was no punishment, no time out that he had to endure – just forgiveness, mercy and grace.

Despite all that was natural, Joe reached out and took His hand, repenting and feeling his heart pierced with a sorrow so deep that a physical pain overtook him. For one brief moment, he saw his own sin and shame suddenly covering this Man in front of him who had been clothed in white, holy perfection. "No!" Joe cried out into the still forest air, his spirit unable to hold back at the sight of One so holy covered in such filth.

And then it was gone. The man was again clothed in the stunningly white clothing, and the shame, the sin was nowhere to be seen. *"You have been washed white as snow,"* the Man said, touching the top of Joe's head. *"Your sin is now as far from you as the east is from the west. I have restored you to innocence. Arise and follow Me once more. There is no shame, no condemnation for those who are in Me."*

Joe lay with his face in the damp soil for a long time, letting forgiveness wash over him, letting Jesus realign the wrong things within him, letting Jesus speak tenderly to him. He had never experienced such freedom, such forgiveness, such a nearness to the LORD. He had never known His God in this way, and Joe stayed down at His feet for a very long time.

As he worshipped face down in the dirt, Joe was filled with a new humility that came from knowing that he was weak, and that he had only been forgiven – saved – by grace.

He was not the golden boy he had grown up thinking he was. It meant nothing that he had been good his whole life, that he had gone to youth group, that he prayed and read his Bible, that he had lived rightly, that he had longed to introduce people to Jesus. As good as he had been, as good as he could ever be, he had been saved by grace and not of himself.

A religious pride that he had unknowingly wrapped around himself in a cloak of self-righteousness, had shattered. It had been replaced by a worn, plain cloak of humility, yet it settled over him sweeter than anything ever had.

Finally, when he stood, his face was marked with mud, but his heart and spirit were clean in a way they had never been. He traced the initials carved in the tree and suddenly had a memory of Jessi tracing them, just as he was doing now. He had not thought of her in several hours, and even with the guilt, the shame and even the anger gone, he stared at the initials and whispered, "Why?"

His heart had changed, but still the memory of her was raw

and carried great pain. "Did you take her away to save her?" That new thought was the most bearable explanation that he had come up with yet. But while it was bearable, it was still wrong.

With the hot summer sun beating down on him and the wind rustling the leaves far above him, he finally knew the truth – God hadn't taken Jessi away to save her. He sent her away to save Joe. In His kindness, He had sent her away. It was not His anger, not His judgment, but His mercy.

Epilogue

Five years later…

Jessi woke slowly, fighting her way out of the fog of her dreams. She rubbed her tired eyes and they felt gritty. She yawned as she pushed herself to a sitting position. She was on her black suede couch, the shades were drawn tight, and the apartment was dark and quiet.

Her mind ran over her last few hours in Kentucky, the flight home, the ride on the bus, the walk from the bus stop, and…Joe. She spun and checked the clock. It was almost four. She was suddenly nervous as she looked at the telephone. After so many years, would he call?

She grabbed her cell phone and hurried into the bathroom to take a shower. Either way, she had things she needed to do. She took a long, hot shower, then put her makeup on, did her hair, and got dressed. She was unpacking her suitcase and sorting her clothes into piles of laundry when the telephone split the silence. She reached for it with shaking hands, an odd sense of the past settling over her.

"Hello?"

"Hey! Jessi?" Her heart raced. It was a deep familiar voice that made her stomach flop.

"Yeah, this is Jessi." There was a pause.

"It's Joe."

A NOTE FROM ANN

Dear Reader,

Like many of America's young people, I come from a "broken home." Addiction, divorce, moving, changing schools, peer pressure, insecurities and self-image problems were all a part of my growing up years. Trying to figure out who I was, where I was going and what life was about felt like an uphill battle, especially as things constantly seemed to be changing around me.

Now, in my early 20s, I look back and I see God's goodness, His protection and His merciful guidance in every phase of my last two decades. I see that, with His strength, my mom – likely the strongest woman I've ever met – was able to hold things together and make life wonderful, even when circumstances were not. I see purpose in every questioning moment and every painful experience.

I can now laugh about the time I missed my chair and fell on the floor in front of the entire class my freshman year of college, the time I messed up the ending of the school melodrama with painfully good intentions, and at the pictures where my hair was a bit too big and I was a bit too chubby. Although the passing years have shed light on the reality of my youth, I'll never be too far removed to remember that they were sometimes hard, emotional, unsteady years of my life.

In the pages of this book, Jessica's story is not my story. Parts of it are similar to my story, parts are similar to what I watched friends go through, and parts are simply reflections of the lives of so many in my generation and the generation after me. Sadly, divorce, loneliness, leaving everything and everyone you know to go somewhere new, and feeling cut off from your parents is common. Dating is a game that continues to become more intense and the stakes continue to get higher. Purity and abstinence are viewed as more abnormal than the alternative, and men and women have often been with multiple others by the time they marry.

In a similar way, Joe's story is not my own; however, I had to figure out how to be pure in an impure generation, and hold true to my convictions while helping those around me who were lost and hurting. These are things my friends dealt with also, along with the rest of America's Christian youth. It's so easy to start out with good, even Godly intentions, and soon find yourself in a mess.

In high school, faced with these realities, I started dreaming about this series – a series that could capture a sliver of real life, that was entertaining, but also that people could relate to and take something from. As I wrote *Glendale* during my senior year of high school, I started to hope that this series would serve to answer questions, give a bigger perspective, bring healing or lead to an encounter with the very real God for even just one reader. Almost a decade later, as it's finally being made available to the masses, I still hope that's the case. I don't want to write just to entertain. I want to write to aid in the healing process, to give hope that an unseen God is living, breathing and speaking, to shed a different light, and to keep others from going down a road I know to end in heartache. I hope and pray that in some way this book and this series have touched your heart, entertained your mind and left you somehow different than you were before you read it.

And for those of you who are interested in delving in a bit deeper, you can visit my website for questions meant to facilitate conversations about the undercurrents of this book.

Although I love to write, I write for my readers. With that constantly in mind, I would love to hear from you. I enjoy having people stop by my website, getting emails and postal mail, hearing from you on facebook and getting to know you, so please, always feel free to drop me a note!

Until next time, may the LORD of Hosts bless you and keep you and cause His face to shine upon you!

Ann

www.anngoering.com
ann@anngoering.com
www.facebook.com/AuthorAnnGoering

LOOK FOR THESE OTHER CAPTIVATING NOVELS BY

ANN GOERING

THE GLENDALE NOVELS

The Glendale Series

Glendale

A New Day

Promising Forever

Mothers of Glendale

One Desire

Gray Area

Silver Lining

www.anngoering.com

A Special Preview of *A New Day,* Book II

Jessica Cordel stood facing her bedroom door, feeling as if it was the only thing that separated her from that which wanted to consume her, overtake her and pull her back down into the pit she had lived in for the first fifteen years of her life. In reality, the only thing on the other side of her door was her dad and step-mom.

When she had awakened that morning, it took a few moments to realize where she was and what was real. At first, she thought she was fifteen again, her mom and dad were at work, and she would have the house to herself. Then she remembered.

Her father, a senator who was always too consumed with work to have time for his family, had an affair with Jari, a young girl in his office. He had thrown Jessi and her mother out and married his new girlfriend. Jessi and her mom, Carla, had moved back to Carla's hometown and lived there a year – a year that had turned out to be a life changing, magical and remarkable year for Jessica.

After a lifetime of being lonely and consumed with an unfulfilling quest for pleasure, she had found family, belonging and depth. And she had found love. When she moved to Glendale, Joe Colby had been a challenge – the golden boy who didn't date. As the months wore on, though, he became her lifeline, her best friend and eventually, her lover.

Which, she reminded herself, was the reason she was back in her old room in D.C. When Joe had abandoned all he held dear, when he had laid aside all of his convictions, morals and dreams in a flawed plan to keep her in Glendale after her father demanded her return, she had realized just how deeply she loved him. And she realized that really loving him meant leaving Glendale and leaving him. If she had stayed, he would have given up everything he had ever wanted, and she couldn't live with that. More than anything else, she wanted him to be happy.

The knock came again, drawing her back to the present, and she warily walked over and opened the door.

"Good morning, Jessica," her dad said tightly.

"Bill," she answered, her tone dull. His eyes snapped as he looked at her, but he took a deep breath before speaking.

"Call me Dad, as you used to – and as you should."

"You don't deserve that title," she told him.

She may have returned to D.C., but that decision had nothing to do with her father's threatening demands. Her heart had softened during her year in Glendale, but now, as she looked at him, she felt the hardness coming back.

Desperate to stop it, but unsure of how to curb her wrath, she stood absolutely still, unflinching under his intense gaze. She let the indifferent facade come across her face and the numbness overtake her. She hated feeling like this, but didn't know how to be the girl she had become in Glendale back in D.C., in her father's house. Everything was different here. Those who were soft got trampled on and hurt; allowing the hardness to return was the only way to survive.

"Deserving has nothing to do with it," he answered, his voice sickeningly pleasant. "You won't call me Bill again, is that understood? Now come have breakfast with Jari and me. I have to leave for work soon."

She shook her head in disbelief. "Do you think I'm happy to see you? Do you think I want to be here? Do you realize that I had a life in Glendale – that I had friends and I *liked* it there? Why do you think I would want to come back here and live with you and your girlfriend?"

She could see that her last comment burned him. "She's my wife, Jessica!"

"Oh, that's right. Just like mom was. For how long, Bill? Are you going to wait until she gives you her youth, the best years of her life, and then trade her in on a newer model? Is that how it's going to work again?"

His face grew red. "You are grounded, young lady."

She threw up her hands. "What would I do if I wasn't? Grounding me is no punishment, Dad! My life is back in Glendale, not here in D.C."

He spun around and marched out of her room, slamming

294

her door so hard the house shook. She crossed the room and locked the door quickly, not wanting to give him the opportunity to think up a response and come back in to spew his venom at her. She sank to the floor in front of her door and started to cry. Since she had cried herself to sleep after arriving the night before, she wouldn't think she would have any more tears, but they still came.

"I chose this," she reminded herself. "I made the decision to come back here." She wished it wasn't true, but it was. She could have been lying in her bed in Glendale, her mom puttering around getting ready to leave for work down the hall. She could have gone swimming with Joe's sister Kara and gone down to the river with Joe like she had the night before last.

She remembered the look of passion in his pale green eyes – passion for her – and the shame. As she remembered the deep shame and the grief in his eyes, she felt sure that her decision had been right.

No matter how horrible her dad made life for her, no matter how much her heart ached, no matter how deeply she longed for her life in Glendale, she had made the right decision. Of that, she was sure.

Joe had forsaken his God for her and sacrificed his everything on an altar built in her name. She shook her head. She couldn't let that continue. She wasn't enough for Joe Colby.

Although she didn't know or understand his God, she knew that somehow his God was big, limitless and fulfilling. She felt small and shallow. Joe wasn't like other boys. He was different. He was more intriguing, handsome, confident, and full of purpose than anyone she had ever known. No, she would never be enough for him if she was his everything, and she couldn't bear that. She wanted him to be happy, fulfilled and content, even if that meant she had to be out of his life.

One thing was certain, though. If she was going to live back under her father's roof, she had to get rid of any softness that had crept into her heart during her time in Glendale and replace it with steel. Otherwise, she knew she would never survive.

GLENDALE SERIES

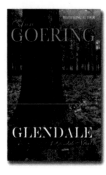  

The Glendale Series wrestles with the age-old dilemmas of love, faith, family, forgiveness and growing up in a fresh story format. With relationships that grip readers' hearts as they reflect raw realities plentiful in our society, and an ending that will keep readers on the edge of their seats right up until the end, The Glendale Series is one girl's unforgettable journey to health, wholeness and joy.

MOTHERS OF GLENDALE

The Mothers of Glendale Series tells the personal, emotional, and sometimes painful stories of three special women introduced in The Glendale Series. Glendale mother figures Jari, Carla, and Hannah are each on their own journey, with their paths weaving together with one another to create a beautiful tapestry of faith, hope, and unconditional love. With raw realities that women face every day, covered by the grace of a very big God, Mothers of Glendale takes readers a step further than new love to the weathered and deeply beautiful land of seasoned marriages, motherhood and saying goodbye to a full life, well-lived.